Luther Arkwright
Parallel Lines

8 Multiverse-Spanning Missions

By

Chad Bowser, Anthony Boyd, Scott Crowder, Bruce Mason, Pete Nash, Bryan Steele, Lawrence Whitaker, and John White

Luther Arkwright and all prominently featured characters herein and the distinctive likenesses thereof are trademarks of Bryan Talbot and used by Design Mechanism with Permission and Under License.

Mythras is a trademark of The Design Mechanism Inc.
All rights reserved. This edition of *Luther Arkwright*: *Parallel Lines* is copyright © 2017.

This book may not be reproduced in whole or in part by any means without permission from The Design Mechanism, except as quoted for purposes of illustration, discussion and game play. Reproduction of the material in this book for the purposes of personal or corporate profit, by photographic, electronic, or other methods of retrieval is strictly prohibited.

Published under license in the UK by Aeon Games Publishing
games.aeonbooks.co.uk

ISBN 978-1-91147-124-0

Credits

Luther Arkwright Created by Bryan Talbot

Developed and Written By
Chad Bowser (*Hot Metal & Methadrine*), Anthony Boyd (*This Corrosion*),
Scott Crowder (*Mattanit*), Bruce Mason (*Bridge Over Troubled Parallels*),
Pete Nash (*Hanging on the Telephone*), Bryan Steele (*NuAtlantis*),
Lawrence Whitaker (*Mjollnir, Silver Pictures Move So Slow*), and John White (*One Way or Another*)

Editing & Proofing
Carol Johnson

Design and Layout
Alexandra James

Artists
Bryan Talbot, Colin Driver, Brian Koschak, Ronan Salieri and John White,
Brian Koschak appears courtesy of Outland Entertainment

Playtesters
Richard Barton, John Bell, James Biltcliffe, Shannon Carr, Darla Charlot, Kris Charlot,
Colin Driver, Tim Evans, David Finch, Katherine Fisher, Paul Fisher, Matthew Forbes, Philip Gaul,
Chris Gilmore, Erich Glinker, Óisin Hannigan, Jude Hornburg, Randall Hayes, Beau Hughes, Sean Jenkins,
Keith Laidlaw, Brandon Lowe, Garrett Madgett, Chris Marsh, Ewan McMahon, Brad Milburn, Pete Nash,
Blain Neufeld, Andi Newton, Lorne Oliver, Tim Other, Carl Pates, Pete Robson, Chad Rohrbacher,
Dan Ruffolo, Michael Schloss, Bob Thoms, Ben Turner, Howard Tytherleigh, Dan Voyce, Lawrence Whitaker

Special playtest thanks go to the regular team at *Dan's Books and Games, Cobourg ON*,
and players at *OSCON 2016, LozCon 2016* and *PeteCon 2017*

Contents

INTRODUCTION   4
  Mjollnir   4
  The Missions   10

MATTANIT   11
  Overview   11
  Background   12
  Agent Briefing   12
  Salem, Mass   13
  Goin' South   17
  The Devil's Swamp   19
  The Alien   20
  Returning to Zero-Zero   21
  Mattanit Technology   22
  Non-Player Characters   23

THIS CORROSION   27
  Overview   27
  Background   28
  Botany Bay   29
  On the Road   32
  Nine By Nine   37
  Non-Player Characters   40

HOT METAL & METHADRINE   47
  Overview   47
  Background   48
  Briefing   50
  Arrival   51
  The Street   52
  The Squat   54
  The Dealer   55
  Empire Down   55
  The Alph Flophouse   57
  The Plant   57
  Georgy-845's Skyscraper   59
  Conclusion   60
  Non-Player Characters   60

ONE WAY OR ANOTHER   65
  Overview   65
  Briefing   66
  The Hunt for Red Octobriana   67
  Trans-Siberian Express   68
  Strangers on a Train   71
  End of the Line?   76
  A Lady Vanishes   78
  Conclusion   78
  Non-Player Characters   79

SILVER PICTURES MOVE SO SLOW   87
  Overview   87
  Passengers and Crew   89
  Events   95
  Concluding the Scenario   101
  Airship Key   101
  Non-Player Characters   106

NUATLANTIS   114
  Overview   114
  The Kingfisher   116
  Welcome to NuAtlantis   118
  Sunday Girl   122
  Presidential Invitation   123
  The Banquet   123
  Sabotage!   125
  Please, Please Help Me   126
  A Presidential Decision   126
  Conclusion   126
  Non-Player Characters   127

BRIDGE OVER TROUBLED PARALLELS   130
  Overview   130
  Fire Walk With Me   134
  Exploring Edinburgh   135
  The Forth Bridge   143
  There's No Place Like Valhalla   147
  Games Master Notes   147
  Non-Player Characters   149

HANGING ON THE TELEPHONE   154
  Overview   154
  Buzby Murders   155
  My Name is Bren, Mr Bren   159
  Underground, Overground   160
  The Fancy-Dress Shop   161
  The Great Balloon Race   163
  Conclusion   164
  Non-Player Characters   165

INDEX   168

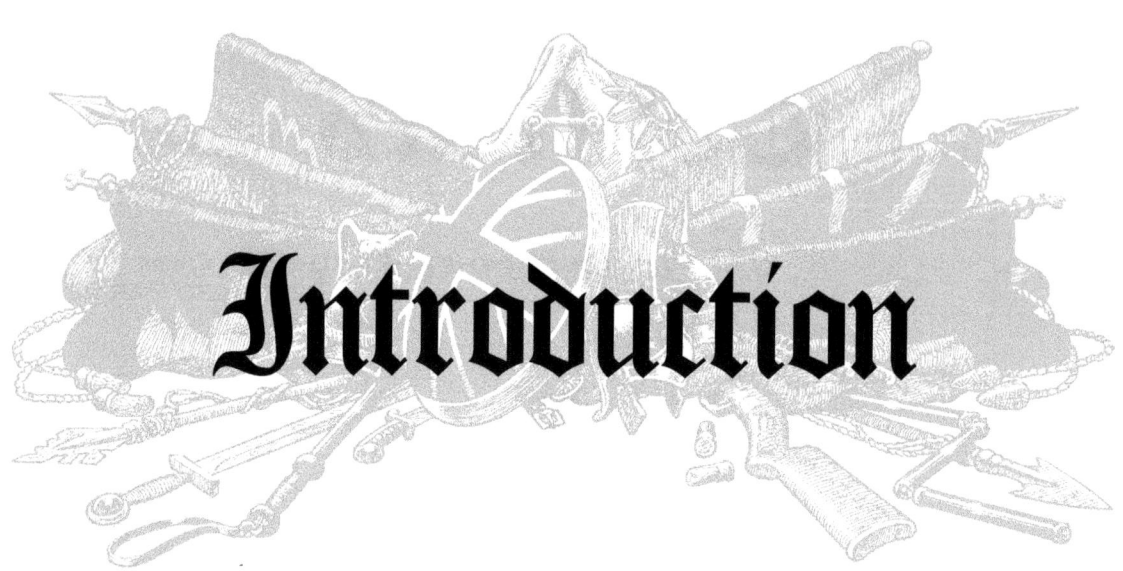

Introduction

PARALLEL LINES is a series of missions for Valhalla Agents in the *Luther Arkwright* roleplaying setting for the MYTHRAS rules. Each mission is a self-contained scenario that can be played independently and in any sequence, although the order of presentation suggests a natural running order to create a full campaign. Here in the introduction, we have provided a ready-made sub-agency of Valhalla, *Mjollnir Section*, that offers a cohesive gateway to each mission, a support network, access to resources, and a set of non-player characters that provide consistency from one mission to another. Use of Mjollnir is entirely optional; none of the scenarios suffer without its use.

While the characters – henceforth the *Agents* – can move from one mission to the next, we do recommend a little breathing space between each, and perhaps the insertion of other adventures of the Games Master's own devising. Some of these scenarios are tough and may require recuperation time afterwards; a couple flow together naturally, creating extended missions.

Not all the missions are concerned with thwarting Disruptor plans: indeed, some have no connection with the Disruptors at all. While Valhalla is actively engaged in monitoring Disruptor activity, W.O.T.A.N watches for any and all multiversal anomalies, whatever their nature, and Valhalla sends Agents to investigate where the circumstances warrant it.

Before running any of these scenarios, read through carefully. Some are quite complex and rely on finding certain clues for success. Give the Agents lots of chances to find these clues; while success should never be guaranteed, it is churlish to reward poor dice rolls with failure. Allow several chances to discover clues so that the characters are not set-up to otherwise fail.

One of the scenarios, *Hanging On the Telephone*, relies on several subliminal clues found in other scenarios: these are noted in boxed sections subtitled *Buzby Murder*. All will become clear when reading through the *Hanging on the Telephone* mission.

Mjollnir

W.O.T.A.N continually monitors the parallels for anomalies: strange events, disturbances and phenomena that may indicate Disruptor activity or could be the result of other forces unrelated to the Disruptor network. Investigation is always needed; sometimes by field teams native to the parallel in question, but on other occasions a specialised team is sent instead. These teams form Valhalla's *Mjollnir* section, so-called because, like Thor's hammer, they strike rapidly and return. Mjollnir teams are not intended to remain embedded in a single parallel for very long; instead, their tasks are to Investigate, Assess, Inform, and, if possible, Rectify. If they cannot rectify (and with extensive Disruptor influence this is often the case), a highly experienced and trained Agent, such as Luther Arkwright or a Rose Wylde, is sent for a prolonged period.

If desired, the characters are Agents of Mjollnir Section forming a cohesive team. This gives them a reason for working together and the rest of this introduction provides necessary background on Mjollnir that can be shared with players as the Games Master wishes.

Structure

Mjollnir comprises several departments, as the organisation chart opposite shows.

Command

Mjollnir is commanded by Freyr Lingstadt. Native to Zero-Zero, Freyr is an experienced field agent who, due to injury, has been forced to retire from direct operations. Mjollnir is her baby, and she selects the Agents who become Mjollnir Mission Teams. She reports to Valhalla's Executive Committee directly and occupies the rank of Programme Strategy Director, placing her on a par

Introduction

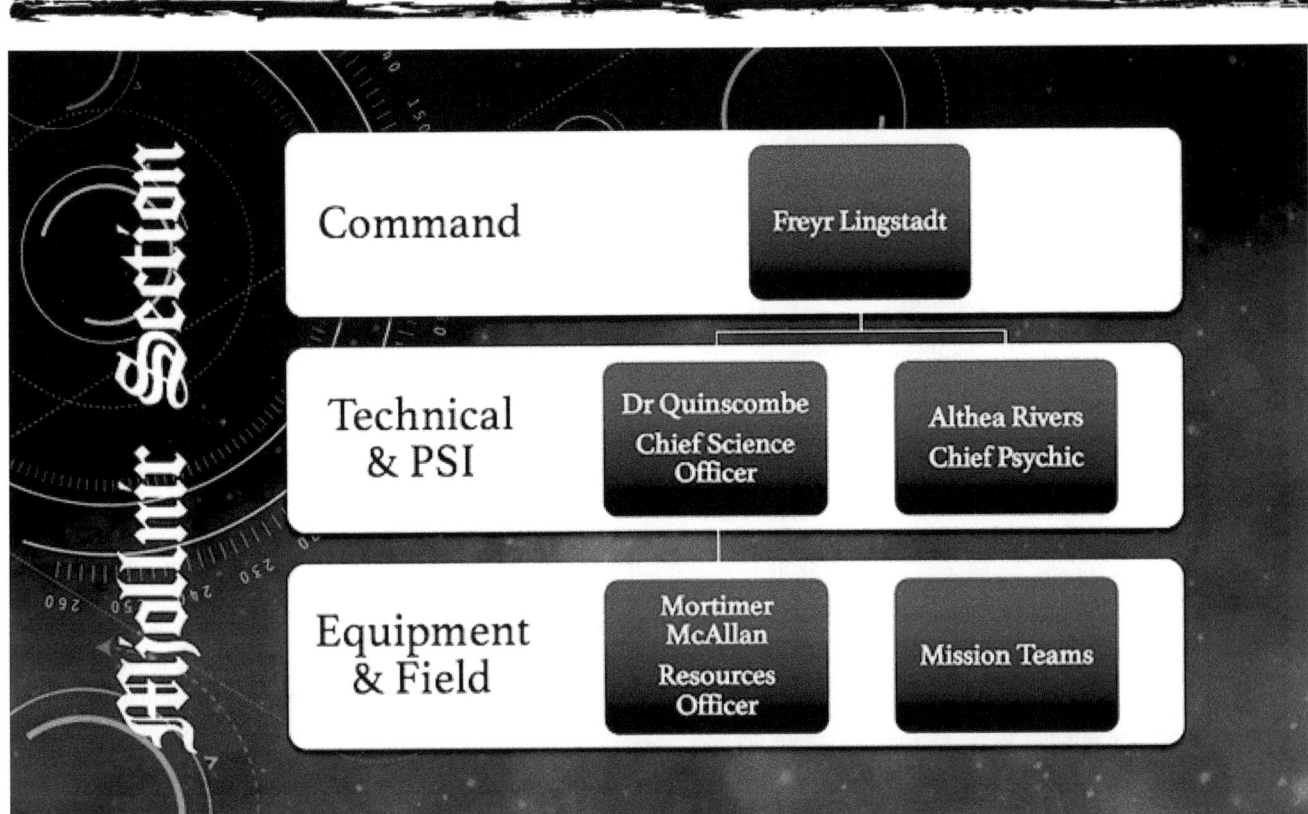

Mjollnir Section

with Karl Merkel. She has a considerable annual budget and the operational autonomy to communicate directly with W.O.T.A.N, conduct her own research and development, and direct her own psychic team. By contrast, Merkel is responsible for the deep-cover field agents, such as Arkwright, which creates a natural breakpoint between Mjollnir's activities and Valhalla's wider remit. Nevertheless, Freyr and Merkel are often in conflict over mission parameters, and Merkel has complained several times about Freyr allowing Mjollnir (both Agents and support units) to go too far.

Freyr is described more in the Personnel section on page 7.

TECHNICAL & PSI

Answering to Freyr Lingstadt are Doctor Leyton Quinscombe and Althea Rivers, heads of the Technical and PSI units, respectively.

Technical is responsible for developing all necessary science and technology to enable Mjollnir's mission, meaning that it has the developmental capabilities needed for trans-parallel transportation and travel. Under Quinscombe's guidance, the unit has developed The Van Mk II, which is capable of both parallel and spatial relocation, meaning it can shift to a specific set of geographical coordinates without needing to be physically co-located first. This makes The Van considerably more flexible, but the technology is still in its final experimental stages before being fully adopted by Valhalla. Quinscombe has also been developing several new methods of trans-parallel travel in conjunction with Althea Rivers, that do not rely on the cumbersome Van technology.

PSI Unit is headed by Althea Rivers, a powerful psychic who, like Rose Wylde, can contact her parallel selves, as well as being skilled in telepathy, psychometry, and several other talents. She provides psychic support from Valhalla Nova where it is needed and can call on other psychics as required, depending on the talents or disciplines to be employed. Like Freyr, she was a field agent and worked with Freyr on the now infamous Loki operation, which led to both women having to retire from direct involvement with the Disruptors.

More on Quinscombe and Althea can be found in Personnel.

EQUIPMENT & FIELD

The Equipment Unit works closely with Technical, but is responsible for outfitting Mjollnir Mission teams with the appropriate clothing, currency, and equipment for a given parallel. Given the infinite diversity of the task, this is no mean feat, and so Equipment's head, Mortimer McAllan, has a direct link with W.O.T.A.N's analysts so that accurate assumptions can be made regarding modes of equipment, currency, dress, styles, and so forth to be fashioned. He then has superb links with Valhalla's technology teams to get requisite items fabricated, along with external manufacturers who believe they are working for a highly eccentric historian and specialist museum curator.

The Field Units are the Mission teams themselves, and they report directly to Command. Freyr likes each team to have one of its number be the Mission Coordinator, acting as the main point of contact and organisation. Mjollnir has several mission teams; if a team suffers a casualty, a replacement from a reserve team can easily be drafted in as a replacement, equipped with a full briefing on mission histories.

Operations

Mjollnir Missions tend to be vanguard investigations that may or may not hand over to more specialised Agents depending on the severity of the circumstances. The main task of any mission team is to investigate and understand the circumstances as fully as possible before reporting back to Valhalla so that more detailed plans can be made.

The four pillars of a Mjollnir mission are:

- *Investigate*: Understand the local circumstances, agencies, and individuals involved, related power or control structures, technology, socio-political circumstances, and potential consequences of action and inaction.
- *Assess*: The feasibility for direct or indirect Valhalla action, along with what nature this action should take. For example, can a field agent or team of Agents native to the parallel be used, or are more specialised resources needed?
- *Inform*: Report back, as fully as possible, to Mjollnir Control on investigation and assessments, enabling next steps to be taken.
- *Rectify*: If – and only if – there is no other alternative, a Mission Team can attempt to rectify things through decisive action. This must usually be sanctioned by Mjollnir Control, and only if all other scenarios have been explored and exhausted.

Freyr Lingstadt enforces these four pillars rigorously. Anyone who transcends their mission brief without due authority from her is liable to be expelled from the section, usually returning to menial duties. Each Mission Team is therefore expected to exhibit rational, dispassionate judgment and act accordingly. Lingstadt would rather that a mission abort than compromise itself, compromise innocent lives, or compromise the ability for other Valhalla Agents to assume responsibility for the task. However, every so often it is necessary for a Mission Team to go above and beyond. This can create tensions elsewhere but, as long as there are sound reasons, Freyr is willing to be flexible. Mjollnir is vital to intelligence gathering, but this does not make her Agents impassive observers: sometimes they have to act, and if that means occasionally breaking the rules, then she will judge each case on its merits.

Mjollnir Section operates from the Heisenberg wing of Valhalla Nova. This is a small, self-contained area of the Valhalla Nova arcology that has its own sleeping quarters, briefing room, laboratories, and PSI facilities. It is self-sufficient in most regards, and when not in the field, Agents can lodge here and be fed, rested, and participate in other activities. Curie wing does not have its own medical facilities; these are shared with the rest of Valhalla.

Resources

Mjollnir can call upon the equipment listed in the *Luther Arkwright* rules, pages 75-79. It also has the experimental Van MkII, which has been modified to be able to move spatially while in transit between parallels, to arrive at coordinates distinct from its point of origin. This is only possible while in planar transit; the Van II cannot translocate to another geographical point on the same parallel, or fly/drive overland. Despite this limitation, it makes the Van far more flexible although it does have some teething difficulties. On a couple of occasions, The Van has materialised kilometres away from its destination (sometimes a few, sometimes several hundred). In other respects, the Van II is the same as that described on page 76 of *Luther Arkwright*.

McAllan's Connections

The jovial, charismatic Mortimer McAllan is incredibly well-connected, both within Valhalla and without. If an Agent requests or needs a particular piece of equipment, or to have an existing, mundane piece of kit modified, McAllan can usually arrange it, either by outsourcing the work, or using his own small team of technicians to work on it. He usually needs a week's notice, and getting him to agree requires a successful Influence roll. If an Agent wants something very complicated, or something that might be out of keeping with a parallel (a concealed laser in a 19th Century musket, for instance), then apply grades of difficulty to the Influence roll according to the request. McAllan can refuse, but if he believes there is a genuine need, is usually obliging. He is especially fond of good single malt whisky, and a bottle of something rare can make the Influence roll easier.

While McAllan can certainly help with technology and general equipment, where he shines is clothing. McAllan holds that clothes can make or break a mission, since nothing causes more suspicion than a conspicuous or incorrect garment. McAllan has an immense database of fashions and styles from a huge array of parallels. His database has a special algorithm that can accurately predict particular modes of dress or cut requirements, based on W.O.T.A.N's calculations, reports from field agents, and a huge array of historical documents. McAllan can usually ensure that every Agent is suitably attired for a mission before they leave Valhalla, and he takes great pride in the abilities of the tailors and dressmakers who work for him.

Psychic Support

The PSI unit consists of Althea Rivers and her assistant, Anahita Sanjeev. Together they psychically monitor mission progress where possible as both Althea and Anahita are connected with their Other Selves through their innate Empathic Links. Althea is a telepath and can use her abilities at distance via her Empathic Link as long as the version of herself on a parallel is aware and open to the multiversal bond between all Althea Rivers.

If other psychic abilities are needed, Althea can usually source them from within Valhalla, but it is not possible to have a psychic seconded to a Mission Team just because the characters might request it. Psychics are a precious and highly valued resource in Valhalla, and not to be used like equipment.

Personnel

Freyr Lingstadt

Freyr is a tall, blond-haired Norwegian woman in her early 40s. Her hazel eyes are captivating, and she favours delicate mascara and eye shadow to accentuate them. Clearly in very good shape, Freyr has an aura of authority that marks her as someone not to mess with, although, when off-duty and with a glass of good wine, she is open, sociable, and funny.

Freyr has been with Valhalla for more than 20 years and was an experienced field operative. Much of her time was spent on parallel 77.41.84 where, along with Althea Rivers, she infiltrated a Disruptor cell led by a psionically powerful Knight who was only ever identified as *Loki*. Freyr and Althea were close enough to assassinate Loki and destroy the Disruptor plot (which involved destabilising several governments in strategic, yet fragile alliances), but something went wrong. Their covers blown, both women were arrested. Althea managed to escape and get back to Valhalla, but Freyr was drugged, tortured, and subjected to psionic interrogation that would have broken a lesser person. She managed to escape with Rose Wylde's help, but on return to Valhalla needed several years of psychotherapy to recover from the ordeal.

Loki, the Disruptor Knight, escaped and is still at large. Freyr has vowed to track him down and bring him back to Zero-Zero for interrogation and incarceration, although she will settle for his death – accidental or deliberate. All her Mjollnir Mission Teams are under orders to uncover every scrap of intelligence they can pertaining to Loki, and Freyr is confident he will, one day, be brought to justice.

Professor Quinscombe

A professor of transplanar sciences, 'Prof Q' is a thin, elderly man who suffers from curvature of the spine, meaning that rather than being the tall fellow he was in his youth, he is now somewhat stooped. This has not dwindled his immense enthusiasm though, and Prof Q is a voluble whirlwind of gesticulations, random trains of thought, wild-eyed grins when he hits on something fascinating, and a sure, sincere belief that everyone is as thoroughly interested in planar science as himself. A typical sentence from

Freyr Lingstadt	Attributes
STR: 13	Action Points: 3
CON: 12	Damage Modifier: +1d2
SIZ: 14	Prana: 14
DEX: 15	Tenacity: 11
INT: 15	Movement: 6 metres
POW: 14	Initiative Bonus: 15
CHA: 13	Armour: None

1d20	Hit Location	AP/HP
1 – 3	Right Leg	0/6
4 – 6	Left Leg	0/6
7 – 9	Abdomen	0/7
10 – 12	Chest	0/8
13 – 15	Right Arm	0/5
16 – 18	Left Arm	0/5
19 – 20	Head	0/6

Skills	Passions, Traits & Dependencies
Athletics 44%, Brawn 39%, Bureacracy 75%, Drive 80%, Endurance 60%, Evade 51%, Insight 70%, Locale 60%, Mechanisms 60%, Perception 75%, Pilot 48%, Survival 65%, Stealth 48%, Unarmed 77%, Willpower 69%	Passions: Loyalty to Valhalla 95%, Loyalty to Agents 80%, Obsessed with Loki 90% Traits: Self-Awareness, Tenacious Dependencies: Risk-Taking 70%

Combat Style & Weapons			Traits & Notes	
Firearms (Pistol, SMG) 74%				

Weapon	Damage	Range	Ammo	Fire Rate/Load
9mm Pistol	1d6+1	50/100/200	9 (magazine)	1/3

Dr Quinscombe	Attributes
STR: 9	Action Points: 3
CON: 11	Damage Modifier: 0
SIZ: 16	Prana: 9
DEX: 8	Tenacity: 9
INT: 18	Movement: 6 metres
POW: 9	Initiative Bonus: 13
CHA: 15	Armour: None

1d20	Hit Location	AP/HP
1 – 3	Right Leg	0/6
4 – 6	Left Leg	0/6
7 – 9	Abdomen	0/7
10 – 12	Chest	0/8
13 – 15	Right Arm	0/5
16 – 18	Left Arm	0/5
19 – 20	Head	0/6

Skills	Passions, Traits & Dependencies
Athletics 20%, Brawn 20%, Drive 30%, Endurance 44%, Evade 21%, Insight 37%, Engineering 106%, Mechanisms 99%, Perception 42%, Probabilities 89%, Science (Mathematics 88%, Physics 98%, Parallel Physics 104%), Willpower 49%	Passions: Loyalty to Valhalla 85%, Loyalty to Agents 81%, Obsessed with Planar Technology 90% Traits: Technical Dependencies: Tobacco (pipe) 44%

Combat Style & Weapons
None.

Quinscombe begins with 'Ah, I'm very glad you asked me that' even if one didn't.

Despite his obvious eccentricities (he wears a monocle, a shabby, leather-patched green cardigan, and flannel trousers several sizes too large), he is extraordinarily brilliant. One of the team that perfected W.O.T.A.N, he has gone on to specialise in planar travel. The Van was his idea, and The Van Mk II is his latest development. But his overriding desire is to replicate psychic translocation technology on a personal scale, so that *any* Valhalla Agent can shift parallels using a handheld device or via ingesting some form of chemical that helps effect quantum transference. His experiments have met with mixed success. One (non-human) test subject was somehow transmuted into a goldfish, while others have emerged physically sound but psionically traumatised. Nevertheless, his two latest developments (aside from the Van) have been given permission for live testing with human subjects and are relatively safe. They are explored in their relevant scenarios.

Althea Rivers

A striking indigenous Australian woman, Althea is a gifted telepath with a natural empathic link with her other selves. Like Freyr, she was a field operative until the failure of Operation Loki led to the catastrophic collapse of the political order on 77.41.84 and reverberations across dozens of parallels, triggering either extreme left wing or right wing activity, depending on the parallel.

Althea retired from field work after Freyr's capture by Loki-controlled militia, but was instrumental in psychically coordinating her escape and safe return to Zero-Zero. Althea is an empath and acutely sensitive to emotional energy. She finds herself adopting, unconsciously, the speech rhythms of whoever she converses with, and picks up on surface emotions with no effort at all; a simple Insight roll is all that is needed for Althea to deduce and understand how someone *truly* feels.

Her experiences on 77.41.84 wounded her, but she did not need the extensive psychotherapy Freyr required. Instead she channelled her energies into setting up a way to track Loki wherever in the multiverse he might try to go. Over the ensuing months, through her Other Selves, Althea established a network of Valhalla-loyal contacts, spies, and informers who would be on the lookout for a medium-height, russet-haired, strong-jawed, impeccably dressed man, most likely with a slight German or Austrian accent, who is obviously cultured, refined, but also cruel, manipulative, and keen to place himself close to seats of power. She circulated the many aliases Loki uses and steadily, reports trickled in. Loki was still at large, still manipulating and still bent on completing whatever plan the Disruptors had charged him with.

This work strengthened Freyr's resolve and with Althea, she convinced Valhalla to establish Mjollnir Section to supplement such intelligence gathering and have the ability to move quickly, without relying on solitary, embedded Agents.

Althea Rivers	Attributes
STR: 15	Action Points: 3
CON: 14	Damage Modifier: +1d2
SIZ: 12	Prana: 12
DEX: 12	Tenacity: 12
INT: 15	Movement: 6 metres
POW: 12	Initiative Bonus: 11
CHA: 11	Armour: None

1d20	Hit Location	AP/HP
1 – 3	Right Leg	0/6
4 – 6	Left Leg	0/6
7 – 9	Abdomen	0/7
10 – 12	Chest	0/8
13 – 15	Right Arm	0/5
16 – 18	Left Arm	0/5
19 – 20	Head	0/6

Skills	Passions, Traits & Dependencies
Athletics 65%, Brawn 45%, Deceit 66%, Endurance 45%, Evade 30%, Insight 60%, Oratory 51%, Perception 60%, Survival 45%, Stealth 62%, Unarmed 47%, Willpower 30%	Passions: Loyalty to Valhalla 65%, Love Freyr 70%, Hate Loki 85%
	Traits: Psychic, Self-Awareness
	Dependencies: Drugs (Cocaine) 38%

Psionics	
Telepathy 85% (Mental Scan, Mind Probe, Telepathy)	Although she doesn't need to, Althea usually snorts a line of cocaine before using any of her psychic powers. She is quite open about this, and her addiction is under control.
Empathy 81% (Empathic Link, Feel Emotions, Mental Shield)	

Combat Style & Weapons	Traits & Notes
Small Arms (Pistol) 65%	

Weapon	Damage	Range	Ammo	Fire Rate/Load
.38 Pistol	1d6	50/100/200	6 (revolver)	1/3

Mortimer McAllan

Large, affable, jovial, and with a permanent twinkle in his beady grey eyes, 'Uncle Morty' McAllan is as well-connected as they come on Zero-Zero, seemingly knowing anyone who is anyone *worth* knowing. He is loud, theatrical, and therefore bonds well with Quinscombe, becoming as enthused about the professor's discoveries as the professor himself. Morty is technically adept in his own right; a dabbler in half a dozen technical disciplines, but also a keen student of etiquette, protocol, fashion (especially the fashions of the military, royal courts, and chambers of government), and fine living.

Introduction

These things make for the consummate fixer. If Mjollnir needs something fabricated, whether it's a modified cell phone or a dress uniform of the King's Fusiliers, Morty can oblige.

He has never been a field agent for Valhalla, and has never left Zero-Zero; before joining Valhalla, he was the director of a repertoire company in the north of England, and one that was noted for its astonishing stage special effects and exquisite costumes. It transpired that Morty McAllan was the genius behind both, and with some contrivance he was persuaded to come and work for Valhalla where his penchant for tinkering would be indulged in undreamed ways. His connections in finance and politics helped too; whenever Valhalla has needed high level help, Morty has simply called in a few favours, or thrown a lavish party with the right people invited, and the problem has soon been resolved.

Morty tends to fill an entire room with his presence, and sulks when the spotlight is not trained on his incredible bulk. He calls everyone *Darling*, peppers his conversations with shameless name-dropping, and adores tales of heroism and derring-do. He makes no secret of the crush he has on one Captain Arkwright, and always makes sure he is present at any social function in Valhalla Nova Arkwright is scheduled to attend.

Mortimer McAllan	Attributes
STR: 13	Action Points: 2
CON: 16	Damage Modifier: +1d4
SIZ: 18	Prana: 10
DEX: 7	Tenacity: 10
INT: 16	Movement: 6 metres
POW: 10	Initiative Bonus: 14
CHA: 17	Armour: None

1d20	Hit Location	AP/HP
1 – 3	Right Leg	0/7
4 – 6	Left Leg	0/7
7 – 9	Abdomen	0/8
10 – 12	Chest	0/9
13 – 15	Right Arm	0/6
16 – 18	Left Arm	0/6
19 – 20	Head	0/7

Skills	Passions, Traits & Dependencies
Acting 75%, Art (Fashion) 90%, Athletics 18%, Brawn 39%, Courtesy 90%, Deceit 68%, Endurance 75%, Evade 22%, Influence 85%, Insight 76%, Forgery 77%, History 82%, Mechanisms 90%, Oratory 81%, Perception 69%, Science (Electronics) 45%, Unarmed 21%, Willpower 53%	Passions: Loyalty to Valhalla 62%, Crave Attention 80%, Hate Rudeness 85% Traits: Technical Dependencies: Attention 78%

Combat Style & Weapons
None

> ### Loki
>
> Loki has various aliases: *Pieter Klass, Hans Krupcht, Erik Schmeisser* and *James De Vere* are four known to Valhalla. He is a handsome, strong-jawed man, usually of Germanic/Prussian aristocratic heritage although he has been known to claim British ancestry.
>
> He is a ranking Disruptor Knight, active across several parallels, and seemingly with an open remit to foment chaos according to some larger plan that runs separate from, but complementary to, wider Disruptor schemes such as the hunt for Firefrost. He is a clever, calculating, and shadowy operative, making full use of henchmen, elaborate cover stories, and keeping as much distance from the unpleasant dirty work as possible.
>
> Loki is a talented psychic, with Thought Implantation being a known speciality. He seems to enjoy exposing people to their deepest fears and even takes a sadistic delight in doing so. Always suave, frequently charming, and unerringly polite, he is nevertheless a ruthless operative responsible for countless murders across the multiverse.
>
> For the *Parallel Lines* missions, Loki is a shadowy influence rather than a definite presence; the Agents will not encounter him directly, although his reach extends through several of these adventures. Therefore no game statistics are provided for him because he is not intended to be encountered as a non-player character. Loki will turn up in further **Luther Arkwright** scenarios though, and so *Parallel Lines* serves to introduce him as a mysterious arch-enemy who, in the very best tradition of villainy, manages to elude capture....

USING MJOLLNIR

Mjollnir is intended to be a backdrop rather than a main player in the missions contained in *Parallel Lines*. Details are kept vague so that Games Masters can develop the section is much or as little as needed. There are some obvious tactical uses should they prove necessary.

- *Briefings*: Each mission is introduced and briefed by Freyr Lingstadt; she is the constant from one mission to the next. Her loyalty to her Agents means she will pull strings to help them whenever she can, but she is no fool; Agents who act recklessly or carelessly risk her wrath.
- *Rescue*: If the Agents find themselves in a very tight spot, Mjollnir can help extract them. There is always a fallback position if needed.
- *Intelligence*: Althea and her PSI Unit can offer psychic insight in the form of clues to help out with leads now and again – especially useful if the Agents get stuck.
- *Equipment*: Morty McAllan never lets his Agents go unprepared; he, along with Quinscombe, act as Mjollnir's 'Q Branch', ensuring they have the gadgets needed.

Otherwise, Mjollnir is a connecting device; a way of bringing groups of characters together and giving them the common support needed to get the job done.

The Missions

Parallel Lines consists of 8 missions, each a scenario that can be played as part of the sequence or on its own.

Mattanit
Sent to rescue a stricken Valhalla undercover operative, the team encounters strange goings-on in the New England swamps. Is this genuine witchcraft, some Disruptor plot, or something else entirely?

This Corrosion
When the Van materialises in a blasted parallel Camargue, the Agents find themselves in a race to get to safety before a savage warlord can take his revenge. That is, if the mutated horrors don't get them first.

Hot Metal and Methadrine
Sent to investigate potential Disruptor activity in a balkanised Britain, the Agents find themselves knee-deep in murder and corruption.

One Way or Another
In order to retrieve information vital to finding Loki, the Agents must board the Trans-Siberian Express to get a fellow Agent to safety. But the luxury of an epic rail jiourney is soon tarnished by violence and mayhem.

Silver Pictures Move So Slow
Ensuring a royal diplomat of the Ukrainian Imperial household reaches London safely means boarding the *Empress Katerina*, an airship with an eclectic passenger manifest. Does Loki have agents of his own onboard? Are there other agendas in play?

Nu-Atlantis
In an underwater arcology, scientists are preparing to debut a revolutionary treatment that will enhance latent psychic abilities. This is of considerable interest to both Valhalla and the Disruptors, and the Agents are sent to investigate the importance of the discovery.

Bridge Over Troubled Parallels
A serious breakdown of the fabric of the multiverse is traced to a parallel Edinburgh under the jackboot of a totalitarian regime. The Agents are against the clock to locate the source of the rupture and neutralise it – or witness first-hand the collapse of reality.

Hanging on the Telephone
In smog-choked southwest London, someone is murdering random people and leaving them clothed in bizarre costumes. The Agents must uncover the murderer and get to the bottom of a sinister conspiracy, while avoiding becoming victims of it themselves.

This Corrosion follows on from *Mattanit,* and *Silver Pictures Move So Slow* follows on from *One Way or Another*. *Hanging on the Telephone* has links with several of the previous scenarios and is recommended to be played last in the sequence.

Mattanit

Parallel 08.24.63 has been rife with fear and savagery stemming from ignorance and superstition. Progress has been stymied and oppression of the masses is brought upon willingly by the oppressed in the name of God and His followers. Now one of Valhalla's own is put in danger, because this collective madness has been mixed with an alien influence. It is time for other Agents to act.

Overview

Parallel 08.24.63
British Empire Variant
Disruption Likelihood: 30%

This mission is set in late October, when the days are getting shorter, but before the snow comes. The Agents are sent to rescue a Valhalla Agent accused of witchcraft, leading to an incredible discovery of major interest to the Valhalla Project.

Games Masters may wish to have the Agents (or one of them) know Sarah Burroughs, perhaps even romantically. She is not a member of Mjollnir Section, but deep field agents do return to Zero-Zero from time to time for briefings and health assessments. This is entirely optional of course, but a potential liaison between the characters and Sarah can assist with the dramatic tension needed for a rescue.

If this option is used, then Agents should be given some advanced information on Sarah and perhaps include her particular talents as a mystic. How much information is up to the Games Master to decide.

Non-Player Characters

- *Sarah Burroughs*: The Salem 'witch' is a Valhalla Agent who is a gifted psychic who can track down psychic emanations... if the colonists don't drown her first.
- *Daniel Barwick*: A formerly possessed guide wandering the wilderness; his knowledge of the area was stolen by an alien.
- *The Engineer*: An alien being – the Mattanit – trying to repair a damaged star ship.

Timeline

1. The Agents are briefed on parallel 08.24.63.
2. The Agents are sent to the parallel where they must rescue Agent Sarah Burroughs.
3. The Agents escape Salem and head south.
4. The Agents cross the Hockomock Swamp.
5. The Agents face a strange foe.
6. The Agents must get back to Zero-Zero.

Areas to be Covered

- Salem – A bleak puritanical Protestant town.
- Sarah's cabin – A spartan cabin hidden in the woods outside Salem.
- Boston – A major port. Clues as to the nature of the disturbance can be found here.
- Battle site – Colonial troops rebelled from a British General possessed by a Mattanit.
- A Mohican Village – A refuge with spacious wigwams and simple living.
- Hockomock Swamp – A dank and dangerous morass, especially at night. Within it, a crashed spaceship lies dormant.

Background

In parallel 08.24.63, an alien race evolved on a distant planet and developed star travel. These beings, who feed on synaptic and psychic energy, eventually found their way to Earth's rich biosphere during their quest of galactic expansion. As fate would have it, a micrometeorite inflicted critical damage on their star drive and their ship crash landed in the Hockomock Swamp, south of Boston, Mass. The inhabitants of this parallel have only developed technology equivalent to the late 18th century. North America has been colonised for fewer than 150 years. Native Americans control much of the continent with British colonials only controlling the eastern seaboard. The British Empire is the preeminent political and military force in the world and the sun never sets upon the Union Jack. It is Pax Britannica.

The four crash-landed aliens left their best engineer behind to attempt repairs while they set off to explore and conquer this new worlds and turn its inhabitants into a psychic food source. The aliens quickly came into contact with the neighbouring Algonquin tribes who named these beings the Mattanit, which means 'The Spirit of Evil'.

The Mattanit can possess the bodies of their victims and drain all knowledge from them (skills, memories, and so forth.). In this way, the Mattanit learned enough to realise the best way to subjugate humanity is to possess the Queen of England.

The local Valhalla Agent, Sarah Burroughs, a mystic living outside Salem, was investigating strange rumours (disappearances and abrupt odd behaviours) and sudden manifestations of psychic energy that seemed to radiate from the south, affecting both natives and colonists, but now she has gone dark after a distressing transmission. The Agents have been hastily gathered with two mission priorities: find and extract Agent Burroughs and get to the bottom of what's going on in 08.24.63.

Agent Briefing

Freyr Lingstadt summons the Agents to the Mjollnir briefing room in Zero-Zero. She is very tense indicating something serious is afoot. Without the usual formalities of a typical briefing she immediately directs their attention to a large screen where she plays the last TPT broadcast of Valhalla Agent Sarah Burroughs, a local mystic on 08.24.63. Burroughs is shown recording her last transmission:

'I think they're coming for me next. Two weeks ago, they hung five women accused of witchcraft. Three days later, they piled stones upon a man. He took two days to die. Word came that General Blair sailed from New York and has seized Boston. I sensed his dread presence nearby already. I sense another, as well. I think I've found the source... Oh no! They're in the trees! They're coming! Send help!'

The recording stops and the Agents are briefed on the parallel.

Witch World
Designator: 08.24.63
Classification: British Empire Variation
Cultural Type: North American
Political Type: Lawless
Technological Type: Pre-Industrial

'08:24:63's point of divergence is twofold,' Freyr says. 'First, the ancient astronomer Ptolemy died at birth; thus, his direction-finding principles were not available to aid navigators in long sea voyages. Consequently, the New World was never discovered. Second, in 1588, the Spanish Armada defeated the Kingdom of England. With the Protestants being oppressed, innovation and free thinking stagnated. Technological advances were set back centuries. The Protestants, renaming themselves 'The Pure', went underground for the next two centuries, not only persevering, but gaining widespread popularity despite Catholic attempts to root them out.' She pauses to flick through different images on the view screen showing current day pictures from the parallel; the Agents see something quite primitive in nature – at least 250 years behind Zero-Zero, and maybe more.

'Finally, when the abuse of the Inquisition grew too intolerable, the Pure rose up and overthrew the Roman Catholic Church in a short, bloody, and merciless campaign. Catholicism ceased to exist almost overnight. Great Britain suddenly found itself as the seat of power of a Protestant Empire that spread over all of Europe. Exploration flourished and the New World was discovered soon after. Before long, the Union Jack flew in every corner of the globe. Many of The Pure felt called by God to convert the New World savages and so they began the colonisation of the Americas. As Britain became more cosmopolitan, tension rose between hardcore colonial Purists and the ruling elite back home. Despite this, The Pure remain loyal subjects of the Crown.'

THE MISSION

Sarah has a mystic talent that allows her to sense psychics, making her perfect for locating possible candidates for the Valhalla Project. A week before this briefing, she reported she'd sensed powerful and unexpected psychic emanations coming from the south. Shortly thereafter, strange events started. The populace thought the Devil was loose in Salem. Sarah was told to investigate, but did not get a chance to report her findings before she was taken by the locals.

W.O.T.A.N needs to determine whether this is a Disruptor incursion or the mad ramblings of a superstitious, backwoods parallel.

The Agents must dispatch immediately to rescue Agent Burroughs and find out what is really happening on 08.24.63. Quinscombe intends to use this mission as a test-run for the Van II. It should be able to transport the Agents from Zero-Zero's London directly to a location outside Salem, Mass, traversing both parallels and geographical distance in a single operation. 'We've tested it on automated settings and with some laboratory subjects, and it's worked just fine. I tested it myself to take a trip to Margate on 25.04.57 and treated myself to a lovely meal of fish and chips. You'll be *perfectly* fine. Just keep an eye out for anything strange and I want a full report on how it all went when you return.'

The Van II is prepared while the Agents get themselves ready. Morty McAllan has had costumes suitable for the parallel hastily prepared, and the Agents are allowed to take black powder weapons suitable to a frontier land of the late 17th Century. As a cover story the Agents are fresh-in from England via Boston and looking to set-up trade contacts at Salem port. It's a common enough occurrence and a couple of forged letters from the East India Company support the story.

The Van II looks almost identical to the Mk I version, save for a redesigned power system and updated controls, readouts, and guidance equipment. Wishaw, an assistant to Quinscombe, gives a crash-course in how to activate the basic settings and the emergency return sequence. In essence though, the Van II is fully automatic and there is little for the Agents to do. One of them is given a small communications device, rather like an elaborate fountain pen with a set of twist controls near the cap. 'This is a beacon and remote activation device that you should use to bring the Van back to get you when ready,' Wishaw says. 'Twist this ring like so, and we should have the Van materialise within 100 metres of your location. It will avoid any intervening structures and arrive in the largest open space, so be careful where you are when calling it. It takes about 10 minutes from the point of activation for it to arrive.'

And what Quinscombe and Wishaw say is true. Van II operates exactly like Van I, rapidly transporting the Agents across the parallels with the weird lengthening and twisting sensation one never quite becomes accustomed to.

However, when it arrives in 08.24.63, it materialises half a kilometre north of Salem, and about three metres above the ground. Alarms inside the Van blare a quick altitude alert before the Van thuds to the earth with a heavy crunch. The Agents are strapped into safety harnesses so arrive unhurt, but the superstructure of the Van is buckled at the bottom and some of the machinery sparks and splutters worryingly. Once the Agents have disembarked, the Van grinds out of existence as it returns to Zero-Zero. The process is usually smooth, but the fall has damaged some of the circuits and the transition is jerky and stilted; there is some nervousness that the Van is too badly damaged, because repairing it on a technologically under-developed parallel will be a tough call indeed. Thankfully though, it dematerialises leaving the Agents in open country not far from the port of Salem.

Given the proximity, and the fact that this is relatively open country, there is a chance the Agents' arrival will be seen. The arrival is in daylight hours, and there is a 30% chance of someone being nearby when the Van appears.

Any Agent familiar with the United States notes the referrals to 'Mass' instead of 'Massachusetts'. This is intentional. In this parallel, the colony is known simply by *Mass* as a throwback to the power of the Church. Should an Agent accidentally use the longer, home-parallel nomenclature, locals will surely begin to wonder about them – placing the Agents and the mission under even greater scrutiny.

SALEM, MASS

Salem, Mass, is a wealthy port town comprising merchants and clergy centred around a town church known locally as the Meeting Hall. The town proper is home to fewer than 200 people; the bulk of Salem's populace live in nearby farms. The surrounding countryside is typical of New England farmland of the time: scruffy and untidy. Boundaries wander and tree inconveniently punctuate the landscape. Homes are made of sturdy wood; the forests are still dense and plentiful here. Yards tend to be surrounded by picket fences, many in disrepair. Life is hard, despite its dockside wealth, and property maintenance isn't a high priority. Overall, Salem is a dreary place, sullen and bare by design. One dirt road passes through the centre of town, with muddy paths leading off.

The strange events to the south have sparked fear and hysteria in the populace. Townspeople are watchful and disapproving. Anyone observed doing anything out of the ordinary is treated with suspicion or labelled an agent of the Devil.

SARAH'S FATE

Sarah has been captured by the Salem authorities and interred in the local goal. From the time of their arrival, the Agents have two hours to locate Sarah and try to spring her from prison; if they do not, she is taken by the angry mob to the bridge where she is found guilty of witchcraft, trussed, and tossed into the icy waters of the river to test her guilt. This results, seemingly, in Sarah's death, but as a trained mystic she is able to control her bodily reactions to remain alive long enough for another rescue attempt from the

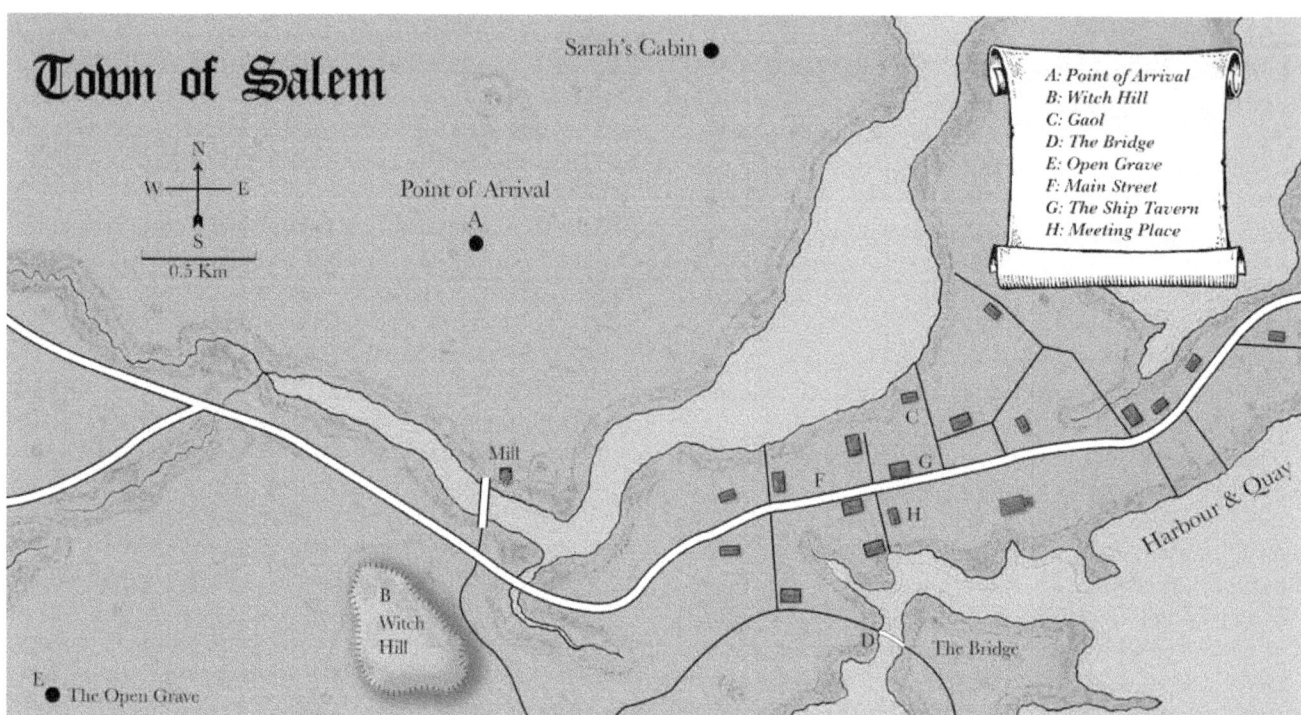

shallow grave her body is tossed into. Thus, the Agents have two options for the rescue; a gaol-break or a grave robbery. If the do not rescue her, Sarah rescues herself, but believing that her call to Valhalla for help has gone unheard, she makes her own escape, heading to the Mohican village described later in the scenario.

Thus, what the Agents do when they arrive in Salem is crucial. Obviously the whole town knows that Sarah is to be executed, but there is a chance for the Agents to rescue her before this happens. If Games Masters want to make things more dramatic, then the Agents can arrive as Sarah is being thrown into the river.

Witch Hill

As the Agents enter the greater Salem area, they pass several empty gallows upon a low rise. This is Witch Hill, where 'proven' traffickers with the Devil (most often through suspicion of witchcraft) are executed savagely and left for the populace to witness. Unless they are moving in concert using Stealth, patrolling watchmen stop them and ask their business. Wrong answers lead to arrest.

The Agents should look the part due to their clothes, but a few convincing Influence skill tests go a long way. Unless they have a credible answer (looking for work, coming to buy passage on a ship, etc.), the patrollers try to detain them, taking them to the Salem Meeting Place. Use the statistics for three 'Pure' as guards on page 24 if an altercation transpires.

Main Street

If the Agents make it into town unhindered, they find it mostly deserted. In the centre of the road, outside the Meeting Place, is a set of four stocks and two pillories. They appear well used but are currently unoccupied. All the businesses are locked up. A young couple rushes past the Agents: 'We're going to be late! The witch might already be dead!'

Buzby Murder

Outside the gaol stands a town crier, taking the opportunity to bellow out local news as people gather for the execution. Along with warnings against harbouring witches and the sighting of a falling star the week before, an astounding £5,000 reward is offered for the capture of the Polka-dot Pirate. So named for his white spotted red headscarf, this daring rogue slaughtered an entire company of dragoons en-route to Concord and made off with the gold bullion they were escorting – five years long overdue back pay for the colonial army. Someone in the crowd mutters that the pirate must have had the help of the devil, since the heavily laden cart tracks vanished mere yards from the mud-churned ambush site.

Salem Gaol

The gaol is built of thick hand-hewn oak timbers and siding. It has six double-occupancy cells. It stinks, is rat-infested, and the wrought iron bars of each cell are sturdy and strong. Each cell is secured by an iron padlock, with Ned the Gaoler, a burly brute, holding the keys to each lock on a thick leather belt. Despite the security inside, Ned is the only guard, and if the locks can be picked and Ned overwhelmed, there are no further guards to deal with. Each cell has a skylight set high on the wall, and covered by an iron grill. It's easy enough to climb up to the skylight to peer into each cell to see if it's occupied.

If the Agents arrive before Sarah is taken for execution, this is where she can be found. She occupies the last cell in the block and sits on the bare wooden bunk, dejectedly, but still with a certain sense of calm. She has not yet given up hope of a rescue by Valhalla. If the Agents arrive before she is dragged off to the Bridge for trial and execution, she can help create a diversion to aid in any rescue attempt. Of course, there is a high chance of being seen, leading to an angry pursuit by pitchfork and torch wielding locals.

If the Agents are caught, this is where they are brought before their own trial at the Meeting Place. Depending on timing, being caught might be in everyone's interests, as it will certainly help them find Sarah, although escape will be all the harder as they need to spring themselves from gaol as well as Sarah.

The Meeting Place

The Meeting Place serves as the religious and social centre of the town: town hall, church, and courthouse. It is here that the Agents will stand trial, if necessary. It can hold up to 60 people on hard benches, and its plain wooden walls are otherwise not noteworthy in construction.

Any weapons and equipment confiscated from the Agents is held in the Meeting Place under lock and key in one of the small backrooms. In another backroom is a small armoury where muskets and cartridges are kept for use by the Salem militia. There are eight muskets in total, but around 200 cartridges, packed into a straw-filled chest.

The Ship Tavern

The Ship is the local tavern. It has a couple of rooms for rent, serves the locally brewed dark ale, and is usually busy with regulars and itinerants from the harbor. Tonight, it is subdued as most are gathering at the Bridge for the witch trial, but there are some diehards, such as Norman and Clifford, who never leave their stools if they can possibly help it.

The landlord is Samuel Malone, a Bostonian who came to Salem in disgrace several years ago. He's an ardent womaniser, and any female Agents come under his flirtatious scrutiny. He's affable enough, and engages in conversation, wanting to know where the Agents hail from, their business in Salem, and, more importantly, why they're not at the witch trial. 'Should be a good one,' he says. 'Local girl'. If pressed (Influence rolls), he reveals her name as Burroughs, although he has trouble remembering her first name. Clifford or Norman, two of the fixtures and fittings of The Ship, quite readily let it be known that Sarah is either at the gaol, just been taken from it, or is at the bridge, depending on how long the Agents have taken to get to this point. If local help is needed from these three, they can be bribed with money or alcohol, to cause a diversion or a similar distraction as long as it doesn't involve them getting hurt.

If the Agents question Norman or Clifford at any length, they find both men have nothing to say about witchcraft or Sarah Burroughs, but a Hard Influence skill roll can get either to mention seeing 'lights in the sky' a while back. It seems whilst Norman was languishing the stocks for public drunkenness, he witnessed something (the alien ship, but he does not know this) fly overhead towards the south. Although everyone in Salem thinks he is crazy, an Insight roll reveals his truthfulness. Clifford didn't see the strange light, but Malone, who talks to a lot of people, says he heard other reports of a very bright shooting star heading towards the south.

The River

West of town is a stone arch bridge that spans a section of the North River. A huge crowd – the entire town it seems – has gathered there. As the Agents approach, they overhear various townsfolk speculating on the witch's alleged crimes. Several claim to have suffered ailments, mishaps and accidents that could only be the result of spells cast by a witch. 'Burroughs,' one of the locals spits. 'Devil's whore, no doubt of it. Milk of all my cows made sour after she visited the farm. Never trusted her. Let her drown, I say.' The townsfolk have tied a rope around Sarah and dropped her off the bridge into the river. Her right thumb is bound to her left big toe. A successful Insight or Swim roll shows that this ensures that she couldn't swim or otherwise keep herself afloat except through witchcraft – the undeniable proof they are looking for. A tall man, the magistrate, holds a small mirror up to her dripping face, then shakes his head. He declares her dead, 'Goody Burroughs, may God have mercy on your soul.' At this point, two town watchmen unbind her and carry the body to the shallow grave indicated on the map. A Perception roll indicates something not quite right about Sarah's 'corpse'; the Agents need a much closer look to know what.

The majority of the mob disperses, leaving a cadre of truly dedicated locals – the pious and the perverse – to gawk at her burial.

The Shallow Grave

The watchmen fall back several metres after tossing the body in the grave. At the grave site, locals line up to peer at the body. To get a closer look or learn more about 'Goody Burroughs', the Agents must either wait their turn for about 15 minutes or make an Influence roll to move up the queue. While working the line, they learn that 'Goody Burroughs' was caught fornicating with the Devil, that she mated with livestock, and that the Parish Minister's daughter Abigail Warren was struck ill by the witch's evil eye. An easy Influence roll reveals that much of the 'witch's' craft took place at her cabin in the woods a few kilometres away. Any attempt to get precise directions to Sarah's home arouses suspicion, unless craftily hidden within a Deceit skill roll.

Viewing the body reveals a lovely young woman who is obviously not breathing, lying peacefully in a muddy hole.

Anyone who makes a Healing or Science (Physiology) roll notices that she doesn't look like a drowning victim: no blue lips, swollen tongue, and so on. Not only that, but she is trying to conceal a shiver. Sarah is still alive.

If no one else is nearby, or if the Agents cause a diversion, Sarah opens her eyes, breathes deeply, and whispers, 'Thank Newton! I h-hope you brought d-dry clothes and a p-plan to get me out of here! I'm s-so c-cold!' If asked how she survived, she shivers and winks, 'I'm-m a w-witch, remember?'

GRAVE ROBBERY

Getting Sarah out of her grave could prove difficult without a clever plan. Within a few minutes, the grave-side crowd disperses and a gravedigger carelessly fills the grave with loose dirt. A well-timed Influence skill could convince the gravedigger to hand off his duties (and shovel) to the Agents. Without a good cover for mucking about with the grave, it takes several Stealth and Deceit rolls to keep onlookers from noticing their 'grave robbing'.

Once out of the grave, Sarah insists they return to her cabin so she can gather her notes and belongings, which are 'vital'. She notes once the locals discover she's missing (as they most assuredly will), they will burn the house to ground to banish her 'evil spirit'. 'They've purged two other witches in the same way,' she says ruefully. 'So they'll do the same to me.'

Sarah's disappearance will be raised at some stage by a nosy local, and the alarm raised, rousing 15+1d10 angry villagers with pitchforks and torches to give chase. They gather at the Meeting Place where the magistrate, Josiah Choat, harangues them to pursuit. Three villagers are handed rifles from the armoury. The mob isn't subtle in its approach, rushing after the Agents or, if the Agents were not seen, marching directly on Sarah's cabin to burn it down and cleanse their community, killing anyone foolish enough to stand in the way.

If the Agents don't realise that Sarah is still alive or spent too long incarcerated, Sarah rescues herself. Her disappearance goes unnoticed until dawn. In that case, finding her requires several difficult Perception rolls and at least two Tracking rolls; Sarah does her best to cover her tracks.

> ### Sarah's Powers
> Sarah's unique ability is to sense psychic disturbances over long ranges; it is a form of the *Sense PSI* talent, but is peculiar to her. This makes her receptive to those who might make good Valhalla Agents, but also makes her sensitive to creatures like the Mattanit, which feed on, and exude, psionic energy.

SARAH'S CABIN

Sarah's home is a modest, single-room log cabin. Inside the cabin is a small bed, fireplace, and a few meagre possessions. The psychic obviously lives a spartan existence.

Nearby is a small barn, meant for a couple of goats or pigs, but that has clearly been empty for some time. A search of the barn with a Hard Perception check reveals a wooden trap door hidden beneath the mouldy straw that leads to a surprisingly dry cellar. The cellar is but a single 4 by 7 metre room. Here is where Sarah keeps her TPT, a small, portable version, hidden in an old, locked chest. A table takes up one corner of the room, a map of the coast showing Salem, Boston, and Hockomock Swamp unrolled upon it. Hockomock has been circled with the word 'Here?' in neat handwriting next to it. Any Agents with a skill at handwriting analysis can match the lettering to Sarah. On the wall hangs a Jager rifle.

If she's with them, Sarah quickly dons dry clothes, stripping immodestly in front of the Agents whilst telling them to grab provisions. If the Agents find and inspect the cabin and barn first, Sarah arrives shortly thereafter.

Either way, Sarah explains that they must hurry – it's only a matter of time before the townsfolk come to burn down her cabin. If pressed about how she survived being drowned, she explains that she spent time among the indigenous people of the region, and they taught her some of their mystical techniques for survival. These equate to a Path of Focal Yoga (see *Luther Arkwright*, page 69).

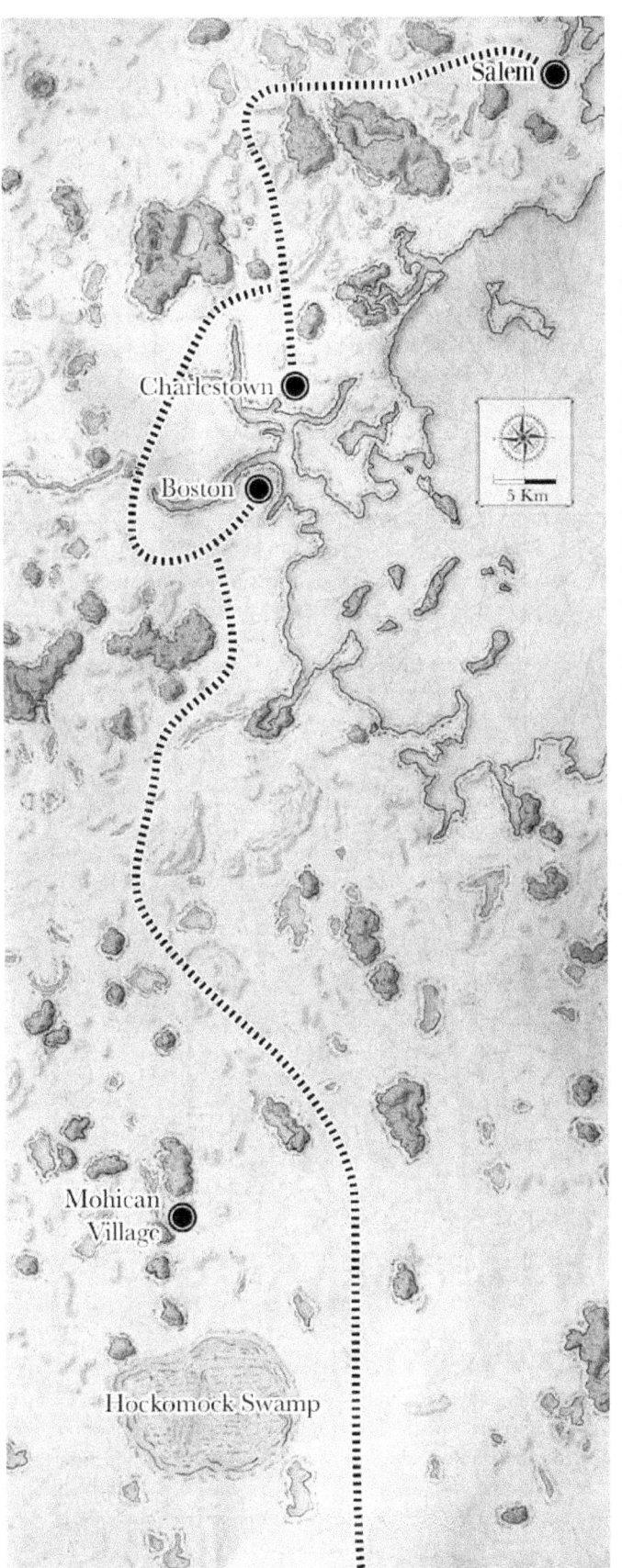

GOIN' SOUTH

It is 85 kilometres from Salem to the Hockomock Swamp, following the road that leads to Charlestown and then Boston. It takes the team two days to ride there on horseback, four days travel on foot. Once the Agents get far enough away from Salem to have effectively evaded pursuit, Sarah briefs them.

'One of my talents is sensing people who are touched. People like you. This is a dangerous land for such folk, as I'm sure you've noticed. Fear of the Devil is deadly serious here,' Sarah explains. 'But for the last few weeks I've felt something... different, something beyond God-fuelled cruelty. I feel malicious minds so distinct that I don't even need to meditate to sense them. I just *feel* them and from many miles away. They were all south of here at first, but now I feel they have split up. The strongest, and I assume the main, presence is far south. I have friends among the Mohicans who live down there. A while back, they told me of strangeness around Hockomock Swamp. Whatever is going on, that's where it all began, and that's four days' travel from here. Where should we go first?'

It is clear that the team needs to head south towards the Hockomock Swamp. En route, whichever way they take, there are opportunities for encounters as described in the following sections.

THE BRITISH PATROL

Without warning, a patrol of eight British Regulars (see page 24) on horse descends upon the Agents from around a bend or over the ridge of hill. They are moving fast with tense purpose. Unless the Agents use Deceit, Stealth, or Influence to avoid the encounter, the British stop them and demand their business.

If the Agents admit they are headed far south to the Mohicans or the Hockomock, the soldiers shake their heads at their folly, remarking on the backward savagery of the natives and the strange things happening of late. If pressed, they describe mysterious fogs that roll in at odd times and people disappearing and then returning but acting strangely: disobeying simple orders or forgetting the most basic things. One man forgot his wife and children; another forgot how to talk. If asked about the British Empire or their leadership, they refuse to speak further, saying they've wasted enough time on idle chatter already and tell the Agents to move along.

If the Agents lie, the outcome depends upon both the tall tale and their Deceit skill. A Success means the encounter passes smoothly; Failure, the soldiers act. They are experienced veterans who do not hesitate to resort to violence if they sense danger or trickery. If caught hiding from the patrol or drawing weapons on them, the soldiers ready their flintlocks and demand the Agents lay down their arms. They inform the Agents they are taking them to a nearby gaol to hold them until they can verify their story. Since their story can't be verified in any satisfying way, the Agents need to be quick-witted to avoid being clapped in irons and dragged off.

THE WANDERER

The initial part of this encounter can happen no matter which direction the Agents take, at the Games Master's discretion.

The Agents come upon a colonial wandering in the wilderness, crying out for assistance. His name is Daniel Barwick. He is lost and is looking for his family who are certainly waiting for him. Abby and his three children live in a nice two-storey home, but Daniel can't remember the name of the town. In fact, he doesn't even really know *where* he is. He doesn't remember any place names – Boston, Mass, and even Great Britain mean nothing to him.

The Mind Probe psionic talent can be used to learn something of what happened to Daniel. His mind has been partially wiped, but the method of the wipe does not suggest traditional psionic methods; this is something much more invasive, and much more fundamental. It is the psionic equivalent of amputation: large parts of memory and experience have been ripped away leaving trace residue that appears in snatches without context or coherence.

In reality Daniel is a victim of the aliens. When three of the Mattanit left the swamp in the possessed bodies of Mohican warriors, they came upon a group of fur traders and their guide, Daniel Barwick. They swapped bodies with the fur traders and drained Daniel of some of his memories.

The three Mattanit are at large in the region, but it will take considerable effort to track them. One will eventually possess General Blair and find its way to England and the Queen, while another two remain in Boston and become responsible for a series of unexplained murders.

When Daniel regained his senses after the Mattanit attack, he found himself lying beside three dead Mohicans with no memory of where he was or how to get home. The fur traders were also nowhere to be found.

He can and does tell the Agents about everything that happened after he woke up. The only way he can make sense of what happened is that the fur traders were in league with the Devil and somehow they killed the Mohicans and then placed a hex on him so that he couldn't get home or warn anyone.

Daniel is low on supplies and would appreciate directions to any nearby town. If pressed, he can backtrack to where he buried the bodies. Should the Agents go there and dig them up, there find no wounds or signs of violence, nothing to indicate what the natives died from. Using the Medicine skill only shows the Mohicans died of no illness, wound, or external stimuli. All psychic residue that would indicate the Mattanit involvement here has already faded.

THE MOHICANS

The Agents enter Mohican territory and find a small village that Sarah knows and is on good terms with. She introduces the Agents to the Mohican *sachem*, Makwa. Sarah speaks fluent Mohican and translates as Makwa speaks. The Agents are welcomed into their wigwams for the night.

After a meal, Makwa tells the team that the Hockomock Swamp has always been a holy place. Hockomock means 'where the spirits dwell'. It was here that the white man slaughtered every *Wampanoag* who stood their ground, so that only a few escaped to find refuge with their neighbours the Mohicans. Now the *Mattanit*, the 'Spirit of Evil', lives there. Makwa tells them that they first knew this evil was here after seeing strange lights in the sky and an unnatural fog blanketed the Hockomock.

The Mohicans sent one of their warriors, Etchemin, and his thirty-strong warband into the swamp to investigate. Only three, excluding Etchemin, returned. Those who did were not the same. They refused to speak about what they had witnessed. Instead, they took what they could carry and left, never to be seen again. The fog still covers Hockomock. No one goes near it.

Makwa urges the party not to go into the swamp, but if they cannot be dissuaded, he offers them a carved-out canoe large enough to carry them all. It takes a Hard Influence roll to persuade Makwa to allow one of his scouts to guide them. Use The Mohican statistics (page 25) for an average Mohican Scout.

> ### The Algonquin Tribes of New England
>
> *Algonquin* is a term to describe the numerous tribes whose roots and language are based upon Native American tribes that speak the Algonquian languages. Combined they are the First Nations. The original Algonquin people live in Quebec and Ontario, Canada. Algonquin tribes, however, have many names and live in many places. The Mohican are an Algonquin tribe that lives in New England; the Wampanoag are another. In this parallel, the Wampanoag were massacred at Hockomock and the survivors took refuge with the Mohicans to the west. The Mohicans and the few Wampanoag survivors resettled the Hockomock area soon after. The Mohicans live in small round houses called wigwams. The men wear tunics over a loin cloth with ankle-length leggings. The women's leggings reach down to their knees. All wear moccasins. The Mohicans are farmers and hunters, living off of corn, squash, moose, and small game as well as fish. They were among the first Native Americans to become proficient with flintlock weapons and actively trade for them with the Dutch and British.

THE DEVIL'S SWAMP

The Games Master should keep track of the time on this journey as it impacts how the action unfolds. There are 11 hours of daylight, and the Agents must navigate the swamp and find their answers before dark; everything gets much more difficult and dangerous after sundown. This swamp has the potential to inflict levels of Fatigue if the Agents aren't ready to use Luck Points early and often.

One of the Agents should be designated as navigator and attempt a series of Navigate rolls at Formidable difficulty due to the thick, unnatural fog. Other Agents can use Navigation skills to aid the main navigator. With each failed roll, an hour passes and the Agents become more lost in the swamp. With each successful roll, only 10 minutes pass and the team experiences an encounter. A critical success means the Agents proceed immediately to the next encounter with minimal time passage. A fumbled Navigation roll means two hours pass.

The swamp is truly terrifying after the sun goes down. The Agents cannot navigate effectively in the dark, forcing them to tie up their boat and hold-up for the perilous hours. Swamp fog as thick as smoke settles quickly and the eerie cries of wildlife echo all around. During the night hours in the Hockomock, the Agents' senses are assaulted from all sides, meaning Navigation rolls are considered Herculean, and Perception skills are always Formidable. Additionally, all Agents lose one point of Tenacity from the concentrated hate from the nearby Mattanit.

Encounters

Daytime encounters occur in the following order:

1. Swamp gas erupts from a pocket of clay and mud. The Agents suffer asphyxiation as per Mythras, page 71. They must use the Task Round system (Mythras, page 66) to successfully boat out of the area. First, calculate how long each Agent can go without breathing. At least one person must row the boat to get it out of the gas; others can augment with their own Boating skills by taking up oars. This is considered strenuous activity for calculating how long they can go without air. Every 5 seconds, make an easy Boating roll. For each successful Boating roll, they travel 25% of the distance they need to get out. It doesn't matter which direction they row; the gas is invisible and rolls along the surface evenly in all directions. Each 25% increment represents the distance they go in the direction they choose, even if this is back the way they came. To activate her Denial (Air) talent, Sarah must meditate and cannot help the Boating roll until she's done. After that, she can row long after the rest have collapsed. Her Boating skill is 24%.

2. The top of a massive boulder juts out of the water. It is inscribed with strange, unreadable petroglyphs. Sarah says it's called Dighton Rock. Even the natives don't know who carved those symbols. Many copies have been made of the Dighton Rock carvings, but no two copies are ever the same because the inscriptions have been worn with time. Anyone may attempt to copy the petroglyphs if they have writing utensils and make a Herculean Willpower roll or a Formidable Art roll. Understanding the petroglyphs requires at least 4 weeks of study and a Herculean Insight roll, and at this point induces the student to astrally project, entering a dimension of space time occupied by the ancient shaman who carved the rock. If the student is willing to spend a year with the shaman (leaving the body in a catatonic state for a similar period), he or she gains the Totemic Connection Mystical Path of Enlightenment (*Luther Arkwright*, page 69).

3. A Turtle of Unusual Size (page 25) rises from the water to investigate the Agents. The turtle is the size of a motorcar and rocks the boat making it unstable and possibly sending Agents into the water unless they make a successful Athletics roll. Failing to do so means a dunk in the swamp, giving the turtle an opportunity to make a single attack on the target. A Swim roll is required to get back in the boat or outmanoeuvre the turtle.

4. Day turns suddenly to night. The stars are visible overhead even though the sun should still be shining. This effect last for two hours. A chill frost rimes the boat and Navigation rolls become Herculean. Each Agent must roll Endurance or lose a level of fatigue to the cold. There is no explanation for this mystical darkness.

5. An unnatural, mechanical whirring noise can be heard through the fog. It is hard to pinpoint its exact direction. Roll Perception at Formidable difficulty; if any Agent succeeds, the navigator can roll the next Navigation roll at Standard difficulty in an attempt to find the source of the strange noise. The noise is coming from the Mattanit Engineer attempting to restart the crashed ship's EM Drive. The Engineer hopes to get it running without the Ancestor Coil, so he can at least use the ship around as an all-terrain vehicle, but by the time the Agents arrive, he will not have found success (see The Starship and The Ancestor Coil).

6. A small island suddenly looms out of the fog, not more than 12 metres across. With a successful Perception roll, the Agents spot a Mohican warrior hunched over an odd futuristic vehicle of some sort, the source of the noise in encounter 5. The Mohican looks and up and the noise stops. This is the crash site for the Mattanit ship. Once the Agents arrive at the island, they can proceed to The Alien.

The Alien

There is one Mattanit-possessed human present as the Agents approach. The body is that of the Mohican *Sachem* Etchemin, and the Mattanit possessing his body is The Engineer trying to repair the ship. Thus far, it has been unsuccessful in repairing the Ancestor Coil.

The island is where the Mattanit ship crashlanded and has remained ever since, under the protection of The Engineer. When Etchemin and his Mohican warband came to investigate the swamp, the Engineer stalked them, devoured their minds, and saved Etchemin's body for himself. It has been aware of the Agents' presence in the swamp ever since they arrived, but has chosen to wait for them to come to it, rather than stalking them as it did with the Mohicans.

The Engineer's tactics are simple. Pretending to be Etchemin, it lures the Agents close enough to use its Neural Neutraliser, which renders a target painlessly and silently unconscious for several hours, allowing it to psychically feed at leisure. Anyone who resists the Neural Neutraliser is targeted by the Mattanit's Sap Vigour talent to slow them down so that the Neural Neutraliser can be used again. The Engineer also uses Etchemin to defend and attack physically with the Mohican's own weapons.

The Engineer's main role here is to defend and repair the spacecraft. It has been patiently working on the part known as the Ancestor Coil, but the process is delicate and requires time as the alien must cannibalise other parts of the ship to effect the repair.

If given the chance to occupy the mind of one of the Agents, or even Sarah Burroughs, the Mattanit understands that here is an opportunity for it to learn all about inter-dimensional travel, greatly extending its species' reach. It is quite prepared to abandon its current endeavours to travel to Zero-Zero and is quite happy to use any of the Agents to achieve these ends. The rest, it is content to feed on, leaving behind drained husks that, stripped of intellect and memory, simply starve to death out here in the swamp.

Naturally, the Mattanit Engineer must be stopped. Others of its species are busy infecting this parallel, and there is little the Agents can do about it. But this specimen can be either killed or captured, and taken back to Zero-Zero for in-depth study.

The Engineer thus fights hard, fights to the death, and seeks to preserve its own life. If it can, the alien exits Etchemin's body and flees into the fog, seeking to hide deep in the swamp where it will be almost impossible to track it down. But unless Etchemin's body is killed, it fights with the alien weapon, Mohican weapons, and its psionic abilities to the last.

Sarah wants to take Etchemin alive, hoping to get to the bottom of whatever madness this is. She urges the Agents not to use lethal force, but if it becomes apparent that the Engineer has no such qualms, her view can be changed. Etchemin's personality has long-gone, devoured by the Engineer, but of course, the Agents and Sarah cannot know this until it is too late.

The Engineer might try and pass itself off as Etchemin, perhaps awaiting rescue, but Insight rolls recognise that while it might try to act like Etchemin, it is not. The Engineer is not accomplished in assuming different roles, so any deception it might try to work is soon uncovered.

Once the alien is defeated (or hiding within Sarah or another Agent), the Agents can investigate the island. Here they find the crashed starship. It has been opened up so its internal components can be worked upon. A couple of strange looking tools lie about as well as what looks like a large coil. The coil is obviously damaged. Sense Psi detects the coil as psionically attuned. This is the Ancestor Coil and it is integral to the Mattanit ship's operation. See the description on page 21.

THE STARSHIP

The ship vaguely resembles an amphibious car (about the size of a 2-door sports car), with no seats or recognisable interior. It has wheels for ground travel and retractable fins and propellers for underwater use. The 'hatch' is only a series of small holes into which the Mattanit can vent in gaseous form and thus might not be recognised as such by human observers.

The ship is designed to hold 12 Mattanit, who are of much smaller mass than a human and don't breathe atmosphere or eat (being dependent upon synaptic and psionic energy for survival). As such, the craft is completely useless to humans. There is simply no way for them to fit inside, let alone understand how to operate it.

The ship is powered by a series of d highly advanced, highly compact drives that both Valhalla and the Disruptors would greatly value. The technology is far beyond the comprehension of the Agents, but Quinscombe, other Valhalla technicians, and W.O.T.A.N will have a field day studying it.

MATTANIT STARSHIP
Size: Small (2.5m by 4m)
Hull: 12 *Structure:* 15 (20 when repaired).
Systems: 5
Speed: Impossibly Fast. (Instantaneous acceleration from zero to full speed. This ship ignores drag, gravity, seemingly the laws of physics when in flight mode.) In water, it is Rapid. On the surface, it is Fleet. Note the vehicle currently has no movement capabilities as its power supply is damaged.
Traits: All-Terrain Vehicle, FTL, Enhanced Performance, Spacecraft, Submersible
Shields: None
Weapons: None

THE ANCESTOR COIL

Made from the psychic essence of a thousand deceased Mattanit grafted into this coil-shaped artefact that emanates psychic energy, the Ancestor Coil is what makes distant star travel possible for the Mattanit. It provides both energy for the warp drive and psychic nourishment for the Mattanit during the journey. Anyone with Sense Psi detects huge psychic emanations pulsing from the Coil, and it is this that Sarah has been sensing for some time.

This Ancestor Coil's energies have begun to fade. Just as the ship came out of warp, at micrometeorite pierced the hull and struck the Coil, causing a critical leak of psychic energy. The Mattanit were barely able to reach Earth and execute a controlled crash land in the Hockomock Swamp.

If the Coil is handled by a human Agent, the following happens: The Coil seems to come alive in the hands. The handler sees dark shadows swirling about the device and suddenly feels its psychic energies flowing from the Coil and into the body. Before the handler can drop the device, he or she begins to see a vision of a faraway world; a barren planet. Two moons hang in the sky, one red, one white. A distant, dying star struggle to survive.

At that point, the Ancestor Coil's remaining psychic energy is spent. It is rendered completely useless and even the Mattanit can no longer repair the device. Further handling of the Coil has no effect.

The handler should also make a Formidable Willpower roll to resist the insidious, malevolent power inherent in the Coil. Failure results in Level 3 Psionic Trauma event (see *Luther Arkwright*, page 50). Irrespective of how much Tenacity is lost, the victim gains the Delusional Condition, believing him or herself to be the reborn collective intelligence of the Mattanit intellects contained within the Coil. The victim no longer considers him or herself to be human, and believes it must feed on sentient minds to survive. This mania is not real of course, but requires significant therapy to cure.

If no one handles the Coil, it bleeds out the last of its energies in a few days, becoming completely inert.

Returning to Zero-Zero

Having discovered the secret of Hockomock Swamp and saved Sarah, return to Zero-Zero is simply a matter of summoning the Van. It arrives after about 10 minutes, materialising close to the Agents with an accuracy that it failed it demonstrate when it brought them to this parallel.

The Mattanit ship is too large to fit into the Van and the Agents lack the equipment needed to be able to attach it to the Van's exterior. More importantly, there is no way of knowing how the Van would handle with another mass attached to its exterior, so it is best to use the various navigational recording devices inside the Van to note the ship's coordinates on this parallel, and hand the problem over to Quinscombe. If the Agents are adamant that they will try to salvage parts of the ship, it takes 1d6x6 hours to disassemble any of the alien technology effectively, and requires an Engineering roll to stow it safely. On return to Zero-Zero, Quinscombe will be livid at such experimentation (although, see the next scenario, *This Corrosion*; getting back is not as immediate as one might think) without consulting him first.

The best course of action is to leave the starship where it is, and salvage it later, when time and resources are available. This also offers the opportunity for some of the remaining Mattanit to return to guard their valued property.

Are We There Yet?

The Mk II Van was damaged in its arrival on this parallel. Although the superficial damage was repaired by Quinscombe's team, further faults were not spotted, and it's navigation systems decided to malfunction on the return trip, sending the Agents spinning off to the war-torn parallel of *This Corrision*.

> ### And the Other Mattanit?
>
> The Mattanit ship brought 12 individuals to Earth. One of them died in the crash, and its body has already been absorbed into the Ancestor Coil. The remaining four stayed by the ship, assessing the local environment when the Mohicans led by Etchemin arrived to investigate the strange light they had seen. The Mattanit made short work of the warband, possessing four of the men and feeding on the rest (their decomposing) bodies float in the reed beds of the swamp. Leaving the Engineer behind to work on fixing the ship, the other Mattanit, posing as the Mohicans, fanned out in all directions to learn more of this world and how it can be exploited.
>
> As mentioned on page 18, three of them came across the fur traders and Daniel Barwick, and the remaining seven have split up, with four headed to Charlestown in the north and three to New York in the south. Their presence will cause havoc on this parallel and tracking them down can be the purpose of an extended mission Games Masters can develop separately. One of the Mattanit controls General Blair and intends to take control of England's Queen Anne, while the rest are focused on seizing control of important notables in Charlestown, Boston, and New York. This subtle invasion may even appear to be a Disruptor plot, but it is not.

Mattanit Technology

Neural Neutraliser

A small black oblong device the size of a thumbdrive, the Neural Neutraliser packs a huge psychic wallop. Once activated (by squeezing the sides of the device), it generates a wave of psionic energy that acts on the brain of anyone caught in it's field of operation - 15° arc with a range of 15 metres. Anyone caught in the beam must succeed in a Formidable Endurance roll or lose consciouness for 1d6 minutes, which is long enough for a Mattanit to possess a victim or begin a feeding session.

The field disrupts the local air, giving the beam a coherence similar to a dark mist that means it can be evaded with Acrobatics or Evade rolls. This effect is peculiar to the device's operation in Earth's atmosphere and does not happen elsewhere. While this makes the weapon avoidable, it does not prevent the Mattanit from using it.

The Neural Neutraliser has a limited charge. It can operate continuously for 10 combat rounds, or in a directed pulse mode for a total of 6 bursts. The device is small enough to be concealed in a palm, and its operation with the smoky trail generated by the energy field, may make it appear that the user is creating some form of magical force from his or her hand.

Fog Generator

The Fog Generator is a device that can be used to generate a thick, harmless fog that covers up to 6,000 hectares of land. The Mattanit use it to hide their presence while they establish themselves on a new planet, and here in the Hockomock swamp is no exception. The machine is portable; a crystalline globe about the size of a grapefruit and peppered with thousands of tiny apertures. A small control panel on its base controls its operation and it requires a Hard Insight roll to understand its purpose and operation (see *Luther Arkwright*, page 79). When active, the globe emits a series of chemical spores that react with the local atmosphere, resulting in the dense fog. The device has a chemical capacity for six months of fog generation before needing to be refilled, and inherent sensors detect when the fog is likely to dissipate and produce another chemical burst. A full 6 hectare seeding lasts for about 24 hours before another burst is required.

Non-Player Characters

Sarah Burroughs

Sarah Burroughs is a deep field agent native to this parallel but recruited several years ago and trained at Zero-Zero. She is naturally sensitive to psychic emanations but is not herself psychic. Instead, Sarah has studied with several mystics in both the Americas and Europe, learning a form of Focal Yoga.

She has lived near Salem for only a few months, drawn there by the rumours of witchcraft that, she knows, usually indicate nascent psionic potential. She was unable to save the women who were accused of being witches and actively opposed the brutal regime behind the persecution. This led to her own downfall and the events that brought the Agents to her rescue.

Sarah is tough and resourceful. Little scares her, and she is quite capable of handling herself in this male-dominated society. She is not afraid to speak her mind and, on this occasion, it has caused her a great deal of trouble. She will not be deterred though, and Sarah is disdainful of the foolish and the bigotted.

Sarah Burroughs	Attributes
STR: 10	Action Points: 3
CON: 14	Damage Modifier: 0
SIZ: 13	Prana: 14
DEX: 15	Tenacity: 14
INT: 16	Movement: 6 metres
POW: 14	Initiative Bonus: +16
CHA: 15	Armour: None

1d20	Hit Location	AP/HP
1 – 3	Right Leg	0/6
4 – 6	Left Leg	0/6
7 – 9	Abdomen	0/7
10 – 12	Chest	0/8
13 – 15	Right Arm	0/5
16 – 18	Left Arm	0/5
19 – 20	Head	0/6

Skills	Passions, Traits & Dependencies
Athletics 30%, Boating 24%, Brawn 23%, Commerce 61%, Endurance 43%, Evade 60%, First Aid 31%, Home Parallel 67%, Influence 35%, Insight 35%, Language (English) 100%, Language (Algonquin) 50%, Lore (Animal) 62%, Mechanisms 36%, Mysticism 51%, Meditation 52%, Perception 55%, Ride 34%, Stealth 61%, Swim 24%, Survival (Wilderness) 58%, Willpower 43%	Passions: Loves Horses 66%, Loyalty to the Valhalla Project 80%, Hates Superstitious Ignorance 40% Traits: Perceptive (Psychic Energy) Dependencies: Risk Taking

Combat Style & Weapons	Traits & Notes
Frontiersman (Flintlock Rifle, Flintlock Pistol, Dagger) 45%	Skirmisher Trait

Weapon	Damage	Size/Reach	AP/HP	Effects
Knife	1d3	S/S	2/3	Bleed, Impale

Weapon	Damage	Range	Ammo	Rate/Load
Flintlock Rifle	2d6	20/200/500	Single Shot	1/4
Flintlock Pistol	1d8	10/20/50	Single Shot	1/4

Ned the Gaoler

A corpulent man sporting a vast walrus moustache, Ned cuts an imposing presence but is slow on his feet and in his wits. He takes great pleasure in incarcerating people, especially the women recently accused of witchcraft, and enjoys humiliating those who spend time in his cells. He frequents the Ship's Tavern where he boasts of his captives and how he has taunted them.

Ned the Goaler	Attributes
STR: 16	Action Points: 2
CON: 9	Damage Modifier: +1d4
SIZ: 18	Prana: 10
DEX: 7	Tenacity: 10
INT: 8	Movement: 5 metres (gammy leg)
POW: 10	Initiative Bonus: +8
CHA: 6	Armour: None

1d20	Hit Location	AP/HP
1 – 3	Right Leg	0/6
4 – 6	Left Leg	0/6
7 – 9	Abdomen	0/7
10 – 12	Chest	0/8
13 – 15	Right Arm	0/5
16 – 18	Left Arm	0/5
19 – 20	Head	0/6

Skills	Passions, Traits & Dependencies
Athletics 18%, Brawn 75%, Endurance 33%, Evade 30%, Influence 36%, Insight 29%, Language (English) 100%, Perception 41%, Stealth 28%, Unarmed 65%, Willpower 43%	Passions: Cruelty and Humiliation 80% Traits: Brutal Dependencies: Violence

Combat Style & Weapons	Traits & Notes
Thug (Fists, Headbutt) 65%	None

Weapon	Damage	Size/Reach	AP/HP	Effects
Fists	1d3+1d4	S/S	As for Arm	Stun Location

The Pure

Use for the Angry Mob, the town watchmen, and Daniel Barwick as needed. The Pure arm themselves with whatever tools are close at hand, typically pitchforks and torches. They are easily worked into a religious fervour and cannot be reasoned with.

The Pure	Attributes
STR: 10	Action Points: 3
CON: 9	Damage Modifier: 0
SIZ: 11	Prana: 10
DEX: 13	Tenacity: 10
INT: 11	Movement: 6 metres
POW: 10	Initiative Bonus: +12
CHA: 11	Armour: None

1d20	Hit Location	AP/HP
1 – 3	Right Leg	0/4
4 – 6	Left Leg	0/4
7 – 9	Abdomen	0/5
10 – 12	Chest	0/6
13 – 15	Right Arm	0/3
16 – 18	Left Arm	0/3
19 – 20	Head	0/4

Skills	Passions, Traits & Dependencies
Athletics 39%, Brawn 30%, Endurance 30%, Evade 30%, Influence 30%, Insight 33%, Language (English) 100%, Perception 33%, Stealth 33%, Unarmed 45%, Willpower 40%	Passions: Hate the Different 80%
	Traits: Bigoted Ignorance
	Dependencies: Feeling Righteous

Combat Style & Weapons	Traits & Notes
Mob Rules (Pitchfork, Musket) 55%	None

Weapon	Damage	Size/Reach	AP/HP	Effects
Pitchfork	1d4+4	M/L	2/4	Impale

Weapon	Damage	Range	Ammo	Rate/Load
Flintlock Musket	1d10	15/100/200	Single Shot	1/4

British Regulars

Arrayed in their signature red coats and polished black boots, these soldiers are spooked by the odd things that have been happening and may be a bit more trigger happy than usual. Their job is to patrol the road from Boston.

Redcoats	Attributes
STR: 12	Action Points: 3
CON: 13	Damage Modifier: +1d2
SIZ: 13	Prana: 10
DEX: 13	Tenacity: 10
INT: 11	Movement: 6 metres
POW: 10	Initiative Bonus: +12
CHA: 11	Armour: None

1d20	Hit Location	AP/HP
1 – 3	Right Leg	0/6
4 – 6	Left Leg	0/6
7 – 9	Abdomen	0/7
10 – 12	Chest	0/8
13 – 15	Right Arm	0/5
16 – 18	Left Arm	0/5
19 – 20	Head	0/6

Skills	Passions, Traits & Dependencies
Athletics 58%, Brawn 45%, Endurance 56%, Evade 48%, Locale (Mass) 40%, Perception 61%, Stealth 49%, Survival 51%, Unarmed 58%, Willpower 39%	Passions: Loyal to the Crown 60%
	Traits: None
	Dependencies: None

Combat Style & Weapons	Traits & Notes
British Regular (Flintlocks, Bayonet) 75%	Formation Fighting

Weapon	Damage	Size/Reach	AP/HP	Effects
Bayonet	1d4+2+1d2	M/L	6/8	Impale

Weapon	Damage	Range	Ammo	Rate/Load
Flintlock Rifle	2d6	20/200/500	Single Shot	1/4

Mattanit

The Mohicans

Natives of the region, a few survivors of the Wampanoag massacre led them to resettle this area. The Mohicans are highly attuned to their environment, knowing the land and its soul intimately, but being superstitious with it. Despite this they are brave fighters and good and loyal friends to those who display respect and courtesy. Sarah knows them well and is friendly with the local tribe.

The statistics here are for a typical warrior, and they also serve for Etchemin, who is possessed wholly by the Engineer Mattanit, and fights at 76% rather than 66%. Note that Etchemin/Engineer also has a Neural Neutraliser (see page 22).

Mohicans	Attributes
STR: 14	Action Points: 3
CON: 13	Damage Modifier: +1d2
SIZ: 12	Prana: 13
DEX: 14	Tenacity: 13
INT: 12	Movement: 6 metres
POW: 13	Initiative Bonus: +13
CHA: 11	Armour: None

1d20	Hit Location	AP/HP
1–3	Right Leg	0/5
4–6	Left Leg	0/5
7–9	Abdomen	0/6
10–12	Chest	0/7
13–15	Right Arm	0/4
16–18	Left Arm	0/4
19–20	Head	0/5

Skills	Passions, Traits & Dependencies
Athletics 46%, Boating 52%, Brawn 24%, Conceal 21%, Customs (Algonquin) 71%, Dance 44%, Deceit 23%, Endurance 52%, Evade 66%, First Aid 28%, Influence 40%, Insight 40%, Language (Mohican) 68%, Locale (Mass) 88%, Perception 49%, Ride Horse 88%, Sing 45%, Stealth 78%, Swim 52%, Survival 67%, Unarmed 65%, Navigation 75%, Tracking 79%, Willpower 37%	Passions: Loyalty to Tribe 60% Traits: Superstitious Dependencies: None

Combat Style & Weapons	Traits & Notes
Mohican Warrior (Flintlocks, Dagger) 66%	Skirmishing

Weapon	Damage	Size/Reach	AP/HP	Effects
Dagger	1d4+1+1d2	S/S	6/8	Impale

Weapon	Damage	Range	Ammo	Rate/Load
Flintlock Musket	1d10	15/100/200	Single Shot	1/4

Turtle of Unusual Size

A turtle the size of a small car has been sighted many times in the Hockomock swamp. This one is an ornery cuss that likes to let people know he's around. He'll knock them out of their boats and take a bite out of them if he gets the chance. He's not a killer, however, and having shown everyone who's boss of this swamp, he swims away.

Turtle	Attributes
STR: 36	Action Points: 3
CON: 15	Damage Modifier: +2d8
SIZ: 52	Prana: 14
DEX: 17	Tenacity: 14
INS: 11	Movement: 6 metres
POW: 14	Initiative Bonus: +14
	Armour: Tough Skin and Shell

1d20	Hit Location	AP/HP
1	Right Hind Leg	4/14
2	Left Hind Leg	4/14
3–15	Body	9/16
16	Right Fore Leg	4/14
17	Left Fore Leg	4/14
18–20	Head	4/14

Skills	Passions, Traits & Dependencies
Athletics 34%, Brawn 102%, Endurance 80%, Evade 34%, Perception 24%, Stealth 33%, Swim 100%, Survival 67%, Willpower 38%	Passions: Hate Intruders 70%

Combat Style & Weapons	Traits & Notes
Ancient Mutant Ninja Turtle (Bite) 70%	Formidable Natural Weapons

Weapon	Damage	Size/Reach	AP/HP	Effects
Bite	1d12+2d8	E/M	As for Head	Sunder

The Mattanit

Mattanit means 'Spirit of Evil' in the Algonquian tongue, and to humans it is entirely applicable to this alien race. The Mattanit are parasitic psychic vampires, feeding on the energy of a host in the form of their memories and experiences. In their natural form, Mattanit are only a metre high and resemble a cross between a bipedal cat with the head of a manta ray. Their bodies are dark skinned and mottled, with glowing red and amber eyes. Their hands terminate in three, long fingers with complicated joints. Their legs are short and thin, but capable of propelling the alien at a nimble turn of speed. All Mattanit are naturally psionics and have the abilities Drain Prana, Intangibility, and Sap Vigour. They feed by merging physically with a host, their forms integrating the spinal cord and brain of the victim. Mattanit prefer to merge with an inert or unconscious target, and so use their weapons and Sap Vigour abilities to render a potential host powerless, before commencing the merging process. If a target is conscious, it requires the host to resist with Endurance vs the Mattanit's Intangibility skill. If the resistance fails, the Mattanit becomes one with the host and seizes complete mental and physical control of the body. If the resistance succeeds, the Mattanit must find another host or render this one inert before it can try again. Merging with a host takes around 30 seconds and is a level 2 Psionic Trauma event to witness; if experiencing it, then it is level 3.

Once it is one with the host, the Mattanit feeds using its Drain Prana. Memories and recent experiences go first, absorbed by the alien where it collates and digests them before feeding on the energy they provide. Then the Mattanit drains the rest of the brain of psychic, emotional, and electrical energy until all that is left is a lifeless husk. The Mattanit can continue to inhabit the body, controlling it like a puppet, or abandon it to find a new one.

Their own world is dying, and the Mattanit seek a new home – or several – to colonise. Earth is not perfect, but it intrigues the aliens, and they see great potential for seizing control of the planet and enslaving so many delicious food animals. They have no inkling of travel through the dimensions, so learning of the possibility will be of huge interest to them.

Mattanit	Attributes
STR: 1d3 (2)	Action Points: 3
CON: 1d6+6 (9)	Damage Modifier: -1d8
SIZ: 1d3+1 (3)	Prana: 20
DEX: 3d6+6 (17)	Tenacity: 20
INT: 2d6+8 (15)	Movement: 8 metres
POW: 4d6+6 (20)	Initiative Bonus: +16
CHA: 2d6 (7)	Armour: None

1d20	Hit Location	AP/HP
1 – 3	Right Leg	0/3
4 – 6	Left Leg	0/3
7 – 9	Abdomen	0/4
10 – 12	Chest	0/5
13 – 15	Right Arm	0/2
16 – 18	Left Arm	0/2
19 – 20	Head	0/3

Skills	Passions, Traits & Dependencies
Athletics 65%, Brawn 8%, Conceal 35%, Deceit 75%, Endurance 36%, Evade 51%, Influence 69%, Insight 85%, Perception 66%, Stealth 90%, Survival 54%, Unarmed 12%, Willpower 80%	Passions: Conquer and Feed 90%
	Traits: Psionic
	Dependencies: Vampirism

Psionics	
Mattanit Psionics 90% (Drain Prana, Intangibility and Sap Vigour)	When in possession of a host, the Mattanit assume all physical skills (STR, CON and DEX based) at the host's percentage.

Combat Style & Weapons	Traits & Notes
Mattanit Predator (Neural Neutraliser) 80%	See Neural Neutraliser, page 22

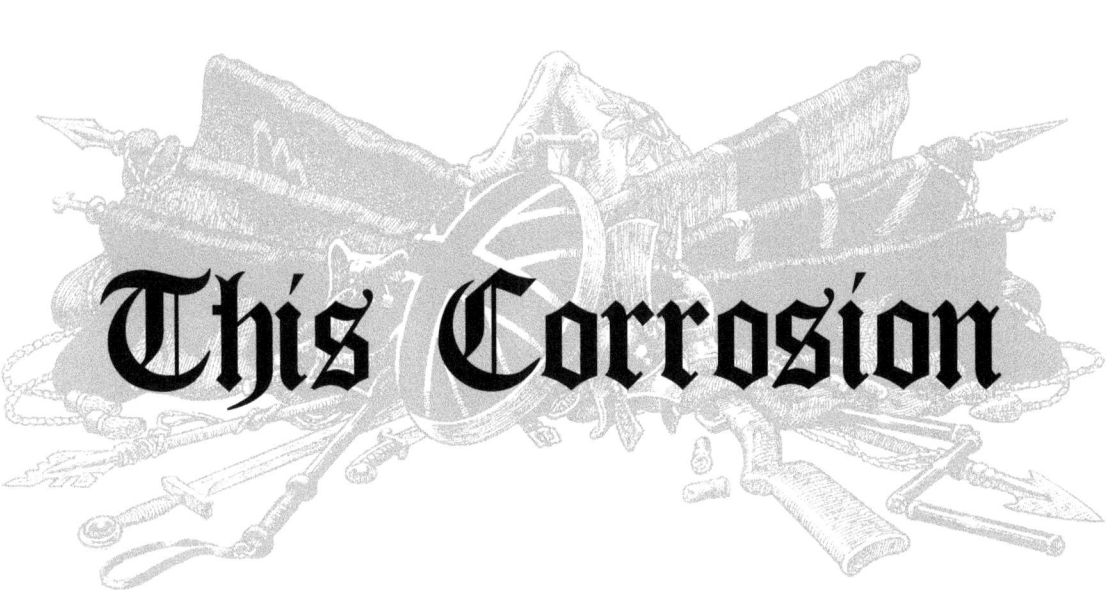

This Corrosion

Hatred of a thing is not the same as feeling its fetid breath condensing on your frozen face. Even with the best intentions, sometimes you need to face something to learn to hate it, and in so doing, learn to fight it. Learn to do what it takes to win: whatever it takes.

OVERVIEW

Designator: 07.99.54 (Time Slip)
Classification: Europe in Flames
Cultural Type: Northern Europe
Political Type: Bureaucratic
Technological Type: Industrial Age

The Agents arrive by mishap in the war-torn Camargue to witness bravery, quest for freedom, contend with monsters, and hear a call to heroism and sacrifice. The survivors experience the threat of the Disruptors and their corrosion of the human spirit first-hand. This is a journey that will change them and show the Agents, in no uncertain terms, what they fight for.

NON-PLAYER CHARACTERS

- *Kyland the Warlord*: Warlord and self-proclaimed ruler of Europe. His army is heading for Aigues-Mortes chasing dreams of powerful technology. Join him or die!
- *Vehemence Drake*: Leader of a slow but powerful steam caravan following a fabled path to freedom. She is quick and incisive, and seeks any advantage she can. That advantage is the Agents.
- *Aref*: Part of a growing revolutionary movement from Kyland's camp. Cautious and clever, with an eye for a person's quality. He believes in the Agents.
- *Number Nine (or the Hermit)*: Hermit and living legend mythologised for surviving in the open on his own. He has a secret score to settle with Kyland and needs the Agents to make it happen.
- *Grime*: Strangely cheerful warband leader in Kyland's service. Positively vengeful if his adolescent will is thwarted. He would shoot the sky for raining if it would bleed. He is on the trail of the caravan.

KEY POINTS/TIMELINE

1. The Van malfunctions, stranding the Agents.
2. Rib Ripper strikes!
3. The caravan arrives, meet Aref and Vehemence Drake.
4. A warband patrol attacks.
5. The Agents join the caravan or set out on their own.
6. The Agents run afoul of Grime's warband.
7. If captured, the Agents face Kyland to receive his ultimatum: Join or die.
8. They meet Number Nine and learn of his plan to defeat Kyland.
9. An attack is launched near Aigues-Mortes.
10. Cruel Departure.

Areas to be Covered

- The Camargue – This scenario is entirely set in this marshy region of Southern France and is focused on a caravan of refugees crossing it whilst fleeing for the coast.
- Botany Bay – The arrival point of The Van is a ruined commune 46 kilometres from Aigues-Mortes, near the ashes of Fourques and infested with foul things.
- Aigues-Mortes – An ancient coastal fort the refugees claim is the port of departure for the promised land.
- The Battlefield and the Hermit's Cave – A salt-flat on which men fight and die for buried secrets and unknown power.

Background

It is assumed that *This Corrosion* follows *Mattanit*. It takes place as the Agents are returning to Zero-Zero from the Hockomock Swamp. If running *This Corrosion* independently, some quick changes are needed. Two suggestions are the following:

- *Ignore any mention of the Mattanit and its ship. Start the scenario off with a brief statement that while in transit to another parallel, something has gone wrong. The Van is malfunctioning and after several painful seconds, the Agents find themselves stranded on Parallel 07.99.54 with uncertain chances for rescue.*
- *Stage it as a rescue mission for a wounded Agent. After recovering their downed comrade, The Van malfunctions on its return to Zero-Zero. Substitute any mention of the Mattanit and its ship with reference to the unconscious and injured Agent.*

Starting with a Bang

Arrival occurs with no warning and no time to rest or recuperate from the last assignment. Stressed and disoriented, the Agents have slammed through the frying pan and are nuts-deep in the fire. The Agents may wish to recover or take cover; these options are unavailable. Bad things are all around, and they are hungry, cruel, or both. The Agents must move to stay alive.

Some groups may possess the means to escape this parallel for another parallel. In the first few moments of play, it is important to give them reasons to flee the crash area, but not flee the parallel. If this scenario is about something, it is the conscious choice to oppose the work of the Disruptors wherever it is found. The Agents will experience a few days of hell, but will get to leave. That cannot be said for the natives of this blighted place. Who will help them if the Agents do not?

Europe in Flames

The Agents have been thrown into the middle of a warlord's quest for dominion and a legendary hero's quest for redemption for having armed and set the warlord on that path. Fleeing across their path are brutalised and desperate slaves who are taking life and sanity in their own hands to risk a dangerous escape to the south coast of France, and Africa beyond.

The Europe of this parallel has fallen into a heavily industrialised chaos of warring feudal states. On the rise now is the merciless warlord, Charles Kyland, backed by fanatical warriors, the fervent aid of the animalistic Once-Men, and advanced weapons of war. He has been burning his way across central Europe unchecked, crucifying and immolating his foes, and pressing the conquered into the service of his brutal army. Slaves in his service know no end of depravity. A thorn in his side is a man called the Hermit, also referred to as Number Nine for the tattoo on his face. Blamed for every failure or problem, this nearly legendary figure has become an icon of hope for refugees and slaves alike. Unlike anyone else, including the Warlord, Number Nine can survive alone in the wilderness without armed escort.

Disruptors have been watching this parallel slide further towards chaos and have chosen occasionally to help it along by randomly providing unbalancing weapons technology. They also interfered decades ago by unleashing the worst horrors of their genetic experiments into the wild via a massive portal, which still remains hidden away in the Camargue. The Warlord has recently become aware of what he believes is a cache of weapons technology and correctly believes Number Nine to be making use of it to oppose him. His army, under the shadow of his dread airship, is on the move to end this threat and obtain the technology once and for all. If the Hermit has his way, it will be the last thing the Warlord ever does.

The Hermit actively opposes the Warlord, but is only one man. He confides in no one and explains nothing. There are rumours about his motivations and abilities, ranging from him being a ghost to him being the Warlord's brother. He is known to target technology over soldiers, and to be more active in freeing technicians and learned men from Kyland's slavery than others. The truth is that Number Nine and Kyland grew up together in service to another cruel warlord, and through Number Nine's inventiveness and ability in understanding and applying the principles of advanced technology they were given by mysterious 'benefactors', Number Nine empowered Kyland's rise to the man he is today. Number Nine is consumed with regret and responsibility. He must end what he started, if he can find a way.

> ## Objects in Space
>
> As Time Slip is a parallel where Earth is out of sync, shifting between parallels using psychic or mytsical abilities has the undesirable result of arriving in the void of space. Offering strong hints to their unusual location is advised in such cases; some are provided in the text.
>
> For details of this parallel, known anecdotally as *Time Slip*, see *Luther Arkwright*, page 136.

The Camargue

This region of France on the coast of the Mediterranean Sea has never been heavily settled, and comprises mainly treacherous salt marshes, swampland, and unpredictable terrain. Given to narrow, winding roads at the height of civilisation, things have not improved. The largest settlement is in the ruins of Arles. Kyland has taken it as an operations centre, built fortifications, foundries, and factories, and is now launching the next phase of his war with the crucifixes of his enemies burning to light the way.

The locations in this scenario are less than 50 kilometres apart. This parallel, however, turns that on its ear, making the short trip into a gruelling slog, where terrain and fauna work together to eradicate travellers. Decades of neglect, warfare, and the damage wrought by its titanic monsters have battered this region into a hellhole of mud, grasping vines, and roads that go nowhere. Despite this, a beacon of civilisation still burns in Aigues-Mortes.

Aigues-Mortes

The walls and towers of this rectangular fortified city still stand despite the fall of Europe. The city's small population and well-trained militia keep the salt marsh relatively clear of larger threats, mainly by luring them elsewhere or redirecting them towards other threats. With great effort, they are able to survive inside the walls, and keep the Canal Viel and harbour clear. Maintaining the fields has become an impossibility due to an influx of Mud Lurkers and other horrors. Trade with the Kingdoms of Africa is essential. As the flames of war are fanned by Warlord Kyland, desperate bands of refugees are expected, but few have appeared.

Malfunction

The the damage the Van sustained when arriving near Salem is responsible for shorting out its planar interchange systems. Quinscombe's team did not have enough time to fully find and rectify this damage before the Agents summoned the Van to bring them back. This leads to surges and losses in power that not only disrupt the transit of the device between parallels, but send it hurtling out of sync in space as well. As luck would have it, The Van succeeds in finding an Earth to appear on.

Botany Bay

Blue and white light blinds the Agents in a series of electrical discharges that arc from the cargo containers, around the Agents, and along the pyramidal frame of energy conduits that provide power to The Van's steering components. Split-second flashes intercut randomly: drops from high altitude that roil the stomach, glimpses of deep space that unseat the mind, and moments of deep cold with waves of sizzling heat that compete to sear the skin, over and over. Then, through it all, a sense of falling comes to dominate,

> ### Parasites
> Any time the Agents are prone or low to the ground, make an attack by a Wriggler. See page 44 for details. These are small, segmented creatures with a hard shell about their heads. Often targeting eyes, they invade the bodies of warm-blooded creatures to nest in their kidneys. Agents unable to remove them before they reach a kidney require modern surgery. Locals often wear protective goggles.

until finally – after a seeming age of paralysing vertigo – impact. Have the Agents make Unsettling Fear checks (Willpower at Hard) to determine any loss of Tenacity.

The Agents are disoriented as they are thrown clear of The Van. Roll a Hard Endurance check. Success indicates Winded. Failure indicates Tired. A Critical Success avoids more Fatigue, while a Fumble indicates Wearied. If already feeling equal or greater effects of Fatigue, their condition worsens by one rank on a Failure or Fumble. The Agents are dizzy, with ringing ears. They have slight burns in places and patches of steaming frost on their clothing. They fall across a weed-strewn clearing under a storm-grey sky. The ground beneath is a mix of cobblestone and mud, disrupted by ragged tufts of grass and tangled patches of thorny plants.

The clearing was once a yard that ran between greenhouses, now ruined, collapsed, and weathered. Countless plants grow with abandon over everything, obscuring terrain details and the outlines of foundations. Atop the ruins is a large wooden sign split by the drunken lean of a rusted metal clock tower pulled down by vines. On one side of the tower, a gently creaking sign remnant reads 'Botanique' and on the other, reads, 'Baie'. The middle of the sign has long since rotted away. The time on the clock's oxidised face reads one minute to twelve. Far on the south-eastern horizon, the vague outline of massive smokestacks can be made out, along with the dark orange glow of vast fires. At the base of the clock tower, wanted posters flap fitfully in the breeze. One bears an image of a man with a number nine tattooed on the side of his face. Another is for a man dressed as a French chef brandishing a wooden spoon. Both men are wanted dead.

> ### Buzby Murder
> Unfortunately for the Agents the bottom half of the wanted poster for the man with 9 tattooed on his face has been torn off. The chef's poster is still intact however, having been pasted up in the last day or so. It reads thusly: 'WANTED dead for an act of criminal cooking. A reward of 15,000 Francs is offered for the individual known as the Iron Chef, who served a bombe glacée at the Kingdoms of Africa trade meeting dinner, resulting in the deaths of all attending delegates when it surprisingly exploded.

The Van is on its side. Its mechanical displays reveal the Parallel Designator of 07.99.54 and geographic coordinates. The

Agents may be able to assess that they are near Fourques in the Camargue region of southern France with a Navigation check, and a check of para knowledge from any relevant skill reveals information on the parallel. The power source is melted. Some cargo carriers were dislodged and bits of equipment and survival gear were scattered nearby (The Van, *Luther Arkwright*, page 76). The flares destroyed the mimetic cover and TPT, but only singed the case of four newly added Universal Translation Matrix devices. Beyond it, the clearing cuts off sharply into a freshly dug trench of prodigious width and depth, wreathed in a greenish steam with a bitter scent. (See *Trench Digger* on page 45 for details.)

The bleak clouds above undulate in a chilling breeze from the east that carries the bitter odour of the trench away while bringing scents of hot metal and the dry-nostril smell of steam. A cacophony of gears, boilers, tyres, and desperate voices registers in echoes and growing proximity in the Agents' ringing ears.

Situation Normal...

Before the group can react to the noise, a Rib Ripper attacks from ambush (check Perception at Formidable). This human-sized, vaguely cephalopodic creature has six powerful tentacles and a sharp prong on its underside, which it uses to implant the endoparasitic larval stage of its young in warm-blooded hosts its size or larger. It seeks to do so, then escape so that it can guard the host whilst hiding. See page 43 for details.

After the defeat or disappearance of the Rib Ripper, the mechanical and human noises should rise to the forefront. Through the obscuring greenery, the Agents see the tops of a preposterous caravan of steam-powered vehicles trailing thick smoke and jets of churning steam. The caravan is moving at speed and arcing towards them, on course to smash through the foliage and right into them and The Van. A Perception check shows that the lead driver cannot see the Agents or the trench, but is signalling for the caravan to stop – perhaps to assess battle damage or reassign guards as it looks like it has seen recent action. Even so, it is touch and go if the vehicles can stop without some minor collisions with the Agents, The Van, or each other. Any timely signal by the Agents forestalls accidents. If they do not signal, a damaging crash between the two central vehicles occurs, requiring repairs taking one additional hour. A Fumble could cause further damage to The Van.

Refugee Caravan Vehicles:

Steampunk Land Ironclad Tenders #10, #11. #50, #59
Hull: 11 *Structure:* 70
Speed: Sluggish
System: 4
Traits: Ground Vehicle, Construction (All-Terrain), Cargo, Weaponised, Enhanced Performance
Shields: None
Weapons:
Forward and Rear Gatling Guns x4
Central Mortar (Munitions) x4 (5d6 500/1000/2000)
(Salt Bomb) 2d6 + Intensity 3 Acid to Diggers

Description: Squat, broad, and built to last, these Large vehicles use powerful engines and massive ribbed tyres to crawl wherever they are needed. Intended as tenders for Kyland's tanks. They have a plow, front and back winches, and an articulated crane with cargo claw. These four have been modified with weapon turrets, catwalks, and access ports between the interior cargo spaces. They take a crew of eight to run and three-person teams for the turrets.

The caravan includes four huge, steam-driven, military construction vehicles showing signs of hasty modification and weaponisation. The storage compartments of ammunition loaders and

---

How Much Fighting?

This scenario is framed in brutal violence. This, however, is not its purpose. Agents can die anywhere. It's what they do that matters, and the Agents can make a difference here, while at the same time learning why that difference is so important – even if just on a personal scale. Make the conversations, the labour, and the lingering glances meaningful. Make the losses and fear powerful. Make the desperation, the dependencies, and the desire palpable.

Living or dying, make sure the characters show their players what they are fighting for. It's not about violence, it's about passion and resistance.

heavy-equipment haulers have been repurposed to protect huddled refugees. Flat tops have been fitted with catwalks and turrets front and back, with a mortar turret in the middle. The crew and refugees are haggard workers and guards in brown coveralls. The refugees seek escape with their families from Kyland's growing dominion, hoping to reach the free kingdoms of Africa. To get there, the refugees need to make their way to Aigues-Mortes for passage on trading vessels, trade which keeps that fortified city out of the grasp of greedy warlords.

UNIFORM CULTURE

Everyone is attired in brown workers' uniforms with yellow numbers on the back and two parallel slashes of red across the shoulders. Each person has repaired the worn-out attire in different ways giving a carnival air to the group. Vehemence Drake's crew wears red handkerchiefs around the left bicep as insignia. Everyone is tired and dirty. People are packed in like sardines or prowling the catwalks between gun cupolas scanning for threats. The caravan is well armed, but not all of these weapons have operators.

Leading the refugees is a middle-aged woman of obvious confidence and physical ability, Vehemence Drake. Drake was once a trained and oath-sworn protector of travellers in a far northern kingdom, but since its fall she has been selling her services to Kyland as a mercenary peace-keeper. When she learned of the atrocities of his war of expansion, Drake began to devise a way to extricate herself from his grasp, and take as many victims with her as she could. An assignment to guard a rearward re-arming and repair facility gave her the opportunity she needed. With caution and cleverness, Drake made it possible for the captive technicians there to secretly modify four giant tank tenders for refugee transport and self-defence. Last night, Kyland's tanks were called up to take position in Arles as his infantry began to mass for a push to the south. Her second in command, a shadowy man called Aref, is no stranger to risk and deception. He has slowly created a network of contacts and allies across Europe for years. With his help, Drake arranged for this 'caravan of refugees' to fall behind in the confusion. This morning they neared Fourques and managed to split off to head for Aigues-Mortes. Two things spoil their plans. The first is, unknown to them, Kyland's army is making for Aigues-Mortes by a different route. The second is that Kyland's vicious Steam-Charioteers, under the lead of teen fanatics like the finger-collecting Grime, are scouring the countryside looking for deserters, spies, and traitors.

Drake, dark goggles around her neck, introduces Aref while the crew works. The Agents, lacking uniforms and Kyland's mark, are demonstrably not in league with the Warlord. Drake needs fighters, but also lacks mechanics, engineers, and medics. She wants to determine quickly if the Agents are dead weight or not. Aref is quiet at first, assessing with shadowy eyes. In dreams, Aref has had contact with Agents of the Valhalla Programme before. Even if these Agents do not identify themselves, they trigger something in him. Aref attempts a dreamed code phrase, 'Do you remember

> ### Replacements
>
> For crew, there are six remaining drivers, five gunners, two mechanics, eight coal-tenders, and four lookouts, each risking injury and building fatigue every moment. They are addressed using their worker numbers or a specific physical detail like 'bright blue eyes' or 'missing teeth' – the Games Master should note these details and encourage the players to come up with and use such nicknames for each Non-Player Character. Some have been provided.
>
> In these close quarters, or in the hard labour at an obstacle, each makes their presence felt. That flash of bright blue eyes or the audacious grin of absent teeth is sorely missed when they are killed. The Agents will need to fill those voids. There are 10 refugee passengers per vehicle of varying ages from 10 to 50.
>
> *Number 802 'Cauliflower'*, a balding man in his late 40s, is the lead driver. He tugs a cauliflower ear when stressed, and has the red-stained lips of those who 'carry the 'Baby' (a potent drug, see page 34). He is down to his last few doses, but is the sort who shares everything.
>
> *Number 236 'Flat Nose'*, a lean and glittery-eyed gunner on the last vehicle, has the ruins of a once-proud nose flattened across her lined face. In her 50s, she misses nothing and is the sort to shoot first, then again, and questions be damned. She works hard and keeps her guard up.
>
> *Number 1159 'Tenor'*, has a waxy complexion and lips stained bright red from 'Baby. A coal-tender, he spends most of his time in the belly of the lead vehicle, singing to his partner as they suffer in the heat. His voice, though untrained, is heart-breaking in its clarity and emotiveness.

a time when Angels...?' He expects the counter phrase, 'Do you remember a time when Fear...?' Introductions get interrupted here, but no matter how events go, Aref will be for including the Agents in the caravan, if only to satisfy his curiosity.

IS IT MONDAY?

The sudden sound of gunfire cuts through the noise of the caravan. Four Steam-Chariots crash through the shrubbery and vines, drivers firing and screaming 'Kyland!' Drake and her crew can repel them, but without the Agents' aid, they take heavy losses.

Each Chariot has a human handler, the Charioteer, and a Once-Man chained like a rabid attack dog. See page 46. The Chariots are armed, low-slung, steam-powered trikes with the engine between the driver and his living weapon. The handler drives and also controls the front-mounted Gatling gun. The Once-Man rides in a cupola on the other side of the engine, straining to fight, leaping around the cupola with startling agility and reckless hunger for release. Once released by the handler, they fight fiercely, fast, and frenzied, first against opponents, then against their handlers. The handlers are hardened to putting their living weapons down once they have served their purpose, namely, eviscerating the enemy.

The Charioteers are all action and little thought, unlike Grime, a more capable threat whom the caravan is sure to encounter later on the trail. Their tactics are simple: circle the

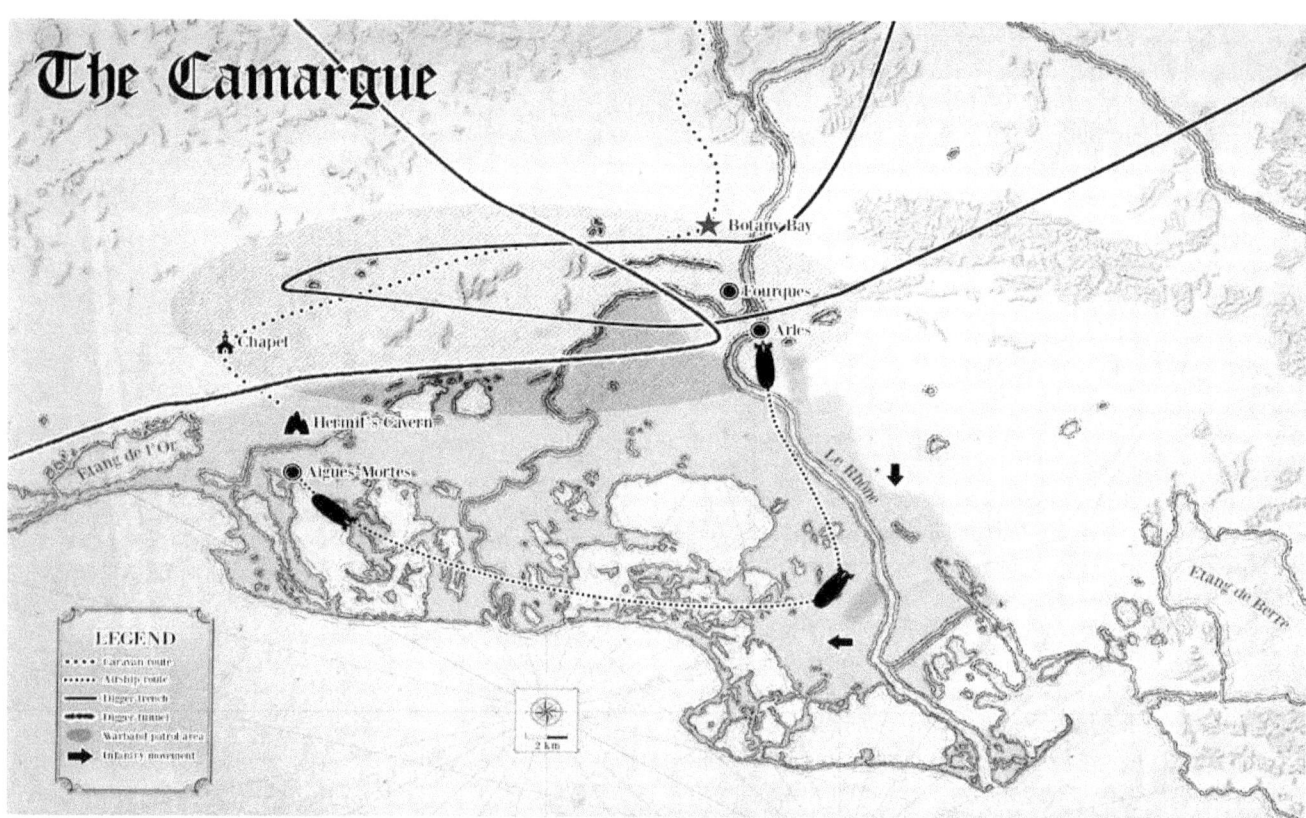

A larger version of the Camargue map can be found on page 172

caravan and shoot. In the clearing, Charioteers release the Once-Men who hurtle straight for the gunners in the turrets, crossing 15 metres of open terrain in a sickeningly short time. Moving faster than a human should be able to, they revel in any damage they take, like the pain fuels them. If the Once-Men survive and overcome the gunners, they dive into the passenger spaces to tear at the refugees without mercy. The Once-Men are brutal and relentless; they won't stop until killed. The handlers direct Gatling gun fire at the vehicles, but as the guns are largely stationary, fixed forward, the handlers must circle and weave to get a bead on targets.

These Charioteers are completely unprepared for return fire from heavy weapons; they expect to be the only side with Gatling guns. Treat them like Rabble if a defence with Gatling guns is mounted. If driven to flee, the Charioteers make their best speed to Arles to report. If captured and forced to talk (threat of abandonment in these wilds is one means of effective persuasion), the Charioteers can reveal the following: Grime's brutal warband also patrols this region, a tank battalion has been moved up to protect Arles, and there is a supply depot in a chapel midway to Aigues-Mortes on this route. They also know Kyland is heading south to seek a cache of technology and that he has raised an already high bounty on his domain's number one enemy: The Hermit, Number Nine. They do not know what is relevant to the interrogators and reveal information in the order presented here.

Need a lift?

If the Agents acquit themselves well, Drake and Aref seek to persuade the Agents to join them. Drake offers transport, including The Van, to Aigues-Mortes, 'the only safe haven in the Camargue and the portal to Free Africa'. She describes Africa as a place of peace and prosperity. Aref reinforces this, mentioning a technological renaissance there. One additional argument they make is that Rib Rippers and other creatures are a fairly common 'nuisance' and sleeping rough in the Camargue is suicide. If the Agents did not make a good impression, one of them needs to make an Influence check opposed by Drake's Willpower (50%) to get a ride. If they enlist Aref's aid beforehand, the Agent receives a 10% bonus to the roll. If they cannot sway her, have Drake make a Standard Insight roll before departing to discern more of their character, possibly changing her mind.

The caravan cannot make the short trip to Aigues-Mortes quickly because of its rate of speed, creature assaults, warbands, obstructions, and the lack of contiguous roads due to Diggers. There are no signs or route markers. Rain is due, and when it rains, there is mud. The mud is home to many deadly things.

If the Agents do not join the caravan, walking cross-country makes them targets of monsters and gives warbands opportunities to find them. Worse: where do they go? A parting shot from the caravan as it clatters away gives them some direction, 'They say the Hermit, Number Nine, dwells near here. God won't help you, but he might!' See Capture or Death!?, opposite.

> ### Capture or Death
>
> Should the Agents end up on their own for any reason, events rapidly lead to capture or death. Warbands like Grime's patrol regularly and are under orders to bring deserters before Kyland (any lone groups are assumed to be deserters no matter their appearance or protests). Agents not killed by the wildlife are increasingly likely to be found by Grime's patrol. Start at 30% per hour and increase by 20% every two hours. If subdued, prisoners are taken to a temporary camp of tents in the shadow of Kyland's airship (see the faction route map, opposite) and given the opportunity to 'Join or Die'.
>
> Joining Kyland means handing over and explaining their technology, and assisting him in using what he finds in the Hermit's hidden cache near Aigues-Mortes. Chances of the Agents gaining access to the cache depend on earning the Warlord's trust. If successful, they face the Formidable challenges of recognising the gate and repairing it – if they can persuade Kyland that such a thing benefits him. Details for Warlord Charles Kyland can be found on page 42.
>
> Escape and evasion before or after capture is very possible for resourceful Agents and after an initial period of dogged pursuit by soldiers and Once-Men, they are left for dead in the wilderness as the army presses onward. Kyland's focus is on finding the Hermit's cache of technology. No one has time for dealing with prisoners.
>
> If the Agents win their way free with skill, stealth, trickery, and luck, they once again find themselves alone with all the horrors of this world between them and safety unless they follow the path cleared by Kyland's forces. Even then, displaced menaces abound.
>
> If they are unable to escape and refuse to join Kyland, they are crucified and used to adorn the Warlord's airship, making the trip towards Aigues-Mortes in agony that way. Despite the extreme nature of their punishment, opportunities for escape exist. In addition to the Agents' own capabilities, crew members with loyalties to Aref's beleaguered information network may assist them. Aref's spies surreptitiously question the Agents about their identities and if satisfied the Agents warrant aid, take them down, treat the worst of their wounds, and help them sneak off the airship in crates of supplies for Kyland's troops. The airship is a military vessel on alert. Kyland wears his iconic battle armor and is flanked at all times by an honor guard of 6 Once-Men.
>
> If they escape capture, prison, and/or crucifixion, and evade recapture by patrols and death by creature attack, Number Nine appears, showing them 'secret ways' around Kyland's forces towards Aigues-Mortes. He is obviously pleased to have found them and claims he needs the Agents' help to stop the Warlord.
>
> *The Hermit's Request*
>
> The Hermit's 'secret ways' follow the deeper tunnels of the Trench Diggers and so avoid the dangers of the surface. The trip is long and does not allow for rest. The air is stale with a bitter scent. Number Nine makes 'Baby available if the Agents want it. Test Endurance at one-hour intervals at Strenuous Effort. Depending on where they start, the Agents have as far as 25 kilometres to travel through uneven underground passages with acid pools and the growing risk of collapse or a Digger encounter. There is a 10% chance of a collapse every hour, which increases by 10% each hour until one is triggered. Working through a collapse adds time to the journey (an additional hour per collapse). Failed Formidable Perception checks expose the Agents to weakened acid for one Turn. A collapse brings a 30% chance of encountering a Digger. Diggers are immense creatures with powerful claws that secrete acid from glands in their hide. See page 45 for details.
>
> As they run, the Hermit explains his responsibility for Kyland, how he set plans for placing superior technology in the Warlord's hands as a younger man, allowing the cruelty of the Warlord to spread unstopped. He begs for the Agents' help in ending it. Number Nine wants the Agents to help activate a massive weapon left by the beings who brought the monsters. If they help, Number Nine promises to help the Agents return home.
>
> At the end of the journey is a careful foray across a salt marsh in the fresh sea air to a hidden set of steps concealed by grass, piles of salt, and stones. Beneath is his cavern, a huge space filled with advanced technology (see page 38, The Hermit's Cavern) that the Agents recognise as being not of this parallel, suggesting Disruptor interference. Getting a good look at Number Nine in the cavern reveals a strong family resemblance to Dr. Quinscombe.

ON THE ROAD

The journey from Botany Bay is 46 kilometres as the crow flies. Given the conditions and that predatory species plague the Camargue, travel to Aigues-Mortes takes the rest of this day and most of the next – if not longer. It is a gloomy, chill noon. Darkness falls before 8 pm.

If the Agents join the caravan, Drake wastes no further time on conversation; she is a person of action. Her whistle gets everyone's attention and sends unwholesome creatures scurrying in the undergrowth. Issuing orders, she turns to the Agents as if to assign them to tasks. Overhead, the chuckling calls of a murder of 8 crows echoes the heavy threat of the cloudy sky. Breaking off to watch their mocking passage overhead, Drake shakes her head at some internal monologue before telling the Agents, 'Aigues-Mortes is just 46 klicks, if you believe the birds....'

The first obstacle is the Digger's trench. The caravan is carrying metal sheets long and strong enough to fashion a bridge over it, but applying this solution takes time, effort, and cleverness. Drake asks the Agents to contribute skill if they have it or muscle if they haven't. Agents versed in Engineering, Mechanisms, or Science should have something to contribute, as the crew, under Drake's direction, secures the metal plates to span the trench, and then recovers them for use next time. The challenge is of Standard Difficulty and takes four hours. One hour to deploy the plates, another to get them in position, one more to navigate across the makeshift bridge, and one final hour to reclaim and load the plates on the vehicles again. Coordinated aid can reduce this time. Opportunities to display leadership and improve efficiency abound. Fumbles lengthen the manoeuvre by two hours due to confusion and arguments. Failure means a minimum of four hours is required. Success means the time is reduced by one hour, and a Critical indicates that two full hours can be saved due to the Agents' efforts.

Team rolls are appropriate for setting up the bridge, increasing or decreasing the time needed. A Sorting roll is appropriate for handling NPC drivers navigating it (Mythras, page 52).

Roll a Hard Drive (Crawler) check to cross the bridge, modified by driver condition. Fumbling propels a vehicle into the trench. The recovery operation for such an outcome would take all night and part of the next morning if attempted. Failure indicates trouble keeping straight while crossing, which adds 30 minutes per vehicle that fails and 15 minutes per vehicle yet to cross due to nerves and second-guessing. Success indicates crossing without problem, using the proper care. A Critical shaves 15 minutes from the total time needed.

JOURNEY CONDITIONS

OBSTACLES

The caravan follows intermittent tracks rarely better than mud and loose gravel. These ruined roadways are washed out in places or sunken in others. Stretches appear solid but are actually deep mud. Bridges have been destroyed by warbands, weather, or the region's giant predators. Every stream and river must be crossed with effort and imaginative application of the arts of driving and engineering. Feel free to add others, but do not let the problems of the road become boring for the players. Frustrate the characters, not the players. Once the frequency of challenges is established, shift them to the background and bring interaction and encounters to the forefront.

In motion or at rest, the noise of the caravan attracts attention from Kyland's warbands or bands of feral Once-Men, even at rest. Warbands of scouts handling Once-Men patrol the region searching for deserters and threats. The greatest threat amongst Kyland's roving warbands is a small unit of four Steam Chariots led by a teen psychopath named Grime. He has a quick grasp of tactics and nothing exists for him but pursuit and capture. Blonde and weathered with brilliant green eyes, he is easy to spot, and his reputation for mutilating his prey has spread throughout the region.

The caravan also attracts predators large and small. In motion, its noise can lure Rolling Horrors. At rest, leaking boilers and repair work can attract Mud Lurkers, Rib Rippers, and Wrigglers.

See the creatures section on pages 43-45 for details.

> ### 'Baby
>
> 'Baby is a powerful stimulant with a terrible cost in deferred exhaustion. Users' lips are stained a rich red by a concoction sucked from pouches of dark moss. If kept dosed, only one level of Fatigue is incurred for every two and Tenacity checks are reduced by one grade. An Endurance check increasing by one grade per day is required for continued use. Doses last one hour. Failure returns all the deferred Fatigue. Fumbling doubles the amount of Fatigue. Success allows continued dosing. A Critical allows continued dosing or a chance to sleep through the ill effects. 'Baby is potent, both physically and psychologically, with seemingly benign side effects. Those addicted to narcotics or activity face a 20% penalty when seeking to resist it or overcome an addiction to it.
>
> *Application:* Ingested
>
> *Potency:* 70
>
> *Resistance:* Special (Endurance)
>
> *Onset time:* 1d4 minutes
>
> *Duration:* 1 hour
>
> *Effects:* Reduces earned Fatigue and decreases grade of Tenacity checks
>
> *Conditions:* Exhaustion; 'dropping the 'Baby' returns deferred fatigue, strongly addictive (initially 30%)
>
> *Antidote/Cure:* Can be counteracted by the careful application of a depressant in correct doses, but the fatigue debt must be paid.
>
> The use of 'Baby is common, and under the current circumstances of cheap lives facing such odds, every edge is to be sought. All of the drivers are 'carrying the 'Baby', as are the lookouts. There is a good chance that any given refugee or crew member has at least 2d4 doses of it, and the willingness to share when things get bleak. Aref has stockpiled a large supply of 30 doses, which he has hidden away in the second vehicle. He doesn't use himself, but if the caravan pushes on without resting, he offers it to those who must stay awake and alert, downplaying its side effects and addictive properties.

Track all time spent stopped. Kyland's forces are headed to the same destination by a different route. Obstacles are 1d3 x 10 minutes apart at the caravan's ponderous rate of speed.

DAYLIGHT HOURS

Driving is mostly a frustrating and painstaking application of power and brakes through twisting ruins of roads. Frequent stops are needed to clear obstacles, such as downed trees, or cross streams or sunken sections.

Stopped, the caravan takes time to get in motion again and runs the risk of getting mired as its weight settles in the mud or soft earth. Where there is mud there are Mud Lurkers. Mud Lurkers are hard to spot and strike with sudden speed from hiding. They have a dark, segmented exoskeleton and two large claws that grip prey for the creature's blood-draining bite. It is able to prey on larger creatures by virtue of the necrotising venom it secretes with its bite. See page 45 for details.

Nighttime Hours

The caravan has limelights for the perpetually cloudy nights. These are frequently rendered useless by thick fog, trees, and uneven terrain. Going is doubly slow, requires scouts on foot, and draws risks from poor navigation and predatory species. Warbands do not travel at night, but encampments are all over the region. In addition, feral Once-Men are attracted to the light and noise.

Checks

Drive (Crawler) rolls for the caravan in most conditions or stressful situations are Hard. Rain increases the Difficulty by one. Medium Effort Fatigue rolls for drivers and laborers are needed every three hours.

Progress

Any obstacle could delay the caravan enough that night falls before getting free. Drake must decide to stop or press on. Drake is up for running like a bullet to the ocean, but knows even dosed on 'Baby not all of her charges can keep up. Despite the risks, stopping at night is something she considers only if persuaded.

At each stop, the connections between passengers, born of shared need and desperation becomes more evident. Each face tells a story of fear, loss, torture, and the desire to be free. Working together to clear obstacles with numbered passengers and crew members leads to conversations which reveal the horrors of this parallel, the threat of Warlord Kyland, the promise of Aigues-Mortes and Africa, or the legend of Number Nine. Fatigue is seen harshly warring with determination. The refugees are on the run, but they will not be run to ground without a fight. They look to Drake as a deliverer, but every soul will fight tooth and nail to be free.

Number 773, 'Harness', a young, muscle-bound mechanic, bears the ruins of both lower arms and hands across his belly in a tight leather harness. He helps in every way he can, lending a shoulder to push, or a watchful eye over the children, but the look in his eyes shows both his ongoing pain, and the freshness of his loss.

As the adults work, unnumbered children test the safety of mud with sharp sticks and fearful expressions under the watchful eyes of Number 3728, 'Pock'. A teen, her forehead splashed with acne, she takes her responsibility as guardian very seriously. All the numbered children look to her, protecting the young, unnumbered ones with makeshift weapons. The closer to Aigues-Mortes, the more frequent the Mud Lurker attacks. Numbered children lecture unnumbered ones on common signs of giant predators. Unnumbered ones are identified by features. Keen-eyed Agents note that numbering seems to coincide with the onset of puberty.

'Blonde One-eye', a feisty girl of perhaps 8 years, is both afraid of and thrilled by finding and killing threats in the mud with the others. She is shy around strangers, but has a self-sacrificing nature urging her to protect others.

Number 1293 and 1294, 'Smile' and 'Grin, serve a hot broth and stale bread rolls at stops. Siblings (likely twins) in their thirties, each has a kind word to everyone about how hard they are working. Their numbers are a deep blue, and no one seems to expect the androgynous pair to do any labour other than this. Investigation reveals that they worked as 'pleasurers' and are treated as if fragile.

Obstacles and Observations

A section of road blasted by artillery shells before the last rain must be carefully circumnavigated. There is a 50% chance of rain that lasts 1d6 hours. A duration of 4+ hours increases all time penalties from obstacles by half and requires an Endurance check to resist Fatigue from the chill. A failed Drive roll means getting stuck in mud and having to dig out. Success takes two hours to free the vehicle. Failure takes twice that. A Critical cuts the time by half, and a Fumble leads the caravan drivers to feel the vehicle must be abandoned. Shifting passengers and necessities to the remaining vehicles takes an hour and means that during any encounter, people are riding on top of the vehicles for lack of space, and are unprotected.

Lookouts and sharp-eyed Agents spot the brassy glint of metal and slowly recognise one crater to be the remains of a tower with a screw-track worked into its armoured exterior that once allowed it to be raised above or lowered beneath ground level. Time has eroded interior and exterior features of the tower, but shell fragments carved bright scratches in the corroded armour, exposing gears and levers of a retractable weapons mount, and the tangled remnants of a fluted cannon of baroque design. If the Agents take the time to explore inside, they find twisted metal vies with mud and bones inside the ruin, nothing with shapes that make sense, except racks of corroded weapons with long muzzles and triggering studs suggesting energy projectors of some kind. Outside in the mud, Blonde One-eye finds a rusted shell of a helm with open flanges crafted to evoke the tusked visage of a boar when closed.

Not far past the tower, a section of road is washed out, requiring a metal plate to cross. Grime's Steam Charioteers find them as the crew gets to work. See page 42 for details of Grime, his warband, and their Once-Men. Grime knows his band is too small to deal with Drake, so his Charioteers try to snatch refugees for interrogation by Kyland. Their plan is hit and run, taunt and shock. They note crew members, Drake, and the Agents, but do not capture them. They try to wound Drake whilst escaping with captives. They do not unleash their Once-Men until they move to withdraw, sacrificing them to escape. Grime's sole goal is to snatch one or two refugees and go. Wounding Drake would be a bonus.

The next 2 kilometres of travel offer two similar washouts and a section of road needing to be cleared of a rockslide. Each obstacle adds 1d4 x 10 minutes of delay.

After 5 kilometres more, the remains of a large band of refugees, identified by tattered uniforms, are seen scattered in every direction. Numbers on the backs are a dark orange, but the parallel slash markings indicating Kyland slaves are the same. Any crew member reveals if asked, or Aref volunteers the information, that the colour indicates workers from a logistics group. The ground in the area is flattened in broad swathes metres wide and spattered with blood, mud, and body parts of various sizes. There are no intact bodies. Roll Unsettling Horror checks.

The Agents hear gasps of 'Rolling Horror' throughout the caravan. Rolling Horrors are massive tubular monsters with grasping tendrils that are extruded to animate dying human bodies as a form of armour. For more details, see page 44. Far to the side of the site, a slime-coated trench is evident. Older crew members speculate that a battle between a Trench Digger and a Rolling Horror would be the sort of hell both creatures deserve. Some wonder if a Digger scared the Horror off. It is unusual for so many remains to be left behind. If burying the remains is suggested, Drake states that the dead take care of their own. She understands the need to maintain morale, however. If the Agents push her to stop, she considers it.

If they stay or go, the lookouts suddenly spot cracking ground and hear rumbling deep in the earth over the sounds of the caravan. Everyone recognises signs that the Trench Digger is still here (see page 45). The terrain is in fair condition, so the caravan drivers may use their vehicles as weapons against the creature if it blocks them. The Digger has a 60% chance of surfacing beside the second vehicle, causing the need for Drive checks if in motion. On a Critical, it either surfaces under a random stationary vehicle, flipping it, or ahead of the moving caravan, causing collisions. The Digger is drawn only to the carnage on the road, so it does not pursue unless badly injured, which causes it to frenzy.

Drivers seeking escape face obstacles like fallen trees and rubble. Failure means damage is sustained in the escape, but movement is not prevented.

HORROR ON THE HILL

Once the Digger threat is behind them, the rough patches give way to a decent track, enabling the caravan to roll on for nearly an hour before the road rises between rolling hills. Speed is slowed again. One of the hills is topped with a picturesque stone chapel, a glint of new steel highlighting its steeple. This site is one of many waystations for Kyland's iconic airship. It houses ammunition and canned food for his forces, and used to be guarded by two warbands, both of which have fallen to the predation of a Rolling Horror (see page 44). Tracks of Chariots cut through tall grasses around the chapel, but all seems quiet. Observation at a distance determines that the steeple has been recently augmented as a communications and airship mooring tower. Kyland's red slashes can be seen on the roof as the caravan draws near. Inspection is needed to find the cache of supplies. The chapel is 60 metres from the road, up a gentle, grassy slope. If it did not rain earlier in the day, it starts now. If the rate of travel seems too fast, use the rain to add delays.

Depending on the Agents, events could play out differently. Options follow.

A MOMENT TO PREY

If investigating, the Agents note signs of the chapel being used as a cache, but need to enter the building to determine what is stored there. The Rolling Horror shrieks as they reach the top of the hill. It is visible at the bottom of the far side of the hill surrounded by the wreckage of Chariots and soldiers; its scale encourages retreat. Roll Disturbing Madness checks. The Horror accelerates slowly up the back of the hill, taking one Round, before shattering the

> **Quick Sand and Mud Hazards**
>
> Pedestrians failing a Hard Perception check become trapped in quicksand. The hazards are 1d6+1 metre deep. The trapped sink ½ metre immediately, with a rate of ½ metre per Round unless they make a Standard Athletics check to spread themselves prone. Three rolls are needed to escape. Failure causes further sinking. Two consecutive failures increase the Difficulty by one grade.
>
> Mud hazards have a 50% chance of including Mud Lurkers.
>
> Escape provides a Difficulty reduction of one grade for future Perception checks.

chapel in a spray of stone. It takes a Round to recover, giving the Agents more time to retreat.

The creature chases the caravan, its hunger immense. Movement rates may result in a battle on the hillside. Early on, Grime's warband arrives, if they have not been killed. Grime uses the distraction of the Horror to try to snatch more captives but his warband is caught up in the creature's assault and consumed. This should give the Agents a chance to gain distance or get the caravan moving.

HORROR ON THE ROAD

If the caravan does not stop to investigate the chapel, they have a slight edge. In motion, the noise of the caravan obscures the screams of the Horror's armour, and the caravan is big enough to make the Horror cautious. Each time the caravan stops, the Horror has a chance to close. Desperate to feed, it wastes no time, but it knows to wait until dark to attack large prey. Each stop tempts it further. If stopped for more than an hour, or if night falls, the Horror attacks. If neither occurs before the end of the road, it stalks them unseen, but not always out of earshot.

STEEPLE CHASE

Once past the chapel with the Horror in stealthy or open pursuit, Grime's warband (or another if they were killed) approaches from ahead. They are tired and desperate. All thoughts of capture are gone; they are out for blood with as much show as possible. They launch their attack by unleashing the Once-Men and gunning for defenceless targets.

As blood is spilled, the Horror is unable to resist any longer and comes rapidly writhing into the path of the caravan, extruding the bodies of its recent meals through its skin. It is unafraid of the Chariots and smashes two of them to fragments against the sides of the caravan vehicles as it shrieks into view. It may feel threatened by the vehicles if the drivers use them to attack; check the Horror's Willpower (30%) modified by its Passion to Feed and Grow (75%). While present, its tendrils seek to snatch up warriors and refugees alike. Recognising someone as part of the Horror's body amplifies the Terrify effect of the Rolling Horror, raising it to Shocking (Madness check). Luck Points may reduce the Intensity by 1. The effect on the refugees and crew as they see the victims' faces, even those of Grime's warband, on the flailing bodies whipping madly about the Horror as it rolls is heart-rending. The screams and taunts of the bodies mingle, making it uncertain if they want release or company. If the Horror stays to fight, it does so until its vitals, sensory organs, or brain are Seriously Wounded, and then flees.

END OF THE ROAD

The Camargue is a place of shifting pathways and lost direction. When the caravan reaches the salt marsh surrounding Aigues-Mortes, there is no road. There is no forward passage for the vehicles. The refugees have to go on foot through marsh, quicksand, and shifting hillocks of false land, facing all the predators that lurk within. Far out over the Mediterranean, a glimmer of blue sky beckons.

Kyland's banners of crimson parallel slashes wave under the bulk of his airship. The refugees have eight hours minus the time lost during the trip to reach the fortress. Crossing the marsh safely takes two hours. This likely means the Army has reached the fortress first, engulfing but not besieging it. Searchers with dogs comb the marsh directly ahead of the army, towards the caravan. Kyland's force seeks Number Nine's secrets. They now believe a cavern lies beneath the marsh and they intend to find it.

> **The Road to the Sea**
>
> There are destroyed bridges every few kilometres along the ruins of the road from the chapel to the sea, and stretches where trees and debris from stone walls block passage. Bridge crossings are easier to handle than the trench crossing, taking no more than two hours at worst. Each road blockage takes 1d4 x 10 minutes to clear using the caravan's massive plow blades. It is simple but gruelling.

NINE BY NINE

The Hermit's solo war against Kyland is almost over.

If the Agents travelled to the marsh with Number Nine, he guides them to the caravan as it approaches from the side farthest from the army. Number Nine hurriedly urges the Agents to help him escort the caravan survivors stealthily to the cavern while the army is preparing the siege of Aigues-Mortes. The caravan crew are inclined to follow the Hermit and readily agree when he implores them to help operate his weapon, a massive pyramidal frame that will rise out of the marsh to destroy Kyland's terrifying airship.

If the Agents are with the caravan, the Hermit greets them as the caravan slows to a halt at the end of the road. He readily recruits the survivors, ideally Drake and Aref if they have made it this far, to assist him and offer protection. He implores the Agents, whom he claims to have seen in dreams, to come with him to his cavern where he has a weapon waiting to battle Kyland along with a means to send the Agents home. As per the *Capture or Death!?* text box on page 33, Number Nine explains the situation with

Kyland and uses all his manipulative ability to seek the Agents' help. He is drawn to The Van and any Mattanit technology if those items have survived the trip. He is relieved to see them and asks anyone skilled in Engineering or Mechanics to assist him in rigging a connection between the items and his 'weapon'. He does not care if told they are nonfunctional, he values them for another property, claiming they 'increase the effect'.

In either case, once in the cavern, he reveals the weapon is actually a gate and the Agents' role in the plan is to take positions high on its superstructure and be shifted, along with Kyland, into the hands of the Valhalla Programme. Expecting them to refuse, Number Nine tries to manipulate the Agents' Passions to get what he wants without having to waste time on further explanation.

MOTIVE, METHOD, OPPORTUNITY

Number Nine sincerely desires to stop Kyland, but he is being deceitful when he says he is activating a weapon. The device is actually a massive gate the Disruptors used to bring monsters to this parallel from The Dark. Number Nine plans to shift Kyland, his airship, The Van, and the Agents to Zero-Zero. The airship is the symbol of Kyland's power. With it and Kyland 'destroyed', Number Nine knows the army will founder as the Once-Men will turn on the soldiers without Kyland to lead them. The fate of Aigues-Mortes is less certain.

With Empathic Link, Number Nine contacted his Zero-Zero self who, in turn, implored Dr. Quinscombe to aid this parallel, namely, by showing him how to use the cache of advanced technology against Kyland. Quinscombe agreed for a price: he would show Number Nine how to use the gate as a weapon, in exchange for Number Nine rescuing the Agents and their cargo. A sign of good faith was helping Number Nine complete a primitive TPT. At the right time, Number Nine will be instructed through gate activation, step by step. Number Nine believes the Agents will want to stay, which is why he is not straight with them about the device, which would send them home against their will. He sees them as heroes who would not act to save themselves when weaker folk need protection, even if they are not.

Unknown to Number Nine, Quinscombe intends for the gate to move everything to a lifeless parallel where no further harm can be done and from where he can recover any remaining Agents.

STRANDED?

If the Agents refuse to be shifted with Kyland's airship, they need to devise their own way home or adapt to life here. Either way earning the good will of Number Nine would help. If they survive the battle, the cavern holds tools for repairing The Van as well as the means to survive a parallel shift into space long enough to be retrieved. With Number Nine's help, this process could perhaps be arranged in a few months.

If Number Nine fails to shift Kyland, his army washes over the fortress as if its defences were not there and raids the cavern. Only the bones of the crucified bear witness afterwards.

THE HERMIT'S CAVERN

Inside the cavern are technological wonders in many stages of restoration. Gear and scavenged parts are piled all around, with narrow pathways between. There is order and arrangement here, but it is not immediately obvious. In the shadows beyond the focal point of the pyramidal gate array are partially assembled frames of ornithopters and immense, sealed-environment transports. To the side, archaic lances lean drunkenly among one another, a precarious still-life. Diagrams of towers, patterns for riding gear for giant birds, and schematics for all manner of devices curl haphazardly, pinned to every surface. On the far side of the cavern are the gate controls, lit by the glare of a TPT without a signal. Stacked around it are crates of Kyland Model 9 Frag Pistols (*Luther Arkwright*, page 106) and ammunition (fragmentation blast radius 1 metre).

The gate can target any large objects within 100 metres. What it targets, as well as anything in direct contact with the gate, is pulled into a blinding tunnel of positive and negative forces to be shifted elsewhere.

If the Agents agree, Number Nine starts the power sequence for the gate and then rushes them to get in position on its superstructure whilst The Van is posit. Outside, the raucous calls of Kyland's army are rising. In just a few minutes, the gate will rise up out of the marsh to shift Agents and Airship away from this place. Moments before the shift, a bark of laughter from the stairs stops Number Nine cold.

THE MAD GOD

Kyland is here to kill and plunder. If the Agents escaped him earlier, Kyland snarls at the sight of them, but known or unknown, their presence with Number Nine infuriates him. So driven is he, that Kyland has personally led the forces seeking the cavern. As perverse as luck is, he has found it.

Flanked by a personal guard of six Once-Men, Warlord Kyland, fully armed and armoured for battle, strides down into the cavern with a bellow of, 'At last!' echoing out of a wolf's head helm. Infantry (as Grime, page 42) and bloodhounds are heard scrabbling above.

At his shout, the Once-Men leap to the attack as Kyland locks eyes with Number Nine. With a cry of 'Keep working!', the Hermit vaults up onto the rising frame of the gate, counting on being pursued. He taunts and insults Kyland, seeking to enrage and lure him on. Kyland rushes onto the rising gate from the stairs and begins clawing his way up after his enemy. Both men receive cover (4 AP) from ranged attacks as they climb. Firing into the gate structure will damage it on a Fumble from the Agents or a Critical from enemy fire. The Hermit intends to Translocate away from the gate if it is activated; he has no intention of leaving his home.

It takes two people three rounds to activate the gate. Quinscombe hesitates to send instructions through the TPT until he is certain the Agents and their cargo are in contact with the gate or until he witnesses the ferocity of the Once-Men. Drake and Aref,

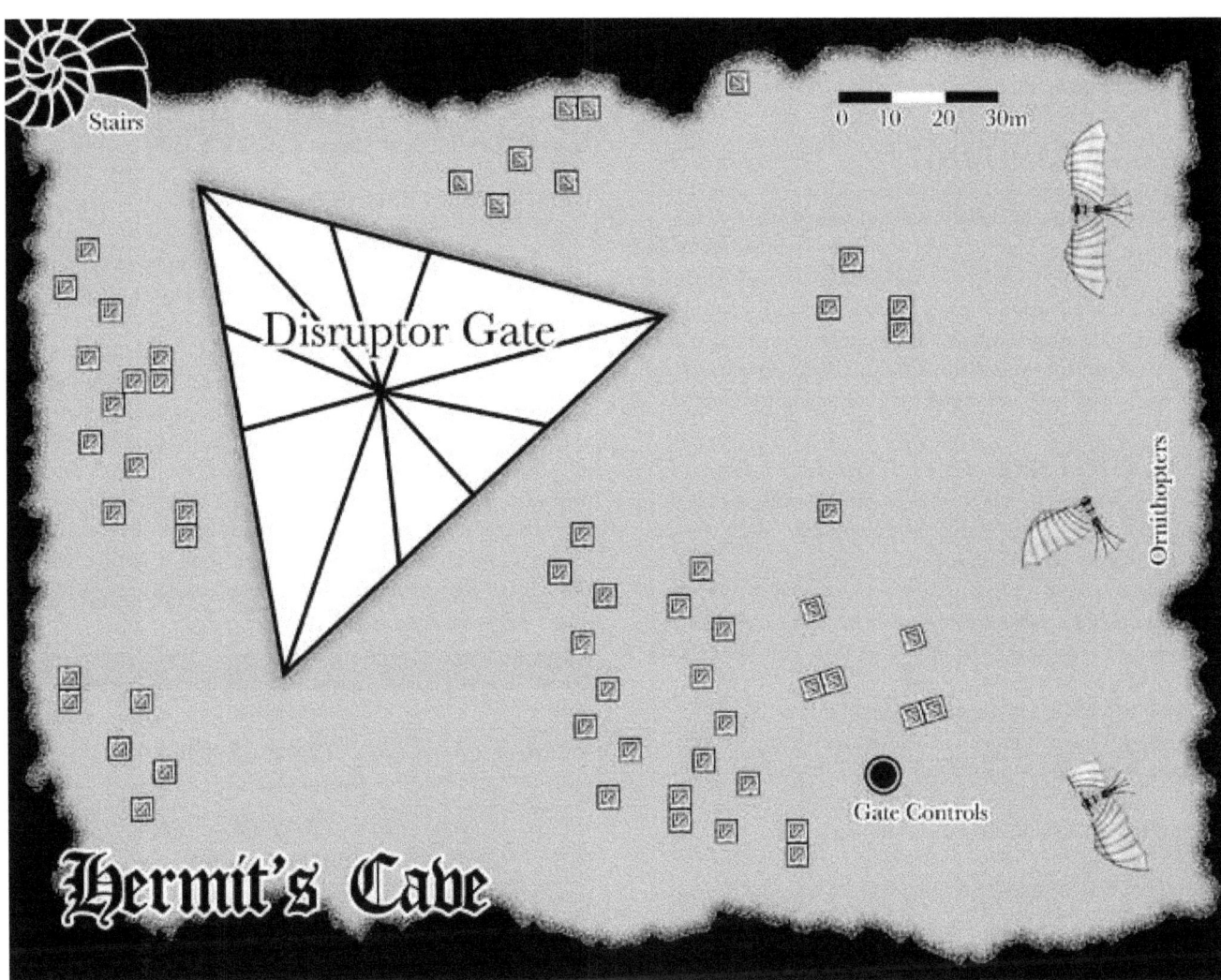

or other survivors, urge the Agents to climb after the Hermit as the cavern roof splits open and a salty rain of marsh water and mud spills in thin streams around the base of the gate. Through the gap, everyone sees the massive airship with weapons ready drifting lower and closer, just 150 metres away. Sounds of battle being joined across the marsh at the walls of Aigues-Mortes augment the growing electric hum of the gate as it powers up. The Once-Men attack in threes without mercy or thought of surrender, choosing the nearest refugees. They only stop if they witness the death of Kyland by the gate or by violence. As Kyland climbs, the airship holds fire. Should Kyland, easily recognisable to the airship crew by his armour, be seen to fall or move away from the gate, the ship no longer hesitates to open fire.

To help Aigues-Mortes and turn the Once-Men besieging it against Kyland's infantry, the airship must be destroyed. To those who see it from the field of battle, destruction of the airship is the destruction of Kyland. Assuming Aref and Drake are present, they are as conscious of this link as the Hermit and urge the Agents to target the ship, as fighting and dying spreads through the cavern.

Drake guards Aref as he and a survivor the Agents care for ready the gate.

What do the Agents do?

If the Agents do not climb the gate, they stand amongst the carnage the Once-Men are making of the non-combatant survivors, and face the swelling ranks of an army between them and Aigues-Mortes. Firing on the Once-Men risks hitting survivors and damaging precious equipment. If Kyland catches Number Nine, the two battle unarmed using their psionics, dangling high above the marsh. The infantry squad holds position outside the cavern as reinforcements and the airship converge on the area.

If the gate is not activated, or if the Agents are defeated and they survive to be captured, they are hauled back to Arles to be used as particularly gruesome examples of Kyland's sense of justice: crucifixion. Opportunities for escape exist as before. If the gate effort fails, but Kyland is slain, or if the gate is activated and the airship destroyed, survival is still not assured as the marsh is full of Once-Men and vengeful soldiers. Aigues-Mortes is spared a dedicated and organised siege, but may not be free of danger, yet. Careful defence of the cavern, even if the Hermit does not survive the battle, may in time, allow the Agents to end that danger and eventually make their way home.

Gated Community

If the Agents are in contact with the gate as it activates, their view of the siege and airship slows down and is drained of all colour. Forces surge along the walls of Aigues-Mortes as smoke rises from within. Heat is leeched from the Agents as they streak into black and white entanglements of energy along a coruscating corridor of silent noise. The Agents cannot discern more of what happens as they – for an instant – cease to exist before being deposited in the coldness of space like sand through a wildly spinning hourglass.

Out of Time

The agony of transit becomes asphyxiation. The stars are blocked by the rupturing airship. Roll a Disturbing Fear check. Instants later, the Agents feel an impact and vanish to reappear floating in the narrow confines of a small white room, with a space-suited figure scrambling to clear the way for medics. On a display behind him, alarms flash urgently. A clock reads 11:59. The Agents black out.

Days later, once out of treatment for exposure and the effects of the Disruptor transit tunnel, the debriefings begin. The Valhalla Programme expects the Agents to put this behind them.

Can they?

Consider new or altered Passions to reflect what has happened.

Non-Player Characters

Vehemence Drake

One of few survivors of a northern land now ash, Drake was trained in a monastic order known as *The Wardens*, who protected travellers on treacherous roads. The order fell and Drake found herself a mercenary for a time. When working for coin brought her under Kyland's thumb, Drake could take it no longer. She has turned his own technology against him and is heading for the promised land with refugees in tow. Drake is a harsh woman with no idea of what freedom or peace mean. Raised fighting, she cannot fathom a world without it. She appears heroic to the caravan, but the truth is she wants to hold the power herself. She lives every moment as if it were her last and expects others to do the same. She prizes quick and incisive intuition, quickly losing patience with debate. Her thick dark hair is shaved on the sides and kept short. Her features are sharp.

Vehemence Drake	Attributes
STR: 10	Action Points: 2
CON: 18	Damage Modifier: -1d2
SIZ: 10	Prana: 12
DEX: 15	Tenacity: 12
INT: 11	Movement: 6 metres
POW: 12	Initiative Bonus: +13
CHA: 11	Armour: : Leather Clothing, Advanced Ballistic Vest, tinted goggles

1d20	Hit Location	AP/HP
1 – 3	Right Leg	2/6
4 – 6	Left Leg	2/6
7 – 9	Abdomen	5/7
10 – 12	Chest	5/8
13 – 15	Right Arm	2/5
16 – 18	Left Arm	2/5
19 – 20	Head	0/6

Skills	Passions, Traits & Dependencies
Athletics 55%, Brawn 20%, Endurance 56%, Evade 50%, Influence 52%, Insight 65%, Navigation (Land) 60%, Mechanisms 60%, Meditation 60%, Mysticism 60%, Perception 42%, Stealth 30%, Survival 23%, Unarmed 70%, Willpower 50%	Passions: End Chaos 60%, Destroy Enemies 70%, Find a Home 60% Traits: Mystic Dependencies: Activity 60%

Mysticism	
Focal Yoga: Augment Warden Combat Style, Invoke Denial (Fire), Invoke Indomitable, Invoke Pain Control, Enhance Fatigue, Enhance AP, Path: Warden Training (Militant Monastic Order)	

Combat Style & Weapons	Traits & Notes
Warden (Unarmed, Pistol, Rifle) 80%, Heavy Weapons 40%	Skirmisher Trait

Weapon	Damage	Range	Ammo	Rate/Load
4-Barrel Pistol	1d8	10/20/50	4	1/4
Rifle	2d6	20/200/500	6	1/4

AREF

Called Aref, his actual name is R.F. Ban (for Raymond Foster). This idealist – whose eyes seem always to be in shadow – has made contact with Agents unwittingly more than once. Reliable, equitable, and carried by an unwavering belief in a better future, Aref was slowly building a network of informants and proto-revolutionaries across the continent with dreams of one day unleashing a cleansing fire. Drake's emancipation of the workers and plan to seek Africa has inspired him and he will help her or die trying. He has dark hair and is tanned.

Aref	Attributes
STR: 11	Action Points: 2
CON: 10	Damage Modifier: -1d2
SIZ: 9	Prana: 12
DEX: 12	Tenacity: 12
INT: 13	Movement: 6 metres
POW: 14	Initiative Bonus: +13
CHA: 17	Armour: : Leather Clothing, Advanced Ballistic Vest, tinted goggles

1d20	Hit Location	AP/HP
1 – 3	Right Leg	2/6
4 – 6	Left Leg	2/6
7 – 9	Abdomen	2/7
10 – 12	Chest	4/8
13 – 15	Right Arm	2/5
16 – 18	Left Arm	2/5
19 – 20	Head	0/6

Skills	Passions, Traits & Dependencies
Athletics 45%, Acrobatics 40%, Bureaucracy 50%, Courtesy 70%, Endurance 70%, Engineering 40%, Evade 40%, Medicine 60%, Influence 65%, Perception 90%, Sleight 59%, Stealth 80%, Unarmed 55%, Willpower 60%	Passions: End Chaos 70%, Foment Revolution 30%, Find a Home 60%
	Traits: Alternate Persona (Spy, Warrior, Rebel, Lover)
	Dependencies: Authority 58%

Combat Style & Weapons	Traits & Notes
Dirty Tricks (Unarmed, Knife, Garrotte) 55%, Pistol 65%	Improvised Weapons

Weapon	Damage	Range	Ammo	Rate/Load
Revolver	1d8	10/20/50	6	1/4

Weapon	Damage	Size/Reach	AP/HP	Effects
Knife	1d4-1d2	S/S	6/8	Impale

CARAVAN CREW

Any ethnic background and aged from 20-40. They wear the remains of brown worker coveralls with large yellow numbers on the back and two parallel red slashes above the number along the shoulders.

Caravan Crew	Attributes
STR: 10	Action Points: 2
CON: 9	Damage Modifier: 0
SIZ: 11	Prana: 10
DEX: 10	Tenacity: 10
INT: 11	Movement: 6 metres
POW: 10	Initiative Bonus: +11
CHA: 11	Armour: Leather

1d20	Hit Location	AP/HP
1 – 3	Right Leg	2/6
4 – 6	Left Leg	2/6
7 – 9	Abdomen	2/7
10 – 12	Chest	2/8
13 – 15	Right Arm	2/5
16 – 18	Left Arm	2/5
19 – 20	Head	0/4

Skills	Passions, Traits & Dependencies
Athletics 30%, Brawn 40%, Drive (Crawler) 60%, Endurance 40%, Navigation (Land) 30%, Perception 40%, Stealth 30%, Unarmed 60%, Willpower 20%	Passions: Escape Kyland 40%, Loyalty to Drake 60%

Combat Style & Weapons	Traits & Notes
Pistol 50%, Unarmed 60%, Heavy Weapons 40%	None

Weapon	Damage	Range	Ammo	Rate/Load
Pistol	1d8	10/20/50	6	1/4

CAPABLE REFUGEES

As for Caravan Crew, but treat as Rabble (MYTHRAS page 111).

Grime

A teenage, leather-clad warband leader, Grime has a quick grasp of tactics, and a propensity for singing misunderstood lyrics of popular songs of the past. Nothing exists for him but the pursuit of deserters. He is followed at all times by a tight-knit crew of similarly attired pubescent warriors, spoiling for a fight. He is blonde and weathered with brilliant green eyes.

Grime	Attributes
STR: 11	Action Points: 3
CON: 9	Damage Modifier: 0
SIZ: 12	Prana: 11
DEX: 14	Tenacity: 11
INT: 11	Movement: 6 metres
POW: 11	Initiative Bonus: +13
CHA: 13	Armour: Leather

1d20	Hit Location	AP/HP
1 – 3	Right Leg	2/5
4 – 6	Left Leg	2/5
7 – 9	Abdomen	2/6
10 – 12	Chest	2/7
13 – 15	Right Arm	2/4
16 – 18	Left Arm	2/4
19 – 20	Head	0/5

Skills	Passions, Traits & Dependencies
Athletics 55%, Brawn 53%, Drive (Crawler) 95%, Endurance 54%, Evade 58%, Locale (The Camargue) 52%, Perception 65%, Stealth 40%, Survival 60%, Unarmed 60%, Willpower 40%	Passions: Love Praise 50%, Loyalty to Kyland 80%, Loyalty to Warriors 30% Dependency: Collecting Fingers 90%

Combat Style & Weapons	Traits & Notes
Warband Charioteer (Dagger, Weighted Net) 50%, Pistol 60%	Mounted Combat

Weapon	Damage	Range	Ammo	Rate/Load
Hand Flamer	1d8	3/10/40	Incendiary	1/4

Weapon	Damage	Size/Reach	AP/HP	Effects
Kukri	1d4+2	S/S	6/8	Bleed

Warband Warriors

As per Grime, but treat as Underlings (MYTHRAS page 111) and arm them with Pistols.

Charles Kyland

Kyland intends to rule Europe at any cost and is amassing the technological might to do so. At night, his warriors dance fierce dances of deeds and deaths around towering fires and twisted steel gantries erected in base camps under the eyes of crucified enemies. By day, messages of control and domination echo out from crackling loudspeakers on his massive airship as his forces of men and Once-Men blacken the land behind it. Grey-haired and muscular, his short stature is soon forgotten in the force of his convictions. As a call-back to a legendary age, Kyland wears a snarling wolf-head helm in battle.

Kyland	Attributes
STR: 16	Action Points: 3
CON: 9	Damage Modifier: +1d2
SIZ: 10	Prana: 13
DEX: 11	Tenacity: 13
INT: 14	Movement: 6 metres
POW: 13	Initiative Bonus: +13
CHA: 15	Armour: Ballistic Vest, Leather Clothing, goggles Battle Armour: Advanced Combat Armour (6 AP all locations)

1d20	Hit Location	AP/HP
1 – 3	Right Leg	2/4
4 – 6	Left Leg	2/4
7 – 9	Abdomen	4/7
10 – 12	Chest	4/6
13 – 15	Right Arm	2/3
16 – 18	Left Arm	2/3
19 – 20	Head	0/4

Skills	Passions, Traits & Dependencies
Athletics 55%, Brawn 53%, Drive (Crawler) 54%, Endurance 64%, Evade 58%, Influence 82%, Locale (The Camargue) 52%, Perception 65%, Stealth 40%, Survival 60%, Unarmed 110%, Willpower 50%	Passions: Subjugate Europe 70%, Crucify Number Nine 60% Traits: Psychic Dependency: Competitive 84%

Psionics	
Martial Mind 66% (Body Fortress, Mental Shield, Psychic Wrack)	Out of affectation, Kyland always dons his wolf helm to use his psionics.

Combat Style & Weapons	Traits & Notes
Blitzkrieg (Dagger, Unarmed) 110%, Pistols 80%	Swashbuckling

Weapon	Damage	Range	Ammo	Rate/Load
Frag Pistol	1d8 (1m)	3/10/40	Fragmentation	1/4

Weapon	Damage	Size/Reach	AP/HP	Effects
Dagger	1d4+2+1d2	S/S	6/8	Bleed, Impale

NUMBER NINE

The Hermit, Number Nine, is marked by an irregular tattoo of that number from his right temple to his jawline and circling his eye. No one knows who he was, but he is seen as a legendary protector of travellers and a thorn in the side of the Warlord. The truth is he was once the friend of a younger Charles Kyland and the discoverer of a stockpile of advanced technology left by the Disruptors. Believing Kyland a visionary, he shared many devices that the two investigated. Seeing the use to which the Warlord eventually put this knowledge, Number Nine disappeared and swore to undo his mistake. His white hair, still dark at the temples, is neatly tied back.

Number Nine	Attributes
STR: 11	Action Points: 3
CON: 15	Damage Modifier: 0
SIZ: 11	Prana: 15
DEX: 16	Tenacity: 15
INT: 12	Movement: 6 metres
POW: 15	Initiative Bonus: +14
CHA: 10	Armour: Leather Clothing, Heavy Hooded Robes, Skull cap, goggles

1d20	Hit Location	AP/HP
1 – 3	Right Leg	2/6
4 – 6	Left Leg	2/6
7 – 9	Abdomen	3/7
10 – 12	Chest	4/8
13 – 15	Right Arm	3/5
16 – 18	Left Arm	2/5
19 – 20	Head	4/6

Skills	Passions, Traits & Dependencies
Athletics 55%, Brawn 53%, Engineering 54%, Endurance 50%, Evade 56%, Insight 70%, Locale (The Camargue) 80%, Perception 85%, Stealth 110%, Survival 110%, Unarmed 70%, Willpower 80%	Passions: Help the Needy 60%, Atone for Kyland's Reign 70% Traits: Psychic Dependency: Discipline 75%

Psionics
Empathy 60% (Empathic Link, Mental Shield, Sense Psi)
Translocation 50% (Intangibility, Translocate)

Combat Style & Weapons	Traits & Notes
The Tyranny of Evil Men (Unarmed, Knife) 70%, Pistol 65%, Shotgun 90%	

Weapon	Damage	Range	Ammo	Rate/Load
.50 Pistol	1d12	50/100/200	Hollow Point	1/3
12 Gauge Shotgun	3d6	20/100/200	Armour Piercing	1/-/8, 3

RIB RIPPER

A human-sized cephalopod with 6 powerful tentacles that lurks in damp, overgrown locations. Brownish-black on the surface with a lighter brown underside, Rib Rippers match colouration with their environs. Preying on vermin, they could be beneficial but unfortunately, they use humans as hosts for the endoparasitic larval stage of their offspring. Rib Rippers do not harm a host once a larva has been implanted and instead stalk them as protectors for the 3-6 days it takes the larva to complete metamorphosis and eat its way out. Hosts suffer effects of blood loss at a rate of one level of Fatigue every four hours unless they make an Endurance check, which increases in Difficulty grade each day. When the larva is ready to emerge, it inflicts 1d6 points of damage directly to the location in which it was implanted. A Hard Surgery check is needed to remove the larva from the host safely. Failure indicates the larva has compromised a major blood vessel and removal inflicts 1d6 points to that location. A Fumble causes the larva to retaliate, inflicting 1d4 points to the location and burrowing deeper. Attempts to remove the larva noted by the Rib Ripper enrage it and causes it to attack in defence of the larva (and the host).

Rib Ripper	Attributes
STR: 3d6+6 (17)	Action Points: 3
CON: 3d6+6 (17)	Damage Modifier: +1d2
SIZ: 2d6+6 (13)	Prana: 7
DEX: 3d6+10 (27)	Tenacity: N/A
INS: 2d6+6 (13)	Movement: 6 metres
POW: 2d6 (7)	Initiative Bonus: +20

Abilities: Formidable Natural Weapons (Tough Entangling Tentacles), Camouflaged, Multi-limbed (2 additional Combat Actions when Grappling), Grappler, Regeneration (1d3 HP / day including lost limbs)

1d20	Hit Location	AP/HP
1-3	Front-left Tentacle	3/6
4-5	Centre-left Tentacle	3/6
6-7	Rear-left Tentacle	3/6
7-9	Front-right Tentacle	3/6
10-11	Centre-right Tentacle	3/6
12-13	Rear-right Tentacle	3/6
14-16	Upper body Surface	4/8
17-18	Head	3/6
19	Lower body Surface	2/7
20	Endoparasite Prong	3/5

Skills	Passions
Athletics 84%, Brawn 47%, Endurance 64%, Evade 78%, Perception 47%, Stealth 67%, Survival 54%, Track 77%, Willpower 53%	Passions: Protect Implanted Host 75%

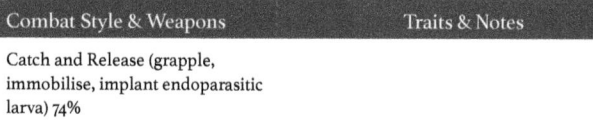

Combat Style & Weapons			Traits & Notes	
Catch and Release (grapple, immobilise, implant endoparasitic larva) 74%				

Weapon	Damage	Size/Reach	AP/HP	Effects
Tentacle (Constrict)	1d6+1d2	M/T	As for Tentacle	Grip, Pin Weapon
Tentacle (Grip)	N/A	M/M	As for Tentacle	Grip, Take Weapon
Prong	1d6+1d2	M/T	As for Prong	Impale

Rolling Horror

Rolling Horrors are solitary by nature and few in number. Rippling fleshy tubes coated in ichor, mud, and blood, Rolling Horrors adorn and protect themselves with extruded and animate corpses, and move in surges. The flailing bodies and limbs of dying/dead victims serve as armour, weaponry, and the source of the creatures' power to Terrify (*Luther Arkwright*, page 50). No one is ever surprised by the attack of a Rolling Horror, as they can be heard coming from quite a distance. They are frequent visitors to Time Slip's many battlefields and charnel houses. They have learned to seek out loud and continuous noises. They leave nothing but flattened soil and shattered remains of whatever objects stand in their way. The dead they take with them. As they move, their outer coat of corpses whips about forcefully. These extrusions are typically attached at the shoulders and hips (but sometimes by other parts) so that the limbs and head flail about horribly. Its attack is to roll over its opposition, projecting twisting and twining tendrils to entangle and pull victims into a maw it forms to Engulf them. They use their armour of corpses to communicate with, taunt, and lure prey into fatal mistakes, goading them to press attacks they cannot win, and dissuading them from striking at the helpless victims behind which the body of the creature hides.

Rolling Horror	Attributes
STR: 3d6+30 (51)	Action Points: 3
CON: 2d6+20 (31)	Damage Modifier: +2d8
SIZ: 3d6+30 (51)	Prana: 7
DEX: 3d6+6 (17)	Tenacity: N/A
INT: 2d6+6 (13)	Movement: 12 metres
POW: 2d6 (7)	Initiative Bonus: +15

Abilities: Engulfing (up to SIZ 26 ingested and later extruded as a part of the Horror), Grapple, Terrifying (Tenacity: Madness at Disturbing Intensity), Trample

1d20	Hit Location	AP/HP
1–3	Tendrils	0/15
4–6	Fleshy Mass	6/16
7–9	Vital Organs	6/17
10–12	Tendrils	0/15
13–15	Sensory Organs	2/15
16–18	Fleshy Mass	6/16
19–20	'Brain'	6/16

Skills	Passions, Traits & Dependencies
Athletics 98%, Brawn 131%, Endurance 92%, Perception 44%, Survival 45%, Willpower 30%	Passions: Feed and Grow 75%

Combat Style & Weapons			Traits & Notes	
Engulf and Consume (Roll Over, Flailing limbs, projecting + entangling + pulling tendrils, gaping maw) 98%				

Weapon	Damage	Size/Reach	AP/HP	Effects
Flailing Limb	1d12+2d8	M/S	2/10	Stun Location
Maw	2d6+2d8	H/T	0/15	Engulfing
Tendril	1d2+2d8	H/L	0/15	Grip
Rolling Crush	4d8	E/T	4/16	Trample

Wriggler

Wrigglers resemble maggots, with a hard shell encasing the head. If any part of the body is separated from the rest, pieces grow a new body and head. If the head is destroyed, the creature dies. They burrow into living flesh using a rigid proboscis, which releases a mild anaesthetic oil, preventing most potential hosts from noticing the attack (Stealth check). If one point of damage is done, they enter the body to first burrow inward and then toward a kidney to nest at a rate of one hit location per day, inflicting a damage of one per location. They can be cut out of limbs with a successful Medicine check and simple tools. In the head, torso, or abdomen, complicated surgery is required to remove them. Their preferred entry point is the eye, but any location will do.

Wriggler	Attributes
STR: 1	Action Points: 3
CON: 1	Damage Modifier: N/A
SIZ: 1	Prana: 10
DEX: 12	Tenacity: N/A
INS: 15	Movement: 1 metre
POW: 10	Initiative Bonus: +14

Abilities: Regenerate (If the body is cut apart in any way, each part reforms as a new Wriggler in a few days. If the head is destroyed, it dies.)

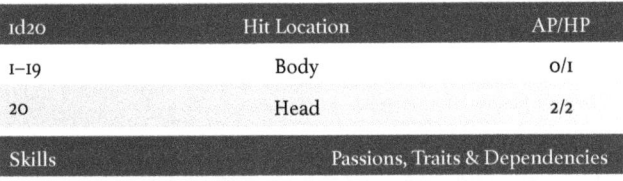

1d20	Hit Location	AP/HP
1–19	Body	0/1
20	Head	2/2

Skills	Passions, Traits & Dependencies
Endurance 32%, Perception 60%, Stealth 80%, Survival 46%	Passions: Find Host 85%

Combat Style & Weapons	Traits & Notes
Burrow Deep 75%	

Weapon	Damage	Size/Reach	AP/HP	Effects
Proboscis	1d2-1d8	-/T	-	Inject Anaesthetic

Mud Lurker

Mud Lurkers wait motionless, submerged in large communities of 20-40 Lurkers. They do not cooperate intelligently, but do share large kills. Mud Lurkers feed on the blood of warm-blooded animals and possess a necrotising venom in their bite that increases blood flow and produces hallucinations. Lurkers have a limited capacity to expand the mud around their communities by breaking up soil and introducing fluids from dissolved carcasses and their own strange secretions. Rainy season is a time for great expansion. Lurkers have a dark, segmented shell, long legs, and four large claws. They move by quick scuttling and sudden leaps.

Mud Lurker	Attributes
STR: 2d6+4 (11)	Action Points: 3
CON: 2d6+6 (13)	Damage Modifier: -1d2
SIZ: 1d6+3 (7)	Prana: 4
DEX: 2d6+4 (11)	Tenacity: N/A
INS: 2d6+6 (13)	Movement: 3 metres
POW: 1d6 (4)	Initiative Bonus: +12

Abilities: Frenzy (warm-blooded creatures), Vampiric, Venomous (Application: Injected, Potency 60%, Resistance: Willpower, Onset time: Immediate, Duration: 1+1d3 hours, Conditions: A necrotising poison manifests as hallucinations as the flesh around the bite experiences Maiming. The hallucinations build in intensity rapidly before dissipating.)

1d20	Hit Location	AP/HP
1–3	Right Rear Claw	3/4
4–6	Left Rear Claw	3/4
7–9	Abdomen	3/5
10-12	Chest	4/6
13–15	Right Front Claw	3/4
16–18	Left Front Claw	3/4
19–20	Head	4/4

Skills	Passions, Traits & Dependencies
Athletics 52%, Brawn 38%, Endurance 34%, Evade 52%, Perception 47%, Stealth 54%, Survival 47%	Passions: Feast! 90%

Combat Style & Weapons	Traits & Notes
Lurk and Lunge (Claw, bite) 52%	

Weapon	Damage	Size/Reach	AP/HP	Effects
Claw	1d4-1d2	M/M	As for Claw	Grip
Bite	1d6-1d2	M/T	As for Head	Inject Venom

Trench Digger

These clawed, burrowing, elongated mouths are mobile digestive systems protected by a glistening hide resembling a rocky crust. They never stop moving. Trench Diggers seek decayed matter and find their way to cemeteries, battlefields, cultivated lands, and the trash dumps of communities if precautions are not taken to lure them in safer directions. If charging through a problem does not destroy it, raising part of its massive body to slam down on the offender probably will. In worst-case scenarios, the massive beast burrows deep into the earth then rises up under opponents to bite from below. Damage to its Acid Glands causes acid to affect the location or object that caused the injury. The creature and its trenches exude a bitter odour that stings the nostrils.

Trench Digger	Attributes
STR: 2d6+20 (27)	Action Points: 3
CON: 2d6+15 (22)	Damage Modifier: +1d8+1d6
SIZ: 2d6+40 (47)	Prana: 11
DEX: 2d6+10 (17)	Tenacity: N/A
INS: 2d6+3 (10)	Movement: 8 metres (6m digging)
POW: 3d6 (11)	Initiative Bonus: +14

Abilities: Burrower, Engulf, Trample, Acid Discharge (Application: Contact, Damage 1d6, Duration: 1d3 Combat rounds), Vulnerable (Salt acts like Strong Acid)

1d20	Hit Location	AP/HP
1–3	Left rear leg	5/13
4–6	Right rear leg	5/13
7–9	Acid Glands	3/7
10-12	Left leg	5/13
13–15	Right leg	5/13
17–18	Mandibles	6/10
19–20	Head	4/13

Skills	Passions,
Athletics 74%, Brawn 104%, Endurance 63%, Perception 60%, Stealth 62% (Underground only, always at Hard+), Survival 51%	Passions: Churn the Earth 65% Feast on Decay 50%

Combat Style & Weapons			Traits & Notes	
Plow through and Pulverise (charge, body slam, claw, mandibles) 60%				

Weapon	Damage	Size/Reach	AP/HP	Effects
Trample	2d10+2d6	E/T	As for Leg	
Mandibles	1d6+1d8+1d6	H/S	As for Mandible	Engulf
Claw	1d12+1d8+1d6	H/M	As for Claw	
Slam	1d12+1d8+1d6	E/S	5/13	Acid

Once-Men

Once-Men are neither man nor beast, but rather an irradiated and corrupted fusion of both. Slight and agile, they run unclothed in packs, preferring to hunt at night. They are malformed and their rough, pale skin forms spurs and is mottled with sores and tumours. Their faces are a blend of human and animal with flattened features and projecting teeth. Nothing quite fits together properly. They are extremely vicious and move with incredible speed in their attacks, but at rest show tribal behaviours. In combat, ferals fight in threes, seeking easy targets first, tearing through them without mercy. Eventually, Once-Men turn on their handlers if all other targets are exhausted. They do not stop fighting until all potential targets are dead. When loosed from a warband, they pair up if possible. Communication is mainly via grunts and howls. They obey strength, and in this region, have come to view Kyland as a god. They would follow him to the end of the Earth and jump off if he asks.

Once-Men	Attributes
STR: 18	Action Points: 4
CON: 9	Damage Modifier: +1d4
SIZ: 14	Prana: 11
DEX: 18	Tenacity: N/A
INS: 11	Movement: 8 metres
POW: 11	Initiative Bonus: +15
CHA: 13	Armour: None

1d20	Hit Location	AP/HP
1 – 3	Right Leg	0/4
4 – 6	Left Leg	0/4
7 – 9	Abdomen	0/5
10 – 12	Chest	0/6
13 – 15	Right Arm	0/3
16 – 18	Left Arm	0/3
19 – 20	Head	0/4

Skills	Passions, Traits & Dependencies
Athletics 50%, Brawn 25%, Endurance 40%, Evade 25%, Locale (The Camargue) 40%, Perception 60%, Stealth 50%, Survival 60%, Unarmed 60%, Willpower 25%	Passions: Love Battle 50%, Loyalty to Kyland 80%

Combat Style & Weapons			Traits & Notes	
Tooth and Claw (Club, Dagger, Claws, Bite after Grapple) 85%				

Weapon	Damage	Size/Reach	AP/HP	Effects
Club	1d6+1d4	M/S	4/6	Bash, Stun
Claws/Spurs	1d3+1d4	S/T	As for Arm	Bleed, Grip
Dagger	1d4+1+1d4	S/S	6/8	Bleed, Impale
Teeth	1d3+1d4	S/T	As for Head	Grip

Hot Metal & Methadrine

A world ravaged by the fires of industrialisation and the greed of the wealthy faces a new foe, an addictive drug that destroys everything it touches.

OVERVIEW

Parallel 00.01.98
Post-modern Corporate Ascendant Variant
Disruption Likelihood: 24.6%

Parallel 00.01.98 is a technologically advanced parallel, but one where big steel rules. Skyscrapers – massive floating palaces – scrape the heavens with their turbofans whilst on the ground enormous city-factories grind away night and day, producing coke and iron to fatten the oligarchs' pockets.

Meanwhile, in the shadows of the smokestacks, a new drug has taken hold: *Pretty Baby*. Dealers push it with the motto, 'Live Fast and Leave a Gorgeous Corpse'. Pretty Baby is ravaging the population, and W.O.T.A.N calculates a 24.6% chance of Disruptor involvement.

Into this walked Valhalla Agents Michel Eldritch and Petra Palmer. Tasked with tracking down the Disruptor influence, they were unprepared for what they found; there was no Disruptor involvement. Pretty Baby is a home-grown narcotic. Eldritch decided to sample Pretty Baby to see for himself what its effects would be. He was unprepared for the consequences; the drug has driven him mad, and Eldritch is now convinced that Pretty Baby should be spread far and wide. Working in concert with its manufacturer, Georgy-845, Eldritch is preparing to use The Van loaned to them to shift between the parallels, spreading the drug's influence. Petra discovered this insane plan and paid with her life. Before she could report back to Valhalla, Eldritch faked his own death to throw the Valhalla Programme off the trail of the real events, and then attacked Petra, forcing her to take an overdose, triggering a cardiac arrest.

Eldritch is now at large on parallel 00.01.98. He is waiting for the right time to meet with Georgy-845, his new benefactor, and show him the wonders of transparallel travel. There is no doubt that in such an unstable state, Eldritch and Georgy-845 will come to the attention of the Disruptors and fall into their clutches. The Agents must therefore discover what happened to Eldritch and Petra, destroy the source of Pretty Baby, and then prevent its spread across the multiverse.

NON-PLAYER CHARACTERS

- *Michel Eldritch*: A Valhalla Agent believed to have been killed on 00.01.98. In reality, he faked his own death and joined forces with Georgy-845, one of the oligarchs of the parallel and the manufacturer and distributor of Pretty Baby. Eldritch is selling his knowledge of the parallels to Georgy-845, along with The Van he and Petra had brought with them. Eldritch is conniving and brutal but ultimately cowardly. If he encounters the Agents who are investigating his 'death', he tries to portray himself as an innocent pawn caught up in events whilst selling the Agents out to the local security thugs. He uses the alias Andre-300 in this para.
- *Georgy-845*: An unscrupulous oligarch and drug manufacturer and distributor. Born into a life of privilege, all Georgy-845 wants is to increase the output of his factories. When one of his chemical engineers came up with a performance-enhancing drug that would greatly increase output, Georgy-845 immediately put it to use. Rather than marketing it as a required supplement, he came

up with the brilliant (to him) idea of selling it as an illegal drug, Pretty Baby. Not only does Georgy-845 make money from the sales and the increased output, but the users think they're getting one over on the oligarch by using a banned substance. Georgy-845 is a short, muscle-bound man in tailored suits. He's intense, quick to anger, and not used to being disobeyed. Georgy-845, who goes by the street name DJ-20, is the only one in his family who knows about the true origins of Pretty Baby. If he dies, the distribution pipeline crumbles.

- Mathias-015: A low-level Pretty Baby dealer with useful contacts throughout the ward. He got into the business to supplement his woeful income as a factory drone. He fell hard for Petra, as Lisl-418, and when he found out she and Eldritch were using him to stop Pretty Baby, he told DJ-20. He quickly regretted it, realising he loved Lisl-418/Petra more than he loved the money and status his dealing brought him. He still pretends to be loyal to DJ-20, but has joined the resistance. He comes across as a strange combination of sleazy and sincere, not unlike a used car salesman.
- Petra: Although Petra is dead at the start of the scenario, she plays a major role, namely, that the Valhalla Agents think they are travelling to the para to save her. Her friendship with Mathias-015, under the alias of Lisl-418, set in motion events that could see the downfall of one of the parallel's most powerful oligarchs.
- Zulu: The leader of the resistance. The group is a motley band of fighters whose primary tactics are to deface CCTV cameras and speakers and spray graffiti. Zulu long ago cast off her given name of Jamie-178 when she faked her own death in a racing accident to be reborn anew as the resistance leader. Now, she chooses to go by the final letter of the phonetic alphabet, the last thing she hopes the oligarchs hear. Despite her determination, Zulu really has no clue how to lead a resistance or fight a battle. She will be grateful for any assistance the Agents can offer.

MISSION STRUCTURE

This is, at its core, a murder mystery. As such, the Agents may not proceed through it in a linear fashion. They may flow from location to location, sometimes doubling back as they follow the clues. The Games Master should not hide any important clues behind rolls. But that does not mean the Games Master should hand out clues with no effort on the part of the players. The goal is to create the right balance of challenge and progress: frustrate the Agents, not the players. If the Agents need a clue to move the plot forward, are in the right spot to find a clue, and indicate that they are looking around, they should find the bare minimum needed to forge onwards. Of course, ancillary clues and other important details require an appropriate Perception or other skill check. The Games Master should also consider ways to introduce multiple avenues for revealing key clues should the Agents take an unexpected path through the scenario.

KEY POINTS/TIMELINE

1. Day -1: W.O.T.A.N receives the psychic transmission from Petra. Petra is killed by Eldritch.
2. Day 0: The Agents receive their briefing.
3. Day 1: The Agents arrive on 00.01.98 and begin their investigation.

Most clues in this scenario are fluid and can be found in any order. The clues lead to a showdown with Georgy-845, which most likely takes place on his Skyscraper.

AREAS TO BE COVERED

- The Flat: The apartment where Petra was killed.
- The Chicken Hut: The local eatery and meeting spot for Petra and Mathias-015.
- Alph Flophouse: Where Eldritch went to ground.
- Empire Down: A large bar, hangout for racers, and HQ for the resistance.
- Pretty Baby Plant: The repurposed factory where Georgy-845/DJ-20 has the drug manufactured.
- Aerodrome: The airport that services oligarchs flying to and from their skyscrapers. Where Eldritch hid The Van.
- Georgy-845's Skyscraper: A decadent Elysian paradise guarded by heavy weapons. It's where Georgy-845 calls home and from which he runs his empire.

BACKGROUND

The Agents of Valhalla don't always play catch-up. Often it may seem that way, Agents racing to a parallel to stop whatever nefarious scheme the Disruptors have come up with this time. Sometimes, W.O.T.A.N calculates which paras seem most likely to attract the Disruptors and dispatch Agents to forestall any geopolitical events that that might entice Zero-Zero's implacable foe to intervene.

In the case of 00.01.98, W.O.T.A.N calculated a 1.86% probability of potential instability related to the emergence of a new narcotic. Thus, Petra and Eldritch, a team who had worked together successfully before and was adept at undercover espionage, were sent to investigate. Intriguingly, W.O.T.A.N's calculations of instability have increased since the pair arrived on the parallel, and in the past few days, have increased significantly. Then, word came of Eldritch's death and the odds of instability spiked.

Unknown to the Valhalla Programme and the Agents, this is due to the mental trauma and distortion Eldritch has undergone.

The escalation in W.O.T.A.N's calculations matches his descent into megalomania: the Valhalla Programme itself is, on this occasion, the source of the instability.

The Iron Oligarchy

Designator: 00.01.98
Classification: Corporate Ascendant
Cultural Type: Northern Europe
Political Type: Capitalist Oligarchy
Technological Type: Industrial Age

The point of deviation from the standard timeline for para 00.01.98 was the early Cold War. Rapid industrialisation after World War II never abated. Factories grew and became cities unto themselves, stretching across political borders until the countries became irrelevant in the face of the needs of the corporations.

Now the world is divided into six wards, but for the purpose of the mission only the North-East Ward is important. It is divided into two classes; the workers and the owners. The workers comprise 98% of the population, slaving away in factories before going back to their company tenements and shopping in their company stores. They live in narrow, smog-choked streets. With what little free time they have, they spend it driving fast cars, hopping the massive trains that connect the disparate sectors of the North-East Ward, and watching blood sports for entertainment. Each worker wears a dark blue jumpsuit with a corporate ID, comprising the worker's name and a number, stencilled across the back.

Security teams patrol the streets to ensure that everybody who is supposed to be at work during their shifts is. They patrol the streets with truncheons, checking work cards against the master schedule on their tablets. If someone is determined to be truant, the security teams are authorised to use whatever force they deem necessary to get that person to work. Security personnel are dressed in black fatigues and rigid riot helmets, black visors covering their features.

The owners have risen above it all. Literally. The few with the money and the power live in skyscrapers; large airships, playing between them, blot out what little sun manages to leak through the smog. For those rare occasions when the oligarchs deign to walk amongst the lowers, they use air cars that cruise silently above the grimy asphalt. The oligarchs wear whatever they want, and it is always very well made.

The economy the average worker has to survive through is bleak. The oligarchs control the supply so they charge what they want. The currency, Corporate Store Credits, is shortened to *Corp Creds*, or *CC*. If this currency had any value anywhere else in the multiverse, each CC would be worth a pence. Unfortunately, the workers only bring home a few hundred CC a week.

From a cultural and fashion perspective, 00.01.98 is very similar to the 1970s in Great Britain. Cars are large and collars are larger.

The North-East Broadcast Network

The oligarchs know that a happy workforce is a productive workforce. They wholeheartedly acknowledge that it takes teamwork to make the dream work. To that end, they created The North-East Broadcast Network, a radio station that is played in every factory, meeting room, flat, and street in the ward. The only way to shut off its incessant pop music is to smash a speaker. Each speaker is also equipped with a CCTV camera that transmits data in real time to the local security office. Thus, smashing a speaker has drawbacks, usually in the form of a retaliatory security force curb stomp. When an important message needs to be disseminated to the masses, a monotone voice interrupts the music. The Games Master is encouraged to pepper some interruptions throughout the game to amplify the surreal feel of the dystopia. It can also offer an interesting means to provide clues to the Agents.

Sample announcements to set the tone:

'Peanut butter will be reduced by 10 Corp Creds in all company stores north of Huxley Park for the next eight hours.'

'Heavy rains are expected this evening. Slickers and galoshes are recommended.'

'An automobile accident on Viaduct Ypres-12 has occurred. Alternate routes are encouraged. Security personnel are alerted of this accident, so it does not count as a valid mitigation to truancy.'

'Employee Zamyatin-127 was recently promoted to shift manager at Factory Marrakech-18.'

'Factory Kiev-104 is under lockdown while reports of a cowboy firing weapons is investigated by security personnel.'

'Employee Mathias-015 at Factory London-96 has been congratulated on 12 days without a workplace accident.'

'Southern Ward security forces attempted a hostile takeover of Factory Marrakech-18, but were stopped by Employee Zamyatin-127.'

'Spies for the Far Western Ward have been spotted. If you see any dressed [description of the Agents], please report them immediately to the nearest security personnel. Any worker who provides leads that result in execution will be granted a day off from the factory.'

The resistance is able to occasionally broadcast messages through the speakers, usually by taking control of one of the broadcast offices. They try to be as disruptive as possible in the short time they control a station. Needless to say, the response by security personnel is swift and brutal, so much so that the resistance usually takes a station, sends a few broadcasts, and then flees before any response arrives. Here are some sample resistance messages the Games Master can splice into the game:

'At least 400 people died from Pretty Baby overdoses last month. Stay safe out there and don't take the drug!'

'Zulu has destroyed Factories London-91 through London-98. All workers are given a holiday.'

'Resistance has liberated the shops north of Waterstone. All groceries are free for the next two hours!'

'The other wards have cast down their oligarchs. Rise with the resistance!'

'All truancies will be forgiven today. Ask your local security personnel how!'

'Rumours of a cowboy loose in Kiev-104 are greatly exaggerated. Management requests all employees wear chaps and paper badges tomorrow to make up for the cowboy deficiency (see Buzby Murder, page 56).'

THE GEOPOLITICS OF 00.01.98

Politically speaking, the world is very stable. The six wards have become so focussed on producing material goods for export to the other wards that it's practically a closed system. The owners know that open conflict will only cause instability so they negotiate it away as much as possible. However, they know the workers need a channel to vent their frustrations, so they fabricate announcements of wars with other wards. Naturally, the ward making the announcement always wins. It's no use to have workers think they're losing a way. They might get angry with the owners.

PRETTY BABY

Pretty Baby is a highly addictive synthetic drug. Those who use it almost always become addicted after just a few uses. Its dealers use the mantra, 'Live fast and leave a pretty corpse', because it's accurate. Any Valhalla Agent who uses it runs the risk of developing an immediate strong dependency. The first time they use it, a Willpower check is needed to see if the addiction is staved off. The second and subsequent uses, for those who aren't addicted, is a Hard Willpower check. Once addicted, they develop a Dependency of 40%+1d10%, which means they must indulge in Pretty Baby at least once a week or start suffering Fatigue as per the rules in *Luther Arkwright*, pages 45-46.

The primary benefits are an immediate boost to Endurance and Perception. Users are instantly more aware of their surroundings. All Endurance and Perception tests for the next 24 hours are Easy. In addition, the Agent receives a permanent increase of 1 to Charisma. The Charisma augmentation manifests as seeming benefits in health and vitality: glossy hair, glowing skin, clear eyes, full red lips, and the heightened production and release of pheromones that make the user more sexually alluring. The most useful benefit from Pretty Baby, at least as far as the oligarch is concerned, is that it allows a person to go 48 hours without needing sleep.

Unfortunately, Pretty Baby burns out its users very fast. Once those 48 hours are over, the person succumbs to sleep within an hour. Usually, just enough time to wend a way home in a hazy mental fog. At this time, an Endurance check is required. If successful, the user sleeps like a rock for the next 1d10+4 hours. If the Endurance check fails, the sleep lasts for 2d10+8 hours.

A standard dose is 0.5 ml. Anything over that amount runs the risk of an overdose. If 0.10 ml or greater is taken, the user must make a Hard Endurance check or immediately go into cardiac arrest. In addition, once Charisma has increased by 3 or more points in toto, the user must attempt a Hard Endurance check or immediately suffer heart failure due to overexcitement. The Hard Endurance check is repeated each time the user's Charisma increases with the same risk of a heart attack.

For average people on this parallel, a cardiac arrest is almost always fatal. They don't have easy access to trained medical professionals. However, Valhalla Agents might have a medic with them who can save them.

Once addicted to Pretty Baby, the rules for decreasing a Dependency can be used to wean a person off the drug.

BRIEFING

Freyr Lingstadt summons the Agents to the briefing room. Althea Rivers is already present, and she plays a psychic transmission received from Agent Petra Palmer, a deep cover Agent on parallel 00.01.98. The transmission shows a woman some of the Agents may recognise as Agent Michel Eldritch lying in a pool of blood, the result of a shot to the head, the blood pooling like a grotesque thought bubble and the shadow of an enormous chicken dwarfing his body. A paper bag with the phrase *'stes like chi'* is clutched in Eldritch's hand. The view pans up from the smoking gun in Petra's hand to the neon lights outside a partially boarded-up window before everything goes black. It appears Eldritch has been murdered and Petra looks to be involved.

'Agents Michel Eldritch and Petra Palmer.' Freyr says, flatly. 'Experienced field Agents with a knack for deep undercover work. Petra's an empath and Eldritch is – or was – able to rapidly assimilate large amounts of complex data. This empathic transmission suggests Petra killed her partner for reasons we need to establish. They were investigating a new narcotic rife among the workers of an industrial parallel. Your job is to bring back Eldritch and Petra, and finish whatever they've started. They have a Van there with them; that needs to be located and brought back too.'

Althea explains what else is known. Based on W.O.T.A.N's predictions, and what Agents Petra and Eldritch learned and managed to transmit previously, a new synthetic chemical/drug, street name Pretty Baby, is laying waste to the lower class of this parallel, particularly in the North-East Ward, an industrial super-city stretching from England in the north to Ukraine in the east, Syria in the south, and Morocco in west. W.O.T.A.N's predictions are that the drug is of Disruptor manufacture and is being used to undermine the North-East Ward so that the Southern Ward, which comprises sub-Saharan Africa, South America, and Antarctica, can invade and supplant the North-East Ward's influence on the geopolitical scene.

Not long before this last image was received, Eldritch and Petra reported they made contact with a Pretty Baby dealer, Mathias-015, and had secured samples of Pretty Baby they planned on bringing back for analysis. All that has changed, though. The priority mission is Eldritch and Petra. The secondary objective is to cut off the supply of Pretty Baby.

Freyr concludes the briefing. 'We can't be sure that this *is* Disruptor involvement. Look into it. If it is a Disruptor operation, it carries some of the hallmarks of Loki, so I want details. If it isn't, then we need to know if the Disruptors are aware of what's happening on 00.01.98 - because it's *precisely* this kind of chaos that attracts a bastard like Loki.'

ARRIVAL

The Van delivers the Agents to a poorly lit alley in the midst of rundown section of the ward with four-metre-high piles of refuse along both walls, leaving only a narrow passage down the centre. The glow of neon lights and shouting spill in from beyond the mouth of the alley. A unit of eight security personnel is assaulting a group of five workers who are running late for work. Shouts of 'Show us your card!' and 'Shut up when I'm hitting you!' can be heard.

The Agents have a brief moment to get their bearings as The Van returns to Zero-Zero before a person in blue coveralls is thrown into the alley and three men in black fatigues pursue him. The security personnel continue to beat the man when he's down for two Rounds before one of them notices the Agents (unless they have hidden). The Agents' clothes immediately set them apart as outsiders and the security personnel demand to see their identity cards. The security personnel do not take 'no' for an answer.

If the Agents manage to hide, or do not intervene of their own accord, the beatings continue for three more Rounds until the security personnel kick the worker a few times and command him to get to work. He limps off as quickly as he can.

If the Agents fight, the security personnel have no qualms about fleeing, leaving any downed comrades to their fate if necessary. They are not paid enough to cope with actual resistance.

The worker being beaten in the alley is Armando-888, a member of the resistance. He does not hang around even if the Agents help, but does note these strangers and, if any intervention they stage works, word spreads back to Zulu, giving her a favourable impression of the Agents.

> ### Eldritch & Petra's Van
> Valhalla protocol dictates that when a Van must remain on a parallel for any length of time, it is hidden somewhere close by for easy access, but that is not the case with Eldritch and Petra's Van. The mimetic cover has been left behind, in the vicinity of where Eldritch and Petra made their base, but The Van itself is gone. Eldritch, working with Georgy-845, has moved The Van to a distant airfield. This put it beyond Petra's reach for use in Eldritch's forays across the multiverse to distribute Pretty Baby. Georgy-845 is fascinated by this technology and sees himself as becoming ruler of many, many worlds. It is therefore under heavy guard and is not be easy to access.

CLOTHING

Mortimer McAllan hasn't had the time to fabricate the jumpsuits worn by most of the parallel's populace, so the Agents need new clothes if they want to fit in. The most direct options to get to the information they want are to acquire either security personnel fatigues or worker jumpsuits. Workers' clothes can be found in company shops for the low, low price of 500 CC. Security personnel fatigues have to either be taken off security personnel or bought on the sly in pawn shops. If the Agents find a pawn broker willing to admit to selling them, they cost 10,000 CC. The Agents are likely to be short on funds at the outset, so barter is a viable option. Items from Zero-Zero would be highly desirable to the brokers (exotics appeal to the owners) and the Agents could work out very favourable trades.

A third, and very dangerous, route exists. The Agents can try to infiltrate the oligarchs. The Agents would need to steal clothing from a posh shop, which are only found on the skyscrapers or at the closely guarded city centres where the oligarchs like to slum, or off an oligarch. The other problematic factor is that, at least within a specific ward, the oligarchs all recognise each other by name if not face. Posing as an oligarch from a far distant ward, perhaps the South-Western Ward with interest in importing Pretty Baby would work well.

If the Agents go undercover as oligarchs, they learn some damning information about the parallel. The war between the wards is completely fabricated by the oligarchs to keep the workers loyal. Nothing drums up loyalty like a desperate struggle against a monolithic foe. The oligarchs fabricate war casualties to parade in front of the workers. Criminals are trussed up like enemy combatants and paraded as captives. The sick and dying are executed by the oligarchs in 'war games', where the oligarchs hunt them like game on their skyscrapers. The munitions plants provide the weapons the oligarchs use in the war games. They also periodically fire off large volleys to remind the workers that war is close to home.

SECURITY PERSONNEL

As long as the Agents blend in and do not cause too much of a stir, security personnel do not go out of their way to bother them. There is high turn-over at the factories as people are shuffled around by the oligarchs, so new faces aren't unexpected. More to the point, though, security personnel, for all their thuggish ways, are paranoid that a worker will bring a case against a security team, citing the security team as the reason the person is late to work. Tardiness is not tolerated by the oligarchs and if a worker can make a convincing case of being late because of security team harassment, that team could find itself cleaning the chemical toilets, or worse.

Enterprising Agents can hack the system to retrieve dossiers on various people. There are no dossiers on the oligarchs.

- The dossier on Mathias-015 has a picture of him and points him out to be a troublemaker that might warrant extra surveillance in the near future – it's possible that he's connected to the Pretty Baby problem.
- The dossier on DJ-20 is very vague. It says there are no records of him prior to a year ago. It's believed he is the main pipeline for Pretty Baby coming into the ward. He might be an agitator from the Southern Ward.
- Zulu is the single greatest threat to this ward's safety. She is a skilled assassin responsible for at least 20 deaths (this is false). All attempts to infiltrate her organisation have failed. There's a very blurry photograph that could be of anybody.
- Armando-888 has a picture in his dossier. He is the man being beaten when the Agents arrive. He is listed as a known truant who is habitually late for work and therefore disruptive to the productivity of the ward.
- The file on Pretty Baby is surprisingly thin. The security personnel consider it a major problem and list the symptoms of use and general pathological description of an overdose victim (see page 50). It surmises that there is a complex web of suppliers and dealers tracing back to DJ-20. This is partly false. Yes, DJ-20 is the main supplier, but he's an oligarch whose real name is Georgy-845, However, the supply chain isn't nearly as robust as the security personnel believe it to be.
- There are no dossiers on Petra and Eldritch's alter-egos, Lisl-418 or Andre-300.

However, if Eldritch learns that other Valhalla Agents are on the parallel, he assumes the Agents have come for him. To save his own hide, he alerts the security teams that there are dangerous spies from another ward trying to undermine the oligarchs. At first, Eldritch supplies descriptions of Zero-Zero style clothing. Once he learns their identities, Eldritch provides those to the security personnel.

Although the world is industrialised, the technology level is below that of Zero-Zero. The text-based computer terminals can be hacked with Computer checks. The communications systems used by the security teams can be interfered with by successful Comms checks. Engineering or Electronics can be used to override the basic electronic locks on doors.

THE STREET

Beyond the alley where the Agents arrive, the street is quiet, garishly lit by an endless parade of neon signs: a sleeping bull with z's rising from its snout for a flophouse called 'Roadside Attraction'; a guitar vibrating with CC signs for Lux Life, a pawn shop; and a large animated chicken crawling inside a bun with a large speech bubble reading 'Tastes Like Chicken' for a Chicken Hut; and large neon lips blowing a kiss for Squatweiler's Love, an adult video shop, unfortunately, part of the neon is flickering, making it look like the lips have a fever blister. A few groups of workers returning from shifts make their way along it, window shopping. Between the shops are several run-down flats with names like 'Vinge Acres', 'Okorafor Estates', and 'Bradbury Suites', many with boarded-up windows.

If the Agents are still wearing whatever clothes they arrived in, they draw curious stares and hushed whispers. People cross the street to get out of the path of the Agents.

Every hour on the hour, the silence is broken by the roar of an elevated train rushing past. The nearest station is a mile east.

Unless the Agents are on the street at shift change, most people are at work and the security patrol has either moved on or been dealt with. There is the risk of more security patrols taking an interest in the newcomers, guaranteed if the Agents intervened in the recent beating of Armando-888. Reinforcements arrive in a black, unmarked Ford Transit, spilling out of the rear doors with truncheons and riot shields, intent on capturing these subversives. The Agents need to get off the street and find a disguise as soon as they can.

Shift changes occur at 0800, 1600, and 2400 hours. During shift changes, the streets are packed with workers sullenly trudging to

> ### Finding Petra
>
> The Agents should be focussing their search on Petra, as at this point, they believe Eldritch is dead. The Agents are equipped with Polaroid photos of Petra and Eldritch to show to locals. There is a 25% chance of a random worker; shop attendant, server, or customer; or other local recognising one or the other. The chances of running to Mathias-015 is 30% as he has been frequenting the Chicken Hut looking for Lisl-418/Petra (see The Dealer – Mathias-015). On a successful ID, they learn their local names – Lisl-418 for Petra or Andre-300 for Eldritch. There is then a 20% chance that this random informant can point out the tenement block where the couple squatted. A Critical Success reveals that the person saw Mathias-015 visit frequently and recently heard fighting. The informant blames a love triangle.
>
> Petra and Eldritch squatted in a dilapidated flat on the fifth floor in the Bradbury Suites. If the Agents correctly deduce the tenement block or enter it by luck and start asking questions, there is a 30% chance of the residents recognising either Petra or Eldritch from the photographs. On a Critical Success, the resident identifies the flat Petra and Eldritch; otherwise, a Persuade or Intimidation roll is needed to get that information. See the Bradbury Flats Residents section.

or from the factory. Security personnel tend to stay on the side lines during shift changes so as not to delay people getting to work. They only intervene when there's an obvious problem, such as a fight, dawdling workers, or vandalism.

Perceptive or Insightful Agents should put two and two together and realise the shadow of the massive chicken seen in Petra's last transmission was from this Chicken Hut sign. Their flat is directly across the street on the fifth floor, overlooking the shop, but clearly in the shadow of the vast sign. The tenement is called 'Bradbury Suites', and a shabby sign, the 'd' missing from the red plastic letters, hangs at an angle above the main doors.

Bradbury Suites is sleazy, crumbling, and anonymous; one amongst hundreds of thousands of such tenements in this ward alone. The internal lights in the corridors work intermittently, and the place stinks of old urine, cheap alcohol, and body odour. The elevator does not work. It sits, doors jammed open on the third floor, and someone has used it as a toilet.

Bradbury Suites Residents

Some of the flats are empty, but most have occupants – even many of those with boarded-up windows. Some sample occupants are listed to help the Games Master flesh out the search. Use these as-is or as a springboard for other memorable characters.

Most of the occupants react more favourably to a fellow worker than security personnel, so if the Agents are wearing fatigues, no one answers a door and everyone does their best to move quickly away from them. The flat doors are flimsy constructs, so a successful Brawn check is all that's needed to beat or kick one in. Shooting out the hinges would be overkill.

Each flat has the same basic layout. The door opens into the front room, a combined living and dining room. The kitchen is straight ahead off the dining room. The bedroom is off the front room and a single bath is near the front door. All rooms except the kitchen have one window. Basic appliances (a cooker but no dishwasher), a small fridge, TV, and telephone round out the accoutrements of the average flat. Tenants are responsible for providing their own furniture, and many go without due to the outlandish fees charged in the company stores. Paint or wallpaper are in bad condition, as are the floors, whether they be sticky, spiky carpet, or warped hardwoods. It goes without saying that roaches, rats, and other vermin vastly outnumber the human residents.

- *Vittorio-089*, a large, shirtless hairy man who is a nursing a bloody nose lives in one flat. He remembers seeing a guy who matches Eldritch's description, but hasn't seen him in a while. If asked what happened to his nose, he looks furtively down at the ground, shuffles, and says something about 'fuckin' spooks', a clear reference to the security thugs.
- *Analissa-753*, a young girl staying home whilst her parents are at work. She has dark, haunted eyes and perpetually tear-stained cheeks and tries to avoid making eye contact. Her flat is bone chillingly cold even though a kerosene heater is burning hotly in one corner. Analissa is a latent psychic who passively absorbs heat and uses that energy to unconsciously scan for other psychics. She doesn't understand her powers, or even that she has powers. If befriended, she admits that the lady several flights above screamed and screamed but nobody heard. Analissa was picking up on Petra's psychic death throes.
- *Mary-589*, a middle-aged drunk who wanders the halls in her underwear. She raves continuously about how the security personnel stole Terrence-084, her husband, in the middle of dinner one night. They came in through the ceiling, zipped him in a bag, and left her a receipt, which she shows anyone who tries to engage her in conversation. She doesn't know Petra or Eldritch, but can confirm that the loud crash a few nights ago reminded her of when they slammed her husband to the ground before taking him into custody.
- *David-36 and John-613*, a pair of Pretty Baby junkies who get their fix from Mathias-015. Both men are in their late 20s and very attractive; they have been using for a while. They are also nearly constantly fixing up, cleaning, and rearranging their flat when not at work, trying to burn off the stimulant aspect of Pretty Baby. They met and disliked Eldritch, who they knew as Andre-300, as something seemed 'off' about him. Petra, Lisl-418, seemed nice enough, though. Both tenants knew Mathias-015 served as Eldritch and Petra's dealer, and they know where Mathias-015 can

be found. If treated kindly, John-613 is prepared to act as a local guide for the Agents.

- The sounds of a baby screaming come from one flat, but no one answers the door. If the Agents enter anyway, they are greeted by a five-year-old boy, Dima-099, pointing a Valhalla-issued vibro beamer at them. Behind him in a crib is the boy's father, Lucca-065, a grown man wrapped in swaddling clothes and screaming his head off, an empty baby bottle tossed on the floor. The Agents have a few rounds to gain the boy's trust before he opens fire. He only has a 15% in combat skills, but he could land a lucky hit. One shot, though, throws the vibro beamer out of his tiny grip. Dima-099 found the vibro beamer under the floorboards in Eldritch and Petra's flat while he was scrounging for food. His father stops screaming if Dima-099 opens fire, and just sits in his cot, sucking his thumb, watching the events with wide, baby-like eyes. Lucca-065 does not communicate, save to burst into tears if anyone shouts at him. His nappy needs changing.
- A giant roach (see page 64) in the bedroom is feeding on the bloated corpse of a female Pretty Baby victim. It creates horrific slurping sounds as it burrows its way into her face. It tries to flee out the front room window.
- *James-444*, an affable older man who is living off the dole after losing a leg in a workplace accident. He gets around on a low four-wheeled furniture dolly by pulling himself along the floor with his hands. The wheels squeak as he paddles around, grating on most tenants' nerves. He knows Petra as Lisl-418, the pretty young lady that lives upstairs on the fifth floor. James-444 is lonely and a huge fan of small talk about anything and everything. He's also a rat for the security personnel – part of his agreement to continue receiving his monthly stipend. If the Agents behave in any suspicious ways, say anything James-444 finds suspicious, or are dressed outlandishly, he calls the security personnel on a cell phone specifically for this purpose. A unit of six security personnel arrive in 20 minutes.

THE SQUAT

The flat that Eldritch and Petra squatted in is on the fifth floor. A faint odour of decay reaches the hall, but that's not too different from the rest of the building. The door is shut, but unlocked.

The flat is thoroughly squalid. A pair of nasty mattresses with thin sheets litter the bedroom. Workers' uniforms hang on pegs, but no two names taped on the breast pocket are the same. The front room has a single electric lamp in one corner and one sunken-in chair that looks like lost a fight with a particularly hateful pitbull. A single end table holds a ratty copy of Eric Blair's Guide to the Wards. The book lists all the exciting 'tourist' locales across the wards in overly positive prose. A photograph of Mathias-015 marks a page with Alph Flophouse and Empire Down on facing pages. The photograph is a profile shot of a late 20s, gangly, watery-eyed, hawk-nosed man with a mop of blonde hair sitting in a restaurant booth with Petra.

The kitchen has numerous shelf-stable canned vegetables, fruits, and proteins as well as a make-shift darkroom for developing photographs. The kitchen also has an overflowing waste bin. There are several Chicken Hut wrappers in the bin as well as a substantial amount of rotting produce. Underneath everything, though, is an empty bottle of Chili Beer. A few blonde hairs are stuck to a smudge of Petra's blood. This is what Eldritch used to club her.

Petra's body is slumped against the wall next to the door. It's been there for two days and some insects have started to feast. Opposite her body is a pool of fake blood with a head-sized void, but no sign of Eldritch's body. Given that the Agents were expecting to find a dead Eldritch, not a dead Petra, and given the squalid conditions of the flat and appalling state of Petra's corpse, this is a Disturbing discovery from a sanity point of view (see Madness and Other Colours, *Luther Arkwright*, page 50). There are several other clues here for the Agents to find.

It is procedure to bring back any recovered fallen Agents to Zero-Zero for burial, so the Agents must arrange that as well. Not only is it a matter of honour to repatriate the fallen Agent, but technologically advanced parallels could learn too much from an autopsy.

Searching the flat unearths a number of clues, as described below.

THE NEEDLE AND THE DAMAGE DONE

Petra holds a 9mm pistol in her right hand. One bullet is missing from the clip, but there's no gunshot residue on her hand. Eldritch slipped a bullet out of the clip, worried that an actual gunshot would attract undue attention. A hypodermic syringe dangles from the crook of her right elbow, the plunger fully depressed. An empty vial lies next to her. A relevant skill check discovers Pretty Baby residue in the syringe and vial. If they found the Pretty Baby victim during their search, they can determine Petra's corpse resembles the other one, indicating a Pretty Baby overdose, though Petra is not as attractive as the other corpse (a skill check reveals she has not been using long). Being right handed, it would be incredibly difficult for Petra to manage to hold onto the gun with her dominant hand and shoot up with her off hand. Any fingerprints on the syringe body and plunger are smudged beyond utility. Close examination of the corpse also uncovers blunt force trauma to the back of her skull. There is no other Pretty Baby in the flat. Petra's Valhalla-issue vibro is not on her either.

THE POOL OF BLOOD

In the gloom of the room, the pool does look like congealing blood with numerous ants crawling around and on it. On closer scrutiny, though, it is too red and too shiny to be several days-old blood. If touched, it is still tacky and has a sugary smell. Eldritch faked his own death with cheap theatrical blood bought from the pawn shop on the street. He did this to elicit a psychic flash from Petra to Zero-Zero. While she flashed, he jumped up and smashed her in the head with a beer bottle. He then jammed the syringe into her arm to force an overdose. He then fled. In his paranoia, he mistakenly assumed that Zero-Zero would write them off. He didn't expect them to send a search party.

Hidey-Hole

When the Petra and Eldritch arrived, they followed protocol to create a hidden location for their TPT and other equipment. Eldritch took the TPT with him when he fled, though, and only some of the easily identifiable cabling remains, dangling from the wall. They pried up a floor-board and hid their Zero-Zero clothes as well as their Valhalla-issue vibro beamers in there. When the Agents search and find the hidey-hole, the clothes are dishevelled and the vibro beamers are gone: Eldritch has one and Dima-099, a young boy from the tenement, found the other and is using it for protection. There is also a coded message on a scrap of paper. Deciphering the message reveals the location where they initially left The Van (see Eldritch and Petra's Van, page 51).

There is no Pretty Baby in the hiding spot.

Matchbook

In the kitchen is a matchbook next to the stove. The cover has 'Empire Down' printed on it and on the inside cover, Mathias-015 scribbled in pencil in a hasty hand. A quick check reveals that Empire Down is a nightclub where many of the street racers and resistance members gather.

Photo

Hidden behind some peeling wallpaper in the bedroom is a photo. It's a blurry, but a swept-wing pusher prop aircraft sits on a tarmac airstrip. The letters 'gy 845' can be barely discerned on the nose. A male, just out of focus, is either handing something to or taking something from a well-dressed man. The out-of-focus man is circled in red and marked with a question mark. The well-dressed man is circled with the annotation 'DJ-20?' The time stamp on the picture is from one week ago.

Petra was suspicious of Eldritch's recent behaviour and followed him. Eldritch went to the ward's aerodrome and met with Georgy-845 in his persona as DJ-20. The picture shows Eldritch receiving a cash advance from Georgy-845 in return for The Van. The same day, Eldritch took delivery of his first batch of Pretty Baby, but Petra had to make herself scarce before she could photograph the proceedings.

The Dealer

There a number of ways for the Agents to locate Mathias-015. If the Agents find the photo of him in the book, they can easily keep an eye out for the distinctive-looking man. If, at any point, the Agents show Mathias-015 a photograph of Petra, a guilty look crosses his face for an instant. The Agents can make of that what they will, but Mathias-015's guilt is only because he feels bad about not building up the nerve to ask her out. He at first assumes one of the Agents is Petra's lover and harbours some jealousy due to his feelings for her. Unless pressed, he tries to pass off Petra as merely a casual acquaintance. If questioned in more depth, his true feelings come spilling out in a blubbery mess of tears, sobs, and throat-clearings.

Once he learns of Petra's death, he is dead-set on believing that DJ-20 (Georgy-845) is to blame, but he doesn't share this information with the Agents. He wants the personal satisfaction of feeling DJ-20's life slip through his fingers. DJ-20 had been asking questions about the new girl that Mathias-015 told DJ-20 was trying to stop Pretty Baby, thus leading Mathais-015 to believe that DJ-20 thought she was an undercover security officer.

First, Mathias-015 has been spending even more time than usual in the Chicken Hut. If there, the Agents find him nursing some biscuits and a fried chicken-meal sandwich. Mathias-015 tells himself that he is waiting to sell some more Pretty Baby, but he's actually worried about Lisl-418 (Petra). He has not seen her in a couple of days and is working up the nerve to go to her flat. As the local Pretty Baby dealer, he knows everybody on the streets. The Agents stick out as outsiders, even if they are in local clothes.

Second, the Agents could spot Mathias-015 near Petra's flat, either already there trying to get up the nerve to knock on her door or following them from the Chicken Hut or the street, relying on his Stealth. If he spots Petra's body, Mathias-015 cannot help but let out a wailing sob. If the Agents move towards him, he runs, purely as a reflex. Mathias-015 had nothing to do with Petra's death, but people like him always get blamed and he isn't stupid enough to stick around. If caught and questioned, a successful Insight roll soon uncovers that Mathias-015 was in love with Petra – a deep infatuation. He thinks Lisl-418/Petra was pretty enough without Pretty Baby and insists he would never have let her use it, though he did sell her 3 vials, which she swore to him were not for her and he believed her. Mathias-015 does say that Andre-300 (Eldritch), on the other hand, was a customer and user.

Third, Mathias-015 spends every evening at Empire Down nightclub selling Pretty Baby. He has a regular table not far from the entrance. It was at Empire Down that Petra first made contact with Mathias-015.

Mathias-015 can be a useful ally, especially if he learns Petra was murdered. He knows the streets of the ward and can get them in touch with the resistance if heavier fire power is needed. Mathias-015 supplied Petra with three vials of Pretty Baby (she intended to take them back to Zero-Zero for analysis); he does not know where they are now.

Empire Down

Empire Down is a multi-storey club occupying a half a city block-sized warehouse near a derelict steel mill. Loud, thumping, almost tribal music, revving car engines, and shouted conversations all add to the oppressive din while strobe lighting, heaving smoke,

> ### Buzby Murder
>
> Despite apparent complicity between the resistance and events at Factory Kiev-104, Zulu has no knowledge of the mysterious cowboy whom she calls the Lone Stranger. If asked about the shooting rampage she will inform the Agents that she'd originally assumed it was they who had laced kilotons of exported food with acute botulism. Unfortunately the other wards have not taken kindly to deaths amongst their workers and Zulu wants the cowboy's head on a platter.

and car exhaust fumes lower visibility. Multiple bars on both levels ensure the alcohol never stops flowing and Pretty Baby is sold openly. Revellers wander among tables on the ground floor or dance to the house band on the upper mezzanine.

At ground level, drivers are racing their cars around the old steel mill. Contests range from two vehicles to however many cars want to race. They compete for the pink slips to each other's cars, credits at the company stores, cash, bragging rights, or the chance to beat the loser to within an inch of his life. Even those without cars can buy their way into racing for a few pounds and are given loaner cars. The Games Master has several options, at its most basic, the races can provide background colour. Agents might want to get in on the action, either as betters or drivers with a loaned or stolen car. The racing grounds can also serve as a treacherous area for a foot chase and manhunt, should Eldritch try to flee, or a car chase should Eldritch steal a car.

Given the poorly lit conditions, few people here would recognise either Petra or Eldritch. However, there are three who do: Rufus-75, the main bartender; Zulu, leader of the resistance; and Eldritch himself.

Rufus-075

Rufus-075 is a gangly man with a multi-coloured mohawk. He is a consummate bartender due to his ability to psychically read people. This allows him not only get the person what they order to drink, but engage them in the right conversations to win them over and earn himself big tips. His souped-up Austin Allegro sits right outside the front door. His keys are in his pocket with a lucky rabbit foot charm attached.

Rufus-075 is a loyal to his friends, and one of those friends is Andre-300 (Eldritch). He covers for Eldritch and try to send the Agents off on a wild goose chase. He tells them he saw Eldritch last night at another club, Alice, on the other side of town. Eldritch looked positively distraught because his girlfriend Lisl-418 had just overdosed on Pretty Baby the night before.

If the Agents use Insight or some other relevant skill to determine the bartender is hiding something, Rufus-075 starts making surreptitious movements with the fingers of his left hand whilst twirling a bottle in his right. Observant Agents can notice the movements and follow Rufus-075's gaze as it flicks upwards. They see a figure on the top mezzanine fading deeper into the crowd.

Rufus-075 tries to stop the Agents from going after Eldritch. His latent psychic powers allow him to command the throng surrounding the bar to stop the Agents from going anywhere (tapping into their fear of outsiders); the press of bodies requires the Agents to succeed in Formidable Athletics rolls to make their way through the wall of people. If they succeed, Rufus-075 opts for violence, producing a sawed-off shotgun from underneath the bar. He wills the crowd part to give him a clear shot at the Agents, and once the gun hoves into view, people run screaming. Rufus-075 shoots to kill – he is part of Georgy-845's organisation and has contacts in the security service who will look after him, so he doesn't care about killing the Agents. If a firefight breaks out, security personnel respond in force in within 1d4 rounds ready to crack every skull in the place, but especially the Agents, because Rufus-075 readily rats them out.

Eldritch

Eldritch is on the upper mezzanine at Empire Down to sell more Pretty Baby as Andre-300. He is using Pretty Baby himself and has suffered a dangerous psychotic reaction to the drug, believing himself to be a saviour who must bring Pretty Baby to the masses (here and beyond), with the help of DJ-20/Georgy-845 and the likes of Rufus-075. This is a complete personality reversal from the sane, sober Valhalla Agent who came to this parallel. His skin glows and his hair is silky-smooth. He feels invincible, self-righteous, and guilt-free. In his Pretty Baby-addled mind, the multiverse should not be denied the delights of this wonder drug and he is the first of many Pretty Baby Messiahs. Underneath though, Eldritch is cowardly and vulnerable. He is easily awed by wealth and power, which is how Georgy-845 corrupted him, and it is what makes him especially susceptible to Disruptor control. Eldritch cannot stop; he must be stopped.

If he spots the Agents approaching (25% chance if the Agents are wearing native attire, 70% if they're still wearing Zero-Zero attire) or sees Rufus-075's signal, Eldritch immediately leaves, making for one of Empire Down's back exits, abandoning his deals, and, accidentally, the keys to his hideout. The keys are stamped with a stylised 'A', for the Alph flophouse, another low-rent tenement in the London district of the ward.

Eldritch flees on foot through the abandoned steel mill to hop a turbine freight train and head to his hideout; he makes his way through the race track deliberately. Anyone who tries to follow must dodge the cars that are racing around the track. It's a warren of decaying buildings, disused smelters, tottering smoke stacks, and rust.

If Eldritch is caught, whether in the abandoned mill, his hideout, or somewhere else, he initially tries to fight back. In his current state, he doesn't care about the secrecy of the Valhalla Programme any longer. He uses his vibro to shoot back, even in a crowded place. Once injured, though, he tries to bargain with the Agents for his safety. All the time though, he paints himself as the victim in all things, a pawn of a much more powerful force. He does not admit to killing Petra, unless there is incontrovertible proof; even then he is more likely to blame Georgy-845 as forcing him to do it.

Zulu

Zulu and ten fellow resistance fighters are at Empire Down, watching the crowds, making their own plans. One of those with Zulu is Armando-888, the worker who the security personnel beat when the Agents first arrived on the parallel. They have a large booth on the mezzanine opposite where Eldritch tends to work. Their booth is cloaked in shadow and cigarette smoke. The group of resistance fighters drink cheap rum, chat, and survey what's going on around them. They've been watching Andre-300/Eldritch for some time, knowing he has connections with Georgy-845. When the time is right, which is not now, they intend to make their move, using Eldritch to get to the oligarch and make a profound example of him.

As leader of the resistance, Zulu has a good idea of what is happening in the ward. She has spies everywhere. She is more than happy to help the Agents, but not for free. Zulu knows she has a tough fight on her hands against the oligarchs, but equipment and tactical support from the Agents would earn her help.

She's eager to see the oligarchs thrown down and the plague of Pretty Baby stopped before more people die needlessly. However, she's not foolish enough to see all her fighters die against the horde of security personnel.

Armando-888's opinion of the Agents colours Zulu's opinion of them and determines how willing she is to lend them aid.

If a fight breaks out, Zulu and her fighters stay out of it, until the security personnel enter the fracas. Then, they make some attacks of opportunity but never endanger themselves, retreating if the fight is going against them. If they see the Agents following Eldritch, Zulu and several others follow, wanting to observe why someone else is interested in him. If they sense the Agents could be allies, they make themselves known.

The Alph Flophouse

Eldritch's hideout is a damp, dank cellar flat in the Alph tenement, several kilometres across the ward from the flat he shared with Petra. He moved in here after killing Petra and making his deal with Georgy-845. Eldritch hasn't been practising good tradecraft and has left some easy-to-find information. The TPT is here, leaning up against a wall. Eldritch started to hook it up, but stopped mid-way through, distracted by a Pretty Baby hit.

This flat has the same layout as the other flats, but Eldritch's only furnished it with a single beaten-up mattress. A half-dozen empty Pretty Baby vials and a single dirty syringe litter the floor next to the mattress. He's added three locks to the door, increasing the Difficulty of kicking it down to Formidable. The bedroom is filled with 40 soggy cardboard boxes. Each box contains 100 vials of Pretty Baby. These are the drugs that Georgy-845 has given Eldritch to spread across the parallels. The damp conditions and soggy cardboard has attracted two giant roaches (see page 64) who crawled in through a broken window. Investigating the boxes arouses their ire.

On the wall of the front room, Eldritch has tacked a map of the ward and circled Georgy's hangers at the aerodrome as well as the Pretty Baby plant.

Hidden in a hold-all, casually tossed into one corner, are several plastic tubes of theatrical blood. This is surplus from his faked death.

The Plant

Pretty Baby is produced in a repurposed pharmaceutical facility tucked in behind several larger steel mills. Georgy-845 is paranoid that his operation will be discovered, so he has six teams of four security personnel patrol the grounds 24 hours a day. All the windows are blacked out and the doors open into vestibules to help diminish the amount of light that escapes. CCTV cameras on the roof pan back and forth.

A security office, with one guard, is immediately past the doors on the far side of the vestibule. In here is a bank of monitors hooked up to the internal and external cameras. There is also a card scanner so workers can swipe in and out for their shifts.

Beyond the security office is the main area, an assembly line of people in white coveralls synthesise Pretty Baby, put it in vials, and package those vials in boxes for shipment to the network of dealers Georgy-845 has around the ward. All this happens under the harsh glow of fluorescent lights and the watchful eyes of a team of four security personnel, patrolling along gantries suspended along the perimeter, looking down onto the factory floor. Along the west wall are drums, some emblazoned with the skull and crossbones symbol for toxic and others with the flame icon, indicating flammable. Pretty Baby itself is not flammable, but some of the ingredients used in the synthesis process are highly explosive. Others release a noxious cloud of gas that causes hallucinations.

Hallucinatory Gas

Application: Inhalation
Potency: 60
Resistance: Endurance
Onset Time: 1d3 minutes
Duration: 1d4 hours
Conditions: The gas causes hallucinations that include the victim's skin sloughing off or bubbling up in pustules that pop, releasing a nast-smelling green ooze. The hallucinations are severe and realistic enough that many people harm themselves scraping at the pustules or scratching at the sloughing skin.
Antidote/Cure: The Regenerate psychic ability can end the hallucinations.

A managers' office is a glass-walled room overlooking the main floor, accessible by steel stairs running up the far wall. It has the books and ledgers as well as two grumpy supervisors who only want their shift to be over so they can head to the bar. They aren't privy to Georgy-845's plan. If the books are inspected, it's clear that production has ramped up in the past week as a new dealer, noted as 'A', has the ability to send the drug to other, more distant markets.

The other room of interest, beyond the bathrooms, is on the east wall. It's the physical plant and pump room. It contains the air exchangers, pbx (telephone exchange), and main electrical junction boxes.

Gaining access to the factory is difficult without a keycard, and only security staff and the workers have them. Even Eldritch has not been granted a card. Close observation of the windows reveal tiny wires running across each window, leading to junction boxes on the wall, obviously an alarm system. Breaking in triggers silent sensor alarms that immediately alert the security teams who converge on the break-in point. If it comes to a fight, they do not take prisoners but do aim to keep one infiltrator alive for questioning by Georgy-845. The security staff are armed with truncheons, 9mm pistols, and 7.62 assault carbines, fitted with suppressors to muffle the sound in the factory area.

The workers work around the clock in eight-hour shifts. The white overalls are only worn inside the factory; at shift's end, the workers change into normal coveralls before leaving, thereby making it look like this is just another routine production facility. Keycards are worn on lanyards around the neck and feature a photograph of the owner, his or her name, and a barcode that provides access to authorised areas.

The factory floor is divided into production, quality control, and packing areas. Bullet-proof Plexiglass walls mark the divisions. The production area is sealed, very well ventilated, and stacked with high-end chemistry equipment used for synthesising the drug. Vast arrays of distillation equipment dominate the area, culminating in large distillation flasks where the clear liquid that is Pretty Baby deposits. The head chemist is an ageing woman with grey-streaked hair pulled back in a tight pony tail. Her name is Heisenberg-502 and she is the genius behind the drug. She oversees the production, adjusting various parts of the production cycle to make sure everything is perfect. Assistant chemists watch and note, ensuring they can keep the process to Heisenberg-502's exacting standards when she is not on duty.

THE AERODROME

It is common knowledge that the oligarchs travel to and from their skyscrapers from the aerodrome. Any worker can provide directions.

The aerodrome on the western side of the London district is heavily guarded at the entrances, but most of the perimeter is only watched by panning CCTV cameras. In addition to the hangers and runways, the aerodrome is also home to several of the North-East Ward's munitions plants. Although all the wards are secretly at peace, a healthy arms race keeps workers busy and makes it easy to sell fabricated wars. Both guns and explosives can be found in the heavily guarded plants.

The aerodrome is where all the gleaming, alloy air cars wait to transport supplies to and from the skyscrapers, and in some cases, human passengers as well. The airfield is ringed with hangers marked with the names of the oligarch to whom they belong. There are four marked Sarah-577, two for LRW-647, three for Georgy-845, a further two for Lady 3Jane Tessier-Ashpool, and many more with other names. Hidden under a tarpaulin is an old motor vehicle, a brilliant red barchetta; a relic from a better, vanished time. All of Georgy-845's hangers are guarded by a pair of security personnel; one of his air cars is purely for personnel transport and is very luxurious with leather seats, velvet wallpaper, and surround sound. It can carry four plus the pilot and co-pilot. It is reserved for Georgy-845 and important guests. This is the pusher prop from Petra's photograph.

Two of the hangers contain air cars, one of which matches the air car from the photograph found in Petra's flat. The third hanger contains the missing Van and crates of Pretty Baby – simply waiting for Eldritch to arrive and start his serious distribution. He makes his way here, eventually. The Agents do not find him here during initial reconnaissance.

The other air car transports cargo. It is much larger and slower, but is still crewed by two pilots. Its cargo hold can hold up to 25 people, though not comfortably. The cargo hold is standing room only. People can lean up against the airframe, but unless there's crates, there's nowhere to sit other than the steel floor. Both air cars have 'Georgy-845' emblazoned on the nose cone.

If the Agents have not found Eldritch yet, he arrives here within 24 hours, intent on starting his work across the other parallels. Of the two Agents, Eldritch is the less technically competent; although he knows how The Van works, he has never used it solo before – Petra has always been with him or the Valhalla Programme has Programmemed coordinates. He has convinced Georgy-845 and others believe that he is a master traveller of the million spheres; it shakes their confidence in him if he fails to activate The Van properly. Plus, Georgy-845 has insisted on sending one of his trusted advisers, Graham-259, to accompany Eldritch on the first mission, so that he can confirm for himself that there are, indeed, other parallels. Graham-259, of course, studies the way The Van works very carefully because, when ready, Georgy-845 wants him to either kill Eldritch or strand him somewhere. There are others Georgy-845 trusts far more than this Baby-addicted murderer.

Georgy-845's Skyscraper

Fully ending the distribution of Pretty Baby requires taking out Georgy-845. To do this, the Agents need to find a way to reach Georgy-845's skyscraper or lure the oligarch down to ground level. The easiest way is to hijack or steal one of Georgy-845's air cars and fly it up. Enterprising Agents can surely find other, more surprising ways. Eldritch has been to the skyscraper and can provide details about its layout and defences. So can Georgy-845's pilots, but they're more reluctant to cooperate.

Each skyscraper is different. Some look like gleaming glass towers, others castles. Georgy-845 is more of a classicist. His skyscraper looks like an ancient Greek agora with a temple at the top of a hill. The area surrounding it is a verdant green forest with bubbling brooks and still blue ponds. Servants dressed as Greek slaves move back and forth making sure Georgy-845, his friends, and his family are well taken care of. If the Agents visit the skyscraper, a large, debauched Grecian feast is occurring, with men and women dressed as satyrs chasing men and women dressed as naiads. Food covers hundreds of feet of tables and servants with trays piled high with more food mingle with Georgy-845 and his oligarch guests. Another person dressed as a minotaur is walking around threatening guests, who mockingly scream for help before a security officer arrives to 'chase' off the monster.

There are also security personnel dressed like hoplites but armed with guns patrolling the grounds. Even more dangerous are the gun emplacements. These fortified locations are disguised as statuary and have either rocket launchers or 7.62 medium machineguns.

The cockpit of the skyscraper is inside a small temple to Apollo in the agora. It takes three pilots to manage all the systems on the skyscraper, but it's similar to aircraft on other parallels, so Agents would only need to succeed at Piloting checks to try to fly the craft. Anything fewer than three pilots, though, causes the skyscraper to lurch, pivot, and become unstable.

The temple on the hill, built to mimic the Parthenon, is Georgy-845's mansion. Despite its classic look, it has all the modern amenities. Georgy-845's wife and two children are in the mansion, avoiding the debauched party as much as they can. His wife Mary-096 says she loves Georgy-845, but finds his incessant pleasure seeking to be tiring and she'd rather not have her children exposed to it.

The Loki Connection

Should the Agents search Georgy's office, which is tucked away at the mansion's rear, they will uncover much paperwork and electronic transmissions pertaining to the Pretty Baby trade. One of the transmissions is an email exchange between Georgy and one James De Vere. De Vere is one of Loki's pseudonyms, and the emails discuss the possibility of De Vere becoming involved in brokering the drug in the Prusso-Baltic Ward. Georgy mentions in one email that he has, via one of his couriers, 'come into the knowledge of some startling technology' that De Vere may be interested in. De Vere replies that contacts of his own would, indeed, be interested in learning more and even perhaps meeting Georgy's courier.

This is clearly a reference to Eldritch, The Van, and Georgy's discovery of an entire multiverse. Of course, none of this is news to Loki, but the chance to capture and interrogate a Valhalla Agent is highly attractive.

If the Agents try to follow-up more on James De Vere then they reach a dead-end. A man of that name was resident in the Prusso-Baltic Ward, but left a week ago and has not been seen since. Loki has left the parallel to pursue another mission elsewhere although he has left behind Disruptor Pawns who would be responsible for capturing and interrogating Eldritch at an opportune point.

Games Masters could easily extend this scenario to include this part of Georgy-845's scheme if they wish.

Conclusion

There are a multitude of ways to conclude this scenario considering the Agents' two objectives: first, find Petra and Eldritch and, second, stop the flow of Pretty Baby. The first goal is easier to achieve than the second. Petra's body should be brought back for burial and Eldritch should stand trial for his betrayal of the Valhalla Programme.

Simply destroying the plant or the available stash of Pretty Baby puts a definite wrinkle in Georgy-845's plans, but he has business continuity plans in place and resumes operations in a few months. A more long-term solution might be to kill Georgy-845, though unless they also apprehend the chemist, production may continue under new management. If the Agents report Georgy-845's security arrangements back to the Valhalla Programme, longer-term plans could be drawn-up to deal with him, most likely involving Arkwright and other more-experienced personnel.

Getting to Georgy-845 should be difficult. His skyscraper is well guarded, but a covert team could storm the place, especially if they have support from Zulu and her fighters.

Another option is to bring Georgy-845 down to the surface. He brings a sizable security detail, but won't be defended by the heavy gun emplacements. The easiest to entice the oligarch to the surface is to offer a sweeter deal than what Eldritch has offered. Georgy-845's greed won't let him refuse.

It's entirely possible that the Agents only find Petra and maybe capture Eldritch. If they fail to recover The Van, Georgy-845's engineers eventually figure out how to operate it and Pretty Baby starts appearing on other parallels.

And, if Eldritch does survive and prosper, Loki's Pawns may well capture him (with Georgy-845's unwitting help), subjecting him to all kinds of torture. Loki himself may use Thought Implant to completely turn Eldritch to the Disruptor cause, using him as a double-agent within Valhalla.

Non-Player Characters

Eldritch

Prior to being hooked on Pretty Baby, Eldritch was an average looking man. He had non-descript features, neatly combed black hair, and an average physique. Once he became hooked on Pretty Baby, he started to change. He now has an aura of glamour about him; he could be a cover model.

However, he's a conniving, cowardly bastard. He will harm or lie to anyone and everyone to ensure that he comes out on top.

His name on this parallel is Andre-300.

Eldritch	Attributes
STR: 15	Action Points: 3
CON: 14	Damage Modifier: +1d2
SIZ: 12	Prana: 12
DEX: 12	Tenacity: 10
INT: 15	Movement: 6 metres
POW: 12	Initiative Bonus: +13
CHA: 11	Armour: Security Personnel Armour

1d20	Hit Location	AP/HP
1–3	Right Leg	2/6
4–6	Left Leg	2/6
7–9	Abdomen	3/7
10–12	Chest	3/8
13–15	Right Arm	2/5
16–18	Left Arm	2/5
19–20	Head	4/6

Skills	Passions, Traits & Dependencies
Acrobatics 40%, Athletics 65%, Brawn 45%, Endurance 45%, Evade 30%, Navigation 30%, Perception 60%, Politics 50%, Sensors 55%, Stealth 62%, Survival 45%, Unarmed 47%, Willpower 30%	Passions: Loyalty to Valhalla 35%, Crave Power 75%
	Traits: Assimilation
	Dependency: Drugs 45%

Combat Style & Weapons	Traits & Notes
Pistol Combat (Ballistic and Energy Handguns) 68%	

Weapon	Damage	Range	Ammo	Rate/Load
9mm Pistol	1d6	50/100/200	9 (clip)	1/3
Vibro Beamer	1d8	10/20/80	Armour Piecring, Knockout, Paralysing	1/-/8, 3

Georgy-845

Georgy-845 is the corpulent and well-dressed oligarch who runs the Pretty Baby racket. Despite his large size, he is quick. His round face and blonde hair are always covered in sweat, and he's continually wiping it away. He's seriously considering paying someone to follow him around with a fan.

He's rich and powerful and he loves it. There's nothing he relishes more than hearing about how rich and powerful he is. He sees Pretty Baby and Eldritch as two ways to get even richer and more powerful.

His street name is DJ-20.

Georgy-845	Attributes
STR: 15	Action Points: 3
CON: 16	Damage Modifier: +1d4
SIZ: 17	Prana: 12
DEX: 12	Tenacity: 12
INT: 15	Movement: 6 metres
POW: 12	Initiative Bonus: +14
CHA: 15	Armour: None

1d20	Hit Location	AP/HP
1 – 3	Right Leg	0/7
4 – 6	Left Leg	0/7
7 – 9	Abdomen	0/8
10 – 12	Chest	0/9
13 – 15	Right Arm	0/6
16 – 18	Left Arm	0/6
19 – 20	Head	0/7

Skills	Passions, Traits & Dependencies
Athletics 65%, Brawn 85%, Commerce 105%, Endurance 75%, Evade 30%, Perception 60%, Politics 50%, Unarmed 75%, Willpower 75%	Passions: Loyalty to Self 95%, Crave Power 75% Traits: None Dependency: Adulation 75%

Combat Style & Weapons	Traits & Notes
Pistol Combat (Ballistic and Energy Handguns) 60%	

Weapon	Damage	Range	Ammo	Rate/Load
9mm Pistol	1d6	50/100/200	9 (clip)	1/3

Mathias-015

Mathias is a gangly, mop-haired man in his late 20s. At first, he was a cutthroat Pretty Baby dealer. But, then he met Petra and started to soften. Now, he's a hopeless romantic, although one without the courage to tell her how he feels. If he learns she's dead, his world crumble and he has no loyalty for anyone he holds responsible for her death.

Mathias-015	Attributes
STR: 11	Action Points: 3
CON: 12	Damage Modifier: 0
SIZ: 13	Prana: 12
DEX: 15	Tenacity: 12
INT: 13	Movement: 6 metres
POW: 12	Initiative Bonus: +14
CHA: 16	Armour: None

1d20	Hit Location	AP/HP
1 – 3	Right Leg	0/5
4 – 6	Left Leg	0/5
7 – 9	Abdomen	0/6
10 – 12	Chest	0/7
13 – 15	Right Arm	0/4
16 – 18	Left Arm	0/4
19 – 20	Head	0/5

Skills	Passions, Traits & Dependencies
Athletics 26%, Brawn 24%, Commerce 57%, Conceal 54%, Deceit 45%, Endurance 32%, Evade 32%, First Aid 28%, Insight 40%, Mechanisms 37%, Native Tongue (English) 100%, Perception 55%, Stealth 38%, Streetwise 52%, Survival 22%, Unarmed 36%, Willpower 32%	Passions: Love Petra 85% Traits: None Dependency: Pretty Baby 58%

Combat Style & Weapons	Traits & Notes
Desperate Junkie (Switchblade, Chain) 44%	

Weapon	Damage	Size/Reach	AP/HP	Effects
Switchblade	1d4	S/S	2/2	Impale, Bleed
Chain	1d6	M/L	4/6	Entangle

Luther Arkwright: Parallel Lines

RESISTANCE MEMBERS

Still few and far between, these plucky members of the resistance fight to see the oligarchs cast down from their skyscrapers. For the most part, they dress like regular workers, since they hold down day jobs in the factory. They're rough and tumble looking, covered in scars from long hours on the dangerous factory floor.

Resistance Members	Attributes
STR: 10	Action Points: 2
CON: 9	Damage Modifier: 0
SIZ: 11	Prana: 10
DEX: 10	Tenacity: 10
INT: 11	Movement: 6 metres
POW: 10	Initiative Bonus: +11
CHA: 11	Armour: None

1d20	Hit Location	AP/HP
1 – 3	Right Leg	0/6
4 – 6	Left Leg	0/6
7 – 9	Abdomen	0/7
10 – 12	Chest	0/8
13 – 15	Right Arm	0/5
16 – 18	Left Arm	0/5
19 – 20	Head	0/6

Skills	Passions, Traits & Dependencies
Athletics 48%, Brawn 25%, Endurance 36%, Evade 28%, Locale (Home Ward) 80%, Perception 41%, Stealth 39%, Survival 31%, Unarmed 38%, Willpower 19%	Passions: Love Freedom 60%
	Dependencies: Pretty Baby 20%, Riskj Taking 55%

Combat Style & Weapons	Traits & Notes
Revolutionary Soldier (Guns and Sub-Machineguns) 40%	None

Weapon	Damage	Range	Ammo	Rate/Load
Uzi 9mm	2d6	600/1000/3000	30 (clip)	-/-/3,3

RUFUS-075

Rufus-075 is the mohawk-sporting bartender of Empire Down. He has a pleasant disarming demeanour, which greatly assists him in his job. He knows his loyal customers and is loyal to them in return.

Rufus-75	Attributes
STR: 13	Action Points: 3
CON: 16	Damage Modifier: +1d2
SIZ: 14	Prana: 18
DEX: 14	Tenacity: 18
INT: 16	Movement: 6 metres
POW: 18	Initiative Bonus: +15
CHA: 16	Armour: None

1d20	Hit Location	AP/HP
1 – 3	Right Leg	0/6
4 – 6	Left Leg	0/6
7 – 9	Abdomen	0/7
10 – 12	Chest	0/8
13 – 15	Right Arm	0/5
16 – 18	Left Arm	0/5
19 – 20	Head	0/6

Skills	Passions, Traits & Dependencies
Athletics 40%, Brawn 37%, Commerce 40%, Conceal 54%, Customs 75%, Deceit 72%, Drive (land vehicle) 61%, Endurance 40%, Evade 34%, Influence 53%, Insight 44%, Mechanisms 50%, Native Tongue (English) 75%, Perception 44%, Sleight 48%, Stealth 40%, Streetwise 44%, Survival 28%, Unarmed 47%, Willpower 46%	Passions: Loyal to Friends 85%
	Traits: Latent Psychic - can read surface thoughts and emotions on an Easy Insight roll.
	Dependencies: Competitive 48%

Combat Style & Weapons	Traits & Notes
Angry Bartender (Bottles, Club, Lighter) 50%	Swashbuckling

Weapon	Damage	Size/Reach	AP/HP	Effects
Broken Bottle	1d4+1+1d2	S/S	3/5	Bleed
Cricket Bat	1d6+1d2	M/M	4/4	Bash, Stun

Weapon	Damage	Range	Ammo	Rate/Load
Flaming Drambuie (Thrown)	1d4 - 25% chance of igniting clothes, with 1d4 damage per round until extingishued	5/10/20	-	-

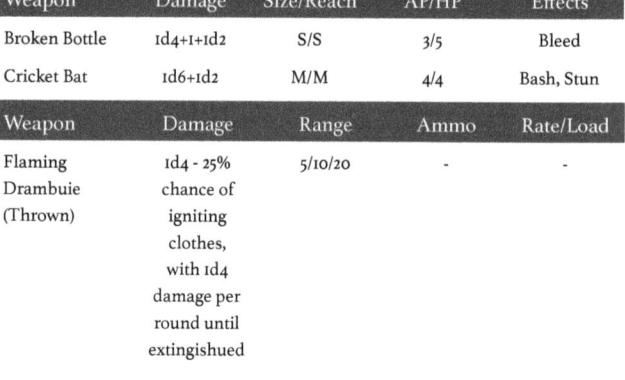

ZULU

Zulu is the leader of the resistance. She's a determined, ferocious leader who believes that all people should be free from the tyranny of the oligarchs. She bears the scars of many battles on her flesh, but the fire that burns deep in her eyes gives her a commanding presence. However, she's reached that point that many resistance fighters reach. If the struggle for freedom were to ever end, she wouldn't know what to do with herself.

Zulu	Attributes
STR: 15	Action Points: 3
CON: 16	Damage Modifier: +1d4
SIZ: 13	Prana: 14
DEX: 17	Tenacity: 14
INT: 18	Movement: 6 metres
POW: 14	Initiative Bonus: +17
CHA: 17	Armour: None - but Security Armour is available if needed

1d20	Hit Location	AP/HP
1 – 3	Right Leg	0/6
4 – 6	Left Leg	0/6
7 – 9	Abdomen	0/7
10 – 12	Chest	0/8
13 – 15	Right Arm	0/5
16 – 18	Left Arm	0/5
19 – 20	Head	0/6

Skills	Passions, Traits & Dependencies
Athletics 65%, Brawn 85%, Comms 65%, Demolition 45%, Endurance 75%, Evade 80%, Perception 70%, Politics 50%, Unarmed 65%, Willpower 75%	Passions: Loyal to Resistance 95% Dependencies: Struggle 48%

Combat Style & Weapons	Traits & Notes
Pistol Combat (Ballistic and Energy Handguns) 60%	Marksman

Weapon	Damage	Range	Ammo	Rate/Load
9mm Pistol	1d6	50/100/200	9 (clip)	1/3

SECURITY PERSONNEL

These black-clothed brutes are the muscle of the oligarchs. They delight in punishing anyone who breaks the rules, no matter how small the infraction. Their preferred weapon is the truncheon because the cracking of bone is much more visceral up close. When needed, though, they don't hesitate to call in flying squads with firearms and flamers. Security personnel of Georgy-845's skyscraper are also skilled in heavy weapons and wear ballistic vests under the hoplite costumes.

Security Thugs	Attributes
STR: 10	Action Points: 2
CON: 9	Damage Modifier: 0
SIZ: 11	Prana: 10
DEX: 10	Tenacity: 10
INT: 11	Movement: 6 metres
POW: 10	Initiative Bonus: +11
CHA: 11	Armour: Ballistic Vests, Helmets

1d20	Hit Location	AP/HP
1 – 3	Right Leg	0/6
4 – 6	Left Leg	0/6
7 – 9	Abdomen	4/7
10 – 12	Chest	4/8
13 – 15	Right Arm	0/5
16 – 18	Left Arm	0/5
19 – 20	Head	6/6

Skills	Passions, Traits & Dependencies
Athletics 38%, Brawn 55%, Endurance 36%, Evade 28%, Locale (00.01.98) 40%, Perception 41%, Stealth 39%, Survival 31%, Unarmed 38%, Willpower 19%	Passions: Love Violence 60% Dependencies: Aggression 65%

Combat Style & Weapons	Traits & Notes
Security Thug (Truncheon, Pistol, Heavy Ordinance) 60%	Formation Fighting

Weapon	Damage	Range	Ammo	Rate/Load
9mm Pistol	1d6	50/100/200	9 (clip)	1/3
7.62 Machine Gun	2d8+2	800/1500/4000	200 (belt)	-/-/22
Flamer Rifle	2d8	12/36/50	8	1/4
Rocket Launcher	4d10	500/800/1500	1	1/4

Weapon	Damage	Size/Reach	AP/HP	Effects
Truncheon	1d4+1	M/S	4/4	Bash, Stun

Workers and Racers

The average working stiffs of the parallel. These people are everywhere just trying to get by. More and more are becoming hooked on Pretty Baby. Some of them are racers, who meet at Empire Down and elsewhere to get a cheap thrill putting pedal to the metal.

Workers/Racers	Attributes
STR: 10	Action Points: 2
CON: 9	Damage Modifier: 0
SIZ: 11	Prana: 10
DEX: 10	Tenacity: 10
INT: 11	Movement: 6 metres
POW: 10	Initiative Bonus: +11
CHA: 11	Armour: Ballistic Vests, Helmets

1d20	Hit Location	AP/HP
1 – 3	Right Leg	0/6
4 – 6	Left Leg	0/6
7 – 9	Abdomen	0/7
10 – 12	Chest	0/8
13 – 15	Right Arm	0/5
16 – 18	Left Arm	0/5
19 – 20	Head	0/6

Skills	Passions, Traits & Dependencies
Athletics 48%, Brawn 65%, Drive 60%, Endurance 36%, Evade 28%, Locale (Home Ward) 80%, Perception 41%, Stealth 39%, Survival 31%, Unarmed 40%, Willpower 19%	Passions: Love Time Off 60% Dependencies: The Company 65%, Pretty Baby 20%

Combat Style & Weapons	Traits & Notes
Pistol 60%	

Weapon	Damage	Range	Ammo	Rate/Load
9mm Pistol	1d6	50/100/200	9 (clip)	1/3

Roach, Giant

A rather unpleasant creature, this roach, the size of a large dog, is a strange anomaly amongst the parallels. It feasts on the detritus of society. It does not hunt, preferring to feed on carrion and human garbage. However, if attacked and unable to flee, it defends itself. It prefers dark, damp environments, but ventures out in search of food when necessary.

Giant roaches do spread disease. It's nothing inherent to the roach, but rather a by-product of their environment. The roaches end up coated with all manner of waste, and because of the amount of filth they can carry on their bodies, the normal human immune system can be overwhelmed.

Application: Contact
Potency: 45
Resistance: Endurance
Onset time: 1d3 hours
Duration: 1d6+3 days
Conditions: The disease starts as a Fever, but after 1d3 hours the victim becomes Exhausted. After 24 hours, the disease reaches its peak and Nausea sets in.
Antidote/Cure: Antibiotics can alleviate symptoms in 1 day, but the victim is encouraged to take a full 10-day course less the disease resurface.

Giant Roach	Attributes
STR: 4d6 (14)	Action Points: 2
CON: 3d6+6 (17)	Damage Modifier: +1d2
SIZ: 4d6 (14)	Prana: 4
DEX: 2d6+6 (13)	Tenacity: N/A
INS: 2d6+2 (9)	Movement: 12 metres
POW: 1d6 (4)	Initiative Bonus: +11

Abilities: Formidable Natural Weapons

1d20	Hit Location	AP/HP
1	Right Rear Leg	4/6
2	Left Rear Leg	4/6
3	Right Middle Leg	4/6
4	Left Middle Leg	4/6
5-9	Abdomen	4/8
10-13	Thorax	4/9
14	Right Front Leg	4/6
15	Left Fron Leg	4/6
16-20	Head	4/7

Skills	Passions, Traits & Dependencies
Athletics 67%, Brawn 68%, Endurance 74%, Evade 56%, Perception 53%, Track 66%, Willpower 48%	Passions: Love Filth 60%

Combat Style & Weapons	Traits & Notes
Roach Attack (Mandibles) 67%	

Weapon	Damage	Size/Reach	AP/HP	Effects
Mandibles	1d3+1d2	M/T	As for Head	Disease

One Way or Another

The Agents find themselves enjoying the comforts available as travellers aboard the Trans-Siberian Express, but, all too soon, they are caught in the schemes and passions of their fellow passengers, one of whom intends that the journey is a fatal one for them all.

OVERVIEW

Parallel: 47.60.67
European Imperial Variant, Ukrainian Ascendancy.
Disruption Likelihood: 99.5%

More details can be found in the scenario *Silver Pictures Move So Slow* on page 87.

Octobriana, an important ally of W.O.T.A.N on para 47.60.67, has received some important intelligence about the Disruptors' activities but was severely wounded in the process. The Agents need to get her to safety using the Trans-Siberian Express to travel across the vast, snow-covered land of the Russian city-states. After encountering various dangers and distractions, the Agents find themselves threatened by the ambush of the train by Cossack bandits who are under the direction of a Disruptor agent aboard the express.

At the end of the scenario, the Agents should get Octobriana to a safe base in Moscow and pass on vital information that is tied to a Disruptor plot to destabilise the parallel.

NON-PLAYER CHARACTERS

- *Octobriana*: Revolutionary warrior woman who is a trusted ally of W.O.T.A.N on this parallel.
- *Count Mikhail Banin*: An aging, blind aristocrat.
- *Galina*: A beautiful young woman who is a noted jewel thief. She is currently posing as 'Vasilisa Pajari', an aristocratic exile.
- *Irena Lazarev*: The personal assistant to Gertrude Valentova.
- *Major Vladimir Korff*: The officer charged with the safety of the *Marshal Suvorov* and its crew and passengers.
- *Modya*: A petty criminal on the run from former associates.
- *Anton Shur*: A Disruptor agent who is also a poet.
- *Gertrude Valentova*: World-famous actress. She is also an unwitting Disruptor pawn.
- *Volkov*: A former warlord with a long history of war crimes and plundering who now fears to leave the sanctuary of the Trans-Siberia Express.
- *Countess Anzhelika Zykhov*: A beautiful aristocrat who is a celebrity socialite and huntress.
- *'Tsarina'*: Female snow leopard that is cadged in a baggage car.
- *'Boyar'*: Borzoi hound of Countess Zykhov.

As Valentova and Lazarev are also Non-Player Characters in 'Silver Pictures Move So Slow', the Games Master must try and ensure that both the individuals survive and arrive in the Ukraine relatively free from harm.

Key Points/Timeline

1. The Agents are briefed on the mission and travel to Sea Cucumber Bay.
2. They travel to the Vladivostok of parallel 47.60.67 where they locate and tend to the wounded Octobriana at her warehouse base, prior to boarding the Marshal Suvorov, the Trans-Siberian Express.
3. The rail journey continues across most of the length of northern Asia, edging round the mysterious Tunguska region. The Agents get to interact with various passengers whilst spending time, literally, piecing together evidence about a Disruptor plot.
4. The train approaches an ambush site at Howling Wolf Pass where Cossack brigands in the employ of the Disruptors attempt to blow up the train and loot the carriages.
5. The Agents continue their journey to Moscow, either aboard the Marshal Suvorov or else improvising other means. Detours or delays result in their being located and attacked by an unmarked combat aircraft.
6. The Agents arrive at Moscow where they leave Octobriana at a safe house where they report to the Valhalla Programme.

Areas to be Covered

- The Yerov Warehouse: Shoddy looking furniture warehouse used as a base by Octobriana.
- Vladivostok Station: The station where the Trans-Siberian Express is boarded.
- The Siberian Steppe: The adventure occurs along thousands of miles of wilderness on the Trans-Siberian railway passes through.
- The Tunguska Wilderness: This is a mysterious, blighted region that the train skirts across during an early stage of its journey.
- Howling Wolf Pass: This location in the Ural Mountains is chosen by Cossack bandits as an ambush site.
- Moscow Station: The destination of the Marshal Suvorov.

Briefing

Freyr Lingstadt gathers the Agents and informs them that Octobriana, an Agent on parallel 47.60.67, has been wounded in action and, besides needing medical assistance, requires an escort to escape from Vladivostok where her activities have been compromised. The journey is to be via the Trans-Siberian Express to Moscow, where a cell of Octobriana's guerrilla fighters and a safe house is based. The TPT at Vladivostok must be dismantled and returned via The Van the Agents use or, if this is impossible, they must ensure that the TPT is thoroughly destroyed.

It is believed that Octobriana's activities have dealt several blows to the Disruptor activities on this parallel, but she has recently obtained some information that may relate to a growing threat to the stability of this parallel and others in its proximity; a premise confirmed by the Valhalla psychics and planners. Freyrs confesses that transmissions from Octobriana have been brief and not completely lucid, and they are unsure of the nature of the evidence held by her. The Agents are consequently instructed to assess the evidence prior to forwarding it, once they reach Moscow.

Designator: 47.60.67
Classification: European Imperial, Ukrainian Ascendancy
Cultural Type: Eastern Europe
Political Type: Communist Oligarchy
Technological Type: Industrial Age
Description: The Russian Revolution on parallel 47.60.67 was suppressed by the more powerful Ukrainians who went on to form an Imperial state to rival Britain. Russia is a set of feuding fiefdoms with the Crimea seeking violent separation from Ukraine. The Disruptors seem to have a special interest in the region, and are believed to be behind a mysterious explosion at Tunguska in 1908, which devastated a vast region of wilderness, following which it has mutated the natural life of the area.

The Van II is being refined, meaning that only a Mark I Van is available for this mission. The Agents are transported to an oceanic scientific complex at Sea Cucumber Bay, an area given over to the production of food and other products from marine resources that geographically conforms to that of Vladivostok on parallels where Russia has colonised that region. Here, equipment is issued and a Van assembled for them in a nearby vehicle park. Morty McAllan and Wishaw accompany the Agents en-route to Vladivostock on Zero-Zero, and in transit, those Agents who do not speak Russian receive a five-hour hypnotic learning session that gives them INT x 3% in the language and allows them to speak it fluently with an appropriate accent, though the skill wears off at 1% a day.

Issued equipment includes sets of clothing appropriate to their destination, some of which is fur lined to provide protection from cold conditions. Amongst the weaponry and passports provided for the parallel is a set of new identity papers for 'Madame Starr', an alias to be used by Octobriana. The team is also given a leather Gladstone bag holding a medical kit appropriate to the parallel and also 12x nano-tech bandages and 12x sustainment cocktails.

If an Agent requests any photographic equipment, then a wooden box holding a box camera and six flash lamps is made available. Include is a set of tweezers, jeweller's eye piece, magnifying glass, gloves, cleaning agents, and a rack for glass plates. A hidden compartment holds a high-tech micro camera, adhesive film, and a light box.

The Van is used to transport the Agents to the interior of an empty warehouse on the outskirts of parallel 47.60.67's Vladivostok at 09:00 on both parallels.

The Hunt for Red Octobriana

The Van materialises in the interior of a cold, dank, warehouse that is only dimly illuminated by faint sunlight defusing through the sacking that screens some high set windows. As their eyes adjust to the gloom, they notice a maze of large wooden crates and unfathomable objects that are shrouded in mildewed dust covers.

Most of the crates and covered piles contain furniture and miscellaneous items from house sales, usually chipped or fire damaged, but a Very Easy Track skill or an Easy Perception roll quickly reveals that various footprints have disturbed the dust of the floor and a Critical success notices a thin trail of blood leading to one of the shrouded objects, which proves to be draped in sheets of muslin. Under this shroud an unconscious Octobriana lays upon a leather sofa. She is half dressed under the leather trench coat she is wearing, her breath stinking of vodka, a revolver in her hand, and a crudely bound, blood-stained dressing on her abdomen. A leather satchel is looped over her shoulder, inside which is a jumble of broken, blood-stained glass negative plates wrapped in a silk scarf. Hidden under the cushion that pillows her head is a dagger. Nearby, the ashes of a wood stove are nearly stone cold. Failing a fast discovery, a careful search of the factory takes 3d6 minutes to find her, during which time a rat has gnawed her left hand, causing 1d3 points of damage.

Once revived, Octobriana informs the Agents that one of her followers claimed to have found important evidence of a Disruptor plot, but on visiting him she found him dying as his room as it was being ransacked by police. During the ensuring firefight, Octobriana killed the police but was wounded, taking a bullet to the stomach. Her friend was beyond help, but managed to gesture to a pile of broken photographic plates on the floor before expiring. Scooping up the plates, the she-devil fled, but the local police, influenced by an unseen hand, are even now combing the city for her. 'Loki,' she snarls through gritted teeth. 'Loki is involved with this.'

The crudely stitched wound needs cleaning to prevent septicaemia and, until Octobriana recovers positive hit points to her abdomen, she is subject to pain and counts as Wearied. She proves to be a poor patient proving argumentative and needing a lot of persuasion to avoid physical activity. The best way to get her to remain sedate is probably by plying her with sufficient vodka or dosing her up with laudanum.

Nearby is a bath chair covered by a sheet and an adjacent crate, when opened, proves to hold a sabre in its scabbard and a wooden-stocked submachine with a full clip of ammunition. Also within is a widow's disguise that includes a veiled headdress that one of her confederates bought her, although Octobriana is loath to use the chair or the disguise. In the leather handbag with the clothing are some pre-purchased tickets for the Marshal Suvorov, which leaves at noon from the city's main station.

Another covered object is a huge, mirrored wardrobe of mahogany, which incorporates a TPT. The device is defective, having been damaged by Octobriana whilst she was in an angry, wounded state and has no visual signal; it only transmits at all if an operator can make a Hard Comms skill test. A small incendiary device incorporated in the device can be triggered to destroy the apparatus and has a timer that can be set from between 30 seconds to 24 hours.

Travelling outside through the falling snow, the disguised Agents are soon able to reach the station safely where all their documentation passes official examination. However, on their approaching the train, a nervous, seedy-looking individual involuntary hisses in fear as he notices something. The Agents quickly realise that the man, clearly a lowlife of some kind, is panicked by a group of six policemen who have reached the platform and are spreading out in pairs. The alerted Agents find that there is enough temporary cover from the crowd to avoid the police if they board the Marshal Suvorov quickly and succeed with an Easy Stealth roll. Failing this, they are stopped and asked for their papers, which should prove to be good enough to fool the police, though discreet bribery speeds up their acceptance.

Modya, the individual who inadvertently warned them, manages to elude any official detection and then stows away in a baggage car of the express.

The Agents remain in danger, however, as the others who are looking for Octobriana are more vigilant. A lurking spy manages to alert the Disruptors to her boarding the train and Anton Shur, their agent, joins the express before it leaves the station. Initially tasked with finding what Octobriana has learnt, prior to killing her, Shur quickly realises given the size of her escort, that he will need assistance. At a stop further along the line, Shur telegrams for an ambush to be arranged so that the Agents can be killed or captured, along with any evidence of the Disruptors' schemes.

Trans-Siberian Express

The *Marshal Suvorov* express is accorded the status of 'neutral territory' by most of the powers of the region, many of whom find it a useful location to conduct deals and treaties or deliver precious cargo, whilst some of the regional warlords along its route have had to be bought off with gold to keep from interfering with its progress. Although diplomats, couriers, financiers, refugees, fugitives, and spies use the Marshal Suvorov as a means of safe transportation across war-torn Russia, others have, seemingly, taken up permanent residence aboard the train. These 'residents' try to cling to a blinkered life of hedonism, gossip, and intrigue; cocooned from the danger and horror that blight the continent, they shuttle to and fro across. Game statistics for the Marshal Suvorov can be found on page 70.

The Trans-Siberian Express on this parallel involves the use of a single express train for the entire 9,289 kilometre journey that normally takes some 11 days. Other cities and towns are visited along the route and stops are made for a few hours during which time water, fuel, and supplies can be loaded and passengers, goods, and mail cargoes exchanged. Many of these are lawless or dangerous places and passengers whose journeys do not end at these locations are advised to keep to the station platforms and restaurants if they feel the need to take a break from being aboard the train. Enterprising individuals might be able to procure items during brief stops or telegraph for them to be made available for purchase at a city store further down the line. The Games Master can choose to limit such activities through outbreaks of bad weather, Disruptor influence, or pure bad luck, insuring that business locations are closed, and telegraph lines and wirelesses are in need of repair.

Much of the route has only a single rail track, though in urban areas, parallel and branch lines exist to facilitate local travel and the movement of goods.

The armoured engine is normally crewed by two of a four-man team of engineers, off-duty members sleeping in the troop cars.

Distances Accrued Between Stations

Vladivostock -
Khabarovsk: 766km
Chita: 938km
Ulan Ude: 3,090km
Irkusk: 3,647km
Tayshet: 4,773km
Krasnoyarsk: 5,191km
Novosibirsk: 5,954km
Omsk: 6,577km
Tyumen: 7,145km
Yekaterinburg: 7,473km
Perm: 7,853km
Vyatka: 8,332km
Yaroslavl: 9,005km
Moscow: 9,289km

The troop cars include simple bunks and firing apertures, and are located at the front and rear of the express. The unroofed areas allow for the machinegun teams to engage aerial targets. A detachment of eight men are housed in each troop car, two men being assigned to its balcony machinegun in all but the most hostile of blizzards, whilst each car provides a sentry for a baggage car and any detachments needed by Major Korff. Each of the balcony crews has goggles, additional winter clothing, and a set of field glasses to aid their watch for obstacles and threats.

The command car includes Major Korff's private quarters, where he has a metal safe. The operations room includes a radio set and a large map of the rail routes. Four pairs of handcuffs are kept here for restraining prisoners arrested on the Major's orders. Firing apertures are located on the sides, and a hatch and ladder is used to access the interior of the cramped roof-top turret, the gun of which fires high-explosive shells. Two soldiers are attached here to operate the turret and two more function as clerks, batmen, and radio operators. Simple bunks are provided for these men. All the military cars have steel doors with an observation slit that is screened by an interior shutter and have strong triple bolts on the inside to secure them.

The passenger carriages and restaurant are luxuriously furnished, though space is limited when the wall-mounted beds are swung down into position. Samovars located in the corner of the carriages provide a welcoming source of hot water for bathing or beverages. The staff compartments are significantly more cramped and spartan. All the doors of travelling compartments for passengers and staff are secured with light bolts on the interior.

Trans-Siberian Express

Scale: 1 square = 5 metres

Restaurant Car

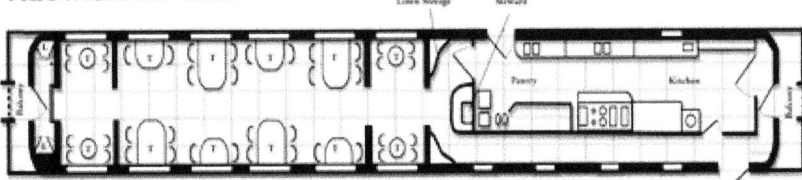

Passenger Car

Command Car

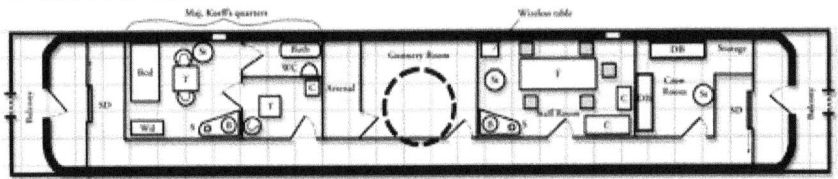

Roof Turret

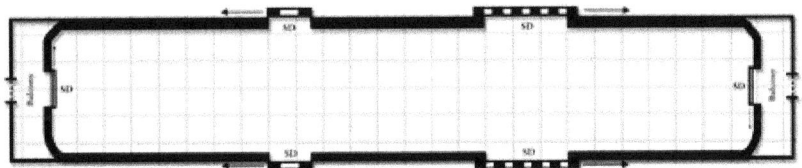

Baggage Car x 2

Troop Car x 2

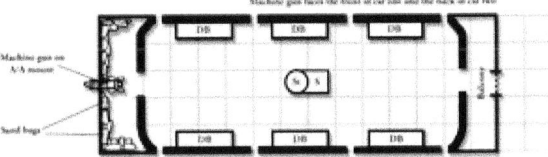

Key

- B. Boiler
- C. Cupboard
- DB. Double Bunk + small lockers
- FB. Folding Bunk
- SD. Sliding door
- S. Samovar
- St. Stove
- T. Table
- Wd. Wardrobe
- •••• Hinged Rail

Volkov's Car

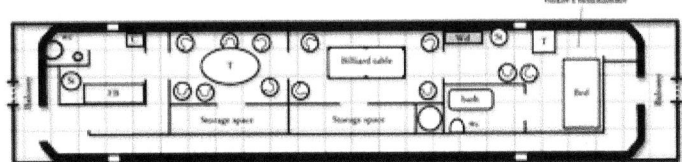

Marshall Suvorov Statistics

Marshall Suvorov	Hull	Structure	Speed Solo/Towing	Systems	Traits	Shields	Weapons
Engine	10 (Large Civilian)	50	Rapid/Gentle	3	Railed	None	None
Troop Car x2	12 (Large Military)	60	–	3	Railed, Weaponised	None	Machine Gun on AA mount
Command Car	12 (Large military)	60	–	3	Railed, Weaponised	None	Turret Gun
Passenger Car x6	5 (Large Civilian)	45	–	3	Railed, Luxurious	None	None
Baggage Car x2	7 (Large Civilian)	45	–	3	Railed	None	None

Train Coupling Sequence

The express is coupled together in the following sequence from its locomotive and tender at the front

1x Troop Car
Engine and Tender
1x Command Car
3x Passenger Cars (Volkov's is first, followed by those used by listed Non-Player Characters and Agents)
1x Restaurant Car
3x Passenger Cars (assorted unlisted passengers and staff)
Baggage Car A (includes Snow Leopard and its cage)
Baggage Car B (includes mail and additional cargo)
1x Troop Car

Some twenty permanent civilian staff are assigned to the train as conductors, stewards and cooks.

The locks in Volkov's private quarters are of Hard difficulty to open with the Lockpicking skill, whilst the doors themselves have a bulletproof metal plate inside that adds 6 Armour Points. Amongst the sumptuous and expensive trappings of his apartment, looted paintings and other art objects are displayed. Inside his sleeping compartment wooden panelling hides a large safe. It requires a successful Hard Difficulty Perception test to locate the hidden door, and the safe itself has a complex set of combination locks that requires a Formidable Lockpicking roll to open. Located within is a large amount of currency and a sizeable fortune in gem stones and jewellery. Documents include material that incriminates various politicians along with a journal of Volkov's activities and his forged identity papers.

The two baggage cars each have a guard assigned. Baggage car A includes a large metal cage, secured by chains to the bed of the car and its door locked by a padlock. Inside is 'Tsarina', a snow leopard that was captured by Countess Zykhov who plans to sell the animal at Moscow. Baggage car B contains lifting gear, tools, and spare track materials for fixing or replacing damaged rail sections and also has an emergency brake that can stop the train.

Passengers' baggage is not searched prior to loading, but the display and use of weapons is not normally tolerated, although Russian officers are allowed to openly wear their regulation side arms and swords. Major Korff is permitted a wide range of latitude in how he deals with criminal behaviour. Troublesome individuals might be asked to leave at the next station or might be arrested and given over to the authorities. High society passengers might merely have to endure a form of house arrest in their compartments, though servants and other 'menials' might find themselves tied or handcuffed to a metal bracket in one of the baggage cars.

Environment

The Games Master can use the following factors to add atmosphere and risks to the adventure.

Passengers find that moving through the carriages is sometimes difficult unless they have a free hand; sudden lurches can tumble individuals off their feet or cause the accidental discharge of a held firearm.

Ice and snow sometimes hinder movement outside the interior of carriages, and perilous and icy blizzards threaten to whip away items or individuals exposed to their screeching fury. Falling or whirling snow can partially or wholly blind vision but, at times, its cover leaves tracks and the biting cold causes the breath of lurking assailants to leave treacherous plumes. Unprotected equipment might suffer from malfunctions if moisture freezes inside the mechanism, whilst inadequately insulated individuals in the open soon suffer from hypothermia. Anyone falling or straying from the moving train in the steppe is in mortal peril.

At some stage in the journey, a villain should need to be chased or attacked by an Agent moving along a carriage roof or a similar perilous route.

Although most of the Marshal Suvorov's journey occurs over a flat, white blanket of snow-covered steppe country, occasional variations of scenery can be rolled or chosen from the following table to add extra drama to incidents.

Random Terrain

1. A long tunnel that extends through a mountain range.
2. A war-torn town that is seemingly abandoned, though possibly the haunt of refugees, bandits, or dangerous predators.
3. A gloomy, dense forest of silent pines.
4. A snakelike track that hugs a sheer mountain range with a precipitous drop.
5. Dismal marsh land that extends as far as the eye can see, which, even in clear summer, is partly shrouded in coiling mist.
6. A long rail bridge across either a steep gorge or a wide river.
7. Deep snow. The line is blocked and a halt of 1d6 hours occurs whilst troops dig a path through it.
8. Bleak, featureless plain. Individuals keeping a constant watch on the landscape or travelling on foot must succeed at a Survival or Willpower roll. Failure results in a deep despondency that inflicts the loss of a Tenacity Point.

Strangers on a Train

Most passengers welcome periods of social intercourse during the long journey. Ideally, each Agent should have the opportunity for at least one significant personal interaction with a Non-Player Character and should be involved in at least one incident. The Games Master can use these opportunities to stoke up suspicions and animosities, preferably involving passengers other than just Anton Shur. Significant encounters might prompt the stirring or explosion of old or brand-new Passions.

During the rail journey, some 50 passengers, including the Valhalla Agents, are aboard the express for a journey leg modified by –1d6 at each leg of the journey after the first.

Roleplay interaction and successful skills might uncover a few pieces of interest about other travellers:

Octobriana

If awake, she wants to abandon her disguise, Each day of the journey, Agents trying to talk her out of this decision must beat her in a contest using a Persuade Skill roll opposed by her Willpower Skill roll. If she is reasonably hale, she feels the need to sate herself by selecting an Agent as a sexual partner for the journey, in any case.

Undisguised she is instantly recognisable to all the travellers and crew, and makes no attempts to conceal her contempt for the bourgeoisie around her. She has a murderous hatred of Volkov that she barely manages to control.

> ### Did You Spill My Vodka?
> The Games Master can find Octobriana useful for provoking arguments or suspicion against other occupants of the train. Although a useful potential ally in a conflict, care must be taken that she does not overshadow the Agents by undertaking roles that they could perform. If necessary, her health can relapse so that she weakens or passes out at appropriate opportunities to ensure the Agents are the main protagonists.

Count Banin

Those making a Perception roll might hear a voice in a foreign language coming from inside Banin's private compartment when he is seemingly alone. Banin is in fact listening to a gramophone record of his late wife speaking in her native Polish tongue. This is a private and personal matter that the Count does not want to discuss with anyone.

Galina

Extended conversations with 'Vasilisa Pajari' might prove an opportunity to see through her false identity. Treat each day of travel spent in her company as a Task Round using Customs (aristocracy) or Courtesy skill rolls opposed by Galina's Deceit skill.

A vanity bag she carries has a secret compartment that needs close examination and a Hard Perception roll to locate. Hidden within is a lockpick set.

Major Korff

His contempt for those employees in his command is obvious. An Insight roll reveals that his appearances often seem to provide some sort of assurance and protection for Volkov. If he learns of Octobriana's presence, he radios Moscow, where the authorities will arrange for her arrest once she leaves the station platform.

Irena Lazarev

Valentova's aide spends most of her time watching over her beloved employer. Individuals showing hostility or contempt towards her mistress are blasted with a withering glare. She is currently teaching herself German and welcomes holding conversations with people proficient in this language. She tries to devote at least a couple of hours a day to clerical work and uses short hand.

Anton Shur

Successful Insight rolls note that Shur is sometimes distracted, either absently fiddling with his pocket watch or doodling in the margins of the book of poetry he often reads from in the evening. In the margins of the book are disturbing sketches of violence and chaos. Anyone studying these images is subject to a psionic backlash and mild Tenacity Damage that could lead to Mild Intensity Madness. Recent doodles show two clock hands set to 12.

If Shur learns that the Agents are examining some evidence or asking questions about Pieter Klass, he may decide to start eliminating them, preferably by causing conflict between the

Count Banin   Galina (Vasilisa Pajari)   Major Korff

Agents and other passengers, but if the opportunity presents itself he may attempt to ambush individuals himself.

Due to a combination of the recent damage to the Disruptors' activities parallel 47.60.67 by Octobriana's terrorist cells and Major Korff's care in keeping his master plan a secret, Shur and his contacts are unaware of the fact that Valentova's safety during her rail journey is essential to the grand scheme of their organisation.

Gertrude Valentova

This spoilt celebrity strives to be the centre of attention and, being a true prima donna, reacts vindictively to any slights she perceives or imagines. Her tantrums can involve throwing crockery or demanding that Major Korff have a clumsy member of the railway staff who has upset her whipped as punishment. Some of the other passengers speculate that Valentova is having an affair with Archduke Kovalenko of the Ukrainian Imperial family, and if questioned on this she merely smiles enigmatically and purrs that 'that would be telling.'

Volkov

His heavy drinking and lecherous interest in attractive female passengers is obvious, but an Insight roll discloses his intense suspicion of strangers. He steers away all discussions about his past. Given Volkov's natural bulk, a Hard Perception roll is needed to notice that he wears a bulletproof vest. He becomes especially paranoid if Octobriana's presence is known to him.

He usually only opens his personal apartment door to his vigilant manservant Ivan, who is required to provide a pre-arranged knock and give a pre-arranged password of each day.

Countess Anzhelika Zykhov

It is obvious that she spends time with Volkov, although an Insight roll determines that she actually loathes him. She also holds Valentova in contempt and mocks her using thinly veiled insults that anyone, except Valentova, can detect with a successful Easy Courtesy roll.

Anzhelika is by turns languid and notably animated, and at odd intervals she visits the baggage car to gaze at her captured snow leopard or else stand on a balcony despite a raging gale. If the train stops in a wilderness, she endeavours to go hunting.

'Boyar'

The Countess' hound often reflects his mistress's attitudes of acceptance, indifference, or hostility towards individuals, going as far as growling and snapping if Valentova attempts to touch him. He howls if psychic activity occurs, and thus, might give a clue to the presence of otherwise hidden individuals he senses.

Picture This

Examination, sorting, and repair of the glass shards that Octobriana obtained are a time-consuming process that cannot be facilitated by individuals attempting it simultaneously. The process of restoring most of the broken pile involves a Task Round of 2d6 hours making a Perception Skill roll. The difficulty of the task varies with the equipment used:

Resources	Difficulty
Has access to a computer that can store the images (may use Computer skill as a secondary skill for the Perception skill roll)	Very Easy
Using photographic equipment.	Standard
Access to magnifying lens, tweezers, etc.	Hard
No tools	Formidable
Assimilation Trait	One grade easier.

IRENA LAZAREV

ANTON SHUR

GERTRUDE VALENTOVA

Successful Psychometry grants the psychic visions that reveal frozen images or a moving tableau based on the original viewpoint of the dead photographer.

The fragments are all from photographs taken at an aristocratic society function. The only plate that has enough pieces to be reassembled in something approaching a whole, reveals a grainy picture of a beautiful woman, Gertrude Valentova no less, where she is in the company of a uniformed man with neatly trimmed hair and a fine, angular jaw. He is wearing the uniform of a member of the Prussian High Kommand and has an iron cross medal under his collar. Valentova is recognised by most Russian individuals from para 47.60.67 and Valentova and Lazarev, should they prove co-operative, are able to name the man as none other than Pieter Klass, a highly influential Prussian officer. Gaining a fuller confidence can elicit the information that Klass has proved very helpful in furthering the starlet's progress through high society and movie stardom. Octobriana and Volkov are both aware of Klass being active in the Prussian Intelligence Service. Klass is in fact the Disruptor Knight known as Loki, and although Octobriana suspects it is him, she has no true proof. Valentova of course, is blissfully unaware of who Klass really is.

At a dramatic point, some of the fragments of a negative can reveal a partial image of Anton Shur talking to the Prussian officer, though as it is blurred by thumbprints and fire damage and a potted plant partially obscures the two men, a Perception roll might be required. Critical success or computer enhancement also shows that a small round object is being passed to Shur.

The Games Master must consider how much the Agents learn of Klass, given his importance to the events in the next scenario. The passengers who know something of Klass, such as Valentova and Lazarev, might prove tight lipped, whilst injury or death at the hands of Shur or bad fortune might silence them at a critical moment before they reveal too much.

DIVERSIONS

As the days pass, Agents may find that they are faced with the temptations of indulging their dependencies whilst aboard the train as halts are infrequent and short. Alcohol, cigars, and cigarettes are for sale at the bar and Andre, a steward, is able to supply laudanum and can also discreetly procure other drugs. Many of the passengers chose to while away time at games of cards; some of them are prepared to gamble for high stakes whilst others find a break from monotony by making assignations in their private quarters or the balconies of carriages.

READ ALL ABOUT IT!

Various newspapers in the Russian language can occasionally be procured along the journey at station stopovers and a few, used, copies might be found in various carriages. The following pieces of information might be of interest to readers:

- *The Alaskan Assassin:* Sarah Putin, The Chairperson of the Russian-American Company and the unofficial governor of the colony, was killed by a rifle bullet to the head whilst she was on a polar bear hunt. The murderer was, according to one eyewitness, briefly glimpsed while slipping away from his ambush point, armed with a scoped hunting rifle and incongruously clad in the garb of a tropical big game hunter despite the arctic conditions. Speculation mentions recent unrest from native Inuit but the editorials also hint at Britain or the USA's territorial designs on the trading colony.
- *Russia's Greatest Love Machine?* Various gossip pieces and photographs can be found about the glamorous actress Gertrude Valentova. Her name is raised as a possible lover of Archduke Rostov Kovalenko of the Ukrainian Royal Family, though some newspapers touch on earlier

VOLKOV   COUNTESS ZHYKOV   MODYA

> ### Buzby Murder
>
> Although a red herring of sorts, this particular Buzby murder will help augment the feeling of paranoia aboard the train. Wiring for more information concerning the murder reveals that the sanity of the witness has been called into question; since claims of the assassin roaming about in subzero temperatures wearing khaki shorts and a pith helmet are clearly ludicrous. Russian secret police are now confining all foreign nationals in the province for questioning, and fully expect to make an arrest if the so-called Alaskan Assassin manages to survive hypothermia. The American State Department has however, expressed extreme displeasure at how US citizens are being treated, threatening a military intervention if not released promptly.

rumoured affairs with celebrity hell raisers such as Nikolai Diamante, Lolo Romana, and Sir Oliver Reid.

Care must be taken by the Games Master that the adventure keeps moving and is not bogged down by individuals wanting to spend several sessions merely roleplaying through dozens of conversations. During the journey, some or all of the various incidents might be selected by the Games Master depending on what themes, complexity, and time are envisaged for the adventure, and the reactions of various passengers to the Agents is modified by what occurs during these incidents.

PSYCHIC ECHOES

On the second day of the journey, the Suvorov proceeds along the outskirts of the Tunguska. Shur seems fascinated with the region and mentions that although strange malformed trees and animals ring the region, little is reliably known about the fog-shrouded interior of blighted forest, though strange, wild tales are told of furtive denizens or mysterious structures. A Perception roll shows that even the snowflakes that are blown against the windows appear sinister as they don't conform to the six-sided perfection expected. If the train stops for any reason in this area, Major Korff strongly advises everyone against straying out of sight of the train.

During this leg of the journey, any Agent with psionic abilities find that they suffer from migraines, nose bleeds, and disturbed dreams for 1d6+4 hours, resulting in any task attempted having an extra grade of Difficulty. In addition, individuals with the Precognitive talent must take an Unsettling Intensity Psionic Trauma test whilst anyone with the Sensitive Trait must make a test at Disturbing Intensity instead. Individuals with precognitive powers receive cluttered images their sleep, some of which might prove to be useful insights into a possible outcome or threat in the near future, such as a nightmare in which the train passes through the mountains the towards a valley from which howling wolves with slavering maws race downwards. While the dreams may hint at Disruptor involvement in the Tunguska explosion, no clear conclusions should be offered via the dreams, just unsettling suggestions.

The atmosphere amongst crew and passengers during this stage of the journey is tense and all the animals on board exhibit nervous behaviour.

THROW MODYA FROM THE TRAIN

During the journey, a stowaway is detected by either Boyar or the train's conductor, and Major Korff has the man, Modya, arrested. When the nervous, grovelling captive throws up over the Major's pristine boots, Korff orders his men to throw the man out of the speeding train. The Agents recognise the unfortunate as the furtive man whose behaviour alerted them to the police sweep of Vladivostok's station. Modya can be saved from this summary expulsion, either by somehow compelling Major Korff's co-operation or by offering to pay the man's passage, a transaction that involves a hefty bribe. If Modya stays on board the train, he is either placed under arrest and cuffed in a baggage car or is expected to keep to the car used for staff.

If rescued, Modya is ostracised by the rest of the passengers but is particularly grateful and eager to assist any Agents who tried to help him. If desired by the Games Master, Modya might stumble onto some vital information or take a bullet meant for one of the Agents.

Note that Modya's death is fated – a chance for angst as the Agents try to save him but ultimately fail. Precognition might reveal this to a psionic individual, perhaps scaring the thief into a funk that actually causes his demise.

MUTANT WOLVES

During an unscheduled stop in the wilds to check a faulty coupling, one of the passengers takes some exercise but strays into a pine forest and draws the attention of a pack of 2d6 famished, mutant wolves and needs rescuing. If similar encounters are needed, other mutated creatures such as bears or eagles can be improvised.

LOST PROPERTY

A passenger discovers the theft of a precious object (see suggestions below). This results in an aura of suspicion falling on the Agents, since they are new and often seen wandering about, until the culprit is discovered and apprehended. Perhaps one of the Agents also loses an item to the burglar. The culprit is Galina, but Shur might use the opportunity to commit another theft to incriminate one of the Agents, Octobriana, or another passenger.

The item can be one or more of the following:

- A Faberge egg with an exterior decorated in onyx, silver, gold, and quartz and fabulous enamelled landscape scenes that incorporates a discreet winding mechanism in the base. Activated, it opens to reveal a golden model of the Marshal Suvorov that runs along a small track encircling a jade map in which the Trans-Siberian line is marked in gold and the city stations indicated by small rubies. The egg was entrusted to Major Korff's care for delivery to the headquarters of the rail company at Moscow.
- A pearl-trimmed jewellery box that belongs to Gertrude Valentova. Inside is a valuable collection of bracelets, necklaces, and rings that were given to her by her numerous suitors. Of paramount importance to Valentova is a sapphire-encrusted golden broach fashioned in the heraldic form of a swooping falcon. It was a gift from Archduke Kovalenko of the Ukrainian Royal Family that she intends to wear on her journey aboard the Empress Katerina in 'Silver Pictures Move So Slow'.
- An emerald necklace that was the part of Volkov's hidden loot. The piece incorporates a locket that shows a portrait of a youthful Count Banin and his wife. Recognising the Count's identity as a young man requires a standard Perception roll, which has an extra level of Difficulty if the Agents have only seen his face whilst he was wearing his dark glasses.
- A pearl and diamond tiara of Countess Zykhov that was in her luggage, but has been worn on some evenings. An individual who looks at it closely and makes an Easy skill roll for Forgery or a Formidable one for Commerce realises that it is actually a clever fake.
- Shur's pocket watch that incorporates a concealed explosive device. Perhaps it is inadvertently activated but precognition of Shur's reactions hint at the imminent explosion?
- Shur's book of disturbing poems and doodles.
- The negative plates that the Agents are trying to piece together.
- A piece of equipment, weapon, or another item of importance to one of the Agents.

NORTHERN LIGHTS

A particularly impressive light display illuminates the north at night, and most passengers and even the various guards choose to sit up and watch it. Their distraction proves useful to Agents and other individuals with nefarious agendas. Perception rolls to notice anything other than the spectacular phenomena requires extra levels of Difficulty. The predominance of red tints leads the more superstitious passengers to view them as ill omens. They may also trigger of any precognitive powers of any psionic-talented passengers on the train.

BORN FREE

As the train slows or stops, Galina decides to free the snow leopard so it can escape into the wilds, possibly soliciting assistance from an Agent. If the attempt is mismanaged, the beast stalks along the carriages, panicking and menacing passengers. Countess Zykhov falls into a foul rage if the cat is lost to her or injured, and develops a homicidal rage against anyone she suspects of the undertaking.

FRIGHT IN THE FREIGHT

If Shur's suspicions have been aroused, he decides to eliminate one or more of the Agents by using the captive leopard. He manages to dope the animal's food with a drug that causes a murderous rage in the feline and then uses a vial of acid to weaken the lock on the cage door. Shur then arranges for one of his intended victims to find an anonymous message that hints at having vital information for them that will be imparted at a rendezvous in the baggage car. The Agent who attempts the assignation, or perhaps another passenger, finds themselves endangered by the berserk animal as it breaks free from captivity. If Shur has been able to lurk in the vicinity, he tries to ensure the death of any Agents by slamming the baggage door shut from the outside and wedging it fast with a purloined tool. If the leopard is not present or

> ### Pavlov's Serum
>
> The drug used by Shur is contained in a metal cigar tube. If he doesn't use it on an animal as detailed here, he might decide to try to spike the meal of a drunken person or else, if especially desperate, take it himself.
>
> **Pavlov's Serum**
>
> This serum was developed by a scientist who was used as an unwitting pawn by the Disruptors. It is a colourless liquid, but has a strong odour of blood.
>
> *Application:* Ingested
>
> *Onset Time:* 1d3 Hours
>
> *Duration:* 2d3 Hours
>
> *Resistance Time:* One Resistance roll.
>
> *Conditions:*
>
> *Debilitation: The user loses 1d3+3 points on CON every hour of duration.*
>
> *Enraged: The user flies into a murderous intent on utterly destroying the object of his rage (treat as Berserk- MYTHRAS, page 183).*
>
> *Hallucinations: The user sees other creatures as a threat that must be dealt with.*
>
> *Antidote/Cure: Anti-rabies drugs can be used but suffer an extra level of Difficulty. If such serums are used to help synthesise an antidote using a successful Chemistry test, then treatment is a level easier.*

healthy enough for Shur's scheme, he lures Boyar, the Countess's hound, into the waggon instead and feeds it the drugged meat.

ECHOES OF WAR

The track passes through the site of one of the innumerable battles of the small wars that blight the northern cities of this continent. Snow-mantled relics of assorted vehicles, rail stock, and crashed aeroplanes litter the site, their components seized up with rust, whilst blizzard-scourged corpses and pitted munitions lie half buried in the iron-hard ground.

If the conflict was comparatively recent, close examination might discover harrowing evidence of atrocities that count as exposure of the Agents to horror of either Mild or Unsettling Intensity.

The chances of success for schemes that involve the cannibalisation of weapons or the creation of a bastardised vehicle from nearby wrecks must be judged by the Games Master.

THE HUNTED

During a stop in the wilderness an Agent leaving the train, possibly whilst engaged in a hunt organised by Countess Zykhov, narrowly escapes death as a shot from an unseen assassin narrowly misses them. The identity of the shooter might remain a mystery. If Suhr is the culprit, he has stolen a weapon, which he then discards or plants to incriminate the owner. Other possible culprits might be trigger-happy or clumsy participants in the hunt, or guardsmen who decide to try and conceal their mistake.

WHITEOUT

During a severe storm that beats against the speeding express, a carriage's window shatters creating chaos as the screaming wind carries billows of snow into the shuddering compartment and lamps are extinguished. Keeping a clear head, Shur finds this the perfect opportunity to make a move. The Games Master could imperil the person the Agents have grown most close with to increase tension.

EAST BY NORTH EAST

Whilst in the wilderness, an unmarked light aircraft is deterred from approaching too closely by bursts of machinegun fire from the train. The Games Master can have it shot and crash in the distance as an indication of the resolution of the train's officer, or could decide that it is piloted by a hireling of Disruptors sent to signal the train's imminent arrival to the Cossacks lurking further up the track.

If the Games Master decides to make the aircraft's presence more dangerous, or if the plane is encountered after the express has been delayed for a few days, use the vehicle and pilot profile on page 85. The aircraft has limited time and ammunition for attacks, so makes only three separate strafing runs unless deterred. Ideally, attacks target weapons crewed by soldiers, allowing the Agents the opportunity to operate the guns as the aircraft makes a fresh attack run.

FIGHTER AIRCRAFT (MILITARY BIPLANE)

Hull: 11 (Large Military), 42 Structure
Speed: Mediocre
Systems: 3
Traits: Airborne, Camouflaged, Weaponised
Shields: None
Weapons: 2x Gatling Guns
Description: This single seat fighter resembles a Heinkel He 49, with the addition of a totally enclosed cockpit. It's all-metal fuselage is painted in a pattern of greys and white, which optimise its chances of escaping detection over the snowy wastes and in the winter sky.

END OF THE LINE?

The Valley of the Howling Wolf Pass, a feature that cuts through the western foothills of the Ural Mountains some 200 kilometres north-west of Yekaterinburg, has been selected as an ambush site by the Cossack bandits sent by the Disruptors. Some 50 Cossacks are ready to derail and storm the express.

The Cossacks have set dynamite charges on the rail, which they attempt to detonate under the train using a detonator box. The Cossack with the detonator is concealed amongst some pine trees some 50 metres from the explosives with a comrade, whilst the remaining bandits wait astride their ponies amongst some bluffs on either side of the track some 150 metres away. One rider on each flank of the ambush lines point is posted as a lookout, well concealed by rocks or a snow-covered clump of brush and pine trees so an observer from the train would need a Herculean success to spot them. The dynamite, if detonated successfully, causes 6d6 damage to the vehicle immediately above it, and automatically wrecks a section of track, derailing the train.

Those with the Precognition Trait experience a vision of the impending calamity, possibly triggered when examining the Faberge egg or viewing the Northern Lights; otherwise, Octobriana whilst idly manipulating her tarot deck suddenly reacts in alarm as she draws a string of ominous cards, focussed around The Chariot and The Tower representing the danger of an imminent collision.

If the Agents are keeping a close eye on Shur, a successful Insight roll notices a sudden excitement come over him and his refusal to meet anyone's eyes. He might decide to move to and destroy the radio in the command car and eliminate the Major just prior to the ambush site being reached. During a conflict, if Shur is still at large, he likely tries to kill Octobriana and the Agents during the chaos.

Persuading Major Korff to halt the train early on such evidence is, at the very least, a Formidable Influence check. Failing that, the Agents would need to use force or cunning to apply the brakes in time. Braking in time safely requires a successful Drive (engine) roll; the earlier the attempt, the better the modifier. If failed, the engine either does not stop or stops on top of the charges. If the line ahead is already blown up, roll on the Loss of Control Table (*Luther Arkwright*, page 113): a roll of 01–50 counts as a roll of 61–70. Each successive car must make a similar roll, until a negative score is rolled; each car after the engine receives a cumulative –10% to its roll. It is also highly unlikely that the Agents can get a crashed engine upright and back on a piece of track.

Damage to different cars in the express can be resolved using the Terrestrial Vehicle System damage table (*Luther Arkwright*, page 111). The Agents and other important Non-Player Characters can be assumed to be amongst the last crew or passengers to be eligible to sustain proportional casualties on a Partial Damage Result. In addition, the Agents only suffer half damage if they succeed at an appropriate skill roll such as Acrobatics, Athletics, or Evade, and none at all if a Critical success is made. Situational Difficulty modifiers include equipment and precautions applicable to a hazard or falls onto cushioning surfaces such as deep snow. If the train car is destroyed, the Difficulty is at least Hard, though especially catastrophic disasters can change this to Formidable or Herculean (Games Master's choice).

Even should the express avoid being derailed or if it stops prior to the explosives, howling Cossacks ride out from ambush, firing off pistols or carbines, whilst some endeavour to drag soldiers or machineguns out of exposed trucks using whips. Many Cossacks attempt to acrobatically dismount and gain access to vehicle interiors or else clamber up onto rooftops, some seeking to overpowering the locomotive's crew to take over the train or force it to stop the train, whichever is more appropriate. If undamaged, the Cossacks attempt to start it up again under their control if it was stopped.

The Games Master is encouraged to adopt a narrative method to resolve the combat that does not directly involve the Agents and ensure that their individual efforts have a significant effect on the overall outcome of the conflict. If randomised rifle and pistol fire is needed against occupants of separate cars, use the table below to determine how many hits are made and then randomise who is hit:

Range	Damage
Close	1d6
Medium	1d4
Long	1d2
Modifiers:	Blizzard, etc. –1 Each speed band over Sluggish –1 Locomotive/Troop/Command Car balcony –1 Troop/Command Car –2

If the express manages to move, which ever direction it takes, the riders have around 10 Combat Rounds of efficient pursuit if the trains moves at Gentle speed plus or minus 1 Combat Round for each speed band of distance travelled each round.

If the Agents look like they are being overpowered, they might consider fleeing across the steppe, captured Cossack ponies proving valuable assets.

Unless Shur makes himself known to the Agents and issues orders for the surviving Valhalla Agents to be bound and kept prior to being handed over to his 'employers', the Cossacks are inclined to massacre them like the other passengers and crew. Valentova and Octobriana prove to be an exception to the slayings; if captured, they are to be kept as prisoners for ransoms, in the case of Octobriana, to one of the many cities who have put a price on her head. If the Agents cannot escape or quickly turn the tables on their captors, the Games Master might decide that Mjollnir Section is needed to effect their rescue.

Back on Track

If the Cossacks are routed, repair of the damaged track should be possible with adequate labour and all the spare track pieces in the baggage car. The delay takes 1d3+3 hours; if the spare track in the baggage car is for some reason unavailable, a further 3 hours delay is needed to take up tracks from the rail line. If the train cannot progress forwards, backtracking takes the express to a junction point some 200 kilometres back to Yekaterinburg from where an alternative rail route allows the express to eventually resume its journey in a westerly direction causing a delay of another two days during which time the train is attacked by an unmarked fighter aircraft (opposite).

If the train is wrecked, another nearby vehicle can be used. The Cossacks have a rail lorry for carrying heavy loads that is kept out of sight during the initial ambush. The cargo bed is covered by a tarpaulin and holds a radio set, an assortment of rations, gasoline containers, basic engineering and digging tools, and a snow plough attachment. Getting the vehicle onto the rails and converting the lorry for rail travel using jacks and mechanic tools take three individuals and requires a successful Mechanisms roll, each attempt taking 1d3+1 hours.

Rail Lorry

Hull: 10 (Large Military), 45 Structure
Speed: Mediocre
Traits: Cargo, Ground Vehicle, Rails
Shields: None
Weapons: None
Description: This two-seater lorry has a cargo bed that is covered with a tarpaulin. The road wheels can be replaced by flanged road wheels and the suspension altered to fit different rail gauges.

A Lady Vanishes

On the approach to Moscow, Octobriana insists that the team leave the train before it pulls into the station. A wise precaution, especially if Major Korff has arranged for the wanted terrorist's arrest. If the Agents disregard Octobriana, perhaps an ally on the train amongst the passengers overhears Korff's instructions to some of his men to apprehend Octobriana at the station. Otherwise, successful Perception or Intuition rolls pick up on wary looks from the military personnel. The Agents could also overhear a radio transmission to authorities.

To halt the train in the outskirts of the city requires luck, or the application of a brake. The train stops by a goods yard that provides decent cover to slip away, and bribery can help ensure that any train staff or soldiers look the other way. The Agents could choose to abandon the train whilst moving. Although it slows down as it approaches the station, those leaping down must make a successful Acrobatics or Athletics roll; Failure results in 1d6 damage to a random location and a Fumble increases the damage to 2d6.

If Korff or Volkov initiated an arrest, a force of twenty railway guards are awaiting the train at the station. Games Masters who want to run a mass combat, but feel that the Agents are outgunned, can add some of Octobriana's revolutionaries to the fray as allies (use the Resistance Member NPC statistics from *Hot Metal and Methadrine* on page 62, replacing the Dependency on Pretty Baby with one for Vodka and giving them a Loyalty to Octobriana of 75%).

> ### Mother Russia; Father Winter
> If the Agents attempt to travel overland on foot or pony back or using a non-railed vehicle for a significant distance, the rail track makes navigation easy, but the overall weather is Freezing with Moderate gales. The Games Master determines any hazards or delays this incurs.

Conclusion

Once in Moscow and free of entanglements, Octobriana quickly takes the Agents to a hideout in the attic of an urban tenement where they can communicate with the Valhalla Programme using a TPT and arrange for a Van to collect them. However, if the Games Master wishes to continue this campaign, the next mission, *Silver Pictures Move So Slow*, continues immediately after reaching Moscow, with the Agents being ordered to the Ukrainian capital of Kiev to ensure a trade delegation arrives safely in London.

The Disruptors, orchestrated by Loki, are playing a long game on 47.60.67. True chaos requires war, and Loki's plan is to bring Europe to its knees by assassinating the King of England. His pawn in this enterprise is a passenger from the Trans-Siberian Express, and so the Agents' experiences of journeying aboard luxurious modes of transportation are set to continue as they board the Empress Katerina, an airship bound for England's capital.

Non-Player Characters

Octobriana

A fierce Mongol warrior and fighter for the Bolshevik cause, Octobriana is one of Arkwright's many contacts (and lovers) across the multiverse. Tough, single-minded and with seemingly insatiable appetites, Octobriana epitomises the revolutionary zeal in the face of totalitarian regimes.

Octobriana is a multiversal constant. Every version of her across the parallels is engaged in the same attempts to effect revolution in whichever country she has adopted or been born into. On this parallel, like her other versions, she has a lusty nature, fierce devotion to overthrowing the incumbent regime, and a deep-seated passion for violence. She also demonstrates some mystical training, and her Mysticism powers are reflected in the character statistics opposite.

She is currently seriously wounded in her abdomen.

Octobriana	Attributes
STR: 16	Action Points: 3
CON: 16	Damage Modifier: +1d2
SIZ: 14	Prana: 12
DEX: 15	Tenacity: 9
INT: 12	Movement: 6 metres
POW: 12	Initiative Bonus: +14
CHA: 12	Armour: None

1d20	Hit Location	AP/HP
1 – 3	Right Leg	0/6
4 – 6	Left Leg	0/6
7 – 9	Abdomen	0/-4 (7)
10 – 12	Chest	0/8
13 – 15	Right Arm	0/5
16 – 18	Left Arm	0/5
19 – 20	Head	0/6

Skills	Passions, Traits & Dependencies
Athletics 68%, Brawn 60%, Conceal 34%, Culture (Revolutionary Classes) 80%, Deceit 37%, Demolitions 66%, Endurance 71%, Evade 55%, First Aid 55%, Influence 36%, Insight 34%, Language (English) 60%, Meditation 38%, Mysticism 40%, Native Language (Russian) 100%, Lore (Tarot) 90%, Perception 58%, Politics 80%, Ride 90%, Seduction 74%, Stealth 60%, Streetwise 52%, Survival 80%, Swim 30%, Unarmed 90%, Willpower 61%	Passions: Love Sex 90%, Loyalty to the Revolution 95%, Hate Bourgeoisie 90% Traits: Unshakeable Dependencies: Sex 70%

Mysticism

Mongol Focused Aggression (Awareness, Enhance Damage Modifier, Indomitable, Pain Control)

Combat Style & Weapons — Traits & Notes

Steppes Horse Warrior (Shortbow, Scimitar) 88% — Mounted Combat

Revolutionary Soldier (Pistols, Sub-Machineguns) 84%

Weapon	Damage	Range	Ammo	Rate/Load
Revolver	1d6	50/100/200	7	1/3

Weapon	Damage	Size/Reach	AP/HP	Effects
Dagger	1d4+1+1d2	S/S	6/8	Bleed, Impale

Count Mikhail Banin

A gaunt, tall, careworn, seemingly ancient, blind man who wears a pair of dark-blue lensed spectacles and always has a cane to hand. He has lost his family and suffered his injuries during the looting of his mansion several years ago. He is polite but detached if approached. His luggage includes some novels written in German and Russian in braille. He relies on Ivan, a demure manservant.

Banin	Attributes
STR: 8	Action Points: 2
CON: 7	Damage Modifier: -1d2
SIZ: 10	Prana: 14
DEX: 9	Tenacity: 12
INT: 13	Movement: 6 metres
POW: 14	Initiative Bonus: +11
CHA: 12	Armour: None

1d20	Hit Location	AP/HP
1 – 3	Right Leg	0/4
4 – 6	Left Leg	0/4
7 – 9	Abdomen	0/5
10 – 12	Chest	0/6
13 – 15	Right Arm	0/3
16 – 18	Left Arm	0/3
19 – 20	Head	0/4

Skills	Passions, Traits & Dependencies
Athletics 17%, Courtesy 65%, Endurance 14%, Evade 18%, Language (English) 40%, Language (French) 65%, Language (Polish) 55%, Insight 50%, Native Language (Russian) 99%, Perception 37%, Politics 45%, Unarmed 17%, Willpower 68%	Passions: Honourable 75%, Love Family 80%, Hate Family's Murderers 75% Traits: Perceptive (Aural) Dependencies: Nicotine 50%

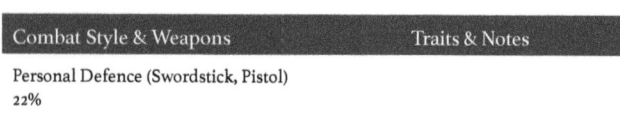

Combat Style & Weapons			Traits & Notes	
Personal Defence (Swordstick, Pistol) 22%				

Weapon	Damage	Range	Ammo	Rate/Load
Pocket Revolver	1d4+1	50/100/200	3	1/3

Weapon	Damage	Size/Reach	AP/HP	Effects
Swordstick	1d6-1d2	S/M	5/7	Bleed, Impale

'Vasilisa Pajari' Galina

This sharp-eyed, pretty woman is actually a thief who is posing as a lesser member of the nobility. She is not a killer by nature but is prepared to do anything to avoid being arrested and tried.

Galina	Attributes
STR: 9	Action Points: 3
CON: 11	Damage Modifier: -1d2
SIZ: 10	Prana: 11
DEX: 17	Tenacity: 8
INT: 12	Movement: 6 metres
POW: 11	Initiative Bonus: +15
CHA: 15	Armour: None

1d20	Hit Location	AP/HP
1 – 3	Right Leg	0/5
4 – 6	Left Leg	0/5
7 – 9	Abdomen	0/6
10 – 12	Chest	0/7
13 – 15	Right Arm	0/4
16 – 18	Left Arm	0/4
19 – 20	Head	0/5

Skills	Passions, Traits & Dependencies
Acrobatics 46%, Athletics 46%, Commerce 44%, Conceal 70%, Deception 57%, Disguise 52%, Endurance 22%, Evade 60%, Gambling 33%, Influence 40%, Lock Picking 54%, Native Language (Russian) 67%, Perception 53%, Seduction 47%, Sleight 80%, Stealth 70%, Streetwise 66%, Unarmed 26%, Willpower 32%	Passions: Love Deception 65%, Contempt for Authority 44%, Covet Riches 85% Dependencies: Stealing 77%

Combat Style & Weapons			Traits & Notes	
Personal Defence (Pistol) 36%				

Weapon	Damage	Range	Ammo	Rate/Load
Revolver	1d6	50/100/200	6	1/3

Major Korff

A tall, arrogant officer, Korff only seems to show respect towards the upper echelons of society. He always wears an immaculate uniform and has his weaponry to hand. He is a ruthless disciplinarian and personally beats or flogs those of his men who displease him.

He is secretly paid by Volkov to pass on any information about individuals who seem to have a particular interest in him and is expected to prioritise the privacy and safety of his paymaster.

Korff	Attributes
STR: 14	Action Points: 3
CON: 15	Damage Modifier: +1d2
SIZ: 14	Prana: 14
DEX: 13	Tenacity: 10
INT: 12	Movement: 6 metres
POW: 14	Initiative Bonus: +13
CHA: 13	Armour: None

1d20	Hit Location	AP/HP
1 – 3	Right Leg	0/6
4 – 6	Left Leg	0/6
7 – 9	Abdomen	0/7
10 – 12	Chest	0/8
13 – 15	Right Arm	0/5
16 – 18	Left Arm	0/5
19 – 20	Head	0/4

Skills	Passions, Traits & Dependencies
Athletics 47%, Brawn 48%, Customs (military) 56%, Drive (speeder) 40%, Endurance 50%, Evade 36%, Language (English) 30%, Language (German) 50%, Lore (tactics) 45%, Native Language (Russian) 65%, Oratory 40%, Perception 36%, Ride 50%, Survival 36%, Unarmed 37%, Willpower 43%	Passions: Love Power 60%, Loyalty to Rail Company 35%, Loyalty to Volkov 30% Hate Disobedience 60% Dependencies: Trademark Weapon (Sabre) 40%

Combat Style & Weapons			Traits & Notes	
Russian Officer (Sabre, Revolver) 70%				

Weapon	Damage	Range	Ammo	Rate/Load
Revolver	1d6	50/100/200	6	1/3

Weapon	Damage	Size/Reach	AP/HP	Effects
Sabre	1d6+1+1d2	M/M	6/8	Bleed, Impale

IRENA LAZAREV

Irena is Valentova's put-upon public relations person, personal assistant, and general dogsbody. Irena is brutally efficient and has a crush on her employer; no-one gets to Valentova without Irena knowing about it.

As she handles Valentova's correspondence, forging her writing and signature is consequently a Very Easy task for her.

In her valise is a German/Russian phrase book, a stock of business cards and photographs for Valentova to autograph, and a makeup kit to use on her patron. She also travels with a portable typewriter and a bag of cleaning materials for the cabin, which includes a bottle of bleach. Her prized possession is a framed and signed photograph of Valentova.

Lazarev	Attributes
STR: 10	Action Points: 2
CON: 13	Damage Modifier: -1d2
SIZ: 10	Prana: 12
DEX: 11	Tenacity: 9
INT: 13	Movement: 6 metres
POW: 12	Initiative Bonus: +12
CHA: 11	Armour: None

1d20	Hit Location	AP/HP
1 – 3	Right Leg	0/5
4 – 6	Left Leg	0/5
7 – 9	Abdomen	0/6
10 – 12	Chest	0/7
13 – 15	Right Arm	0/4
16 – 18	Left Arm	0/4
19 – 20	Head	0/5

Skills	Passions, Traits & Dependencies
Art (make up) 35%, Bureaucracy 88%, Commerce 54%, Courtesy 54%, Craft (typewriting) 44%, Deceit 64%, Drive (Speeder) 33%, Endurance 26%, Evade 22 %, First Aid 34%, Influence 35%, Language (English) 24%, Language (German) 24%, Native Language (Russian) 64%, Oratory 28%, Perception 40%, Politics 29%, Stealth 34%, Streetwise 28%, Unarmed 23%, Willpower 34%	Passions: Love Valentova 75%, Hate Inefficiency 80%, Jealousy 70% Dependencies: Nicotine 45%

Combat Style & Weapons	Traits & Notes

Personal Defence (Pistol) 35%

Weapon	Damage	Range	Ammo	Rate/Load
9mm Pistol	1d6	50/100/200	8	1/3

MODYA

Modya is a short, skinny man with a whining voice and darting eyes that betray his nervousness. He is desperately trying to flee from some of his former associates in The Chill Wind, a Vladivostok-based crime gang.

Modya	Attributes
STR: 9	Action Points: 2
CON: 10	Damage Modifier: -1d2
SIZ: 9	Prana: 10
DEX: 12	Tenacity: 7
INT: 10	Movement: 6 metres
POW: 10	Initiative Bonus: +13
CHA: 8	Armour: None

1d20	Hit Location	AP/HP
1 – 3	Right Leg	0/4
4 – 6	Left Leg	0/4
7 – 9	Abdomen	0/5
10 – 12	Chest	0/6
13 – 15	Right Arm	0/3
16 – 18	Left Arm	0/3
19 – 20	Head	0/4

Skills	Passions, Traits & Dependencies
Athletics 18%, Culture (criminal) 45%, Endurance 30%, Evade 44%, Gambling 30%, Perception 50%, Stealth 50%, Unarmed 21%, Willpower 30%	Passions: Love Secrets 55%, Fearful (Police & The Chill Wind) 68% Dependencies: Gambling 45%, Voyeurism 56%

Combat Style & Weapons	Traits & Notes

None

ANTON SHUR

The Disruptor agent is a seemingly polite but whimsical poet, who sometimes drifts into dark poetry about the human condition. He is a young, handsome man with a strange stare that never seems to focus entirely on the individual he is regarding.

If faced with capture he tries to detonate the explosive device concealed in his pocket watch.

Shur's pocket watch has hidden advanced technology and acts as an explosive device to remove prime targets or commit an efficient suicide. An individual examining the device must make a Mechanisms roll to deduce that it incorporates another device other than the watch mechanism. After that, an Easy Demolitions roll reveals the explosive device, which is primed by setting the main hands to midnight and winding the mechanism backwards, before setting the second hand to detonate the device in a time set between a second to a full minute. The explosion does 2d10/1d10 Disintegrating damage on each target within 3/6 metres.

Shur	Attributes
STR: 11	Action Points: 3
CON: 12	Damage Modifier: 0
SIZ: 13	Prana: 14
DEX: 15	Tenacity: 12
INT: 13	Movement: 6 metres
POW: 14	Initiative Bonus: +14
CHA: 13	Armour: None

1d20	Hit Location	AP/HP
1 – 3	Right Leg	0/5
4 – 6	Left Leg	0/5
7 – 9	Abdomen	0/6
10 – 12	Chest	0/7
13 – 15	Right Arm	0/4
16 – 18	Left Arm	0/4
19 – 20	Head	0/5

Skills	Passions, Traits & Dependencies
Art (poetry) 57%, Athletics 40%, Courtesy 48%, Deceit 76%, Endurance 40%, Evade 55%, Home Parallel 45%, Influence 48%, Insight 70%, Language (English) 50%, Language (German) 60%, Language (French) 70%, Lore (philosophy) 45%, Native Language (Russian) 100%, Perception 75%, Sleight 50%, Stealth 75%, Streetwise 45%, Unarmed 48%, Willpower 75%	Passions: Loyalty to Disruptors 90% Love Poetry 80% Hate Order 80% Traits: Insightful Dependencies: Artistic Expression 55%

Combat Style & Weapons	Traits & Notes
Assassin's Creed (Dagger, Garrotte, Pistol) 75%	Assassination

Weapon	Damage	Range	Ammo	Rate/Load
9mm Auto	1d6	50/100/200	7	1/3
Bomb	2d10/1d10	5/10/20	-	Disintegrate

Weapon	Damage	Size/Reach	AP/HP	Effects
Dagger	1d4+1	S/S	6/8	Bleed, Impale
Garrotte	1d2	S/T	1/2	Entangle

The pocket watch employs similar technology and function to Valentova's powder compact (see *Silver Pictures Move So Slow*) and, like the compact, was issued to Shur by Pieter Klass - aka Loki.

Games Masters might decide to select another passenger as the Disruptor agent, using Shur's template to suggest extra skills, traits, and Passions. In this case, Shur can still be used as an innocent passenger but needs to be altered, removing the items, skills, traits, and Passions connected with acting for the Disruptors.

GERTRUDE VALENTOVA

The glamorous, golden-haired actress Gertrude Valentova is the famous star of the movie 'Gone with the Mistral'. Her name is linked with dozens of affairs amongst many of the crowned heads of Europe. She sports expensive clothes that are tailored to flaunt her figure.

She's currently having an affair with Archduke Kovalenko of the Ukrainian Royal Family. One of her other lovers, Pieter Klass the Disruptor Knight 'Loki', intends to use her as an unwitting Disruptor sleeper agent in a scheme to kill the King of England and the Archduke of Ukraine. She is subject to a Thought Implant placed by Loki that comes into its own in the scenario *Silver Pictures Move So Slow*. The implant should have no effect in this scenario, unless Games Masters wish to make use of it as an additional complication.

Valentova	Attributes
STR: 9	Action Points: 3
CON: 13	Damage Modifier: -1d2
SIZ: 9	Prana: 13
DEX: 15	Tenacity: 6
INT: 11	Movement: 6 metres
POW: 13	Initiative Bonus: +13
CHA: 18	Armour: None

1d20	Hit Location	AP/HP
1 – 3	Right Leg	0/5
4 – 6	Left Leg	0/5
7 – 9	Abdomen	0/6
10 – 12	Chest	0/7
13 – 15	Right Arm	0/4
16 – 18	Left Arm	0/4
19 – 20	Head	0/5

Skills	Passions, Traits & Dependencies
Acting 66%, Athletics 29 %, Dance 68%, Deceit 44%, Drive (Speeder) 33%, Endurance 31 %, Evade 40%, Influence 46%, Language (English) 29 %, Native Language (Russian) 69%, Perception 24 %, Seduction 69 %, Sing 66%, Unarmed 24%, Willpower 36 %,	Passions: Love Fame 80%, Crave Infamy 75% Fear Obscurity 77% Dependencies: Alcohol 33%, Approval 50%, Narcotics 44%, Nicotine 30%, Sex 39%

Combat Style & Weapons	Traits & Notes
Diva Tantrum (anything that can be hurled) 35%	Improvised Weapons

Volkov

This huge walrus of a man is actually a war criminal who is afraid to leave the sanctuary of the express. He is usually buoyed up by alcohol when he meets people and is loud, demonstrative, and brash. Alone he is either maudlin or fearful. He enjoys the use of private quarters and has a substantial stash of jewellery, religious icons, money, and loot from his atrocities, which he keeps locked away in a large safe, along with various false identity papers he can use if he ever has to escape. His winter clothing has small precious stones sewn into the lining that an individual examining the garments would need a Hard Perception test to find.

His door is always locked and even Igor, his single manservant, is not allowed a key. If he feels threatened by an individual, he attempts to browbeat Major Korff into placing them under arrest and detained in a baggage car.

Volkov	Attributes
STR: 14	Action Points: 2
CON: 14	Damage Modifier: +1d4
SIZ: 17	Prana: 14
DEX: 8	Tenacity: 7
INT: 10	Movement: 6 metres
POW: 14	Initiative Bonus: +9
CHA: 12	Armour: Ballistic vest, plus gem and coin-lined coat.

1d20	Hit Location	AP/HP
1 – 3	Right Leg	1/7
4 – 6	Left Leg	1/7
7 – 9	Abdomen	1/8
10 – 12	Chest	4/9
13 – 15	Right Arm	1/6
16 – 18	Left Arm	1/6
19 – 20	Head	0/7

Skills	Passions, Traits & Dependencies
Athletics 42%, Brawn 61%, Conceal 40%, Endurance 38%, Evade 16%, Gambling 48%, Insight 36%, Language (German) 22%, Native Language (Russian) 65%, Oratory 40%, Perception 40%, Politics 45%, Ride 35%, Survival 50%, Torture 66%, Unarmed 48%, Willpower 38%	Passions: Love Wealth 50% Fear Assassins 60% Dependencies: Alcohol 75%, Security Precautions 60%

Combat Style & Weapons	Traits & Notes
Russian Officer (Sabre, Revolver) 77%	

Weapon	Damage	Range	Ammo	Rate/Load
Revolver	1d6	50/100/200	6	1/3

Weapon	Damage	Size/Reach	AP/HP	Effects
Sabre	1d6+1+1d4	M/M	6/8	Bleed, Impale

He openly wears his sabre and pistol, seemingly with Major Korff's consent.

He has a shrewd idea about the state of Countess Zykhov's finances and is trying to blackmail her by threatening to expose her penury unless she agrees to sleep with him during the journey.

Countess Anzhelika Zykhov

Anzhelika is a glamorous, blonde aristocrat but, although the toast of the Russian aristocracies, she is actually bankrupt. She tries to conceal her penury by remaining always on the move, forced to rely on the patronage of others to maintain her lifestyle and pay off creditors. Her clothing is well made and expensive, as are the cigarettes she smokes from an onyx holder. Despite her obvious love of luxury, she revels in the excitement of hunting game in the countryside despite the attendant discomforts. She has no retainer with her but is accompanied by Boyar, her borzoi hound, which responds to a silver ultra-sonic whistle the Countess carries.

Zykhov	Attributes
STR: 9	Action Points: 3
CON: 12	Damage Modifier: -1d2
SIZ: 10	Prana: 14
DEX: 14	Tenacity: 12
INT: 12	Movement: 6 metres
POW: 14	Initiative Bonus: +13
CHA: 18	Armour: None

1d20	Hit Location	AP/HP
1 – 3	Right Leg	0/5
4 – 6	Left Leg	0/5
7 – 9	Abdomen	0/6
10 – 12	Chest	0/7
13 – 15	Right Arm	0/4
16 – 18	Left Arm	0/4
19 – 20	Head	0/5

Skills	Passions, Traits & Dependencies
Athletics 33%, Courtesy 60%, Endurance 24%, Evade 33%, Influence 56%, Language (English) 26%, Language (French) 60%, Language (German) 30%, Native Language (Russian) 64%, Perception 56% Ride 43%, Seduction 66%, Stealth 36%, Survival 36%, Track 40%, Unarmed 23%, Willpower 38%	Passions: Love Luxury 50% Fear Poverty 60% Dependencies: Hunting 36%, Nicotine 28%

Combat Style & Weapons	Traits & Notes
Huntress (Rifle) 53%	

Weapon	Damage	Range	Ammo	Rate/Load
.303 Rifle	1d10	100/300/800	12	1/3

Train Guard Rifles

These men come from a variety of city-states and, although lacking in initiative, usually follow orders unflinchingly. They wear special rifle-green uniforms, but cover these with bulky winter clothing when stationed in the open.

Twenty serve as guards and an extra two soldier-servants are used by Major Korff.

If the Games Master wishes to shorten combat or reduce risk to the Agents, treat any train guards as 5 HP Underlings (MYTHRAS, page 111).

Train Guards	Attributes
STR: 10	Action Points: 2
CON: 9	Damage Modifier: 0
SIZ: 11	Prana: 10
DEX: 10	Tenacity: 10
INT: 11	Movement: 6 metres
POW: 10	Initiative Bonus: +11
CHA: 11	Armour: Greatcoats

1d20	Hit Location	AP/HP
1 – 3	Right Leg	1/6
4 – 6	Left Leg	1/6
7 – 9	Abdomen	1/7
10 – 12	Chest	1/8
13 – 15	Right Arm	1/5
16 – 18	Left Arm	1/5
19 – 20	Head	1/6

Skills	Passions, Traits & Dependencies
Athletics 38%, Brawn 55%, Endurance 36%, Evade 28%, Perception 41%, Stealth 39%, Survival 31%, Unarmed 38%, Willpower 19%	Passions: Loyalty to Train 60%

Combat Style & Weapons	Traits & Notes
Train Guard (Rifle) 60% (all) Machinegun 40% (x4) Pistol 30% (x4)	Formation Fighting

Weapon	Damage	Range	Ammo	Rate/Load
.303 Rifle	1d10	100/300/800	12	1/3

Cossack Bandit

A rowdy band of ruthless rogues who are happy to fight for anyone who promises them easy plunder. They normally prefer hit and run tactics to extended stand up fights. When attacking the train one in ten is also armed with a Molotov Cocktail, which they endeavour to use in the first three rounds of combat and throw using their Athletics skill.

If the Games Master wishes to shorten combat or reduce risk to the Agents, treat any bandits as 5 HP Underlings (MYTHRAS, page 111).

Cossack Bandit	Attributes
STR: 10	Action Points: 2
CON: 9	Damage Modifier: 0
SIZ: 11	Prana: 10
DEX: 10	Tenacity: 10
INT: 11	Movement: 6 metres
POW: 10	Initiative Bonus: +11
CHA: 11	Armour: None

1d20	Hit Location	AP/HP
1 – 3	Right Leg	0/6
4 – 6	Left Leg	0/6
7 – 9	Abdomen	0/7
10 – 12	Chest	0/8
13 – 15	Right Arm	0/5
16 – 18	Left Arm	0/5
19 – 20	Head	0/6

Skills	Passions, Traits & Dependencies
Athletics 38%, Brawn 55%, Endurance 36%, Evade 28%, Perception 41%, Stealth 39%, Survival 31%, Unarmed 38%, Willpower 19%	Passions: Loyalty to Band 60%

Combat Style & Weapons	Traits & Notes
Cossack Bandit (Rifle, Sabre, Whip) 60%	Mounted Combat

Weapon	Damage	Range	Ammo	Rate/Load
.303 Rifle	1d10	100/300/800	12	1/3

Weapon	Damage	Size/Reach	AP/HP	Effects
Sabre	1d6+1	M/M	6/8	Bleed, Impale
Whip	1d2	S/VL	1/2	Entangle

Passengers, Pilot and Staff

This generic template can be modified by adding social skills for passengers or steward skills for retainers and rail staff. Most passengers are well-to-do individuals, though as the train lacks second-class compartments, very few find it convenient or appropriate to take servants with them, some using poorer relatives or associates as 'travelling companions' to undertake menial tasks that crop up on the journey.

It is recommended that most are classed as 5 HP Rabble (Mythras, page 110).

Passengers & Staff	Attributes
STR: 10	Action Points: 2
CON: 9	Damage Modifier: 0
SIZ: 11	Prana: 10
DEX: 10	Tenacity: 10
INT: 11	Movement: 6 metres
POW: 10	Initiative Bonus: +11
CHA: 11	Armour: None

1d20	Hit Location	AP/HP
1 – 3	Right Leg	0/5
4 – 6	Left Leg	0/5
7 – 9	Abdomen	0/6
10 – 12	Chest	0/7
13 – 15	Right Arm	0/4
16 – 18	Left Arm	0/4
19 – 20	Head	0/5

Skills	Passions, Traits & Dependencies

Athletics 20%, Endurance 20%, Evade 20%, Home Parallel 22%, Perception 21%, Unarmed 20%, Willpower 20%

Engine Crew: Drive (steam engine) 50%, Mechanisms 50%

Steward: Courtesy 40%

Body Guard: Unarmed 45%

Pilot: Pilot (Aircraft) 65%

Combat Style & Weapons	Traits & Notes

Self Defence (Pistol) 30%

Weapon	Damage	Range	Ammo	Rate/Load
Revolver	1d6	50/100/200	6	1/3

'Tsarina' Snow Leopard

A snow leopard is a large hunting cat found in parts of Asia that has a pelt that provides good insulation and camouflage in the snow-covered highlands of its territory. Snow leopards and their kin are also kin are also skilled climbers and use trees rocks as a launch place from ambush, aiming to land on the chest or back of the prey, immobilise with both claws and then use Chose Location to attack the head and throat.

They do not normally attack people, preferring flight, though they can retaliate to threats or might be panicked into making attacks as they seek escape.

Snow Leopard	Attributes
STR: 22	Action Points: 3
CON: 13	Damage Modifier: +1d6
SIZ: 15	Prana: 10
DEX: 19	Tenacity: 10
INS: 13	Movement: 8 metres
POW: 10	Initiative Bonus: +16
	Armour: None

1d20	Hit Location	AP/HP
1 – 3	Right Hind Leg	1/6
4 – 6	Left Hind Leg	1/6
7 – 9	Abdomen	1/7
10 – 12	Chest	1/8
13 – 15	Right Front Leg	1/5
16 – 18	Left Front Leg	1/5
19 – 20	Head	1/6

Skills	Passions, Traits & Dependencies

Athletics 60%, Endurance 43%, Evade 65%, Perception 70%, Stealth 90%, Survival 45%, Willpower 43%

Combat Style & Weapons	Traits & Notes

Lethal Ambush (Bite. Claw) 75%

Weapon	Damage	Size/Reach	AP/HP	Effects
Bite	1d8+1d6	M/T	As for Head	Bleed
Claw	1d6+1d6	M/M	As for Leg	-

Mutant Wolf

The wolves of the Steppe country now include aggressive packs of mutated wolves that originate from the borders around the Tunguska region. Life is harsh and favours the survival of those wolves with beneficial mutations. Chaos Features can be generated or selected using the table in Mythras, page 275, or can be abstracted as giving pack members an extra point of armour and increasing the Damage Modifier to +0.

The template below can also be used for Boyar, the Countess's borzoi hound, but modify Prana to 12 and Willpower to 55%, and add the Passion Loyalty (Anzhelika) 80%.

Mutant Wolf	Attributes
STR: 8	Action Points: 2
CON: 11	Damage Modifier: -1d2
SIZ: 8	Prana: 7
DEX: 11	Tenacity: 7
INS: 13	Movement: 8 metres
POW: 7	Initiative Bonus: +12
	Armour: Fur

1d20	Hit Location	AP/HP
1 – 3	Right Hind Leg	1/4
4 – 6	Left Hind Leg	1/4
7 – 9	Abdomen	1/5
10 – 12	Chest	1/6
13 – 15	Right Front Leg	1/4
16 – 18	Left Front Leg	1/4
19 – 20	Head	1/6

Skills	Passions, Traits & Dependencies
Athletics 59%, Brawn 36%, Endurance 62%, Evade 52%, Perception 60%, Survival %, Track 64%, Willpower 44%	

Combat Style & Weapons	Traits & Notes
Pack Savage 59% (Bite, Claw)	

Weapon	Damage	Size/Reach	AP/HP	Effects
Bite	1d4-1d2	S/T	As for Head	Bleed

Silver Pictures Move So Slow

A trade delegation travelling from Kiev to London is marred by strange events that threaten to plunge the Europe of 47.60.67 into war. Can the Agents prevent a major catastrophe?

OVERVIEW

Parallel 47.60.67
European Imperial Variant, Ukrainian Ascendancy
Disruption Likelihood: 99.5%

The Disruptors have targeted 47.60.67 for destabilisation, focussing on the fragile balance of power represented by the Ukrainian, Prussian, and British Empires. Their aim is to assassinate King Alfred II of Britain, directing the blame on a Ukrainian royal visit and trade delegation. Their best psychic agent in this field is the man the Valhalla Programme knows as 'Loki', and he has spent many years building a power base for himself within the infrastructure of the emerging Prussian Empire. On this parallel, he goes by the name Pieter Klass.

Loki has forged a relationship with the famed actress Gertrude Valentova. She has been subjected to a Thought Implant that will compel her to detonate a small but very powerful bomb when in the presence of King Alfred. Her introduction to the king will be through another of her lovers, Archduke Kovalenko of the Ukrainian Imperial House. Kovalenko is leading the trade delegation to Britain that will meet with Alfred II, and he has engineered for his mistress to be aboard the airship taking them from Kiev to London. He intends to enjoy some private time with her during the flight, knowing that the other passengers are discreet. Unfortunately, discretion is perhaps the least of Kovalenko's worries.

W.O.T.A.N has calculated an exceedingly high probability of a disruption spiral focused on Kovalenko. The working theory is that the Disruptors have infiltrated the flight crew of the airship and intend to destroy it as it comes in to land at Battersea Airship Docks. Crimean separatists will be blamed, and the deaths of British civilians gathered to watch the airship's arrival will bring Britain into a war in Europe. While the calculations of disruption are correct, the method of disruption is wrong. Loki has planned carefully, creating a smokescreen to fool the Valhalla Programme. There is a bomb aboard the airship, but it will not be activated until Valentova is introduced to King Alfred. The Agents, therefore, begin this scenario on a wild goose chase.

RUNNING THIS MISSION

The scenario is intended to be a closed-location investigation and thus is structured somewhat differently from other scenarios in *Parallel Lines*. The Agents are forced to integrate with the passengers of the airship, attempting to find and stop the Disruptors. During the journey, a variety of events happen that, when investigated, can help the Agents uncover the real Disruptor agent – Valentova – all the while having to deal with an atmosphere of escalating paranoia.

Read the scenario thoroughly. First comes the briefing from the Valhalla Programme. Character descriptions, motivations, and plots are presented afterwards. Then follows the different events that happen during the flight. Games Masters can pick and choose how many of these take place, but as they are key to the scenario's success, it is recommended they be played out in the sequence offered. Finally, a description of the airship, *Empress Katerina*, along with diagrams, is provided.

Background and Introduction

Designator: 47.60.67
Classification: European Imperial, Ukrainian Ascendancy
Cultural Type: Eastern Europe
Political Type: Communist Oligarchy
Technological Type: Industrial Age
For a description of this parallel, see 'One Way or Another' (page 66).

Briefing

Immediately after the events depicted in *One Way or Another*, the Agents are ordered to remain on 47.60.67. Using a TPT at a Valhalla safe house, Freyr Lingstadt gives the Agents their orders:

1. They have been secured passage aboard the *Empress Katerina*, flying from Kiev to London and must reach Kiev in the next 48 hours. Travel arrangements have been made for them.
2. They must watch the crew and passengers carefully. It is believed a bomb is on board and will be set to explode on the final approach to Battersea Airship Docks, where a delegation of the British Royal Family and government will greet the main Ukrainian delegation.
3. The Ukrainian delegation consists of Archduke Rostov Kovalenko, visiting Britain for the first time; members of the Trade and Transportation ministries, aiming to strike trade deals with Britain over markets in British-controlled China; and a small film crew accompanying the famous actress Gertrude Valentova. The Agents must ensure no harm befalls *any* of these dignitaries, as all are crucial to peace in Europe.
4. Loki is known to be active on this parallel: the Agents must gain as much intelligence on his plans and whereabouts as possible.

A courier arrives within the hour, bringing the documents the Agents need for passage. Their cover is simple: wealthy passengers with business in London who were fortunate enough to attain tickets through contacts in the Ukrainian Air Passenger Service. Feel free to amend the cover story to fit with previous adventures or take into account the Agents' professions and backgrounds. The key thing is that the Agents have a legitimate reason for being on the airship and their credentials are not questioned.

While there is not much time to conduct any detailed research on the voyage, the following facts can be learned from Streetwise or similar rolls:

- This is the first time the *Empress Katerina* has made the voyage to Britain, and it is a hotly anticipated event. The excitement is heightened because Gertrude Valentova is part of the entourage, and the film star is very popular in London.
- The Ukrainian Empire has been attempting to gain access to Britain's lucrative markets in China for some time. The trade delegation, which is the reason for this visit, is there to secure a ground-breaking deal that will seal an alliance between these two empires at the expense of Prussian ambitions.
- Archduke Kovalenko is a playboy aristocrat and a known ladies' man, despite being married for several years. His presence on this mission is symbolic more than anything else.
- A year ago, Ukrainian secret service agents foiled an attempt by Crimean separatists to infiltrate the Kiev Airship Yards.
- The journey to London is to be subject of a short documentary film shot by Otto Schumann, a famed director and friend of Valentova.

The briefing documents for the Agents come with an itinerary:

Day 1
1.30pm – 2.30pm: Boarding. Stewards show passengers to their cabins.
3.00pm: Launch. Cocktails served in the Promenade.
7.00pm: Dinner. White tie. Served in the Dining Room.
9.00pm – 12:00am. Music in the Lounge.

Day 2
6.00am – 8.00am: Breakfast in the Dining Room.
10.00am – 12.00pm: Luncheon and an Audience with Gertrude Valentova, Promenade.
3.00pm – 4.00pm: Invitation to the Control Car.
6.00pm – 7pm: Cocktails served in the Promenade.
7.00pm: Dinner. White tie. Served in the Dining Room.
9.00pm-12:00am. Music in the Lounge.

Day 3
6.00am – 8.00am: Breakfast in the Dining Room.
11.00am: Final Approach to London.
12:00pm: Arrival and Disembarkation.

Note that the itinerary is the scheduled plan of events; what actually happens over the course of the next few days is actually quite different....

In between these activities, the passengers are free to mingle, relax, and enjoy the flight. The documentation notes that the Control Car is off-limits, save with the express invitation of Captain Mors and the scheduled time on the itinerary.

For dinner, the Agents have preassigned seatings, away from the VIPs. Passengers are expected to keep their assigned dinner places; it is frowned upon to try to swap in order to gain any form of social advantage.

NOTABLE PASSENGERS AND CREW

- *Rostov Kovalenko*, Archduke of Ukraine
- *Kommander Gerhard*, Kovalenko's bodyguard
- *Graves*, Kovalenko's butler
- *Ruprecht Volyinski*, High Minister for Trade and Industry
- *Volodymyr Bohdan*, High Minister for Transportation
- *Gertrude Valentova*, film star and Kovalenko's lover
- *Irena Lazarev*, personal assistant to Ms. Valentova
- *Wilhelm Gleb*, secretary to Volyinski
- *Klara Klym*, secretary to Bohdan (and his mistress)
- *Maksim Olesko*, Senior Engineer, Crimean Separatist sympathiser
- *Olga Ruslana*, Head of Security and a member of the Ukrainian Secret Service
- *Anna Thames*, First Officer, *Empress Katerina*
- *Gregor Fedotik*, Head of Hospitality and major domo for the serving staff aboard the *Empress Katerina*
- *Captain Mors*, Chief Officer, *Empress Katerina*
- *Otto Schumann*, Director of Valentova's last film and making a movie documenting the maiden flight of the airship

ROSTOV KOVALENKO, ARCHDUKE OF UKRAINE

A first cousin to Empress Katerina herself, Kovalenko is handsome, charismatic but utterly indiscreet. He has prodigious appetites for food, alcohol, and gambling, and while married with several children, has a string of mistresses. He also has a very short fuse, losing his temper easily, especially when he cannot get his own way. He is used to being waited on hand and foot, and uses his influence with the Empress to both impress and intimidate others. Kovalenko believes he is being sent to Britain to schmooze with King Alfred II, the son of King Edward VIII. Alfred is a man who enjoys the good life, just as his father did, and Kovalenko is looking forward to a week of decadence punctuated by the odd serious chat about trade and banking. Kovalenko cares little for the former, and even less for the latter, relying on Volyinski to brief him. With a natural charm and a few facts, Kovalenko can project a reasonably credible persona, but if challenged, soon turns to bluster and hands all further discussions over to the High Minister.

Kovalenko is also using this trip as a way of spending time with his latest mistress, Gertrude Valentova. The two met at a gala premiere of one of Valentova's films, and the Archduke is smitten. He convinced the High Ministry that Valentova should make the trip to London aboard the airship, using the passage as a public relations exercise; he also convinced the High Ministry that King Alfred of Britain is a big Valentova fan (he isn't, but his daughters are) and that she should be presented to His Majesty. Kovalenko intends to spend the week in Britain bedding Valentova and is manfully trying to restrain himself on the flight over Europe, but simply cannot resist.

Kovalenko is not politically astute and is an outspoken critic of the Crimean Separatists, calling them 'Leftist Militant scum

Other Passengers

Aside from the Agents, who are assigned to double berths, the airship carries a full complement of passengers who are all upper middle class travellers making their way to London. Some are British, some Ukrainian, some American, and some from other European nations. They are not detailed here and Games Masters should add interesting personalities as they see fit. Some ideas are the following:

Schumann's Technicians

Travelling with Schumann are a camera operator, a sound technician, lighting technician, and a make-up artist. They are responsible for all the equipment, which is kept stowed in their berths, including taper recorders, portable editing studio, lights, and so on. They are in awe of Schumann but also hate his dictatorial approach. This is not a fun trip for them.

Inquisitive Journalist

Perhaps this parallel's Hiram Kowalsky is aboard, covering the flight for the New York Times. An ardent republican, his opinion pieces on the aristocrats aboard are scathing, and following Kovalenko's meltdown, he has a ready-made one-page exclusive, unless he can be persuaded otherwise.

British Confidence Trickster

Sir Harrence Fairfax is an East-End petty criminal made good, largely through an illegal Ponzi scheme that never went detected and made him a lot of money. The knighthood is fictitious and could be challenged, exposing him for the conman he really is. Fairfax is loud and crude, fond of breaking wind and making smutty jokes. A real charmer.

Assorted Ukrainian Tourists

These nouveau-rich travellers have paid handsomely to travel in style to London, mainly for tourism and shopping. They are in awe of the royal contingent and continually try to get pictures taken with Kovalenko or Valentova in casual situations, much to the annoyance of Graves and Gerhard. Perhaps a couple are Disruptor pawns, sent by Loki to ensure the master plan works out.

European Love Interest

A very attractive French male or female passenger takes the eye of one of the named passengers, but he or she only has eyes for an Agent and is not backward in coming forward. At an opportune time, the admirer strikes up a conversation and things lead towards a potential in-flight romance, along with opportunities to sneak away from the main areas for some private time. While Agents might be suspicious, there is nothing sinister in this holiday romance; simply a bored passenger attracted to another person, looking for some intimate companionship.

who should be rigorously nerve gassed'. He is therefore a target for separatist reprisals.

For all his faults, Kovalenko is generous and a gifted linguist, speaking fluent Russian, English, French, and German. He also has a wonderful baritone and leads singing after dinner, performing a mixture of opera classics, popular tunes, and a few very bawdy songs.

One fault that becomes apparent during the flight is his susceptibility to powerful psychic residues. The Thought Implant Valentova hosts produces a kind of psionic echo that is detectable by other psychics. The Archduke is not a psychic, but is easily affected by such energies. In the presence of such psychic energy, Kovalenko suffers hallucinations, paranoia, and emotional distress. He seeks the solace of his lover, unaware that she is the cause of this temporary madness. Keeping Kovalenko and Valentova apart is enough to cause the symptoms to ease substantially, but the Archduke is not the kind of man to take kindly to being told who he can and cannot see.

In his affected state, which is whenever Valentova is within 5 metres and he fails a Willpower roll (this is Formidable if side by side with Valentova), one of the following happens:

1. *Kovalenko becomes angry and argumentative. His worst prejudices emerge, and he is disdainful and insulting to all present.*
2. *Kovalenko suffers a hallucination: he sees strange creatures outside the airship attempting to puncture the canopy, or sinister figures hiding in the shadows who might be assassins, whilst experiencing a bizarre hallucination where everyone becomes shrouded in silver light and moves in slow motion.*
3. *Kovalenko becomes violent, taking offence at something someone says and challenging them to a duel there and then. He calls for his cavalry sabre to be brought from his cabin so he can gut the scum who has offended him. He needs to be restrained, as his violent intentions are real enough.*
4. *For no apparent reason, Kovalenko suddenly breaks down and sobs uncontrollably, curling into a foetal position and calling for his nanny.*
5. *Kovalenko suffers a seizure lasting for 1d3 minutes. He shakes, falls to the ground, and suffers 1d4 points of damage to 1d3 locations as he falls and thrashes. When the seizure finishes, he is disoriented and remembers nothing.*
6. *Kovalenko experiences a waking vision of horrible destruction. He suddenly stands, shouts 'Your majesty!' and then recoils in horror as he witnesses an explosion, diving for cover and wrapping his arms around his head. When questioned, his recollection is hazy, save that he saw a mirror and then a blast as though from an artillery shell. He cannot recall if 'Your majesty' was King Alfred or Empress Katerina.*

Once Kovalenko is removed from Valentova's presence, all symptoms rapidly subside. Astute Agents succeeding in a roll such as Insight (at a Formidable grade) note that Valentova is always present when these episodes trigger; however, she is just as horrified as everyone else witnessing them, and even more so if she and the Archduke are alone (and in sexual congress). Valentova has no knowledge that it is a mental implant she carries that causes all this mayhem.

KOMMANDER GERHARD, KOVALENKO'S BODYGUARD

Gerhard is Kovalenko's chief bodyguard. A huge, broad-shouldered, crop-haired brick of a man, he is calm, implacable, diligent, loyal, and deadly. Trained in several martial arts and an expert marksman, he is never more than 2 metres away from Kovalenko and is quick to ensure that he gets in between his royal subject and any strangers. Gerhard cannot be reasoned with, bribed, or diverted. He carries a stiletto, a cut-throat razor, and a Walther PPK and can get, if necessary, a Mauser automatic pistol from his personal equipment.

Anyone who threatens Kovalenko that Gerhard knows about gets the full force of this ex-Secret Service torturer's wrath. When Kovalenko visits Gertrude's cabin, it is the one time Gerhard is separated from his charge, since he is ordered to remain outside the royal cabin to make it look as though Kovalenko is still in there. Gerhard does not like Valentova, nor does he trust her; but it is his duty to protect only Kovalenko's life, not his morals or sexual health.

GRAVES, KOVALENKO'S BUTLER

Britain produces the best butlers in the world, and they are much in demand amongst Europe's royal houses. This is how Graves comes to be working for Kovalenko and has done for the past 10 years. Graves knows *everything* about his employer: how hot his bath must be, how he likes a martini mixed, how long it takes him

to recover after coitus. While Gerhard is in charge of the prince's security, Graves is in charge of his life and is responsible for everything regarding getting Kovalenko through each day.

He despises the actress, but it is not his place to get in the way of his master's wishes. He therefore tries to ensure Kovalenko's activities are never discovered. When something goes wrong, Graves fixes it. He *knows* people who know *people*. There is no one more dependable on the *Empress Katerina*, including the Agents.

Graves suspects that Valentova has some form of ulterior motive and has, in his personal time, been investigating her background. He therefore knows she is engaging in a romantic liaison with Pieter Klass, who has a murky reputation as a spy and interrogator for the Prussian Secret Police. Of course, Graves has no reason to make any of this known, unless it absolutely is necessary to protect Kovalenko's honour and that of the royal family.

In the event of an episode, Graves and Gerhard take charge of Kovalenko's well-being, working quickly to get him away from the public eye and back to his cabin to rest. Gerhard takes it upon himself to warn anyone who might have thoughts about making trouble that he will see to it personally that such troublemakers lose their ability to eat solid food ever again.

RUPRECHT VOLYINSKI, HIGH MINISTER FOR TRADE AND INDUSTRY

A master political operator, Volyinski is young and ambitious. He is the youngest High Minister in the government, having won the coveted Trade and Industry office from under the nose of Bohdan, who was originally earmarked for the job. Volyinski has his sights set on the very highest office: securing trade and export concessions for the Chinese markets, currently under British control, will be a sure way of gaining it.

Sadly, Volyinski has a dark secret: an addiction to heroin that began when he was an economics undergraduate at the University of Belgrade. He has managed to keep his addiction a secret, but his days are numbered. The heroin he has brought with him for this trip is far stronger than his usual supply and he will die of an overdose during the course of the flight. His secretary, Gleb, knows of Volyinski's addiction and is determined to keep it a secret to prevent shame for Volyinski's family. When he discovers Volyinski's body, he immediately implies that this must be murder by poison. (Gleb finds and hides some of Volyinski's heroin and syringes, but fails to hide all the paraphernalia, which can be found by the Agents using appropriate skills.) Of course, the scapegoat for the 'murder' has to be Crimean separatists. Volyinski has been critical of their activities, and as the forthcoming trade negotiations would threaten jobs in Crimea, the separatist movement would stand to gain much through his murder (even though he is not a target and poison is not part of the separatist MO).

Before he dies, Volyinski is guarded but affable. He spends time briefing Kovalenko, but also gets into icy debates with Bohdan. If engaged in conversation, Volyinski never replies with a straight answer to a straight question: he is the consummate politician. Someone with medical knowledge, or a heroin addict, can make an Insight, Medical, or Dependency roll to notice that there's something not quite right with him. If the Agents engage him in conversation, Volyinski always brings the topic around to politics, wanting to hear opinions, provide his own, and generally maintain a subject that interests him, rather than others.

VOLODYMYR BOHDAN, HIGH MINISTER FOR TRANSPORTATION

Bohdan is a tall, ageing politician who has always strived for high office and come up short. High Minister for Transportation is as far as he will get: he knows it and Volyinski knows it – despite the fact that Bohdan has substantially more experience in government. The reason is simple: Bohdan is distinctly unlikable. He is a natural pessimist and an obsessive pedant, rushes to incorrect judgements, and has a talent for making people dislike him. There's something unsavoury in his appearance and demeanour, and he views anyone outside the political class with disdain. He hero worships royalty and is visibly pumped with pride whenever Kovalenko addresses him, but it doesn't take much to recognise someone who is innately self-serving. Whenever the Archduke suffers an episode, Bohdan is amongst the first to rush to his aid, always trying to elbow Volyinski out of the way.

Bohdan is looking for ways to engineer damage to Volyinski's reputation. Discovery of the heroin addiction would be perfect. He knows better than to sabotage the trade talks, but something personal about Volyinski, something to undermine his credibility, would be ideal.

The rivalry between him and Volyinski is well known and palpable – even to outsiders. Bohdan is quick to put-down Volyinski's ideas and always backs (or agrees with) anyone who disagrees with the Trade Minister. Volyinski's death comes as a shock to Bohdan, but he takes this opportunity to step into Volyinski's shoes, asking Kovalenko to name him Acting Trade Minister for the purposes of these negotiations, hoping to be formally declared to the post on return to Kiev. A weakened Kovalenko naturally agrees.

Bohdan is having an affair with Klara Klym, his secretary. It is a mutual arrangement for sex and nothing more. Klym is not devotedly loyal, but neither would she see Bohdan's plans fail: there is a certain degree of respect for his skills, even if his personality is found wanting.

Bohdan snubs the Agents unless he is engaged on his favourite topics: transportation logistics, transport efficiency, rail and air timetables, and the success of the airship Programmeme. He is almost completely incapable of small talk.

Gertrude Valentova, Film Star and Kovalenko's lover

The star of epics 'Petrov the Great', 'Baboushka', 'Gone With The Mistral', and most recently 'Kleopatra' (a Ukrainian-American coproduction, with Ford Harrison as Marc Anthony), Gertrude Valentova is every inch the movie star diva. She is used to getting her own way, and if she doesn't, everyone suffers – either with violent temper tantrums or icy silences and sulks that can last days. When told her preferred brand of moisturiser was unavailable, she refused to leave her trailer on the set of 'Kleopatra' until some was located and shipped over. This took two weeks and cost over 2 million roubles in lost time. Ms. Valentova did not emerge from her trailer once; even her meals had to be brought to her.

She has had many male and female lovers, and Kovalenko is her latest, most aristocratic conquest. Naturally, it must remain a secret (for now – Gertrude does not care about the likely scandal; she simply loves the illicit nature of the liaison and the disruption it will cause when it does become public). She badgered Kovalenko into securing passage on the airship for her and for an audience with England's king, and then insisted that a film crew be allowed to document the voyage.

Throughout the journey, she tries to keep a restrained distance from Kovalenko, but they are frequently in the same room. Their real time together is in her cabin at night, but before that she flirts shamelessly with as many male passengers as she can, which is guaranteed to make Kovalenko jealous (not that he can do anything about it, and Gertrude makes it up to him with much enthusiasm).

Gertrude, like Volyinski, has a drug habit, her choice of substance being cocaine rather than heroin, but she will try anything and, if she can get her hands on some of Volyinski's heroin, she'll snort a little, simply to see what it is like.

Another secret Ms. Valentova has is that she is an unwitting Disruptor pawn. The ranking Disruptor knight on this parallel, one Pieter Klass of the Prussian Secret Service, is known to the Valhalla Programme as 'Loki'. He recruited her when she was a bit-part actress, paying for elocution and acting lessons, and then securing parts for her with a succession of top-notch film directors. Klass is a psychic and has recently lodged a Thought Implant into Valentova's mind that will have her activate a personal explosive device, hidden in a powder compact (a recent gift), when in the presence of King Alfred, killing everyone present in the room. Valentova does not know her role in this terrible plot, and it only activates when King Alfred speaks to her directly, but the Thought Implant can be detected by any other suitable psychic. If Alfred dies, Europe is plunged into war.

This deadly powder compact makes frequent appearances during the flight. Valentova is always adjusting her makeup, and the compact appears so she can touch-up her foundation, delicately checking her appearance in the mirror and dabbing at her cheeks and neck with the soft, cotton pad. The compact is sterling silver and carries an exquisite pattern engraved on the lid: a pair of swans wrapped in an embrace. Inside the lid is an inscription: 'Silver pictures move so slow when you are not the star'. It is clear the compact is new, but it requires significant technical expertise to discover the circuitry hidden inside both the lid and body of the case. It is highly advanced, and a reactant held within the case, coupled with the cosmetic powder, forms a highly explosive compound. On being complimented by King Alfred, the Thought Implant compels Valentova to reach into her purse, remove the compact, twist the lid a full 360 degrees to prime the contents, and then open it. Primed, it explodes on opening, creating a blast causing 3d6 damage to 1d4 locations rolled on 1d10+10 to everyone within a 2-metre radius, falling by 1d6 damage for each metre beyond.

Needless to say, Valentova knows nothing of the terrible secret she carries, although under some form of psychic interrogation, the memories of Klass/Loki planting the mind probe can be resurfaced, although this should be a very difficult task to accomplish.

Valentova remembers the Agents from the Trans-Siberian Express, and, unless they did something to upset her on that voyage, she is both amused and genuinely pleased to see them again, remarking on the coincidence of them being passengers on a luxury vessel once more.

Irena Lazarev

Valentova's personal assistant, Irena, is never far away from her employer, although she keeps a cool distance unless she has to intervene for some reason. She is brutally efficient and has a crush on her employer; no one gets to Valentova without Irena knowing about it. She disapproves of the affair with Kovalenko and uses his 'episodes' to warn Valentova of the dangerous game she is playing. She also knows the powder compact is brand new and a gift from Klass – although she does not know its true nature.

Irena tries to devote at least a couple of hours a day to clerical work and uses short hand. As she handles Valentova's correspondence, forging Valentova's writing and signature is consequently a Very Easy task for her.

Depending on how the Agents conduct themselves, Irena can be an ally or enemy – but she always places Valentova's needs first. She may even be suspicious of the coincidence of the characters being aboard the airship and, if the characters give her cause to be an enemy, she may brief Kommander Gerhard against them.

Wilhelm Gleb, Secretary to Volyinski

Gleb is a middle-aged civil servant with a stooped posture, thinning hair, failing eyesight, but an encyclopaedic knowledge of politics, government, policy, and social etiquette. As Volyinski's secretary (and an old family friend), Gleb is party to most secrets of government and also Volyinski's heroin habit. Gleb is intending to intervene more directly once the trade negotiations are complete, arranging for Volyinski to attend a private clinic in Vienna where he can receive the treatment needed for this addiction. Until then, Gleb watches Volyinski carefully and, when the inevitable happens and the politician overdoses, Gleb cleans up the mess and directs the blame elsewhere, implying the overdose is actually 'murder' by poison.

Despite his short-sightedness, Gleb is a canny operator and political fixer. Blaming Volyinski's death on Crimean separatists is the obvious thing to do, and in preparations for this voyage, Gleb was interested to learn that Maksim Olesko, the senior engineer aboard the *Katerina*, has separatist leanings (although Gleb could not establish any direct links with separatist agents or cells). On discovering Volyinski's death, Gleb does the following:

- Takes all the drug paraphernalia from Volyinski's cabin and temporarily hides it in his own.
- Arranges Volyinski's room to make it appear as though there has been a brief struggle of some kind.
- While attention is elsewhere, Gleb sneaks to the engineering locker used by Olesko where he places the syringe, rubber piping, and sachets of heroin.
- At an opportune moment, lets it be known that Olesko has separatist connections and that a murder made to look like a suicide or an accident is a favoured tactic of the Crimean terrorists. He suggests the crew quarters be searched as a routine precaution.

Bohdan and Klym are suspicious of Gleb's story, but lacking any other form of proof, cannot come up with any alternative suggestions. It goes without saying that, as a professional civil servant, Gleb is a consummate liar, and his reputation as a stringently honourable man means he is even more plausible, no matter how outlandish the accusations may be. And it is all done calmly, diffidently, and with assuredness.

KLARA KLYM, SECRETARY TO BOHDAN (AND HIS MISTRESS)

While Bohdan is unlikeable to most, his secretary, Kara Klym, can see his more positive qualities: namely, ruthless efficiency, single-minded dedication to power, and a forcefulness in the bedroom that she appreciates. They work as a close-knit pair, Klym's administrative capabilities ensuring Bohdan is always well informed and able to argue coherently. She takes pride in this and sees herself as the architect of Bohdan's ambitions. She hates Volyinski because the young upstart secured the position Bohdan should have been given, so when Volyinski winds up dead, she is suspicious of Gleb's assertions, but finds everything works to Bohdan's favour and so is happy to help contribute to making Olesko look guilty.

She is disdainful of everyone else, especially the Agents. She does not like people from outside her political class and disdains those she does not know and is forced to spend time with. It is her task to ensure that no one hampers Borden's moves to secure power, once a vacuum appears following Volyinski's death.

MAKSIM OLESKO, SENIOR ENGINEER, CRIMEAN SEPARATIST SYMPATHISER

A middle-aged, small, but powerfully built man, Olesko is in charge of the smooth running of the airship's engines and systems. What he does not know about the *Empress Katerina* is not worth knowing. He is gruff and matter of fact, and hates slackers. His team of 12 engineers and mechanics fear and respect him in equal measure. He reports directly to Captain Mors and his chief concern is the smooth running of the *Katerina*; he loves the airship like a wife or daughter, and he would never do anything to harm it or those who fly in her.

Yet it is true that Olesko has sympathies with the Crimean separatists. Born in the Crimea, he witnessed the brutal put-downs of local people by the Imperial Army during the food riots of 1974. He knows that Empire cares nothing for Crimea, and he does not trust politicians like Bohdan and Volyinski or royals like Kovalenko. However, Olesko is not an active terrorist: he watches and observes, and intends to report what he sees to those who run the Crimean Resistance once the airship returns to Kiev. This means that whenever he gets the chance, he finds his way 'above decks', where he checks piping, pressure gauges, and so on, carefully observing the goings on. This is how Gleb knows to target Olesko for the blame of Volyinski's death; it is also how Olesko witnesses one of Kovalenko's psychotic episodes (and perhaps even his attraction to the actress), information the separatists will find most useful for future blackmail purposes.

If any harm befalls the airship, Olesko is essential to fixing it. He and his team keep the thing aloft, so ensuring he does not become an isolated or resentful figure is crucial.

OLGA RUSLANA, HEAD OF SECURITY/UKRAINIAN SECRET SERVICE

Reporting to Captain Mors, Ruslana is tall, blond, friendly, but very perceptive and highly efficient at her job. She knows full well that Olesko has separatist leanings, but she also knows he has never nor would ever compromise his duties. She has conducted research into almost everyone aboard the *Katerina*, with the exception of the Agents, so she is very suspicious and wary of them. She takes time to question them (using her charm and easy nature), looking for weaknesses and inconsistencies in stories. When Olesko is blamed for murdering Volyinski, Ruslana puts forward that the Agents might equally be culpable; after all, who really knows them? Where have they come from? Olesko can be explained, but the Agents cannot.

If any violence breaks out on the airship, Ruslana and her team of six security personnel deal with matters quickly. They are armed with rubber-coated truncheons, are equipped with handcuffs, and can access the weapons locker arming themselves with .38 service revolvers. Ruslana also has a pair of long, sharp pins that she wears in her hair, capable of inflicting 1d4 impaling damage.

Anna Thames, First Officer, Empress Katerina

47.60.67's version of Anna Thames found in the *Luther Arkwright* rulebook, she is the First Officer of the *Katerina*, supporting Captain Mors and directly responsible for crew discipline and morale. She is not a Valhalla Agent, but has some psionic capabilities that would most certainly be useful to the Valhalla Programme. She is able to sense psychic energy but is unaffected beyond being able to detect its presence. She is able to determine that Kovalenko's episodes are, perhaps, being triggered by some form of psychic signature, but she cannot explain how she knows this.

For the most part, Anna remains in the Control Car attending to her duties. At dinner, she is seated at the Agents' table, but she is not one for small talk. If asked about the airship and flying, she suddenly comes alive: this is what Anna lives for, and it is obvious that she is a dedicated and capable crew member who will secure her own airship command in the future.

Gregor Fedotik, Head of Hospitality

The gregarious Gregor Fedotik is a consummate host master and entertainer. He knows every art to guarantee service is impeccable, to time, meticulous, and refined. He runs his team of cooks, waiters, and bar staff like a small army. A pocket watch is always in his palm, timing every preparation to the last second. If a mood starts to flag, he is the first to find a way to enliven it. If a guest needs something at 4am in the morning, he ensures they have it. Olesko might keep the ship moving, Anna Thames keep it on course, Captain Mors keep it under control, but Fedotik keeps everything lubricated and sumptuous.

A lofty, well-proportioned man, with a pencil moustache and lustrous black hair, Fedotik moves everywhere at a brisk pace, watch in hand, seeing everything. No speck of dust eludes him; no crease in the serving livery can be too sharp. If guests are not served precisely as they should be, glasses not refilled, dishes not removed, he appears almost as if teleported there to utter the feared words to the waiter: 'Sir. A word. Now. In private.' These indicate a verbal assault from Fedotik that is as ferocious as a machinegun burst or a slap from a scorned lover. To the guests, Fedotik is efficiency on legs, and even the capable Graves recognises the immense talents a man like Fedotik possesses.

Yet in his cabin at night, Fedotik weeps into his pillow. He can never be good enough. Some detail is always lacking. Compliments from guests mask their contempt. His staff hate him. He is a hair's breadth from failure. No one must know these fears. No one must sense them. They are his, and his alone.

Captain Mors, Captain of the Empress Katerina

One of the most experienced pilots of the Ukrainian fleet, Mors was first a fighter pilot who distinguished himself in the wars against Prussia in the 1960s. Afterwards, he moved into civil aviation and excelled at operating the huge airships that ply the world's skies. *Empress Katerina* is his finest commission; the most prestigious of airships, grandest lady of the sky. Mors lives to be aboard her. The air is his home.

A first-rate captain, Mors quietly and diligently makes sure everything runs smoothly. He has planned the route to London so that the airship can take in some of the greatest sights Europe has to offer from the air. His crew is hand-picked so he knows he has the very best flyers in the whole of the Ukrainian empire. Any problem or issue is met with calm efficiency, and Mors relies on Anna Thames, an officer as good as any he has ever met, to be his back-up when he must deal with the tiresome passengers. If he could, Mors would ditch all of the passengers over the English Channel and fly east with just his crew, simply revelling in the beauty of flight and the world unfolding below, but he is a dutiful man who must get his passengers to their destination safely, and so that is what he will do.

Mors rarely interacts with the passengers. He hosts them at dinner and has arranged an hour for people to come aboard the Control Car, but that is all the interaction he wants and needs. He spends most of time on the flight deck or in his study, leaving the tedious business of dealing with people to Anna Thames and Ruslana. They are far better suited to it.

Otto Schumann, Film Director

Schumann, short, clipped, broad, monocle-wearing, is an auteur. He lives for his art. Everything is a performance and, if it is not, he makes it one. He has directed the finest motion pictures in history, and if the critics disagree, that is because they are imbeciles. Only the most intelligent, most discerning, and most sensitive recognise the true genius of his directorial style, his impeccable compositions, his lighting, his dialogue, his vision.

Schumann strides around the airship as though commanding it. He barks orders at his camera operator like a lord to his slaves. He demands perfection when establishing a shot and, when it inevitably falls short of his needs, he takes over the operation of camera and sound, leaving the long-suffering technicians to fume by silently whilst he runs the show.

This documentary of the flight to London might be a simple slice of luxury travel, but Schumann intends to shoot the film with the same intensity he brought to his 4-hour epic 'Gone With The Mistral', the film that catapulted Gertrude Valentova to international stardom as Skarlet Fevre, heroine of the Ukraine-Prussian wars of the 19th Century. His camera never stops rolling, and at night, he edits the earliest footage, creating a masterpiece of cinema verite. Capturing the emotional breakdown of an Archduke and the exposing of a murderous rebel will merely add to the intensity of his finished work. In the odd moments where is not directing, operating the camera, kissing Valentova's hand, or editing, Schumann is practising his acceptance speech for the next Oskars ceremony, where he expects to sweep the honours board.

Schumann is accompanied by Lutz, his put-upon cameraman; Brahms, a sound technician; and Liszt, the lighting and makeup technician. All three must put up with contradictory instructions as well as Schumann's tantrums, domineering manner, and ridiculous perfectionism. Lutz, Brahms, and Liszt rarely say anything and simply try to stay out of trouble. If the Agents show them any sympathy or kindness, they won't forget it and may even be valuable allies for them later, speaking on their behalf or showing them footage that may be important or useful.

The director comes with a great array of camera equipment, including a travelling editing suite with a small viewing screen, splicing tools, and tiny speaker for the audio. This too may prove useful.

EVENTS

The scenario consists of several set events. How the Agents and Non-Player Characters react and respond drives the scenario forward. Games Masters should add additional events of their own devising, if they wish.

EMBARKATION, COCKTAILS & LAUNCH

There is much excitement at the Kiev Airship Fields where the *Empress Katerina* waits to launch. Bands play, the crowds are happy, and a carnival atmosphere has everyone in a good mood. The crew has been aboard for a few hours, making preparations for the passengers. Boarding is conducted via a long, sloping covered gangway that attaches to the passenger quarters within the canopy. Luggage is handled by porters and elevator equipment, but passengers must ascend the shallow stairs themselves. The Archduke's contingent boards first, Kovalenko pausing at the foot of the gangplank to wave to the gathered throng with his flamboyant, feather-covered tricorn hat. Next, the politicians, and then Valentova and Schumann, the director filming the scenes. The crowd roars with adoration as Valentova blows kisses to her fans, taking a little too long to begin the trip up the gangway and causing an official to ask her to hurry along. Finally, the Agents board, and by this time, the crowd has subdued a little, the VIPs having disappeared from view.

A crew member shows the Agents to their cabins. A card in a flowing script invites everyone to a cocktail reception on the Promenade. This is a chance to mingle should the Agents wish to take it.

A six-strong chamber ensemble plays discreet background music whilst the passengers arrive on the Promenade for drinks. Kovalenko is present already and has exchanged his dress uniform for a dapper lounge suit. He stands smoking a cigar and watching the crowds below through the huge panorama windows, waving now and again. Others stand around drinking, and at the bar, liveried wait staff prepare whatever cocktails the Agents want to order, while Fedotik watches from nearby. The cocktails are expertly made and of excellent quality.

Valentova is not present at the cocktail reception, but Schumann is, and he and his cameraman film the proceedings from one end of the Promenade deck. Anna Thames and Ruslana represent the flight crew, and both of them greet the Agents when they arrive for the party.

If anyone tries to approach Kovalenko, Commander Gerhard intervenes, curtly explaining that the Archduke prefers his own space at this time.

After 30 minutes or so, Captain Mors announces over the internal public address system (broadcast externally to the crowd) that the *Empress Katerina* is ready to depart. The engines have been at dull background thrum so far, but now there is a steady increase in noise and vibration as the power is increased. The crowd roars as the mooring lines are released, and the airship rises slowly, steadily, and gracefully into afternoon sky, Mors steering a curving course to gain altitude, maximising viewing opportunities for passengers and the observers on the ground. The genteel music gives way to a stirring melody as the airship gains height, and there are cheers all round as *Empress Katerina* finally heads on a westward course towards Britain.

The gathered passengers remain for around an hour before retiring cabins for some privacy. The politicians conclude whatever discussions they were having; Volyinski remains on the Promenade and spends around 20 minutes briefing Kovalenko on some of the points for the trade deal. Kovalenko looks bored and his gaze keeps flitting towards the entrance where he hopes Valentova might make an appearance. She does not. After a while, Kovalenko excuses himself and Gerhard leaves with him. Bohdan departs soon afterwards, and Volyinski remains on the Promenade sipping a martini and watching the view. He is happy to engage in discussion and small talk if the Agents wish it. Ruslana remains on the promenade drinking mineral water and simply watching everyone. The mood is calm and polite.

Volyinski, if approached, is happy to talk about the flight in general, the trade mission, to a certain extent ('It's vital we gain access to China. Britain has kept it a trophy for far too long'), but is always guarded and never goes too far. Successful Formidable Insight rolls, or Hard Dependency rolls (for drug-dependent Agents) note that Volyinski shakes and sweats a little; he needs a fix soon, but is trying to project as calm and casual an image as possible. When the opportunity arises, he makes his excuses and returns to his cabin.

Dinner

At 6pm, Fedotik announces over the public address that dinner is shortly to be served. This is the cue for everyone to dress. Dinner is a white-tie affair, meaning a highly formal, several-course meal. Arrangements have been made for the Agents to have appropriate attire packed in their luggage, which is by now safely stowed in their cabins.

There are several tables prepared for dinner, which consists of several sittings. For the Agents, the table arrangements are as follows:

Table 1
Captain Mors, Archduke Kovalenko, Gertrude Valentova, Irena Lazarev, Gleb, and Volyinski

Table 2
Ruslana, Bohdan, Klym, Schumann, and his film crew

Table 3
Anna Thames, Gerhard, and the Agents.

Volyinski does not appear for dinner. Gleb waits for a little while and goes to check on him. He says he heard a snore from Volyinski's cabin and pronounces the man simply tired after too much work. At this stage, Gleb is telling the truth; unbeknownst to Gleb, Volyinski is dying, but is not yet dead.

Valentova makes a grand entrance. She is dazzling in a low-cut gown, a string of diamonds around her neck, and a pair of elbow-length black gloves. Everyone stands for her entrance, and Kovalenko holds her seat for her. It is clear he is besotted with her beauty, but she studiously ignores him, focussing on the captain. She makes polite replies to his questions, but eschews any attempts at familiarity.

Dinner is a five-course affair: soup, fish course, meat course, dessert, cheese board. Pleasant music plays from the band, and the guests engage in various topics of conversation. At the Agents' table, Anna Thames is very interested in the varied backgrounds the Agents may have and asks lots of pertinent questions. She answers questions about the airship as far as she can, but becomes tight lipped if the questions become personal or too technical.

Agents making successful Hard Perception rolls notice a couple of things:

- Anna Thames suddenly pauses, fork half way to her mouth, and winces, as though struck by a sharp pain. She shakes her head, assures everyone she is fine, and continues with her conversation. She has just felt the psychic emanations that Valentova's Thought Implant gives out – and shortly before the first of Kovalenko's episodes is triggered.
- A figure dressed in overalls (Olesko), appears briefly at the doorway to the dining room. He does not remain. He is carrying a clipboard and is engaged on a round of checks of various gauges. (He should not be in this section of the airship at all, but could not help himself from catching a glance of Valentova.)
- Archduke Kovalenko suddenly, half way through the meat course, rises to his feet. He is sweating, and his eyes are wide. Roll 1d6 for a random episode (see page 90). Gerhard almost vaults across tables to be at Kovalenko's side. Valentova is alarmed at whatever incident takes place and physically backs away; Ruslana frowns, watches carefully, and then calmly leaves the dining room to secure the area against entry. She dismisses the band whilst securing the area.

Precisely *what* happens depends very much on the nature of the episode. If Kovalenko becomes argumentative, he loudly pronounces that everyone on board the airship are 'fucking imbeciles and separatist traitors! To hell with all of you! I see what you are! Do you take me for a moron?'

If he fixates on one particular individual, randomly choose one of the Agents. From across the room, Kovalenko glares at the selected Agent and screams: 'What did you call me? Say that again you piece of shit! I DARE you!' and starts yelling for his cavalry sabre so he can gut this impudent swine. Dependency rolls from the Agents are certainly needed here, and it takes Gerhard and Bohdan to prevent the Archduke from launching himself at whomever he's targeted – but it may be interesting to have some form of engagement or stand-off. Graves appears shortly afterwards (he takes his meals in his cabin) and he guides the Archduke out of the dining room. Kovalenko calms when he sees Graves, and becomes much calmer as he exits the area (and gets out of Valentova's range of effect).

This episode casts a huge pall over proceedings. Once Kovalenko is out of the way, Fedotik appears and announces that dessert, cheese, and aperitifs are instead to be served in the lounge and everyone should accompany him so that the staff can clean up.

What happens after depends on how the Agents react to Kovalenko's outburst and who they talk to:

Valentova – clearly very upset by the whole thing. She is shaken and drinks quite heavily for the rest of the evening. The more she drinks, the more flirtatious she becomes, but after a couple of hours is encouraged to retire for the night by Irena.

Irena – she is stoic and remains close to Valentova. She knows that her mistress is sleeping with the Archduke and now fears for Gertrude's safety. Otherwise, she has nothing to say. She takes some pleasure in putting her mistress to bed; Gertrude is most beautiful when she sleeps under Irena's loving eye.

Bohdan – remarks at this most odd turn of events but reasons that it is simply tiredness and, perhaps, altitude sickness. He does go to check on Kovalenko after about an hour and conveys to everyone that he is 'quite calm and resting'.

Klym – sits quietly in a corner with a cognac, smoking a French cigarette. She watches Bohdan and, when he decides to retire for the night, leaves shortly after.

Gerhard – remains with Kovalenko on guard outside his door.

Ruslana – watches the Agents carefully, but also watches the rest of the room. She asks the Agents what they made of this incident and notes that it might be a sensible idea not to reveal anything of what they saw to anyone. Ever. All with a glittering smile.

Gleb – Is happy to share a few drinks with the Agents, but is tight-lipped about this outburst. After an hour or so, he excuses himself and retires for the night.

Anna Thames and Captain Mors – after checking on the Archduke, they both return to their duties. They do not gossip.

Fedotik – suggests a game of charades and begins the proceedings by miming one of Valentova's films 'Gone With The Mistral', should any enterprising Games Master wish to try it out on the Agents.

By 11pm, just about everyone has retired for the night. The Agents can do whatever they wish. The night crew for both the control car and engineering takes over the shift until dawn. Anna Thames is in charge of the helm.

NIGHT TERRORS

At about 1am, Kovalenko, recovered from his episode and fortified by several vodkas, decides to pay Gertrude a visit. Against Gerhard's advice, he steals round to her cabin so that they can be together. Perhaps one of the Agents hears something that attracts their attention.

At 1.30am, another episode is triggered, this time while Kovalenko and Gertrude are in the throes of lovemaking. This is another randomly determined episode (but make it a different one to the episode at dinner), and is accompanied by a loud scream from Gertrude as Kovalenko abruptly ceases what he was doing and is overcome by whatever the episode's outcome is. The scream is loud enough to wake all but the heaviest sleepers, and it is obvious where the screams are coming from.

Gerhard has this Walther PPK drawn when the Agents arrive outside Valentova's door. Irena bangs frantically on the walls of the cabin calling to make sure Gertrude is unharmed. The other guests, with the exception of Volyinski, are all awoken and come to see what the alarm is. Once again, Kovalenko needs to be calmed, restrained, and led away from Gertrude's cabin. But this time, the man is naked – as is a very distressed Gertrude – and there can be no denying what has been taking place.

If Kovalenko is violent, he tries to flee the cabin and fight anyone who gets in his way. Only Graves can really calm him. Gerhard does whatever is necessary to protect Kovalenko's life, and that may mean taking action against the Agents.

Gleb checks on Volyinski and discovers his death. He uses the confusion surrounding Kovalenko's episode to gather together and then hide the drug paraphernalia. He does not make the death public. There is a possibility that an astute Agent notices his movements if in the right place at the right time. Otherwise, the death is revealed later.

Ruslana arranges for a sedative to be brought for Gertrude, and Irena stays with the distraught actress for the rest of the night. Kovalenko is returned to his cabin and Gerhard ensures no one gains access to him.

The other guests head for the lounge, where Fedotik mixes some very stiff drinks for everyone and tries to lift the mood with some humorous anecdotes of his time as the maître d' at a very exclusive Swiss hotel. Anna Thames comes to investigate, having been alerted to another incident involving the Duke, and converses with Ruslana for several minutes. Should anyone eavesdrop, they agreed to radio ahead to London and warn that Kovalenko is 'unwell'. Anna suggests making a landing in Paris so that a surgeon can be found, or even turning back. They decide it would be a good idea to seek Volyinski's opinion on this. Ruslana calls over one of the Agents and asks if they would be good enough to rouse Mr. Volyinski as there is a very important matter and they need his opinion. This is, of course, merely a way of having the Agents discover Volyinski's death. If Games Masters prefer, Ruslana herself goes to rouse Volyinski and makes the discovery, but her instincts are to keep this secret from everyone save Bohdan, Gleb, and Klym.

DEATH AT ALTITUDE

Volyinski's cabin is unlocked. Inside, the politician is lying on his bunk, partially dressed, very pale, eyes open, and vomit staining his chest, the pillow, and sheets. It is clear he is dead. His arms are by his side, but checking them reveals the track marks familiar to anyone who is an addict. This is one thing Gleb cannot cover-up, even though he has hidden the syringes and heroin Volyinski brought with him.

A trained physician can easily conclude this is an overdose (though not the type of drug used) and there is considerable surprise that a high-standing politician would be an addict. Ruslana simply shrugs: 'I've seen much stranger things, and politicians are always under some kind of pressure. It does not surprise me at all.'

Searching Volyinski's room does not uncover anything suspicious and certainly nothing drug-related. His desk has papers related to the trade talks stacked neatly to one side, and his briefcase contains more papers relating to matter of state. Gleb takes charge of all of these, later on liaising with Bohdan at the latter's insistence.

When Gleb, Klym, and Bohdan are informed of the death, all three appear shocked. Successful opposed rolls of Deceit for each versus an interrogating Agent's Insight reveals the following:

◦ Gleb feigns shock, but is clearly shaken by the discovery (mainly because he wanted to be the one to make it). He knows something.
◦ Klym is genuinely surprised, but there's something in her reaction that indicates she has little sympathy.
◦ Bohdan is shocked, but moves quickly to take charge. 'The trade talks with London must continue. I will assume charge. I know Volyinski's positions on all trade matters. We will not fail. But I must inform the Duke and send word back to Kiev.'

Anna Thames agrees to have communications sent back and asks Bohdan to draft a brief statement.

At this point, Gleb makes the observation that, perhaps, this was *not* a self-inflicted overdose, but done deliberately by a third party. He notes that there is no evidence of Volyinski owning any drug materials, and there are plenty of people who would want the trade talks to fail. 'Have we a British spy aboard?' he muses, and if any of the Agents are British, or have British accents, he glances in their direction. 'Mr. Volyinski was a superb politician, and not the sort of man to risk such an important round of talks for the sake of a needle! I know he had more self-control than that. No. I think there is more to this. I think we need to be considering the possibility of murder. He was always a staunch opponent of the Crimea separatists.'

Captain Mors is informed of all that has happened, and a hasty conference between himself, the politicians, and Ruslana takes place behind closed doors. If an Agent manages to somehow eavesdrop or even gain a place at the table, Bohdan argues strenuously for the talks to proceed, no matter who has died or how troubled the Archduke might be. He demands that Ruslana investigate everyone aboard who might have even the slightest connection with the Crimean separatists or have a background that is not utterly pristine and corroborated. She agrees, and so, for the rest of the night and until breakfast, she questions all the passengers privately, with the exception of the Archduke.

Each Agent has to convince Ruslana of their innocence. She asks the following questions. The Agents answer by making a Deceit roll at the noted grade, opposed by Ruslana's Insight:

1. 'Where were you between the hours of 4pm and 7pm, and 11pm and 1am? Who can corroborate this?' *(Deceit: Standard)*
2. 'Are you a member of, or sympathetic to, the Crimean secessionists?' *(Deceit: Standard)*
3. 'Are you a member of, or have you worked for, the British Secret Service or a similar covert organisation?' *(Deceit: Formidable)*
4. 'I know that you're hiding something; your background seems off to me. Would you care to come clean now? Tell me what you know or how you were involved and maybe I can help you…' *(Deceit: Formidable)*

Failing questions 3 or 4 immediately places an Agent under suspicion. Ruslana orders a full search of the Agent's cabin and, if any weapons or Valhalla equipment are found, she has the Agent placed under arrest and confined to the cabin under armed guard, until the airship lands, where local police are called. She places two crew members armed with .38 pistols on the door and confiscates all personal possessions, save for essential clothes and toiletries.

If the Agent passes all four questions, Ruslana accepts the explanations and apologises for any inconvenience, but keeps the Agents under watch anyway.

The search is extended to crew lockers. Shortly after breakfast, one of Ruslana's crew members reports that a syringe, rubber tubing, and a quantity of powder have been found in the locker belonging to Maksim Olesko, Chief Engineer.

Ruslana and two armed crew members go to arrest Olesko. Everyone is ordered to remain where they are, but if the Agents want to follow, it is difficult to stop them. Olesko is just waking and preparing for his shift when Ruslana arrives. He panics. His separatist sympathies would spell a death sentence for him, so he resists. Using a wrench, he swings at the crew members and concusses one of them; he then charges past the others and runs into the depths of the airship's maintenance rigging and gantries. It would be insanely reckless to fire a gun in here: hitting a gas bag or piece of machinery would jeopardise the ship. Ruslana wants Olesko taken alive and she needs help. She asks the Agents and other stalwart passengers to aid them in a search.

If so, this entails a cat-and-mouse hunt around the interior of the airship. Olesko knows this place intimately. He can hide, ambush, and move far faster than anyone else. He is inevitably cornered, but not before he has fought for all he is worth with his huge, steel wrench. There are casualties, and all this violence makes Olesko seem more and more guilty, although he vehemently protests his innocence.

Captured, Olesko is interrogated. He was seen snooping around the passenger deck just before dinner the night before ('Maintenance checks! Do you think the passenger deck is immune from malfunctioning?'), and footage shot by Schumman, replayed on his portable editing unit, shows Olesko walking around near the dining room and Promenade, but there is nothing to show Olesko entering or leaving Volyinski's cabin. Gleb, Schumann, or Lutz, the cameraman, can draw people's attention to the existence of footage of Olesko in the vicinity on the previous evening, so it is worth examining the film on Schumann's portable editing equipment.

The politicians decide that Olesko is guilty or, at least, knows more than he is telling. Insight rolls from the Agents show that while he claims to be innocent of killing Volyinski, he is clearly guilty of supporting the separatists. Nevertheless, Ruslana has him cuffed and held, under guard, in the crew quarters until the return to Kiev.

But there is something else.

During dinner, Schumman had the camera running to capture proceedings. He has caught, on film, Archduke Kovalenko's outburst. There, on celluloid, is something very strange. A faint but visible silvery nimbus seems to enshroud both Valentova and Kovalenko. They were sitting at the same table, and this aura wraps around both their heads. Valentova is oblivious to all this in the lead-up to Kovalenko's episode, but once it starts, it seems to thicken around Valentova as she reels back in shock. As it intensifies, it moves with Kovalenko and only ceases when he either loses consciousness or is dragged away. The aura remains around Valentova but is fainter. If any other footage containing the actress is examined (and Schumann has plenty), the same aura is present – faint, but once one knows, clearly visible, unmistakable.

INVESTIGATING VALENTOVA

Following the events of the previous night, Valentova has refused to leave her cabin. What happened to the Archduke was distressing enough, but others witnessing it is mortifying to her. Attempts to see her or even reason with her are met with icy anger by Irena. Convincing either Valentova or Irena to speak is a Task requiring four rolls, each at Formidable against Insight, Influence (or Oratory), Customs (or Courtesy), and finally Willpower. A score of 100 convinces one of the two women to at least speak to the Agents. A higher score convinces both of the women to leave the cabin and take some air. Either way, there is an opportunity for further research.

If any Agent is psychic, the talents of Feel Emotions, Mind Probe, and Sense Danger reveal that Valentova, while not psychic herself, has undergone some form of psionic trauma in the not too distant past. Using Precognition shows a mental picture of a silver powder compact, a crown, and an explosion. Psychometry on the powder compact (which Valentova reluctantly produces on a successful Influence roll) discloses its past: that it was given to Valentova by a man named Klass, that Klass bears a striking resemblance to Loki, and that the compact itself contains some advanced technology and explosive compounds.

Valentova is exceedingly reluctant to speak of Pieter Klass. She knows he is an enemy of Ukraine and that he has a shady past. If pressed, she bursts into tears, Irena becomes outraged, and the Agents are dismissed. If treated gently and with kindness, Valentova is prepared to reveal a little of their liaison: 'He's just a friend...', 'He helped me get better parts...', '...the compact was a gift...', but she has no recollection of any psionic interference. Indeed, it requires deep hypnosis for her to recall Klass initiating the Thought Implant at all.

Should Kovalenko hear that Valentova is under any kind of investigation, he flies into a murderous rage. He emerges from his cabin mid-morning to smoke on the Promenade, under the watchful gaze of both Gerhard and Graves. He refuses to watch the film footage of the aura and threatens anyone who presents any kind of slur against Valentova with a flogging followed by a hanging.

The Agents may know by now that keeping the two of them apart is a good idea. Should Valentova and Kovalenko meet accidentally, or be brought together, a further episode strikes, this time more violent and more prolonged than the last – so much so that Kovalenko needs restraint by at least three people and must be confined to his cabin for the remainder of the journey.

If it is decided that Valentova is a Disruptor pawn, unwitting or otherwise, keeping her under any form of surveillance or arrest is difficult without Ruslana's approval and risks Kovalenko's wrath. Persuading Ruslana that Valentova is a danger is a further Task, requiring Formidable grade rolls against Customs, Influence, Insight, and a Passion (such as Loyalty to Valhalla). Curiously, Anna Thames is much more accepting of any story the Agents propose and can help convince Ruslana that there is something to what the Agents say, no matter how outlandish. Ruslana can therefore order the compact 'taken into protective custody' and recommend that Ms. Valentova remain in her cabin as a mere precaution against Kovalenko's 'illness'.

Ruslana can help with examining the compact too. Equipment can be brought from stores, and making Hard rolls against Mechanisms, Engineering, or an appropriate Science reveals that the compact is a small but powerful bomb. Disarming it requires a successful Demolitions roll, although it may simply be easier to lob the thing out of the airship altogether.

If Valentova (and the compact) are not revealed to be part of a Disruptor plan before the airship reaches London, then the event described in God Save The King, opposite, takes place.

Insurrection (Optional Event)

Olesko's fate is met with mixed reactions by the engineering crew. All of them are loyal to the Empire and they are shocked that Olesko might have had separatist views; but some, a handful, are more loyal to Olesko than they are to Ruslana, Mors, or any interfering politician. They cannot believe Olesko would murder someone, and a group of four engineers decide to break Olesko out of his quarters. Armed with wrenches, spanners, hammers, and other tools, they march on the guards at Olesko's door, beating them senseless. Perhaps shots are fired. It is a foolish move, because this is clearly mutiny, and mutiny aboard an airship carries the death penalty, but these men are so angry at Olesko's treatment, they are prepared to seize control of the airship and change course to somewhere to which they can escape – Ireland, perhaps, or northern Spain. Olesko demands reason, if he's able to, but these mutineers are sick of politicians making life difficult. The airship may therefore be plunged into a stand-off between the mutineers and the crew, with the Agents caught in the middle. The mutineers are outnumbered, of course, and Ruslana and Mors can command weapons to be broken out forcing their surrender. This makes for further complications, possible bloodshed, and is exactly the sort of tactic the Disruptors would delight in, perhaps causing the Agents to suspect even deeper foul play.

Bohdan's Gambit

With Volyinski dead and Kovalenko in a vulnerable state, Bohdan makes a play for power that could have devastating repercussions. Perhaps the Agents overhear the following conversation that takes place in the lounge among Bohdan, Kovalenko, Klym, and Gleb:

- Bohdan petitions Kovalenko to make him 'acting' Minister for Trade and Transportation. Kovalenko agrees.
- Bohdan, supported by Klym, but opposed by Gleb, argues that the trade agreements they have come to secure are too modest: Ukraine wants access to Chinese markets for life, not just ten years, as previously discussed by both sides. If they don't get this, Ukraine will side with Prussia on other matters important to the British Empire. Even Kovalenko thinks this is going too far.
- Bohdan argues that the British Empire has no intention of agreeing the terms that have already been discussed, that this is all a publicity stunt. Bohdan claims Volyinski knew this, but kept it secret because he was weak. Ukraine must make demands that go much further; it is the stronger power, has better ties with Prussia, and so Britain had better listen.

All these lines of thinking, if Bohdan is allowed to present them, could destabilise the delicate political process Volyinski and colleagues spent months building, alienate Britain, and cause Britain to increase taxes on Ukrainian goods and embargo Chinese exports to Ukraine. Tensions will mount and lead inevitably to war. Bohdan must somehow be stopped. Gleb and Klym might persuade Kovalenko to let them take the lead – Gleb on his own is not enough to prevent political disaster from happening.

Here is a chance for the Agents to intervene, with Gleb providing help. If Bohdan can be kicked out of the talks, with Gleb taking his place, the original plan prevails and all is well.

GOD SAVE THE KING

News of some of the events aboard the *Empress Katerina*, including Kovalenko's outbursts, have been radioed to London. The news has reached the government and King Alfred II himself has been made aware of the situation. Alfred is a sensitive and polite man. If Archduke Kovalenko is unwell, His Majesty will go to see him, rather than wait for the formal visit. He takes with him the young princesses Elizabeth and Diana, to meet this important ambassador, but also so they can meet a film star.

Among the flag-waving crowds gathered to welcome the airship is the King, his daughters, and his ministers. They intend to board the vessel, meet the crew, and see for themselves just how ill Kovalenko is. Naturally enough, Ms. Valentova must be presented to the King, and when he tells he how radiant she looks, or some other compliment, she reaches for her powder compact and blows the whole contingent sky-high. Unless the Agents can stop her or propel the King and his daughters to safety.

If Valentova's real part in all this is discovered, London can be forewarned so she never gains an audience with the King and disaster is averted.

CONCLUDING THE SCENARIO

A successful conclusion is the safe arrival of the airship in London, the survival of King Alfred when he greets the trade contingent and attempts to alienate Britain are thwarted. Valentova is unmasked as a Disruptor agent and neutralised – whatever form that takes. Unless the Thought Implant to kill Alfred is removed or dampened somehow, Kovalenko risks further episodes, and if one takes place in front of the King (insults or violent action), it is taken as a sign of aggression by the British and leads to an inevitable breakdown in political relations and a speedy decline into European war. Success therefore hinges on neutralising that Thought Implant – or preventing it from influencing Kovalenko – because even if the bomb in the powder compact is defused, the Thought Implant can still have an effect, even though Loki did not intend it that way.

Volyinski's death was, of course, an accident, and perhaps this can be proven by confronting Gleb and convincing everyone else. If so, Olesko is free from a murder accusation, but his separatist sympathies still condemn him. Perhaps the Agents can free him so that he is not executed as a traitor.

Or perhaps some other ending will emerge – one that cannot be anticipated by this narrative. There is only one way (or another) to find out....

AIRSHIP KEY

This is an Empress-class airship, the pride of the Ukrainian air fleet, alongside the *Empress Anna* and *Empress Olgana*. In design, she resembles the *Hindenburg* of many other parallels. Her statistics are as follow:

- Crew: 40 to 61 (for this voyage, the crew is about 40)
- Capacity: 50–72 passengers (for this voyage, the airship is far below usual capacity)
- Length: 245m
- Diameter: 41.18m
- Volume: 200,000 m3
- Powerplant: 4 × Yukorov diesel engines, 890 kW (1,200 HP) each

Luther Arkwright Vehicle Terms: See Dirigible on page 115 of the Luther Arkwright rulebook.

The *Katerina* lifts using helium, which the Ukrainians are rich in, owing to their dominion over Poland and certain parts of Russia. This makes the airship much, much safer than a hydrogen-based vessel, but also means its lift is less efficient and its payload reduced. The explosion of the US airship the *Richard Millhouse Nixon* in 1979, a hydrogen-lifted dirigible, put-paid to any further airships using hydrogen as a lifting gas.

The *Katerina* is built for luxury. Her passenger compartments are located inside the canopy rather than being slung in a gondola beneath, and they are spread over two decks, one above the other.

A DECK

The passenger deck contains the dining room, lounge, writing room, port and starboard Promenades, 8 single cabins (numbers 1 to 8 on the deck plan), and 17 double-berth cabins. The whole deck is heated from warm air forced from the engine bays around specially designed ducting built into the walls and floors. Pressure gauges are positioned at various points across the deck, and it is these Olesko purports to check on the evening he is spotted roaming the passenger quarters.

The decoration throughout is opulent and in the art deco style popular in the 1980s of this parallel. Sleek lines, sharp angles, and symmetrical patterns proliferate throughout the decor, and it feels thoroughly modern and expensive. Upholstery is Argentinian leather; walnut veneer adorns every table, chair leg, and dresser; and the paintings hanging on the walls are by Hockney, Talbot, and Sienkiewicz.

DINING ROOM

The dining room dominates the entire length of the port side of the passenger deck. It is 14 metres in length by 5 metres wide, and is decorated with paintings on silk wallpaper Sir Bryan Talbot of Britain. The furniture, upholstered in red leather, is

EMPRESS KATERINA

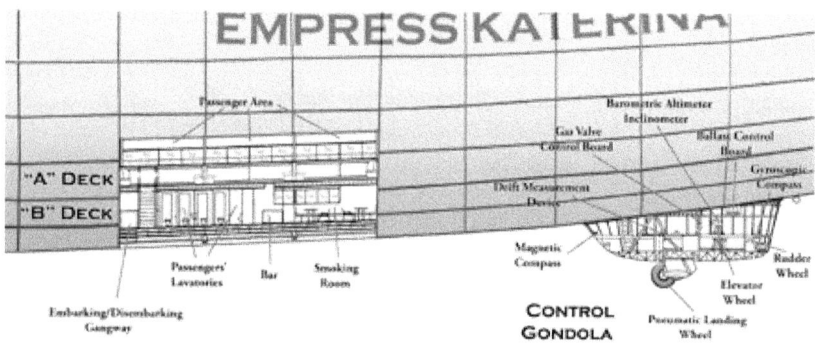

Cabins
1. Kovalenko
2. Gerhard
3. Volyinski
4. Bohdan
5. Graves
6. Schumann
7. Valentova
8. Lazarev
9. Gleb & Klym
10-17. Passengers

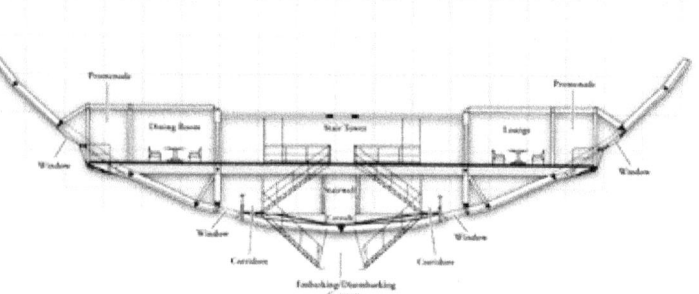

made from aluminium and designed by the famed and exclusive Swedish design house Ikea.

The dining room seats around 26 in relative comfort for dinner, and there are usually three sittings to make sure everyone is fed: 6pm, 7.30pm, and 9pm. Food is served from the serving pantry, which connects with the kitchen via an electric powered dumbwaiter. Passengers can opt to dine in their cabin if they wish, and if so, they can eat at any time between 6pm and 10pm. The lounge can also be quickly converted to dinner seating if needed

Breakfast and lunch are buffet service, with hotplates arranged along the Promenade on port and starboard sides of A Deck.

LOUNGE

On the starboard side are the lounge and reading/writing room. The lounge is approximately 10 metres long, and decorated with a huge, Avant Garde Sienkiewicz mural depicting the history of the Ukrainian Empire in colourful, comic-book format. A representation of the *Empress Katerina* dominates the scene, depicting her against a blazing orange and red sunset. The furniture, like that in the dining room, is Ikea aluminium, but upholstered in green leather.

READING/WRITING ROOM

The reading/writing room is quite small, equipped with Ikea desks and well stocked with handmade paper, fine quality ink, and a selection of monographed fountain pens made by Schaeffer of Prague. Passengers are allowed to keep a fountain pen as a souvenir of their voyage, and each passenger finds, in their cabin, a leather-bound blank notebook that is meant for them to record personal notes and feelings about their journey.

PASSENGER CABINS

Each cabin measures approximately 199 centimetres by 168 centimetres. Most are double berths (9–25 on the deck plan), equipped with bunks, while 8 of them are designed for VIP single occupancy. In each cabin, the walls and doors are made from a thin layer of lightweight foam, covered by a hardwearing cotton fabric. A cabin is decorated in one of three colour schemes —light blue, cream, or delicate green. In double-berth cabins, the lower berth is fixed in place and the upper berth can be folded against the wall when not in use.

> ### Buzby Murder
>
> The headline of a recent edition of The Times refers to a strange murder in central London. A Japanese industrialist holidaying with his family was posing next to the Trafalgar Square fountains for photographs. He was shot with a harpoon from a speargun when a man, dressed in a scuba outfit (complete with snorkel, mask, and flippers), suddenly (and inexplicably) emerged from the fountain, took aim, and fired. The scuba diver then fled into the stunned crowd, shedding flippers and mask, before disappearing in the direction of Charring Cross Station. Police have failed to find the murderer, although the snorkel was found abandoned close to a tobacconist's kiosk.

The single-berth cabins are actually identical, save for not having the additional bunk.

Each cabin is equipped with buttons to summon a steward, a small fold-down desk, and a washbasin made of lightweight white plastic (in the singles berths, it is porcelain, the only difference singles have from doubles) with hot and cold running water. There is a narrow closet covered with a curtain that can hold a limited number of garments. None of the cabins have toilet facilities; male and female toilets are available on the crew and facilities deck below, including a single shower, which provides only a very weak stream of water. None of the cabins have windows, which means passengers prefer the Promenade and lounges to spending too much time in their berths.

Cabin 1: Archduke Kovalenko

A single berth occupied by the Archduke. Only Graves and Gerhard are allowed in here. Both men keep a vigilant watch to ensure no one gets too near. The cabin is surprisingly spartan, aside from the Archduke's travelling trunk, which Graves manages. There are some papers (unread) in a briefcase related to the trade deal, but these are written in Russian and are merely talking points on high-level topics. There are some other notes on King Alfred and the Royal Family, and packed carefully in the trunk are gifts – four Faberge Eggs – for the King, Queen, and two Princesses.

Cabin 2: Gerhard

The bodyguard's cabin is neat and precise. A case is packed with Gerhard's civilian and military clothes, and hidden in a concealed compartment are two spare 9mm handguns and four clips of ammunition, plus a Mauser machine pistol with two clips. Gerhard is always armed with a concealable 9mm Walther PPK pistol, and these spares are in case he is ever disarmed, or needs to arm the Archduke and Graves.

Cabin 3: Volyinski

Volyinski's cabin contains the usual clothing, neatly packed, and all the political papers relating to the trade deal, which are contained in one of two locked attaché cases. Each case is a reinforced affair with a triple combination only he and his secretary, Gleb, know. While one case contains paperwork, the other, beneath his bunk, contains yet more state paperwork (unrelated to the upcoming trade meeting) and a wooden case that holds Volyinski's syringes, needles, and heroin. There is enough high-grade heroin for the next 10 days and, even though Volyinski is normally careful, it is always easy to make a mistake and overdose – which is what happens.

Gleb's plan, when Volyinski's body is discovered, is to clear all the drug paraphernalia from the room and hide it somewhere so that the sordid secret can't be discovered. Everything hinges on Gleb being able to get to the body first so a full clear-up can take place.

Cabin 4: Bohdan

Like Volyinski, Bohdan's cabin is neatly arranged and contains an attaché case of the same style, containing similar papers. Unlike Volyinski's berth, Bohdan only has one attaché case; astute Agents might note this if the opportunity arises.

Cabin 5: Graves

Kovalenko's butler is always on hand. A very light sleeper, he is always aware of the Archduke's movements and knows each and every one of his habits. Graves himself travels lightly; his travelling trunk carries a spare livery (dark suit, grey waistcoat, bowler hat) and personal effects. He also has a second valise containing a full medical kit, sewing and repair kit, specialised items for cleaning (white vinegar, lemon juice, and so on), and the Archduke's shaving and grooming equipment.

When not in attendance on the Archduke, Graves is here, reading the latest London papers and waiting for the next summons.

Cabin 6: Schumann

The dictatorial director is berthed here, and his cabin is an untidy clutter of papers, scripts, scribbled notes for potential shots or scenes, and so on. Amongst the papers are a couple of letters from one Pieter Klass, saying how much he admires Schumann's films, looks forward to their next meeting, and so forth. There are a few things in these letters that might arise suspicion, if the Agents have reason or an opportunity to search Schumann's cabin, they find the following:

- The address on the letters is in Königsberg, the Prussian capital.
- The letters are written in German.
- As well as the signature, each letter has a stamp from a seal: the stamp is two swans in an embrace, very similar to the design on Valentova's powder compact.
- Any agent with Psychometry knows this letter was handled by Loki.
- If analysed at Zero-Zero, the handwriting is confirmed as Loki's.

Schumann knows that Pieter Klass is a high-ranking official in the Prussian intelligence services, but does not know his true nature. He and Klass are meant to be meeting in Berlin in a couple of months' time, when Schumann is scouting for his next picture.

Cabin 7: Valentova

The actress' cabin contains an extremely large bouquet of flowers. These have been arranged in a suitable vase, but a card is still attached to one of the roses that reads, in German:

A safe trip to magnificent London!
PK
PS: I hope my gift helps you to become more radiant by the day.

PK is Pieter Klass, aka Loki. The gift is the booby-trapped powder compact.

The rest of the cabin is filled with Valentova's clothes, packed into a Versace trunk with enough changes for four outfits a day. More clothes are stored in Lazarev's berth.

The Archduke, if given chance, attempts to visit Gertrude here in her berth, although Graves may suggest that it is far safer for Ms. Valentova to visit his berth instead. Whatever happens, their proximity and intimacy is what triggers Kovalenko's incidents.

Cabin 8: Lazarev

Valentova's personal assistant is berthed here, and the cabin is dominated by more of the clothes Valentova needs quick access to during the flight. Otherwise, it is highly functional, with Irena's own clothes (high quality but very plain) and papers relating to the upcoming London itinerary. These detail each function the actress is to appear at, dates, contact names, timings, and so forth. It includes the Royal audiences, and Irena has made careful note of the appropriate forms of greeting to give to the British Royal Family. Accompanying the notes relating to the Royal family is a letter, from Pieter Klass, carrying the same address and seal as the letter in Schumann's room, that offers further advice, in German, to Valentova on meeting with King Alfred.

- *'I have only met His Majesty once, at a State dinner in Königsberg. He is very knowledgeable about Prussian history, so a have included a few anecdotes to help.'*
- *'He is a keen fisherman, I understand, so asking questions about recent fishing expeditions will help engage him.'*
- *'The princesses are huge fans of your films. 'Gone With The Mistral' is a favourite, and young Princess Diana is apparently well versed in your performance in 'On The Waterfront'. Acknowledging all this would be most welcome.'*

Irena keeps a close eye and ear on Valentova's comings and goings, and screens anyone – save Kovalenko – who might try to gain access to the movie star.

In her valise is a German/Russian phrase book, a stock of business cards and photographs for Valentova to autograph, and a makeup kit to use on her patron. She also travels with a portable typewriter and a bag of cleaning materials for the cabin, which includes a bottle of bleach. Her prized possession is a framed and signed photograph of Valentova.

Cabin 9: Gleb and Klym

The two secretaries have been forced to share a berth and have arranged a system for privacy when one or the other needs to change. Their cabins contain an attaché case each with paperwork for the trade deal, but they have nothing else of significant interest here.

Cabins 10–17

These double-berth cabins house the Agents and other passengers. Allocate them as needed.

Promenades

On either side of the passenger deck are the Promenade, featuring seating areas and large windows, which can be opened during flight. Smoking is permitted, given that the airship is helium lifted, but there is also a separate (rarely used) smoking room.

B Deck

Directly below the passenger deck, this level contains the galley; passenger toilet and shower facilities; the crew and officers' mess; and a cabin that doubles as an office for the captain.

The Smoking Room

The smoking room is located on this deck and is painted eggshell blue, with dark blue-grey leather furniture. The walls decorated with Hockney screen prints of poppy fields. Along one side of the room is a railing above sealed windows, through which passengers can observe the landscape or ocean passing below.

The Bar

A portable bar is usually set up on the Promenade, but a permanent bar is also located between the smoking room and the airlock door leading to the corridor on this. If gentlemen desire to retire to the Smoking Room, leaving the ladies to the lounge and Promenade, Fedotik has a bar steward, Howard, open up this permanent bar to serve the smokers. The signature cocktail is the 'Tytherleigh', a heady mix of gin, tonic water, grapefruit juice, bitters, and a twist of cucumber. Shaken and stirred, vigorously. Another specialty is the 'Vitamin Red', which is simply an exceptionally strong Bloody Mary, but expertly prepared over oyster juice and ice.

Officers' Mess

The officer complement of *Empress Katerina* is small, and therefore, so is their mess, which seats three people comfortably in a single sitting.

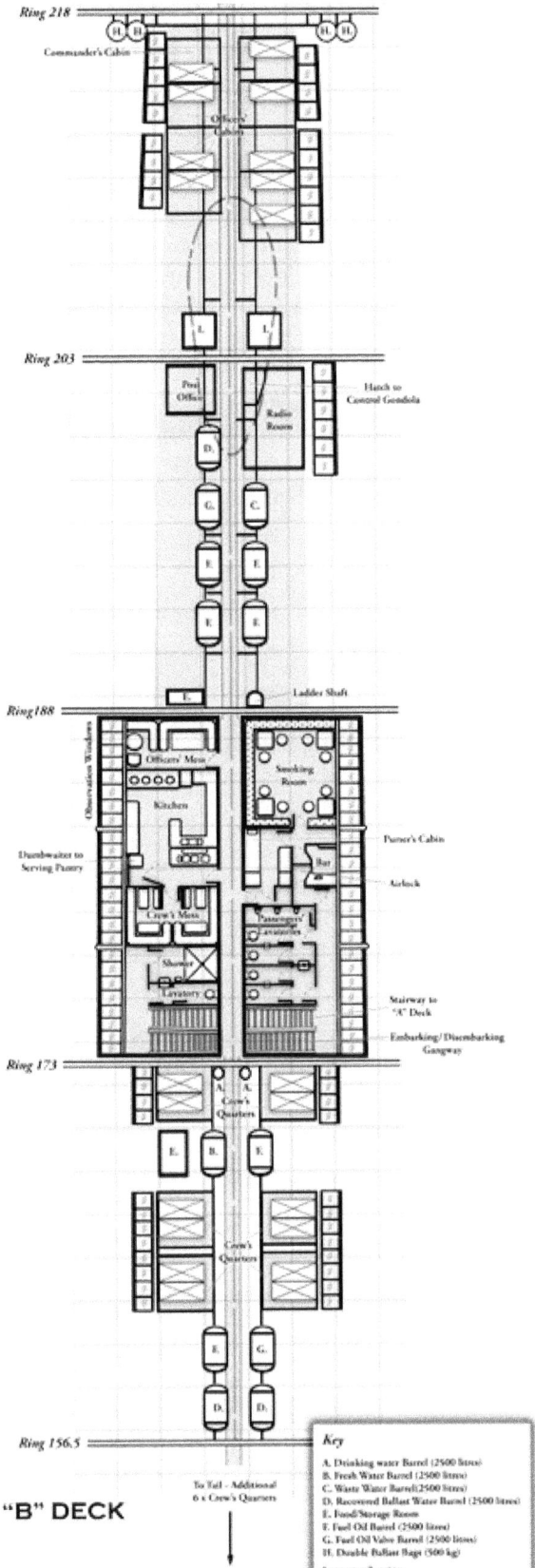

KITCHEN

A riot of activity from dawn until dusk, the kitchen is hot, cramped, and run in two shifts that cater for breakfast and lunch, then dinner (which is always five courses). An electric dumb waiter connects with the serving pantry, eliminating the need to carry food up and down the access ladders.

CREW'S MESS

Able to seat eight at a time, the crew's mess is cramped and functional, with metal tables, banquette seating, and little else. It doubles as a relaxation area when food isn't being served, so the aircrew can kick-back to play cards, chat, and so forth.

SHOWER

This is for passengers and officers only, with passengers having priority.

CREW QUARTERS

The crew quarters are triple-berths with bunk beds. There is precious little room (so private possessions are stored in lockers outside the berths) and precious little privacy.

The officer quarters are fore of the radio room and similar in design to the passenger single berths.

RADIO ROOM

The *Empress Katerina*'s radio room contains long-wave and short-wave battery-powered radios allowing the airship to communicate on most frequencies. It is staffed at all times and has connections with Kiev and London to relay flight details, as well as being able to establish ad-hoc connections with flight centres en route (such as Paris). The radio equipment also includes directional navigation radios located in the navigation room of the control car.

ELECTRICAL ROOM

Electrical power for the *Katerina* is provided by two redundant 100-horsepower diesel engines connected to high capacity generators, located in the electrical room. Electricity feeds through two systems, one at 220 volts and one at 240 volts. Either motor by itself could produce enough electricity for the ship's needs, allowing one to be shut down for maintenance without affecting the *Katerina*'s operation. The electrical room also contained the airship's master gyro compass and a powerful Zeiss searchlight to illuminate the ground or sea below the ship.

THE CONTROL CAR

The control car is the nerve centre for the whole ship and is divided into three sections: the bridge at the front, a navigation room in the centre, and an observation room at the rear.

The bridge is equipped with all the flight and control instruments for regulating ascent and descent, pitch, heading, altitude, and so forth. Anyone familiar with flight controls can soon establish the basic control patterns of the *Katerina*, although flying the craft by anyone who does not have a Pilot Airship (or similar) skill is at Formidable.

The navigation area is equipped with work tables for the navigator, all necessary charts and maps, plus navigation equipment: compasses, a drift indicator, radio direction finding equipment, an altimeter, and various clocks and stopwatches.

Crew Areas and Keel

Other than the control car, the crew and work areas aboard *Empress Katerina* are located along the keel, including work rooms, and rope handling areas for the mooring lines. Fuel, fresh water, and ballast tanks are also located along the keel, as are the cargo storage areas. The keel provides access to the engine bays and the auxiliary control and docking station in the tail. Ladders at various points along the interior structure grant access to the axial catwalk running along the centre of the airship

Searching The Katerina

The Agents may suspect that a bomb has been planted in a strategic section of the airship's engineering: near the ballast tanks, the engine room, and so on. Careful searching takes time and, unless the engineering crew has been persuaded to let the Agents have access to these areas, difficult to do. The Agents need to influence (through bribery, false papers, or other means) the engineering staff – or an officer like Anna Thames – to do a thorough search. Completely searching the areas where a bomb is going to do maximum damage takes about eight hours; going through the entire superstructure takes 12 hours, even with help. It also comes to naught, because the bomb is with Valentova and not located in the superstructure, as believed. Failure to find anything is judged a waste of time and squanders goodwill amongst the engineering crew, unless bribes have been especially good.

Of course, everyone should be relieved that there isn't a bomb, but when it distracts from vital duties and causes panic, it won't be viewed that way. Devious Games Masters could always have a bomb be planted there by genuine Crimean separatists, but it should still act as a red herring for the real threat lurking in Valentova's powder compact.

Non-Player Characters

Archduke Rostov Kovalenko

The Archduke is tall, broad, shouldered, smoky-eyed and exudes a smooth charisma. He is neither tolerant not patient, but expects both virtues in others. He drinks and smokes frequently, enjoying Cuban cigars and very stiff gin and tonics prepared *just so* by the barman. At take off he wears his military uniform but changes soon after into a lounge suit for the remainder of the flight.

Kovalenko	Attributes
STR: 9	Action Points: 3
CON: 12	Damage Modifier: -1d2
SIZ: 10	Prana: 14
DEX: 14	Tenacity: 12
INT: 12	Movement: 6 metres
POW: 14	Initiative Bonus: +13
CHA: 18	Armour: None

1d20	Hit Location	AP/HP
1 – 3	Right Leg	0/5
4 – 6	Left Leg	0/5
7 – 9	Abdomen	0/6
10 – 12	Chest	0/7
13 – 15	Right Arm	0/4
16 – 18	Left Arm	0/4
19 – 20	Head	0/5

Skills	Passions, Traits & Dependencies
Athletics 46%, Courtesy 78%, Endurance 41%, Evade 38%, Influence 78%, Language (English) 44%, Language (German) 68%, Native Language (Russian) 100%, Lore (Strategy & Tactics) 56%, Perception 32% Ride 69%, Seduction 51%, Stealth 31%, Survival 39%, Unarmed 61%, Willpower 31%	Passions: Loyalty to Ukraine 95%, Love Opulence 75%, Hate Separatists 90% Dependencies: Alcohol 30%, Nicotine 55%, Sex 69%

Combat Style & Weapons	Traits & Notes
Ukrainian Hussar (Sabre, Pistol, Rifle) 65%	Mounted Combat

Weapon	Damage	Size/Reach	AP/HP	Effects
Sabre	1d6+1+1d2	M/M	6/8	Bleed, Impale

Kommander Gerhard

Stern, scarred, and bald, Gerhard is a veteran soldier and consummate bodyguard. His grey eyes watch everyone and everything, and there is little that goes unnoticed. He is utterly dedicated to Kovalenko's safety and is prepared to do anything to assure it. He dresses in a dark suit with slate-grey waistcoat.

Gerhard wears a Walther PPK in a shoulder holster beneath his jacket and carries a switchblade in an ankle sheath. He is a Karate black belt and continuous training has left his limbs hardened to blows, giving them the Formidable Natural Weapons trait.

Gerhard	Attributes
STR: 16	Action Points: 3
CON: 9	Damage Modifier: +1d2
SIZ: 10	Prana: 13
DEX: 11	Tenacity: 13
INT: 14	Movement: 6 metres
POW: 13	Initiative Bonus: +13
CHA: 10	Armour: None

1d20	Hit Location	AP/HP
1 – 3	Right Leg	0/4
4 – 6	Left Leg	0/4
7 – 9	Abdomen	0/7
10 – 12	Chest	0/6
13 – 15	Right Arm	0/3
16 – 18	Left Arm	0/3
19 – 20	Head	0/4

Skills	Passions, Traits & Dependencies
Athletics 65%, Brawn 53%, Endurance 64%, Evade 58%, Influence 77%, Insight 80%, Perception 85%, Stealth 75%, Survival 60%, Unarmed 95%, Willpower 78%	Passions: Root Out Traitors 70%, Loyalty to Kovalenko 85% Dependency: Suspicious 74%

Combat Style & Weapons	Traits & Notes
Royal Assassin (Pistol) 89% Knife Fighter (Switchblade) 92% Karate (Hands and Feet) 85%	Assassination Silent Killing Formidable Natural Weapons

Weapon	Damage	Range	Ammo	Rate/Load
Walther PPK	1d6	50/100/200	7	1/3

Weapon	Damage	Size/Reach	AP/HP	Effects
Switchblade	1d3+1	S/S	6/8	Bleed, Impale

Graves

Tall and regal, Graves puts one in mind of a extremely well-bred cat. He moves with a graceful economy of movement not normally associated with so large a frame, but it is his ability to anticipate everything that is so astonishing. If Kovalenko produces a cigar, a flame magically appears as soon as the thing reaches his lips; if he demands a G&T, Graves has already sent word to the barman to have everything ready.

Graves only ever fights as a last resort. His preferred style is boxing, and he is an able pugilist. If inappropriate, he can easily improvise a weapon with anything that happens to be available or nearby.

Graves	Attributes
STR: 15	Action Points: 3
CON: 16	Damage Modifier: +1d4
SIZ: 17	Prana: 12
DEX: 12	Tenacity: 12
INT: 15	Movement: 6 metres
POW: 12	Initiative Bonus: +14
CHA: 15	Armour: None

1d20	Hit Location	AP/HP
1 – 3	Right Leg	0/7
4 – 6	Left Leg	0/7
7 – 9	Abdomen	0/8
10 – 12	Chest	0/9
13 – 15	Right Arm	0/6
16 – 18	Left Arm	0/6
19 – 20	Head	0/7

Skills	Passions, Traits & Dependencies
Athletics 44%, Brawn 32%, Courtesy 110%, Craft (Butlering) 112%, Customs 105%, Endurance 66%, Evade 49%, Insight 89%, Language (French) 75%, Language (German) 73%, Language (Russian) 95%, Lore (Esoteric Trivia) 99%, Native Tongue (English) 100%, Perception 90%, Politics 75%, Unarmed 75%, Willpower 90%	Passions: Loyalty to Kovalenko 95%, Order and Certainty 75% Traits: Quasi-Presience (That strange ability all butlers possess to know and anticipate the needs of the upper crust) Dependency: Tea 35%

Combat Style & Weapons	Traits & Notes
Butlerian Jihad (Anything to Hand) 75% Boxing (Queensbury Rules - Fists) 63%	Improvised Weapons

Weapon	Damage	Size/Reach	AP/HP	Effects
Tea Tray	1d4	S/S	1/3	Stun Location

RUPRECHT VOLYINSKI

Of medium height and bearing, Volyinski is both extremely intelligent and exceedingly perceptive. These qualities have served him well in his meteoric political rise. Of course, he is not without weakness, and his heroin addiction will prove his undoing. Nevertheless, as politicians go, Volyinski is reasonably approachable, reasoably honest, and seemingly open to all manner of discussion.

Volyinski is unlikely to indulge in any form of combat and therefore relies on Unarmed if he needs to defend himself. His addiction makes him restless and causes him to sweat as the need to partake takes hold.

Volyinski	Attributes
STR: 8	Action Points: 2
CON: 7	Damage Modifier: -1d2
SIZ: 10	Prana: 9
DEX: 9	Tenacity: 6
INT: 17	Movement: 6 metres
POW: 9	Initiative Bonus: +13
CHA: 12	Armour: None

1d20	Hit Location	AP/HP
1 – 3	Right Leg	0/4
4 – 6	Left Leg	0/4
7 – 9	Abdomen	0/5
10 – 12	Chest	0/6
13 – 15	Right Arm	0/3
16 – 18	Left Arm	0/3
19 – 20	Head	0/4

Skills	Passions, Traits & Dependencies
Athletics 24%, Courtesy 65%, Deceit 44%, Endurance 21%, Evade 29%, Influence 75%, Language (English) 40%, Language (French) 65%, Language (German) 55%, Insight 50%, Native Language (Russian) 99%, Perception 37%, Politics 99%, Unarmed 17%, Willpower 18%	Passions: Honourable 80%, Loyal to Ukraine 76% Dependencies: Narcotics (Heroin) 60%

Combat Style & Weapons	Traits & Notes
Self Defence 17%	None

Weapon	Damage	Size/Reach	AP/HP	Effects
Fists	1d3-1d2	S/S	As for Arm	-

VOLODYMYR BOHDAN

A sharp contrast with the dynamic young Volyinski, the portly, sour-faced Bohdan has worked long and hard to get where he has and resents those who manage to hijack the fast tracks and surge ahead. Volyinski is a man to be despised rather than admired, and so Bohdan takes great care to appear to be the opposite. He is snobbish to a fault, uninterested in anything that is unconnected with political life, and is a dreadful sycophant, especially where the Archduke is concerned.

Bohdan	Attributes
STR: 11	Action Points: 3
CON: 12	Damage Modifier: 0
SIZ: 13	Prana: 14
DEX: 15	Tenacity: 14
INT: 13	Movement: 6 metres
POW: 14	Initiative Bonus: +14
CHA: 9	Armour: None

1d20	Hit Location	AP/HP
1 – 3	Right Leg	0/5
4 – 6	Left Leg	0/5
7 – 9	Abdomen	0/6
10 – 12	Chest	0/7
13 – 15	Right Arm	0/4
16 – 18	Left Arm	0/4
19 – 20	Head	0/5

Skills	Passions, Traits & Dependencies
Athletics 40%, Bureaucracy 80%, Courtesy 48%, Deceit 68%, Endurance 40%, Evade 35%, Influence 48%, Insight 70%, Language (English) 50%, Language (German) 60%, Language (French) 70%, Native Language (Russian) 100%, Perception 75%, Politics 62%, Unarmed 48%, Willpower 44%	Passions: Crave Power 85%, Hate Volyinski 44%, Loyal to Ukraine 55% Dependencies: None

Combat Style & Weapons	Traits & Notes
Self Defence 48%	None

Weapon	Damage	Size/Reach	AP/HP	Effects
Fists	1d3-1d2	S/S	As for Arm	-

Wilhelm Gleb

Slightly taller than Volyinski, this carefully groomed, balding man is a professional civil servant and not unlike Graves in terms of prescience. It is his job to plan, coordinate, anticipate, adapt, and present solutions for Volyinski to act upon. He is therefore mindful, careful, observant, and, above all, loyal. He knows of Volyinski's addiction to has done a monumental amount to keep it hidden. He will serve his minister even after the minister's death.

Gleb served in the army and is competent if called upon to fight, although he possesses no weapons himself.

Gleb	Attributes
STR: 10	Action Points: 3
CON: 9	Damage Modifier: 0
SIZ: 11	Prana: 10
DEX: 13	Tenacity: 10
INT: 11	Movement: 6 metres
POW: 10	Initiative Bonus: +12
CHA: 11	Armour: None

1d20	Hit Location	AP/HP
1 – 3	Right Leg	0/4
4 – 6	Left Leg	0/4
7 – 9	Abdomen	0/5
10 – 12	Chest	0/6
13 – 15	Right Arm	0/3
16 – 18	Left Arm	0/3
19 – 20	Head	0/4

Skills	Passions, Traits & Dependencies
Athletics 26%, Brawn 30%, Bureaucracy 95%, Commerce 85%, Endurance 30%, Evade 30%, Influence 72%, Insight 58%, Language (English) 84%, Language (French) 66%, Language (German) 48%, Native Tongue (Ukrainian) 100%, Perception 56%, Politics 71%, Stealth 33%, Unarmed 45%, Willpower 40%	Passions: Serve the State 80%

Combat Style & Weapons	Traits & Notes
Ukrainian Officer (Sabre, Pistol) 55%	

Klara Klym

A female version of Gleb, Klara is dark-eyed, fair haired, highly observant, but also politically ambitious. Her affair with Bohdan is nothing more than a career move; Bohdan's lack of subtlety means he will never go any further than he has, but Klara is determined to eclipse him. In conversation, she is polite and reserved, always maintaining a cool facade.

Klym	Attributes
STR: 10	Action Points: 3
CON: 9	Damage Modifier: 0
SIZ: 11	Prana: 12
DEX: 13	Tenacity: 12
INT: 11	Movement: 6 metres
POW: 12	Initiative Bonus: +12
CHA: 13	Armour: None

1d20	Hit Location	AP/HP
1 – 3	Right Leg	0/4
4 – 6	Left Leg	0/4
7 – 9	Abdomen	0/5
10 – 12	Chest	0/6
13 – 15	Right Arm	0/3
16 – 18	Left Arm	0/3
19 – 20	Head	0/4

Skills	Passions, Traits & Dependencies
Athletics 26%, Brawn 20%, Bureaucracy 81%, Commerce 82%, Endurance 30%, Evade 30%, Influence 70%, Insight 60%, Language (English) 44%, Language (French) 71%, Language (German) 85%, Native Tongue (Ukrainian) 100%, Perception 60%, Politics 68%, Unarmed 45%, Willpower 40%	Passions: Serve the State 75% Dependencies: Sex 33%

Combat Style & Weapons	Traits & Notes
Self Defence 33%	

Maksim Olesko

The senior engineer is a small, pugnacious man with greying hair and close-set eyes. He despises the opulence he sees around him aboard the airship and sympathises wholeheartedly with the separatists who spoil for revolution. However he is no martyr and no idiot. Although he wants revolution, he does not want it while flying over Europe. Besides, he loves the airship. He knows every nut, bolt, flange, and girder, and delights in being part of the *Katerina*. He and his engineers keep the *Katerina* in the air, and his professional pride outweighs his politial leanings.

Olesko	Attributes
STR: 10	Action Points: 2
CON: 9	Damage Modifier: 0
SIZ: 11	Prana: 10
DEX: 10	Tenacity: 10
INT: 11	Movement: 6 metres
POW: 10	Initiative Bonus: +11
CHA: 11	Armour: Overalls

1d20	Hit Location	AP/HP
1 – 3	Right Leg	1/6
4 – 6	Left Leg	1/6
7 – 9	Abdomen	1/7
10 – 12	Chest	1/8
13 – 15	Right Arm	1/5
16 – 18	Left Arm	1/5
19 – 20	Head	1/6

Skills	Passions, Traits & Dependencies
Athletics 20%, Brawn 65%, Endurance 56%, Engineering 104%, Evade 28%, Language (English) 25%, Language (German) 41%, Mechanisms 90%, Native Tongue (Russian) 99%, Perception 41%, Stealth 26%, Survival 31%, Unarmed 67%, Willpower 36%	Passions: Loyalty to the Airship 90%, Hate Imperialism 60% Loyalty to Separatists 65%

Combat Style & Weapons	Traits & Notes
Street Ruffian (Tools) 60%	None

Weapon	Damage	Size/Reach	AP/HP	Effects
Fists	1d3	S/S	As for Arm	-
Wrench	1d4+2	M/S	6/10	Bash, Stun Location

Olga Ruslana

A blond ice maiden, the security chief maintains a professional demeanour, being serious and diligent most of the time. When caught off-guard, she is pleasant and easy to talk to, with a mischievous sense of humour hidden by her uniform and duties.

Ruslana carries a 9mm automatic in a discreet waist holster, and a rubber kosh hidden in the pocket of her neat military trousers.

Ruslana	Attributes
STR: 10	Action Points: 3
CON: 14	Damage Modifier: 0
SIZ: 13	Prana: 14
DEX: 15	Tenacity: 14
INT: 10	Movement: 6 metres
POW: 14	Initiative Bonus: +16
CHA: 12	Armour: None

1d20	Hit Location	AP/HP
1 – 3	Right Leg	0/6
4 – 6	Left Leg	0/6
7 – 9	Abdomen	0/7
10 – 12	Chest	0/8
13 – 15	Right Arm	0/5
16 – 18	Left Arm	0/5
19 – 20	Head	0/6

Skills	Passions, Traits & Dependencies
Athletics 56%, Brawn 33%, Endurance 43%, Evade 60%, First Aid 31%, Influence 55%, Insight 78%, Language (English) 75%, Language (German) 50%, Mechanisms 36%, Native Tongue (Russian) 100%, Perception 65%, Stealth 61%, Willpower 70%	Passions: Loyalty to Ukraine 80%, Hates Bullies 70% Loyalty to Airship 56%

Combat Style & Weapons	Traits & Notes
Security Officer (Pistol, Kosh) 66%	Skirmisher

Weapon	Damage	Size/Reach	AP/HP	Effects
Kosh	1d3+1	S/S	2/3	Stun Location

Weapon	Damage	Range	Ammo	Rate/Load
Walther PPK	1d6	50/100/200	7	1/3

ANNA THAMES

Dark haired and quiet, Anna maintains a professional distance from the passengers but is well known to the crew and engineering team. Her loyalty is to the *Katerina* and Captain Mors, and she is focused on the smoothest flight possible with the least amount of fuss. She will certainly engage in conversation, but her attention is always elsewhere, concentrating on the myriad things she needs to monitor during the flight.

Thames	Attributes
STR: 10	Action Points: 3
CON: 8	Damage Modifier: 0
SIZ: 14	Prana: 10
DEX: 15	Tenacity: 10
INT: 16	Movement: 6 metres
POW: 10	Initiative Bonus: +15
CHA: 15	Armour: None

1d20	Hit Location	AP/HP
1 – 3	Right Leg	0/5
4 – 6	Left Leg	0/5
7 – 9	Abdomen	0/6
10 – 12	Chest	0/7
13 – 15	Right Arm	0/4
16 – 18	Left Arm	0/4
19 – 20	Head	0/5

Skills	Passions, Traits & Dependencies
Athletics 31%, Brawn 34%, Deceit 27%, Endurance 36%, Engineering 29%, Evade 28%, First Aid 29%, Influence 64%, Insight 45%, Language (German) 77%, Language (Russian) 48%, Mechanisms 75%, Native Language (English) 100%, Pilot (Airship) 88%, Perception 45%, Stealth 29%, Streetwise 57%, Unarmed 24%, Willpower 44%.	Passions: Loyalty to Airship 80%, Loyalty to England 75%, Hate Captivity 60% Traits: Psychic - although on this parallel, Anna's abilities have not been awoken and she is unaware of her capabilities Dependencies: Routine 25%

Combat Style & Weapons	Traits & Notes
Security Officer (Pistol) 40%	None

Weapon	Damage	Range	Ammo	Rate/Load
Walther PPK	1d6	50/100/200	7	1/3

GREGOR FEDOTIK

Of medium height, his slicked hair and pencil moustache make him instantly recognisable. His concern is entertainment at the finest level, especially with such lauded guests aboard. It is clear to all that when there are smiles and laughs on the promenade, he is at his happiest.

Fedotik	Attributes
STR: 10	Action Points: 3
CON: 9	Damage Modifier: 0
SIZ: 11	Prana: 10
DEX: 13	Tenacity: 10
INT: 11	Movement: 6 metres
POW: 10	Initiative Bonus: +12
CHA: 18	Armour: None

1d20	Hit Location	AP/HP
1 – 3	Right Leg	0/4
4 – 6	Left Leg	0/4
7 – 9	Abdomen	0/5
10 – 12	Chest	0/6
13 – 15	Right Arm	0/3
16 – 18	Left Arm	0/3
19 – 20	Head	0/4

Skills	Passions, Traits & Dependencies
Athletics 26%, Brawn 30%, Courtesy 95%, Customs (Hospitality) 99%, Endurance 30%, Evade 30%, Influence 64%, Insight 62%, Language (English) 84%, Language (French) 88%, Language (German) 81%, Native Tongue (Ukrainian) 100%, Perception 76%, Stealth 80%, Unarmed 25%, Willpower 76%	Passions: To Serve at all Costs 90%, Hate Inefficiency 75% Dependencies: OCD 38%

Combat Style & Weapons	Traits & Notes
Fisticuffs 55%	

Captain Mors

Grey haired and with an imposing physical presence, Captain Mors' owns the *Katerina* from nose ring to rudder. As Olesko knows her physical structure and state, he knows how to coax the best from the airship. He is aware of every creak and groan, every rising and falling note of the engines, and every movement she makes.

Mors	Attributes
STR: 10	Action Points: 3
CON: 14	Damage Modifier: 0
SIZ: 14	Prana: 9
DEX: 15	Tenacity: 9
INT: 16	Movement: 6 metres
POW: 9	Initiative Bonus: +15
CHA: 15	Armour: None

1d20	Hit Location	AP/HP
1 – 3	Right Leg	0/6
4 – 6	Left Leg	0/6
7 – 9	Abdomen	0/7
10 – 12	Chest	0/8
13 – 15	Right Arm	0/5
16 – 18	Left Arm	0/5
19 – 20	Head	0/6

Skills	Passions, Traits & Dependencies
Athletics 36%, Brawn 36%, Endurance 36%, Engineering 51%, Evade 38%, Influence 77%, Insight 32%, Language (German) 99%, Mechanisms 70%, Native Language (Ukrainian) 100%, Pilot (Airship) 95%, Perception 52%, Stealth 27%, Unarmed 44%, Willpower 56%.	Passions: Loyalty to Airship 100%, Loyalty to Ukraine 75%, Hate Separatists 60%

Combat Style & Weapons	Traits & Notes
Luftpirat (Pistol, Sabre) 55%	Skirmisher

Weapon	Damage	Range	Ammo	Rate/Load
Walther PPK	1d6	50/100/200	7	1/3

Weapon	Damage	Size/Reach	AP/HP	Effects
Sabre	1d6+1+1d2	M/M	6/8	Bleed, Impale

Otto Schumann

Short and squat, the film director is a whirlwind of manic energy. Devoted to the truth of the camera, he is determined not to let anyone - save his muse, Valentova - get in its way. Eager to film everything, capturing it for posterity, he ignores everyone in a bid to capture the perfect shot and perfect moment.

Naturally, Schumann wears a monocle, beret, and has a viewfinder hanging around his neck at all times. Sometimes he squints through it simply out of sheer habit.

Schumann	Attributes
STR: 10	Action Points: 2
CON: 9	Damage Modifier: 0
SIZ: 11	Prana: 10
DEX: 10	Tenacity: 10
INT: 15	Movement: 6 metres
POW: 10	Initiative Bonus: +14
CHA: 11	Armour: None

1d20	Hit Location	AP/HP
1 – 3	Right Leg	0/6
4 – 6	Left Leg	0/6
7 – 9	Abdomen	0/7
10 – 12	Chest	0/8
13 – 15	Right Arm	0/5
16 – 18	Left Arm	0/5
19 – 20	Head	0/6

Skills	Passions, Traits & Dependencies
Art (Cinematography) 85%, Athletics 30%, Brawn 32%, Endurance 44%, Evade 28%, Influence 52%, Language (English) 80%, Language (Russian) 41%, Mechanisms 76%, Native Tongue (German) 100%, Perception 60%, Stealth 29%, Unarmed 27%, Willpower 55%	Passions: The Cinematic Arts 90%, Hate Film Critics 95% Dependencies: Shouting 44%

Combat Style & Weapons	Traits & Notes
Artistic Temperament (Fists) 31%	None

Weapon	Damage	Size/Reach	AP/HP	Effects
Fists	1d3	S/S	As for Arm	-

Gertrude Valentova

The actress may well be known to the agents from the Trans-Siberian Express, and if so, she has changed not a bit. Vain, attention-seeking, voluptuous, flirtatious and every inch the silver screen diva. She is looking forward to continuing her affair with Kovalenko at altitude and is struggling to hide her desires. Her Thought Implant is, of course, buried so deep that even she does not know anything about it.

Irena Lazarev

As implacable as she was travelling across Russia, Lazarev watches he beloved mistress like a hawk. There can be no doubt she is in love with Valentova, and anyone catching her in unguarded moments will notice the longing in her eyes, and thinly concealed jealousy when she flirts with the Archduke. Yet she remains professional at all times and in all ways.

Statistics for Valentova and Lazarev can be found in the previous mission on pages 81 and 82. For assorted crew members, engineers and incidental passengers, use statistics for Passengers and Staff on page 85.

NuAtlantis

At the bottom of the Bermuda Triangle in parallel 18.09.26, a secretive undersea community calling itself NuAtlantis has discovered a prenatal neuro-chemical treatment that could revolutionise recruitment methods for either the Valhalla Project or the Disruptors. Secret supporters within the parallel are laying groundwork while Mjollnir briefs its Agents for a high-priority undersea rendezvous.

Overview

Parallel 18.09.26
Technology Ascendant Variant
Disruption Likelihood: 78.4%

In a secretive undersea arcology, a new approach t psionic development has been perfected that, were it to fall into Disruptor hands, might threaten Valhalla's own plans for developing Homo Novus.

Non-Player Characters

The following are Non-Player Characters the Agents meet and interact with during the mission. Game statistics are provided on page 127.

- **Padraig Ventman:** Orchestrating Valhalla operative local to the parallel.
- **Olin Traviche:** President of NuAtlantis.
- **Natalia Parsons:** NuAtlantean scientist, the only expert in the NuGenesis Protocol.
- **Siavan:** Bio-engineer, Disruptor knight.
- **McAvoy:** Bodyguard to Siavan, Disruptor pawn.

Key Points & Timeline

1. Padraig learns of the NuGenesis Protocol and reports to W.O.T.A.N immediately.
2. Valhalla Agents are dispatched to the parallel to either acquire access to or destroy NuGenesis.
3. The Agents meet Padraig, board the Kingfisher, and are escorted to NuAtlantis.
4. The Agents are given a tour of NuAtlantis and explained its strict laws before being assigned housing.
5. The Disruptor agents are revealed as competing for NuGenesis at the same welcome feast the Agents are invited to.
6. The proof that NuGenesis works is borne; agents from all sides are invited to witness.
7. A banquet is thrown to discuss the success and future of NuGenesis, during which nefarious sabotage takes place.
8. The Agents must decide if they need to perform additional measures to claim NuGenesis or destroy any possibility of the Disruptors getting their hands on it.
9. The Agents either get to leave in peace or have to flee NuAtlantis.

Areas to be Covered

- The Kingfisher Exploration Vessel
- The NuAtlantis Undersea Arcology

NuAtlantis

Background and Introduction

Designator: 18.09.26
Classification: Technology Ascendant
Cultural Type: North American/Northern European
Political Type: Academic
Technological Type: Nanotechnology Age

Description: The collective nations of parallel 18.09.26 came together to create a socio-political refuge for scientific advancements in the guise of a neutral arcology. Using the abnormal electromagnetic currents found in and around the Bermuda Triangle, the 'managing rulers' of the experiment built an advanced undersea geo-dome nearly 5 kilometres in diameter. This marvel of worldwide sciences came to contain an entire population of researchers, practitioners, security, and their families. Called NuAtlantis, it became the crown jewel of human advancement in the parallel.

Toying with the human genome, a brilliant neuro-geneticist named Natalia Parsons has unlocked a secret pre-natal series of injections that have shown to produce powerfully psionic infants, a new evolution that would create a race of mythical Atlanteans – the NuGenesis Protocol. Such a miraculous jump in medical science would be a powerful tool in the hands of temporally fluid Valhalla recruitment Agents... or could be perverted into a dangerous Disruptor weapon.

The 'babysitting Agent' native to the parallel learned of Natalia's success with the Protocol and has immediately sent for Valhalla Agents to try and protect the scientist and her discovery.

Unfortunately, Valhalla Nova is not the only agency with spies in 18.09.26, and the Disruptors have also dispatched one of the most clever and charismatic knights to claim NuGenesis. This sinister schemer has orders to make the NuAtlanteans an offer they cannot refuse, which surely complicates things and forces the Agents to decide what to do if they cannot persuade President Olin Traviche to give them NuGenesis – even if that means making sure no one ever gets it.

Agent Briefing

Mortimer McAllen leads the briefing for the team, and he enters the room in a show of exasperation with a pile of paperwork stuffed in his arms, trailing loose pages and fluttering post-it notes. He dumps his stack of pages on the desk unceremoniously, the haphazard tower threatening to topple, and motions to dim the lights.

Mortimer begins a slideshow depicting a beautiful complex of tubes, domes, bubbles, and umbilical hallways all connected underwater to create a dazzling arcology beneath the sea. Pictures of submarines whirring around kelp fields pop up between shots of armoured divers before settling on a large map of the eastern Caribbean Sea, a large section highlighted within the infamous Bermuda Triangle. The pictures shift to images of crisp, clean halls full of chrome, colourful tile, and pieces of art scattered with tan-skinned people in a variety of different-yet-similar uniforms performing a number of tasks.

He goes on to explain that the Agents are looking at ambassadorial pictures taken of NuAtlantis, the single most advanced sub-civilisation in parallel 18.09.26 and the destination of their urgent mission.

NuAtlantis is an ongoing political-science Programme sponsored by their world's greatest superpower nations. Its goals are to further the humanitarian sciences and survivability of mankind in light of melting polar ice caps and rising sea levels. It is designed to weather the loss of dry land taking place on their Earth, and carries a steady living population of well over five hundred families coming and going in 33% shifts every four months. The NuAtlantis personnel are highly trained facets of the overall goal, from those on the security staff to structural engineers and doctors of augmentative biochemistry.

Mortimer steps half into the projection and points to the image of a striking young woman with dark hair, a fair complexion, and a pattern of swirling tattoos in front of her right ear. She is Natalia Parsons and is the focal point of this mission.

Images of scientific data intermingles with pictures of children in a variety of psychological and behavioural tests. Natalia is on hand in each of these images, obviously, the doctor in charge. Mortimer leaves the projector on a picture of a young child of less than six years old levitating a trio of blocks normally used for hand-eye coordination tests. As always, Natalia is in the background, her hand to her mouth and the shine of tears on her cheeks. The look on her face is far more that of a proud parent than of an overseeing doctor. He explains that Dr. Parsons has been trying to chemically instigate psionic evolutions in human beings for years.

Mortimer smiles and says that a local Valhalla Agent on the parallel has reported that, as of nine months before their transition point, she succeeded. Natalia Parsons has unlocked the formulae needed to reliably create powerful psionics in human subjects.

'This information and practice, named the NuGenesis Protocol, is still a privileged secret within NuAtlantis. Not even the other nations of the world know about it yet, making now the time to act – before Disruptor spies can get their talons hooked into it.

'Your job is to ensure that NuGenesis never falls into Disruptor hands. The hope is to bring NuAtlantis into a private alliance with a fake international treaty group, Yggdrasil Incorporated, serving as Valhalla's front on the parallel, ensuring that no one outside the arcology will know about how the process works or even that it exists at all. It is the only way to keep such a powerful tool out of the wrong hands.

'The Valhalla inside man is Padraig Ventman, and he has made arrangements for you to take The Van to the submersible craft *Kingfisher*. *Kingfisher* will then take you over five thousand, seven hundred metres to the ocean floor and NuAtlantis where Padraig has secured security clearance for you.

'Once inside NuAtlantis, your mission parameters are easy: either acquire ironclad rights to NuGenesis or make sure the secret stays on the bottom of the ocean.'

Mortimer looks seriously concerned, his eyes focused on the flickering visage of Natalia, as his tone grows cold. 'It is clear that NuGenesis is the only real priority in the mission, and if the NuAtlanteans do not willingly give you its secrets, you must steal them, and if you cannot manage to steal NuGenesis – you must make sure it never leaves NuAtlantis.'

After a sobering moment of silence letting Mortimer's meaning – the fact that NuGenesis is more important than any number of NuAtlantean lives lost – settle in, he sets one of the mission duffels on the desk. Popping the zip tie, he begins to remove all of the specialised equipment from within to show what the Agents have at their disposal.

Each duffel contains several individually shrink-wrapped packets, each one holding an important part of the mission equipment. Inside are four sets of tailored clothing that match fashion found across most of that parallel's Europe, a powerful dose of infection inhibitors for tropical illnesses, one hour's worth of micro-audio recording equipment, two-thousand locally minted Euro-notes, a single-edged utility/survival knife, and a single application of a transdermally absorbed neuro-sedative that can knock a grown person unconscious for hours. The lattermost comes in the form of a tiny, one square centimetre, one-sided absorption strip sewn into the lining of the duffel – in case it is somehow needed.

'NuAtlantis is not like anywhere you have been before, and your mission could be one of the most important steps towards Valhalla's psionic dominance over the Disruptors and all other foes that may arise across the multiverse.

'I cannot express enough that NuGenesis is the only real priority here. Everything else, and I mean everything, is expendable.

The Van leaves in 20 minutes...'

THE KINGFISHER

The Van brings the Agents to an old warehouse in the port of Miami, where Padraig is waiting for them. He is dressed in worn naval fatigues and a blue knit cap, tapping a stylus against the edge of a clipboard as he quickly reviews stacks or piles of items around him. It is an odd scene: a largely empty building with a folding table and a handful of chairs scattered around it dominate the centre space. Stacks of local newspapers, memo pads full of assorted notes, and an assortment of beers and types of soda decorate the table. Padraig has an instant coffee maker on a side table he uses if an Agent asks.

The Agents can take however much time they need to get familiar with the parallel using the material Padraig has gathered for them. A lot of what he has assembled is about local cultural events like who won the last World Cup, the socio-political

> ### Transdermal Neuro-Sedative Strips
>
> Each Agent receives a single-use dose strip containing a very powerful, fast-acting neurological sedative called azaperone, frequently used to sedate elephants for transport. Each strip has a safety coating that peels off to adhere to any surface and another safety film on the other side that is carefully removed to expose the powerful chemical.
>
> Upon contact with bare flesh (or any liquid), the strip instantly dissolves. When the sedative makes contact with nervous tissue, it is absorbed by the system and makes a quick transition to the brain where it shuts everything down into a near-hibernating state.
>
> *Application:* Contact (skin)
>
> *Potency:* 85
>
> *Resistance:* Endurance
>
> *Onset time:* 2d6+30 seconds
>
> *Duration:* 1d6+1 hours
>
> *Conditions: Unconscious is instant, lasting for the first half of the entire duration. The second half of the determined duration inflicts full-body Paralysis.*
>
> *Antidote/Cure: After the first hour, a successful Healing skill test can reduce the duration by one hour. A secondary Hard Difficulty Healing skill test during the drug's Paralysis reduces its effects from full-body to merely the body location where the drug was introduced.*

state of things in the Eastern Block, the latest and greatest television moguls, and so on. The Agents could spend hours poring over it all. Padraig gladly converses about anything they wish to know about the parallel, though he is often charmingly arch with his replies. When they are ready he calls ahead and a VW bus is waiting for them at the curb. From there, it takes only about 20 minutes to drive to the launching bay where the Kingfisher is berthed.

Padraig's forged visitation paperwork as representatives of Yggdrasil Incorporated expedites things through outgoing customs, and as long as the Agents do not do anything foolish or try to bring recognisable heavy weaponry with them, they pass onto the embarkation platform of the Kingfisher without incident. The platform is a readying point before boarding the large nation-neutral undersea exploration craft that is taking them to NuAtlantis.

The Kingfisher itself is a thirty-metre-long advanced submersible capable of surface travel as well as high-pressure deep manoeuvres. It is crewed by a multinational array of professional marine experts. If engaged in conversation, the crew are polite and informative, but maintain the focus on their duties for the most part. They are not allies or employees of Valhalla, and they know nothing about the Agents' reason for travel.

The vessel is designed to be comfortable for a few days at a time; it is neutrally decorated and furnished with layover bunks and a few private lavatories. The most noticeable feature of the Kingfisher is the viewing lounge in the aft of the vessel. It is a miniature theatre with rows of lifelike electronic screens that receive live footage feeds from dozens of cameras around the hull. Anyone

can come and go in the lounge, take a seat, and watch the ocean pass by in beautiful, digitally enhanced HD video.

Much of the Kingfisher is available to the Agents as they make passage, but there are two areas – the crew supply cache and the helm – that are closely guarded and considered to be off-limits to passengers. Both areas are behind secure doors and often under watch by a dedicated crew member. Crew come and go from these areas frequently, and both are important aspects of the ship's inner workings. The supply cache holds all of the necessary tools and resources the crew may need during a voyage, and it is from the helm that the Kingfisher is piloted and monitored, and all of its important functions are maintained.

The Games Master should note the following:

- One of the Kingfisher's crew is a secret NuAtlantean intelligence agent, and unless the Agents are careful how openly they speak, she might warn her superiors in the arcology of potential subterfuge. A successful Insight test in the first two hours of the journey reveals the overly curious crewmember.
- If the Agents explore the off-limits supply cache, likely needing at least one Stealth test, they can find a small weapons locker containing six sonic pistols (see text box on page 118 for details), holsters for each, and ten sets of emergency diving gear.

After five hours of skimming along the surface at remarkably fast speeds, gentle tones interrupt whatever the Agents are doing and the Kingfisher's helmsman announces the 20-minute warning before beginning the dive trajectory to NuAtlantis. When the vessel begins the dive itself, everyone on board feels the inertial shift in direction and possibly a little vertigo as the vessel evens back out. It is disorienting at first, but the feeling passes in a few minutes.

The spiralling, diagonal dive to NuAtlantis is another 18 hours on board the Kingfisher. Unless the Agents thought about bringing some of their own, the food and drink provided is very basic. Purified water in plastic bottles, protein bars, and dehydrated fruit snacks are about as much as they can find in the passenger supply closets.

Padraig tries to gather the Agents several times during the dive, most often to quickly drag them to the viewing lounge to see some amazing school of fish or coral structure. He has a deep and almost obsessive love for the world beneath the sea. While he has seen all of this many times before, Padraig really wants to share these sights with others – perhaps to find a potential future crewmate or contact.

During the eighteenth hour of the dive, long after the viewing screens have shifted to a light-augmented capture of the depth, Padraig finds each Agent and brings them all to the lounge to watch the final descent into NuAtlantis. He adores the idea of a life under the sea and the concept of what NuAtlantis means

> ### Sonic Pistol
>
> The Persephone Arms mark II sonic pistol is a very popular weapon for naval crews above, in, and under the water. It uses a focussed burst of sound to inflict concussive damage at short range. Designed for underwater use, a sonic pistol doubles its Range when firing completely through a fluid medium. Similar to the stun rifle, a sonic pistol produces an energy field within a 20 metre arc directly in front of the firer. Do not roll for Hit Location. Victims must succeed in a Hard Endurance roll (unopposed) or be incapacitated until the weapon is deactivated
>
> | Damage | Range | Firing Rate | Ammo/Load | Weapon Traits | Enc |
> |---|---|---|---|---|---|
> | See Above | 5/10/25 | 1 | 10/3 | Paralysing, Armour Piercing (4) | 1 |

for the humanity of this parallel, but openly speaks against the experiments that are going on. 'After all, they already live in paradise... why toy with perfection?' he says. During the final descent into NuAtlantis, a successful Hard Perception test by at least one Agent reveals the existence of another, smaller submarine docked in a farther area with the facility. This submarine does not match the style of the NuAtlantean vessels the Agents have seen in their research or the dive.

As Kingfisher slows to accommodate linkages from the pressure docks, the scene displayed on the viewscreens transforms into something wonderful. Iridescent lights shine upon the area, revealing stretches of kelp fields flowing slowly in the current, carefully monitored coral structures that naturally divert flow, and dozens of small, one-person work-submersibles tending to it all. Fish so strange they could be alien lifeforms flit back and forth, joining enormous bottom-feeders and titanic crustaceans to create a backdrop unlike anything on Earth. The Agents get plenty of time to take it all in before confronting the outside of NuAtlantis itself.

NuAtlantis is arranged as several small orbs that spoke off from the central, massive domed structure. The dome itself is pearlescent and covered in hexagonal facets and current-collecting turbines, making the central part of the arcology look like some kind of space station. NuAtlantis glistens and glows brightly enough to illuminate the darkness of the deep ocean for nearly half a kilometre in all directions. It is a literal beacon of light that is figuratively illuminating the path to better humankind in this parallel.

'Get ready to disembark,' Padraig calls over the sound of the magnetic clamps locking the boarding umbilical onto the Kingfisher, 'orientation begins as soon as we get inside. Put on your happy faces, people. It is time to make some new friends.'

Welcome to NuAtlantis

Crossing the 40 metres of pressurised boarding umbilical between the Kingfisher and NuAtlantis is all it takes to initially regulate the Agents to the filtered atmosphere and constant thrum of life support regulators. Immediately before the Agents head inside, Padraig wishes them luck and tells them to be careful, dropping his wry smile for moment. After touring the area and settling in an undersea cove a few dozen kilometres away, he expects to return in 72 hours to pick them back up. Should they require emergency evacuation before that time, the Agents need to take into consideration the 18-hour dive or seek alternate rescue.

The Agents are welcomed to NuAtlantis by two courteous crew members, Stacia and Malcolm. They check each Agent's guest pass before welcoming them officially, complete with gift baskets laden with hydroponic fruits, kelp chips, and dehydrated tea and coffee. After handing out the baskets and dozens of uncomfortably long handshakes, they explains the primary rules and regulations for visitors:

> ### NuAtlantis Law
>
> The following explains the laws of NuAtlantis the Agents could infringe upon during their stay as well as the punishments involved.
>
> *NuAtlantis has an enriched, oxygenated atmosphere and is a completely non-smoking environment:* **100 Euromark fine per incident**
>
> *Visitors cannot stray from clearly marked green sectors after 20:00 without security escort:* **Detainment in brig until 10:00 on the following day; 1000 Euromark fine**
>
> *Non-sonic firearms of any kind are forbidden in NuAtlantis:* **Confiscation of firearm; detainment in brig pending deportation**
>
> *Public inebriation is not tolerated outside of designated hospitality sectors:* **Detainment in brig for 24 hours; 200 Euromark fine**
>
> *Recording classified data of any kind is forbidden in NuAtlantis:* **Confiscation of data; detainment in brig pending deportation**
>
> *Physical violence is a sign of devolved behaviour and is not tolerated outside of sanctioned sporting events:* **Detainment in brig for six hours; 500 Euromark fine**
>
> *Vandalism of NuAtlantean property is not tolerated:* **200 Euromark fine; six hours of community service**

Once the NuAtlantean laws are thoroughly discussed, the initial tour of the arcology begins.

NuAtlantis is designed for ease of travel as well as safety. The central domed portion forms 75% of the arcology's area, with nine smaller mini-domes spoking off from the main section, seven in equal distances around the base circumference and two jutting upwards like towers from the southernmost side. Most of the central dome is considered to be 'green sectors', marked as such by

the stripes along walkways and walls, and contains living quarters, commercial outlets, commissary, and other public access areas – including the guest suites where the Agents are staying during their visit.

The branched mini-domes are classified areas that require specialised clearance or security escorts to gain access. Each mini-dome contains its own specialised reason for being additionally secure, formed into enclosed dedicated offices. The dome branches contain the following types of specific utilities: armoury, filtration, docking/reception, food services, medical quarters, security/brig, and laboratories.

Look and Feel

NuAtlantis bears the aesthetics of a clean, somewhat sterile museum in most places. Alabaster tiles, polished chrome, art, and knick-knacks are omnipresent. All public signs and writings are posted in the three languages of the governments originally involved in setting up the station: first in English, then Japanese, and lastly in Portuguese. Blocks of oxygen-enriching algae are positioned throughout the facility, placed like colourful bricks in the stark white walls, and slow-moving fans push earthy, floral odours throughout NuAtlantis.

To complement its completely self-sufficient power grid, achieved through numerous current turbines and collection points in volcanic vents, NuAtlantis regulates energy consumption via motion-sensing lights, temperature controls, and dual-operation doors in the majority of the arcology. Where activity is at a minimum or a momentary lull, lights go dim, air currents slow, and doors revert to manual activation. In case of emergency, any mechanism that runs on electricity has a hand-cranked mini-generator within a few metres that can be used to temporarily charge a small area of the power grid for a short time.

Inhabitants and Environs

There are three types of people on NuAtlantis: visitors, familial guests, and staff. Visitors, like the Agents, are all required to wear their hosted badges to show they are allowed to be wandering around in the public areas unescorted. Familial guests are the spouses and children of NuAtlantean employees that do not, in and of themselves, fill a role for the arcology; they can be recognised by the shining chrome wristband on their left wrist. NuAtlantean staff wear predominantly indigo-coloured utilitarian uniforms bear a single bandolier-styled stripe of a colour signifying their role in NuAtlantis.

Within the central dome are stacks of dormitories. Public spaces like shops, hotels, bars, and the like are all found on ground-floor levels. Personnel housing and private business offices are on higher floors, accessible by stairs or electric lifts. Some of the world's best ergonomics experts designed the layout and structure of the facility; everything flows and connects together gracefully.

During the tour of the central dome, the Agents are shown all the public locations necessary to their stay on the way to their designated quarters. Each Agent is granted a single-occupancy room and free access to the public eatery on the first floor to the building complex. The rooms are small but well furnished, and come stocked with a small supply of hygiene products and healthy if unfamiliar snacks (kelp chips, dried sardine bites, prawn rice crackers). The doors to these rooms do not come with actual locks, but a small chain can be strung from the inside to thwart accidental entrants.

After shown to their rooms, the Agents are given free access to roam for the remainder of the evening (roughly three hours before the 20:00 Green-only curfew). During that time, they can explore a number of different public areas, speak with NuAtlanteans, or visit different sectors of the facility before turning in for the night. The Games Master should take the following into account as the Agents explore:

- While being shown around, a basic Perception test reveals the general NuAtlantean populace is interested in newcomers, but not overly concerned (unless the Agents do something warranting concern). Visiting guests are rare in the facility, but as long as they have proper escort or passes, they are noted but ignored.
- NuAtlantean guards patrol the outermost walkways and public gathering areas every 30 minutes or so. This gives ample time to Agents wanting to explore when and where they may not be allowed to do so.
- The hand generators can power all basic electric devices on the power grid in a 10-metre cubic area for a number of minutes equal to five times the number of minutes cranked by hand. An easy Mechanisms test can divert this power into an off-grid device or into a makeshift wire-arc that inflicts 1d2 damage per minute cranked.
- Trying to remove a familial guest's ID wristband results in a bright orange semi-permanent dye spurting out in a one-metre radius.
- Bypassing secure doors to get into classified areas anywhere in NuAtlantis require two successful Mechanisms tests to physically bypass the double-airlock-style entry points found throughout the arcology. These dual-layered airlocks are designed to slam shut in case of a hull breach, minimising flooding and collapse until repairs can be made.
- There is a prisoner being held in the brig whilst the Agents are staying in NuAtlantis. Her name is Meghan Royce Willard, a visiting commercial saleswoman from Ireland being detained on suspicion of data-theft until her government can pick her up. She claims innocence, but clever conversation and inquiries can reveal her true intentions – her goal was to steal the regenerating algal filters used by the NuAtlanteans.

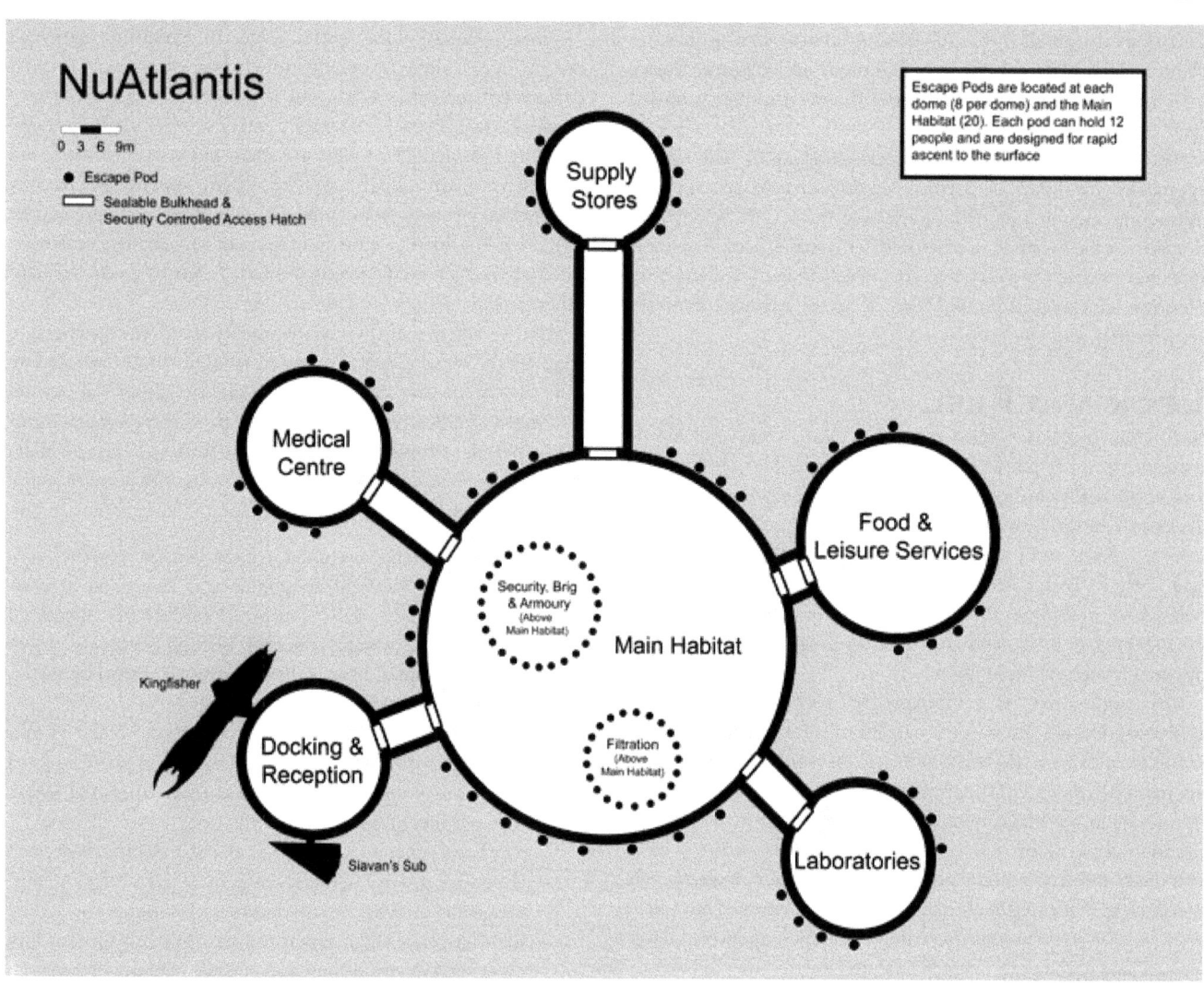

Unexpected Guests

While the Agents are getting acquainted with NuAtlantis and making their preliminary preparations for the mission, the Disruptor agents (who came in on the submarine the Agents may have seen during the Kingfisher's descent) have been held up at docking customs. NuAtlantean entrant protocols are very strict.

The Disruptor sub has two occupants – a powerful psionic Disruptor knight Siavan and her ominous bodyguard, McAvoy. Through the use of her insidious mental abilities, Siavan has secured emergency guest passes for her and McAvoy, convinced the security commission of their sincerity towards NuGenesis and inserted themselves as 'Canadian foreign dignitaries' alongside the Agents. While it was not easy, they also manage to get their large – and extremely private – luggage containers released.

Siavan and McAvoy are escorted to the same general housing area as the Agents, but are given one of the only double-occupancy suites on the block. The nefarious pair enters their temporary space at 18:30, doing so openly and without any semblance of stealth. If any Agents are around and looking across the curving throughway, they see Siavan enter the metallic, prefabricated structure with only a small attaché case. McAvoy however, is carrying two very bulky, heavy trunks, one in each hand – far more luggage than the Agents likely brought with them. McAvoy is a professional bodyguard, and opposed Stealth tests against his Perception might be called for to avoid being noticed – and immediately brought up to NuAtlantean security.

Once the two Disruptor agents have disappeared into their suite, they do not re-emerge until the NuAtlantean staff members come to gather all the visiting scientific emissaries for an official drinks and appetisers meeting, including both the Agents and the Disruptor agents. Until that happens, Siavan and McAvoy hole up in their suite getting their secret and specialised equipment ready for their machinations to unfold over the next few days.

Meet and Greet

After the Agents and the Disruptor agents are settled in, around 20:00, the suite communications speakers rattle to life with conversation-breaking tones until answered. On the other end of the call is Javier Golde, NuAtlantean secretary of guest services, with an open invitation to a special social soiree beginning in 30 minutes.

The event is being held for all visiting dignitaries, social ministry staff, and a few select others. NuAtlantis is holding an evening 'drinks and starters' get together where a select guest list can show their passes and enjoy a few hours of getting to know one another and the free amenities of the facility. It is being held in the Lanternfish Lounge several sections away in the central dome, but well within walking distance for any able-bodied Agents.

Despite its name and the facility-wide ban on smoking, the lounge is dimly lit and made to feel like a smoky bar or tavern. It has ambient music, copious table and bar seating, and two jovial bartenders behind the brushed-nickel bar (Marsha and Carlos). All drinks and appetiser orders are free at the event, with staff being instructed to try and make all attendees feel welcome and to acquiesce to their needs (if possible, and within common sense).

During the meet and greet, Agents with Dependencies based on overeating, alcohol, or other social vices might have some trouble with the free services. This could call for a number of different Willpower versus Dependency contests, especially if the Agents dive into the party atmosphere.

The meet and greet runs from 20:30 until 02:00 the next morning. Throughout those hours, the Agents can enjoy the event and the company of other guests. The guest list is as follows:

- Any Agents that choose to attend
- Three off-duty NuAtlantean guards (Johann, Michael, and Jacqueline)
- The customs official who cleared the Agents
- Siavan and McAvoy
- A dark-skinned, off-duty medical assistant named Terry
- A mid-40s NuAtlantean hydro-therapist named Amanda Hoch with a weakness for red wine
- Holden Colby, a 27-year-old filtration mechanic

The party is intended to be a fun time and offer the Agents a chance to loosen up a bit before the thickest parts of the mission start up on the following day. It also is a good way for the Agents to cement their own alibi stories. If the Agents begin to pry or speak about NuGenesis at all, everyone at the party knows nothing – except for Terry and Siavan.

Depending on the time of night, how many drinks he has had, and the Agents' persuasive skills, Terry might admit to the existence of NuGenesis – possibly even let slip a few minor details about what it means to the NuAtlanteans. He is likely to ironically point out that it is a highly classified secret that seemingly has been leaked to the Agents' organisation and another firm (at which point he gestures to Siavan).

If the topic is brought up at all within Siavan's earshot, she eavesdrops as best she can. The Disruptors did not inform her that others could be competing for NuGenesis, and it makes her far more curious about the Agents. If this happens, or if the Agents ask her directly about NuGenesis, she claims to be a representative for a Canadian neurosurgery firm looking to purchase the NuGenesis process – having learned about it through 'classified channels'. This also makes her want to get closer to whichever Agent seems to be the easiest target for her social (perhaps even psychic) predations.

Siavan is a social butterfly at the meet and greet, making sure that she has some personal interaction with everyone in the lounge. She loves this sort of thing, and her personal skillset is perfect for a gathering like this. The Agents are likely the most interesting people at the party, and Siavan's knack for seduction could lead her to one or more of them rather quickly based on their appearance or conversation. She is drawn to powerful people as they are the most useful to her in the long run. McAvoy stands around silently most of the time, but never lets Siavan out of his sight if able – unless she dismisses him to allow for private time. Siavan never suggests returning to her room for a liaison, instead demurring that displacing her colleague would be rude.

The following apply in investigations of Siavan and McAvoy:

Agents succeeding in an Insight roll while observing or inquiring about Siavan can learn the following facts:
- (Success) She has a subtle air of command that seems to extend to anyone else in her near vicinity.
- (Success) She is a very tactile person, always touching, rubbing, and leaning on the people around her.
- (Critical Success) She looks undeniably similar – perhaps even identical – to an enemy agent from a past mission on a distant parallel.

Agents succeeding in an Insight test while observing or inquiring about McAvoy can learn the following facts:
- (Success) He is utterly subservient to Siavan.
- (Success) He is very strong. If they observed him earlier, they recall he had no trouble carrying all of the luggage in his massive arms.
- (Critical Success) One of his gloved hands is larger and thicker than the other, insinuating a mutation or possibly a hidden augmentation.

Should the Agents try to break in or enter in surveillance on Siavan's suite after they have moved in, they discover advanced countermeasures in place. White noise generators, additional magnetic locking strips on the door, and a micro-camera nodule placed above the suite's only window make the apartment all but impenetrable without significantly difficult Lock Picking, Mechanisms, Sensors, and/or related special Science skill tests.

Around midnight, Siavan leads the room in a loud, boisterous toast to 'The success of NuAtlantis and all those who ally with her'. During the toast (while all eyes are supposedly on her), McAvoy slips out. If any Agents follow, the *Midnight Mischief* section should apply to them.

MIDNIGHT MISCHIEF

McAvoy's instructions are to sneak out of the meet and greet, swing by their suite to pick up a small device and a (stolen) NuAtlantean engineer's toolkit before heading over to the area right outside the security/brig mini-dome gate. If any of the Agents follow him from the gala, they need to be stealthy in tailing him or McAvoy confronts them openly. He is on orders not to be too violent with anyone in the facility until after Siavan gives him the okay to do so – meaning he pulls his punches and avoids causing permanent harm to the Agents.

If the Agents manage to follow McAvoy unnoticed all the way to the mini-dome gating area, they witness him sneak up to an access panel a few metres away from the tunnel seal. Using the tools in a NuAtlantean kit, McAvoy circumvents security measures on an access panel, slips inside, and closes it behind him. He re-emerges a few moments later, looks around to make sure no one is watching, and then heads back to his suite (dropping the toolkit in a recycling dumpster along the way).

Whilst inside the engineering tunnel, McAvoy plants a subsonic device to be activated later. The device, when triggered remotely, sends out a pulse frequency that can shatter the polymer of the dome – and let in hundreds of thousands of gallons of ocean flood into the security/brig mini-dome.

McAvoy uses an advanced electromagnetic suite to bypass the security measures on the access panel and the video surveillance in the area. Unless the Agents have similar equipment on them, NuAtlantean security detects any further intrusions in the access panels and falls upon the trespassers quickly – a wrinkle that very much works against the Agents' goal of getting the NuAtlantean government on their side as allies.

The NuAtlanteans believe their security is impregnable. Should the Agents decide to turn McAvoy in for his actions, the NuAtlanteans run the surveillance tapes of the area (which are filled with static), conduct area scans (which reveal nothing), and simply write off the Agents' accusations as 'drunken ramblings'. Either a single Herculean or three Hard Difficulty Influence skill tests could persuade Guard Captain Jenner to send and engineering team into the panels – where they are unlikely to find anything. The device is physically small and unobtrusive, requiring two Very Hard Perception skill tests to find once inside the engineering tunnel.

SUNDAY GIRL

At 06:45 on Sunday morning, the Agents (and the Disruptor agents) are awakened to rapid knocking on their housing suite doors. They are being roused at such an early hour by messenger escorts sent by Natalia's scientific staff (which could be rough on any Agents that spent a bit too long at the free bar the night before). After a few apologies for the early hour, they are quick to inform the Agents about the impending birth of a special little girl within the next half-hour and urge them to witness the event, as it pertains to their reason for visiting.

The Agents are loaded into a small, electric cart in the street. There is room for Siavan and McAvoy, but if Siavan has had any reason for concern about the Agents (perhaps based on interactions at the meet and greet) and they 'wait for the next one'. If Siavan chooses not to ride with the Agents over to the laboratories, an Insight skill test reveals that she is now oddly wary of the Agents, while a Critical Success reveals that she looks upon them with far too knowing a stare – she knows more than she should and that should worry the Agents.

After a short ride across the central dome, the Agents are brought to the laboratories mini-dome entrance and handed off to a pair of waiting NuAtlantean guards and Terry (whom they should remember from the meet and greet). They remain in the docking ring until all of the Agents and the Disruptor agents to arrive before making elementary introductions between everyone involved.

The guards with Terry wave magnetic scan-wands over all the Agents, Siavan, and McAvoy. The scan-wands are sensitive enough to pick up any metallic objects larger than an ink pen or anything giving off electromagnetic signatures (like active recording equipment). Barring some possible equipment the Agents have on them at the time, only McAvoy sets off the detector, specifically his oversized hand. Siavan quickly produces a 'medical prosthesis' customs card to explain his metallic extremity. If the Agents have something that sets off the scan-wands, they need to do some fast-talking to stay out of the brig, and this surely raises Siavan's suspicions of them.

Siavan is introduced officially as a purchasing representative for Toronto Neurology and Pharmaceuticals; she has been 'invited under unexpected circumstances, like yourselves'. McAvoy is introduced as her assistant and nothing else said about him. After the awkward introductions and a five-minute walk through the docking tube, the Agents are brought to a secured laboratory.

The laboratory of Doctor Natalia Parsons is a perfect combination of chemistry, genetics, and fertility sciences. It is a sterile location with only a few staff scattered amongst two dozen individually sealed rooms, each with specialised equipment for whatever process allotted to it. An Agent with the right type of Science skills can make a basic test to recognise equipment in the laboratory rooms from a variety of fields: chemistry, biology, neuro-science, genetics, and obstetrics.

The Agents are brought to Natalia's NuGenesis Protocol lab and are introduced to the 'good doctor'. Even though she is exhausted from 12 straight hours of working on her project's current birth and shaking from too much caffeine, Natalia greets everyone with genuine smiles and warm handshakes. She is justifiably pleased, as in only a short while, she opens one of the lab's artificial wombs to reveal the most psionically advanced offspring of the NuGenesis Protocol.

While the guests get cleaned up and dressed in one-use yellow scrubs, Natalia describes – in broad strokes – how NuGenesis is applied.

The process begins by selecting two healthy NuAtlantean bloodlines with genetic markers for potential psionic ability. Viable eggs are surgically removed it from the mother and placed it in a nutrient-rich artificial womb chamber to be fertilised by the paternal donor. After a successful fertilisation, weekly infusions of super-concentrated growth hormones as well as a cocktail of gene enhancers are applied to jumpstart certain aspects of the foetus during every minute of the lengthy 48 weeks of gestation. The result, in theory, is a highly psionic child that is removed from the womb at the end of the 48th week.

After the brief discussion, all visitors are brought to a secure room dominated by viewing couches, medical supply tables, and a large cylindrical plastic tube. Inside the apparatus, amidst a spider web of cables, piping and IV bags is a large semi-organic sack of yellowish fluid – containing the shape of a foetal child.

The next 20 minutes are a blur of surgical instruments, medical jargon, and visceral extraction. An Agent with the Medicine skill can attempt a Herculean test to pay close attention to Natalia and learn the surgical side of the NuGenesis Protocol. Even if the rest of the process is lost, they can partially report what they have learned.

At the end of that time, Natalia produces a young, fair-haired girl that looks to be nearly two years of age despite only having just been 'born'. Alice, like all of the artificially birthed beings, has no navel.

After several minutes of poking, testing, and prodding the young girl, Natalia introduces her as Alice. Alice is the seventh successful NuGenesis birth her crew has managed to produce, but the first to spend the full 48 weeks in enhanced gestation, making Alice possibly the most advanced being produced by the Protocol.

Before Natalia hands Alice off to one of her assistants (possibly Terry), the young girl stares intensely at Siavan (and any Agents who are psionic), cocking her head inquisitively and flexing her fingers and toes. Alice can sense the psychic abilities – feel them through the aether – and is curious about the sensation. Although she struggles slightly to stay with fellow psychic beings, Alice is escorted away into a side room.

Natalia is beaming with pride as she takes the guests around the rest of the ward, showing proof that the next NuAtlantean generation will be of a superior stock because of the Protocol. The doctor is beyond pleased with her Programme, almost drunk with excitement to show others her success and is happy to answer basic questions about NuGenesis as she escorts them to several other viewing rooms. In each room, there are six other children – all female by design initially – of ages ranging approximately between three to four years. The children all are involved in learning-based activities, but the last one (Melissa) can be seen levitating a block with dramatic gestures of concentration. Natalia does not interrupt any of the children's studies, but she brings everyone around to see the fruits of her success before ending the tour in an exit lounge. If any Agent has some way of detecting the presence and/or strength of psionic ability, all of the NuGenesis children Natalia shows them register as moderately powerful psychics – Alice terrifyingly so, clearly the strongest.

Any deeper or more technical inquiries (anything that borders on figuring out how to make it work) result in Natalia waiving them off pleasantly before explaining the 'information is proprietary and could only be shared with consent of the President'. A Hard test of an Agent's Insight skill on Natalia during her post-birthing conversation shows how honestly eager she is to share more about NuGenesis; she is only being reserved because too many NuAtlantean people are around and watching.

Presidential Invitation

After as much conversation as needed with Natalia and Terry (although it would make little sense if it lasts less than twenty minutes), an officer from the Office of the President enters the room and puts an end to it. The officer invites everyone privy to Alice's birth to a special social gathering in the banquet hall at 18:00.

The officer makes it undeniably clear: this is a social gathering to discuss the potential future of the now-proven NuGenesis Protocol outside of the NuAtlantean jurisdiction.

After the Presidential officer arrives and invites everyone to the banquet later, the Agents have several hours to investigate and interact with NuAtlantis, the Disruptor agents, and Natalia – the lattermost is remarkably susceptible to the Seduction skill due to her Dependencies.

Siavan spends the hours between the birth and the banquet preparing her for the insidious deeds her and McAvoy have planned, but entertains social relations with the Agents if they attempt to interact with her. At this time, she should be concerned and wary about their presence here, but she is a social manipulator first and foremost. Keep in mind her psionic talents could be very bad for the Agents if she desires to use them, even more so if she managed to make friends with the Agents during the previous evening's meet and greet.

The Banquet

The doors to the President's private banquet hall are guarded by two guards who do not budge or speak more than a denial to speak until exactly 18:00, when they receive the signal to allow everyone inside. If the Agents get to the hall before 18:00, they find Siavan and McAvoy already waiting (they prepared quickly after the invitation and came to wait).

Siavan is dressed for the occasion in elegant dinner attire, with oddly large and elaborate jewellery decorating her ears and neck. McAvoy, however, is dressed the same as always – in a utilitarian jumpsuit, gloves, and a high-collared overcoat.

The doors open and a trio of uniformed servers offer to take jackets or bags before showing the guests to a large octagonal table in the centre of the hall (keeping either arouses suspicion). The table has several elegant place settings arranged upon it amidst a handful of appetisers and a variety of drinks, both alcoholic and not. While everyone is being shown to seats around the table, Siavan nods to McAvoy, who leaves the area (he does not attend the banquet). This is not subtle, and if any of the Agents make note of it, she has any number of quick responses to explain away her assistant ('He isn't feeling well all of a sudden' or 'This just isn't his type of get together' are good examples).

With a Very Hard Perception test made when Siavan whispers to McAvoy, an Agent can read her lips, revealing her order of 'Go. Go and take your position'. This is either to be ready to activate the previously planted device or get one planted to be activated in a hurry, depending on how last evening went.

Once everyone is seated and possibly started filling drinks and starter plates, two doors at the far end of the hall open. Natalia, her assistant Terry, President Olin Traviche, and one of his personal guards enter the room and take up seats around the table. Olin takes an empty seat (if available) next to Siavan, but Natalia and Terry sit anywhere they can. Successful Insight skill tests when the NuAtlanteans join the banquet shows Terry's anxiety about being in a presidential meeting, Natalia has already had a few drinks, pre-celebrating her success (making all skill checks, apart from Seduction, into Hard Difficulties), and Olin is quite interested in Siavan for more than just socio-political reasons.

A four-course meal of hearty seafood, vegetation, and synthetic sweets is brought into the hall by uniformed staff members over two hours' worth of coming and going. While that is underway, Olin addresses his guests with the following statement:

'The good Doctor Parsons has finally perfected the NuGenesis Protocol, and through its use NuAtlantis will change the world. We are going to usher in a new golden age to humanity, and everything we have been working towards here will come to fruition. So much of the world's hope and resources have gone into our beloved arcology, it is wonderful to know we are so close to showing what we have become. Until we have the surface's full support, however, we must be wise and careful in whom we ask to help us further NuGenesis. Your two firms are the first to be interested, despite the clandestine nature of the Protocol. I have invited you here not only to celebrate, but to hear why you want to help us, and how.'

When the President talks about the clandestine nature of NuGenesis and how it was mysteriously leaked, an Easy Insight test reveals a ferocity in his eyes towards Natalia and assumedly her lack of security.

The Agents have as long as they need to talk about what they hope to do to help with NuGenesis and convince President Traviche that the Protocols would be best served with their organisation – and not Siavan's. As that they cannot tell the whole truth about from where they came, it may take some clever storytelling and likely some charm and persuasion to make the Agents seem like NuGenesis' best hope for a future. Traviche reacts well to the ideals of altruism, purity of purpose, and honest goals that will help NuGenesis springboard humanity into the future – also cementing the NuAtlantis project as a worldwide success. This is a political business venture with immense gains to be had.

Siavan interjects her own reasoning from time to time, making sure to deliver her points to the President's satisfaction specifically. She gives counterpoints and reactions to what the Agents are saying, feeding on Traviche's patriotism and Natalia's professional pride. The Disruptor knight weaves all the necessary half-truths about her 'corporation', staying away from science facts that could prove her wrong – happily admitting that she is no scientist, merely the smiling face of NuGenesis' future.

During this conversational back and forth, the Agents undertake a Social Conflict task resolution against Siavan. The Agents use their Deceit, Insight, Influence, Oratory, and Passions primarily against Siavan's use of Deceit, Influence, Oratory, and Seduction skills. The full rules for a Social Conflict can be found in MYTHRAS, page 287. It might seem as though a handful of Agents pitted against the singular skills of Siavan, but her high skill levels, psychic talents, and the sexual desires of the President give her quite an edge.

Just as Olin is about to rule in favour of the Agents or when Siavan

feels it is the perfect time to spring their trap, she sends a secret signal to McAvoy – who has taken up position across from the security/brig mini-dome. A Hard Perception test allows an Agent to notice Siavan pressing one of the gaudy gemstones on her necklace in the 10 seconds before the dome shakes and the emergency claxons go off.

When commanded to do so, McAvoy sends the activation code in his gauntlet and triggers the subsonic device he planted the night before (see Midnight Mischief). The resulting subsonic shock wave tears open the shell of the security/brig mini-dome and its umbilical tube, flooding it with ocean water and setting off emergency alarms everywhere.

Back in the banquet hall, all hell is breaking loose. Drinks spill, the walls shake, lights flicker, and emergency claxons erupt throughout the facility.

A look of abject horror crosses Orin's face as he leaps to his feet. His guards rushing to his side and quickly escort him out of the room to safety. Additional guards enter the room to evacuate the medical staff and guests, as well. While leaving, Olin bids everyone to get to safety and wait for further instructions.

Siavan tries desperately to get escorted out with the President, going so far as to even act like a damsel in distress and cling to his arm. She plays scared, maybe even conjuring up a few tears, and begs for him to get her to safety. Her goal is to hopefully get him alone to further seduce him or place him in a position to use her powerful psychic powers on him – circumventing the NuGenesis negotiations completely. Unless the Agents do something quickly to interject, a single successful Influence skill test on Siavan's part convinces Olin to get her personally to safety.

It does not take much convincing by the Agents to shed their guards after the claxons begin; the guards all have friends and families they want to go check on.

SABOTAGE!

The tidal shielding gives way quickly under the ocean pressure and begins intensely flooding the area. Smaller cracks and leaks from all over within 10 metres of the mini-dome's docking tube, spraying water dramatically on the throughways and threatening further collapse. Safety bulkheads have sealed off the mini-dome itself and emergency repair drones have been dispatched, but it takes 10 hours to replace the shattered dome facet, siphon off the flooded sections, and rescue survivors/retrieve casualties.

Nearly 80% of the current security guards in NuAtlantis are drowned in flooded sections, trapped behind emergency seals, or trying their best to help repairs from the other side of the attachment tube. This allows the Agents – and the Disruptor agents – to move about relatively unhindered in the central dome.

While it is nearly impossible to get into the security/brig mini-dome whilst flooded, the Agents may wish to help with the repairs. Whether part of their plot to gain access to NuGenesis or simply done out of the desire to do good, a handful of successful Engineering and Mechanisms tests go a long way towards cementing the Agents as 'good guys' in the NuAtlanteans' eyes.

If it happens that an Agent or Agents are stuck in the brig when the flooding happens, they drown quickly unless some kind of action is taken. There are over 20 handheld breather units in lockers that pop open during an emergency, each one capable of 30 minutes of air. If an Agent is in this position, a Games Master could create an entire sub-scenario out of the watery survival/escape scene.

The Disruptors' sabotage of the facility opens up several options, especially if Siavan's talks with the President did not go as well as planned. While NuAtlantis is in a state of emergency, the Disruptors make the most of the chaos. The planned course of action is for Siavan to use her deception skills to get in close with Traviche or Natalia, get them in private, and psychically assault them to take control of NuGenesis. If that cannot be readily done, Natalia's assistant Terry is another possible target. If interrupted or otherwise stopped in her attempts, Siavan does not put up more than an argument and instead tries to keep those responsible busy long enough for McAvoy to succeed in his mission.

During the emergency (and the few hours after), McAvoy has a more simplified but far more dangerous role – he must use the lowered security and mayhem to gain access to the laboratories and steal something concrete for Siavan to bring back. If the Disruptor is not under too much scrutiny from the Agents, McAvoy chooses data and records theft. If earlier events are forcing the Disruptors to push the boundaries of risk, McAvoy grabs a medical technician – or better yet one of the young girls NuGenesis has created. If McAvoy does resort to a kidnapping, he brings the heavily sedated captive immediately back to their housing suite to be psychically interrogated later. To avoid onlooker curiosity, McAvoy uses a wheeled cargo cart and a tarp tossed over the captive, something that could be noticed with a successful Perception test.

McAvoy cannot allow himself to be stymied in this burglary. He fights bitterly against anyone who tries to stop him, knowing that the state of emergency should cover all but the most public of conflicts. His orders from Siavan are plainly stated, and he would rather step out an airlock portal than allow himself to be captured. Siavan would much rather McAvoy get away with the captured data/staff/specimens without too much trouble, but she has already given him the clearance to use deadly force to cover his tracks. If it comes to a kidnapping, McAvoy has no qualms about leaving a trail of bodies behind him.

Although the primary damages are focussed on the security/brig area, any depressurisation within NuAtlantis is a major risk to the stability of the whole facility. Throughout the emergency and the following repairs, there is a general feel of chaos, danger, and more than a few 'popped ears' in the central dome. Unless the Agents are directly involved with the repairs or giving aid to the NuAtlanteans, they see that the majority of the inhabitants are staying safe behind re-pressurised doors.

The emergency status is lifted after the first 5 hours of repairs (the claxons are silenced in 15 minutes, leaving only the safety strobes on). Only after his people are safe and the engineers give him the all-clear for public threat levels are messages left for the Agents (and the Disruptor agents) saying President Traviche requires their presence for an official statement at 11:00 the next morning.

PLEASE, PLEASE HELP ME

In the hour after the emergency status of the arcology is lifted, while President Traviche is dealing with the repercussions of the sabotage and signing the orders to get all guests off the damaged facility, Natalia seeks out whichever Agent made the strongest positive impression upon her. If this has not happened in any way, choose one of the Agents at random.

The sabotage of the security mini-dome has proven the existence of a hidden threat to NuAtlantis, and Natalia is fearful (rightfully so) that it has to do with her perfected Protocol. She has come to seek protection from possible attack.

The attack never comes unless something seriously drastic has taken place in the time the Agents have been in NuAtlantis. Siavan was sent here for espionage purposes and McAvoy does not resort to open aggression unless he is ordered to do so or is aggressively confronted directly by the Agents during his possible burglary of the laboratories.

While Natalia is in one of the Agent's care, other Agents could break into the NuGenesis laboratory (possibly using her uniform and ID card) to steal, copy, or destroy the NuGenesis data. Without the ID card, it takes a basic Computers or Hard Mechanisms skill test to break into the laboratory – but not any Stealth tests, as the guards are low staffed and preoccupied. Finding the data requires a Science test.

Natalia stays with the Agents until 10:00 the following morning, giving them ample time to become closer friends, lovers, or potential allies. She leaves in the morning to go speak to the President and give her final thoughts on the matter.

If the Agents have decided to eliminate Siavan and McAvoy to remove that the threat of NuGenesis falling into Disruptor hands, this could be the best time to do so. Getting caught in violent actions in NuAtlantis is not taken lightly, especially in the wake of the sabotage elsewhere. A direct conflict in the open could result in a much bigger problem for the Agents unless they are tremendously careful.

A PRESIDENTIAL DECISION

Traviche has sent for all of his guests – the Agents and the Disruptors – to join him in a conference room at 11:00, 30 minutes before Padraig and the Kingfisher are scheduled to return and pick the Agents up for the ascent to the surface. When everyone has arrived, Olin and six of his guards arrive. Orin directs all guests on NuAtlantis to prepare for early departure. He has decided to revoke all guest passes in light of the attack, but he intends to explain his decision about the future of the NuGenesis Protocol before they go.

Depending on how earlier events took place, President Traviche's decision falls into one of three outcomes:

- If the Agents persuaded Natalia of their good intentions, she has told the President to trust them. He offers to sign an initial exclusivity data contract concerning the Protocol with 'Yggdrasil Incorporated'. This results in Siavan and McAvoy ambushing the Agents on their way to the Kingfisher.
- If the Agents were unsuccessful in making themselves look like the right decision in the eyes of the NuAtlanteans, President Traviche extends data sharing with Siavan and her 'company'. If the Agents do not wish to fail in their mission, they need to stop this from happening. As their parameters were ironclad – by any means possible – this could result in the Agents making some hard decisions in their last half hour in NuAtlantis.
- If either Natalia was not able to report to the President (especially if a body was found, etc.) or the laboratory data were destroyed/stolen, Traviche has no choice but to sadly announce the tragic end of a successful NuGenesis Protocol Programme.

CONCLUSION

After President Traviche has given his final decision, the Agents only have roughly 20 minutes before they need to meet Padraig and get on board the Kingfisher to leave NuAtlantis. This could be an easy stroll down to the docking area, a pitched fight with the Disruptors, or a frantic escape from NuAtlantean guards.

Siavan and McAvoy are on specific orders to obtain NuGenesis for the Disruptors, and while Siavan is not self-destructive enough to take on the whole arcology, she has been given permission to throw McAvoy's life away. She orders her bodyguard to attack the Agents as a distraction so she can steal the NuGenesis data or possibly even eliminate or kidnap Natalia, and get away in her waiting submarine.

If the Agents manage to bring NuGenesis (or at least the exclusivity agreement with President Traviche) back to Valhalla, they can be expected to become the ambassadors to NuAtlantis for future trips to the parallel. They may even one day be called upon to recruit Dr. Parsons and bring her into the operation.

Non-Player Characters

Padraig Ventman

Padraig is a native to 18.09.26. He is a charming man with a hint of sarcasm in a lot of his phrasing. He wears a lined naval coat most of the time, and keeps himself close shaven on both chin and scalp.

He is a skilled combatant with fist and blade, but he hates resorting to anything but his shining smile in most conflicts. This attitude changes when he has to deal with Disruptor agents, but even then, he hates taking a life.

Ventman	Attributes
STR: 14	Action Points: 3
CON: 16	Damage Modifier: +1d2
SIZ: 12	Prana: 10
DEX: 13	Tenacity: 10
INT: 14	Movement: 6 metres
POW: 10	Initiative Bonus: +13
CHA: 14	Armour: Lined Coat

1d20	Hit Location	AP/HP
1 – 3	Right Leg	0/6
4 – 6	Left Leg	0/6
7 – 9	Abdomen	2/7
10 – 12	Chest	2/8
13 – 15	Right Arm	2/5
16 – 18	Left Arm	2/5
19 – 20	Head	0/6

Skills	Passions, Traits & Dependencies
Athletics 55%, Brawn 60%, Endurance 50%, Evade 35%, Locale (Miami and environs) 70%, Navigation 55%, Perception 50%, Seamanship 65%, Sensors 44%, Stealth 42%, Unarmed 60%, Willpower 32%	Passions: Loyalty to Valhall 60%, Loyalty to Friends 48% Traits: Tenacious Dependencies: Alcohol 22%

Combat Style & Weapons	Traits & Notes
Naval Defence (Pistol, Knife, Sword) 62%	None

Weapon	Damage	Size/Reach	AP/HP	Effects
Sabre	1d6+1+1d2	M/M	6/8	Bleed, Impale

Weapon	Damage	Range	Ammo	Rate/Load
Sonic Pistol	Stun	5/10/25	10	1/3

Olin Traviche, President of NuAtlantis

The democratically elected president of NuAtlantis is a tawny-skinned man in his middle 30s with a beard finely sculpted to a devilish point, the edges of which lift upwards whenever Olin smiles. He looks upon the world, especially his undersea empire, with great pride. Traviche is an honest to goodness believer in the ideals behind the NuAtlantis project. He assumed the presidential role from an unfortunately less-than-vigilant predecessor who left things in a state of disarray politically, and has been doing everything in his power to make amends before he hands the reins off to the next president.

Traviche	Attributes
STR: 12	Action Points: 3
CON: 15	Damage Modifier: +0
SIZ: 12	Prana: 12
DEX: 14	Tenacity: 12
INT: 13	Movement: 6 metres
POW: 12	Initiative Bonus: +13
CHA: 13	Armour: ProTek Vest

1d20	Hit Location	AP/HP
1 – 3	Right Leg	0/6
4 – 6	Left Leg	0/6
7 – 9	Abdomen	2/7
10 – 12	Chest	2/8
13 – 15	Right Arm	0/5
16 – 18	Left Arm	0/5
19 – 20	Head	0/6

Skills	Passions, Traits & Dependencies
Athletics 58%, Brawn 36%, Courtesy 88%, Culture (Ducal Etiquette) 90%, Deceit 44%, Endurance 56%, Evade 40%, Influence 68%, Insight 55%, Language (Japanese) 90%, Language (Portuguese) 90%, Native Language (English), 100%, Oratory 78%, Perception 88%, Politics 80%, Stealth 36%, Willpower 74%, Unarmed 36%	Passions: Loyal to NuAtlantis 65%, Oathkeeper 45% Traits: None Dependencies: Discipline 42%

Combat Style & Weapons	Traits & Notes
Self Defence (Pistol) 36%	None

Weapon	Damage	Range	Ammo	Rate/Load
Sonic Pistol	Stun	5/10/25	10	1/3

Natalia Parsons, PhD

Natalia Noelle Parsons graduated top of her medical school class. She was chosen specifically to help adapt the people living in NuAtlantis to longer stays at great pressure and outside of natural sunlight for long periods of time. Her experiments with the human genome led her to the idea and execution of the NuGenesis Protocol.

Dark hair frames attractive features set in caramel skin; her remarkable sapphire blue eyes are always seeking out the next spark of inspiration. She is a bubbly and fun person who loses herself in her work all day long, but then loses herself in a bottle of wine as soon as her guard is down. Like two sides to the same coin, she is utterly devoted to her work until she is not – when she throws herself into nearly hedonistic reckless abandon!

Parsons	Attributes
STR: 11	Action Points: 3
CON: 12	Damage Modifier: +0
SIZ: 11	Prana: 13
DEX: 14	Tenacity: 13
INT: 18	Movement: 6 metres
POW: 13	Initiative Bonus: +16
CHA: 15	Armour: None

1d20	Hit Location	AP/HP
1 – 3	Right Leg	0/5
4 – 6	Left Leg	0/5
7 – 9	Abdomen	0/6
10 – 12	Chest	0/7
13 – 15	Right Arm	0/4
16 – 18	Left Arm	0/4
19 – 20	Head	0/5

Skills	Passions, Traits & Dependencies
Athletics 42%, Brawn 26%, Dance 64%, Deceit 70%, Endurance 75%, Evade 32%, First Aid 44%, Influence 65%, Insight 60%, Language (Icelandic) 90%, Language (Japanese) 90%, Language (Latin) 90%, Language (Portuguese) 90%, Native Language (English) 100%, Lore (NuGenesis) 110%, Oratory 75%, Perception 65%, Science (Chemistry) 95%, Science (Neurology) 95%, Science (Obstetrics) 95%, Seduction 78%, Stealth 32%, Willpower 70%, Unarmed 26%	Passions: Desire to Learn 66% Loyal to NuAtlantis 24% Traits: Savant Dependencies: Alcohol 36%

Combat Style & Weapons	Traits & Notes
Self Defence (Pistol) 36%	None

Weapon	Damage	Range	Ammo	Rate/Load
Sonic Pistol	Stun	5/10/25	10	1/3

Siavan

Siavan (pronounced shih-vaan) is a powerful telepath raised and trained by the Disruptors to serve one primary function – social and mental espionage. She is physically attractive on most levels, empirically beautiful to most cultures, and gifted enough in the psionic arts to make up for any lacking she might have to others.

Siavan's personality is anything she needs to it be at the given moment; she is a social chameleon of the highest calibre. Somewhere deep inside of her lies the true woman, a manipulative creature looking to lash out at the multiverse for her wasted youth, but that is buried behind two decades of layered lies, schemes, and false personas. She is the perfect psychic spy.

Siavan	Attributes
STR: 11	Action Points: 3
CON: 12	Damage Modifier: +0
SIZ: 10	Prana: 17
DEX: 13	Tenacity: 17
INT: 14	Movement: 6 metres
POW: 17	Initiative Bonus: +13
CHA: 16	Armour: Disruptor Slimline

1d20	Hit Location	AP/HP
1 – 3	Right Leg	4/5
4 – 6	Left Leg	4/5
7 – 9	Abdomen	4/6
10 – 12	Chest	4/7
13 – 15	Right Arm	3/4
16 – 18	Left Arm	3/4
19 – 20	Head	0/5

Skills	Passions, Traits & Dependencies
Athletics 54%, Brawn 42%, Conceal 54%, Customs 60%, Deceit 72%, Endurance 45%, Evade 38%, Influence 74%, Insight 54%, Oratory 66%, Perception 60%, Seduction 75%, Stealth 60%, Unarmed 40%, Willpower 65%	Passions: Loyalty to Disruptors 75% Traits: Psionic Dependencies: Authority 35%

Psionics

Empathy 74% (Empathic Push, Mental Shield, Psychic Wrack)

Combat Style & Weapons	Traits & Notes
Disruptor Undercover (Pistol, Knife) 60%	Marksman

Weapon	Damage	Size/Reach	AP/HP	Effects
Stilleto	1d4	S/S	4/6	Bleed, Impale

Weapon	Damage	Range	Ammo	Rate/Load
Sonic Pistol	Stun	5/10/25	10	1/3

NuAtlantis

McAvoy

The silent thug called McAvoy is a Disruptor living weapon and little more. Standing just taller than 2.5 metres and weighing nearly 228 kg, he is a giant amongst most humans. His body is filled with artificial augmentations that make him a powerful creature capable of great violence and personal savagery.

A hard chin, steely eyes, and a bald pate combine with his surgical inability to speak and eternal grimace to make him utterly unapproachable except by those whom the Disruptors have put in charge of him. He is loyal to his 'handler' to the point of self-sacrifice and when set in motion using his secret control phrases, nothing short of death causes him to cease his ordered behaviour.

McAvoy	Attributes
STR: 20	Action Points: 2
CON: 18	Damage Modifier: +1d6
SIZ: 19	Prana: 10
DEX: 12	Tenacity: 10
INT: 11	Movement: 7 metres
POW: 10	Initiative Bonus: +11
CHA: 8	Armour: Augmented Flesh

1d20	Hit Location	AP/HP
1 – 3	Right Leg	2/8
4 – 6	Left Leg	2/8
7 – 9	Abdomen	2/9
10 – 12	Chest	2/10
13 – 15	Right Arm	2/7
16 – 18	Left Arm	2/7
19 – 20	Head	2/8

Skills	Passions, Traits & Dependencies
Athletics 78%, Brawn 88%, Conceal 42%, Endurance 65%, Engineering 55%, Evade 28%, Insight 36%, Mechanisms 75%, Perception 50%, Stealth 30%, Unarmed 55%, Willpower 70%	Passions: Loyalty to Disruptors 100% Traits: Brutal, Natural Armour Dependencies: Sadism 60%

Combat Style & Weapons	Traits & Notes
Overpowering Pugilism (Kosh, Gauntlets, Wrestling) 68%	None

Weapon	Damage	Size/Reach	AP/HP	Effects
Shock Gauntlets	1d6+1d6	S/S	2/6	Armour Piercing
Kosh	1d3+1+1d6	S/S	2/3	Stun Location

NuAtlantean Guard

The guards are staff members that serve as general safety and security agents while inside the sovereign communities of NuAtlantis. They are, above all else, keepers of the peace and helpful pillars of the community. They are the only staff allowed to be armed above a survival knife or tool, and have access to larger sonic weaponry than what is listed here inside the armoury mini-dome.

Guards	Attributes
STR: 10	Action Points: 2
CON: 9	Damage Modifier: 0
SIZ: 11	Prana: 10
DEX: 10	Tenacity: 10
INT: 11	Movement: 6 metres
POW: 10	Initiative Bonus: +11
CHA: 11	Armour: Kevlar Uniforms

1d20	Hit Location	AP/HP
1 – 3	Right Leg	4/6
4 – 6	Left Leg	4/6
7 – 9	Abdomen	4/7
10 – 12	Chest	4/8
13 – 15	Right Arm	4/5
16 – 18	Left Arm	4/5
19 – 20	Head	5/6

Skills	Passions, Traits & Dependencies
Athletics 38%, Brawn 55%, Endurance 36%, Evade 28%, Perception 41%, Stealth 39%, Survival 31%, Unarmed 38%, Willpower 19%	Passions: Loyalty to NuAtlantis 60%

Combat Style & Weapons	Traits & Notes
Train Guard (Sonic Pistol, Baton) 60%	Formation Fighting

Weapon	Damage	Size/Reach	AP/HP	Effects
Baton	1d3+2	M/M	4/6	Stun Location

Weapon	Damage	Range	Ammo	Rate/Load
Sonic Pistol	Stun	5/10/25	10	1/3

Bridge Over Troubled Parallels

Parallel 11.24.10 is an unremarkable backwater with no sign of Disruptor activity. Eighteen hours ago, W.O.T.A.N flashes an outlier alert: a six sigma deviation from normal history has occurred. Fourteen hours later, everything goes critical. According to W.O.T.A.N's calculations, the parallel will collapse within 24 hours and has a 97.4% of starting a chain reaction that will take many more parallels with it. Mjollnir is summoned, briefed, and equipped. They are translocated to the heart of the problem: Edinburgh, 30 April, 1981. Their mission: discover the source of instability and neutralise it by any means necessary. If that means sacrificing a whole parallel, then they have the authority to do so. May Marx have mercy on their stained consciences!

Overview

Parallel 11.24.10
Inverted Cold War Variant
Disruption Likelihood: 97.4%

This scenario challenges the Agents' resourcefulness as they must save a parallel in a race against the clock with no help from The Valhalla Project, no equipment, and just one contact. Agents of almost any experience level can be used; the main challenge is to the Agents' ingenuity

Non-Player Characters

The following are Non-Player Characters the Agents meet during the mission. Game statistics are provided later (see page 149).

- **Hoot the Redeemer:** Owner of Hoot the Redeemer's bar and fortune-telling parlour.
- **The Twins, Jimmy and Jamie Krankie:** Two products of a failed attempt at homo novus.
- **Big Tam:** A republican milkman.
- **Hansie Qualmann:** Big Tam's mechanical genius.
- **The Banksman:** The curator of the Forth Rail Bridge.
- **The Writers Bloc:** A group of radical subversives with a mutual love of writing. One of them is a double agent.

Key Points & Timeline

1. In an unknown parallel, psychic twins are bred as part of a monstrous experiment to create *Homo Novus*. When they reach adulthood, an attempt to waken their psychic powers goes catastrophically wrong. It destroys time in that parallel and sends the twins cascading through the multiverse into parallel 11.24.10, arriving in 1976 local time.
2. The twins arrive in Edinburgh: they are insane and their powers are vastly amplified by the transition. Calling themselves Jimmy and Jamie Krankie, they use their abilities to seize power behind the scenes. They discover that

the Forth Rail Bridge is part of a mandala that can link a myriad of parallels and make plans to finish the bridge to open the link.

3. 4 hours ago: W.O.T.A.N determines that parallel 11.24.10 is at risk of collapse within 24 hours that will trigger a chain reaction across thousands of parallels.
4. The Agents arrive in Edinburgh 11.24.10 by an emergency translocation that goes wrong, leaving them with no equipment, clothes, or way back surrounded by approximately 10,000 revellers at a Fire Festival.
5. The Agents equip themselves and track down their contact: Hoot the Redeemer.
6. The Agents notice increasing temporal anomalies. As they search for the source of the instability (The Forth Bridge), they need to make allies and hide from watchers.
7. Clues lead the Agents to the Forth Bridge where they meet 'The Banksman' whilst having to fend off an attack by psionically uplifted killer chimpanzees.
8. With time running out (literally), the Agents need to find a way to prevent the bridge mandala from opening and infecting thousands of other parallels.

Background & Introduction

One hundred and fifty years ago, in a parallel now destroyed, twins were born as part of a secret breeding Programmeme to create psionically advanced human beings, *Homo Novus*. It succeeded through the use of foul and perverse methods, but the powers remained locked inside the twins. Using technology gifted by the Disruptors, the twins' creator conducted one final experiment. The experiment worked but started a chain reaction that destroyed time in that parallel and sent the twins hurtling between parallels. The twins, calling themselves Jimmy and Jamie Krankie, arrived in parallel 11.24.10 five years ago in 1976, their powers vastly amplified by the transition and driven insane by all that had occurred.

Their transition tore a hole in the Forth Bridge Multiversal Mandala, infecting their new parallel with the same temporal disease that destroyed their home parallel. With their vastly amplified psionic powers, they quickly discovered what had happened and set out to discover the secrets of the Forth Bridge in a bid to determine how to use the mandala to reach other parallels, but they were repeatedly thwarted by the bridge's guardian, 'The Banksman'.

The twins have deduced that if they don't escape the parallel the time fractures will destroy it and them with it. Realising that accessing and opening the mandala would require years of work, they corrupted the Scottish king and his government to gain the resources they needed. Once in place, they determined that the mandala was symbolically incomplete and that they would need the psychic power of thousands of individuals to open the gateway.

They started harvesting psychic power from the inhabitants of Edinburgh through a series of specially modified CCTV cameras and beaming it to the bridge. At the same time, they set to work repainting the bridge to symbolically complete it.

On the morning of 30 April 1981, the twins oversaw the final completion of the paint job using a specially designed paint. This was the symbolic completion they needed and is the six sigma event that alerted W.O.T.A.N. Now the mandala is open and only The Banksman's gradually weakening power is preventing the twins from accessing the whole multiverse and spreading the infection further. The twins plan to open the bridge by channelling the psychic power of 10,000 revellers at the Beltane Fire Festival on the evening of April 30, but the arrival of the Agents disrupts that plan halfway through.

There is not quite enough psychic power to overwhelm The Banksman yet and the twins realise that the time fractures are starting to increase exponentially. Once they recover from the pain and shock of the Agents' translocation, they plan to determine what, or who, exactly disrupted their plans and increase the power to the bridge. One of the twins – Jamie – suggests staging a massacre at a rebellious 'free town' and using the psionic pain from that. The other heads to the bridge to see if The Banksman was behind the sabotage: if so he may finally be able to track the guardian down and kill him, opening the bridge that way.

Time is short for the twins and the parallel itself. If they succeed, they will be free but the temporal infection will also be free to spread across the multiverse. If they fail, they will die along with this parallel but the multiverse will be safe. Once the Agents manage to find out what is going on, it is their job to ensure that the twins fail. But at what cost?

Parallel 11.24.10
Designator: 11.24.10
Classification: Inverted Cold War
Cultural Type: Western European
Political Type: Monarchy
Technological Type: Early Computer Age

Description: an Imperial Russia allied with European royal families opposes a United Socialist States of America. The USSA's greatest ally is The Republic of Greater England under the guidance of its 'Beloved Leader' Chairman Thatch. The United Kingdom was sundered in 1919 when England's communist revolution was stopped at the Scottish border. Now England, glares suspiciously across Hadrian's New Wall at The Free Kingdom of Scotland under the benevolent rule of King Alex 1st. Since the 'incident' of 1961 leading to the Nuclear Wasteland of Wales, an uneasy peace has lasted for 20 years in the 'Untied Kingdom'.

The events of this scenario take place within the Edinburgh of this parallel. Technologically, the parallel is roughly similar to ours in 1981: early home computers, very limited public Internet, no mobile phones. There is more variation in technology than our own Earth. In Edinburgh, one sees steam-powered trams trundling through the streets and horse-drawn drays delivering milk under the shadow of Mons Meg: the greatest gun in the world. Looking out from Edinburgh Castle, Mons Meg can destroy any target within 50 miles (80 km) in just the minute it takes to aim her.

Scotland is ruled by King Alex 1st and has its own parliament, which rubber stamps the king's decrees. The rise to power of the twins, now joint ministers of internal security (MiniSec), has led to increasingly authoritarian policies. The police force has trebled in size, troublemakers are rounded up and held without trial in the cells beneath Edinburgh Castle, and Hadrian's wall has been strengthened in response to the 'threat' of English Terrorists ('E.T.'s'). Using this threat as a cover, the MiniSec has installed an extensive network of surveillance cameras that secretly collect psychic energy and beam it to the bridge.

The Agents' only known contact is 'Hoot The Redeemer' a native of the parallel who is usually to be found in his eponymous bar. Hoot was contacted by a Valhalla Agent by the name of Agent 4th who visited the parallel 7 years ago.

A Note on Psionics

The time fractures infecting the parallel are a form of psionic disease. Any psychic Agent is aware of a continually changing psychic whine sounding like the equivalent of a dentist's drill for the frontal lobes. They find they cannot regain Prana and any attempt to meditate is Formidable. The twins, who are powerful psychics, have had five years to train themselves to deal with the issue. The other problem that psychic Agents face is that the CCTV cameras are highly attuned to psychic energy and rotate to follow them if they ever get within their POW in metres of one.

Agent Briefing

Local time and date for briefing: 19:30 UTC 30-04-1981 Parallel 00-00-00

Freyr Lingstadt summons the Agents to Greyfriars Kirk in Neuer Edinburgh. The hyperloop from the Valhalla complex gets them from London to Edinburgh in a little over an hour, and a ground effect transit takes from the Waverley Loop Terminus to the kirk. It is late afternoon and the team arrives to find heavy security and frantic activity. The graveyard and church are bathed in harsh arc lights. A portable fusion reactor is undergoing its start-up sequence just outside of a tomb as Quinscombe barks orders to scurrying techs. The only calm person appears to be Althea Rivers, who is sitting cross-legged in meditation.

As they are ushered into the church, late-afternoon sunlight streaming through its glorious stained-glass windows, Lingstadt breaks away from an operations table and comes to greet them.

The Agents notice that the ex-church is being hurriedly converted into an operations centre. A huge screen patched into W.O.T.A.N hangs on the far wall.

With no time to waste, Lingstadt provides the following information either directly or in answer to questions.

'Listen carefully team. Eighteen hours ago W.O.T.A.N announced that a six sigma historical divergence event has taken place in parallel 11.24.10. The computer is not able to provide further details but whatever happened is likely to be unique in the known multiverse. Four hours ago at 15:21 local time, W.O.T.A.N revealed that the parallel will collapse within the next 24 hours: cumulative 97.53% chance of collapse by 15:30 on May first 1981 local time to the parallel. Not only that but the collapse has a 97.41% chance of spreading to many other parallels. W.O.T.A.N can't calculate how many are at risk, but a first approximation puts the figure in the thousands.'

Parallel 11.24.10 is nondescript with no more than the usual background amount of Disruptor activity. As Lingstadt's skinny dossier shows, the information Mjollnir Section has is limited and contains little more than the broad socio-political structure.

Valhalla has one potential contact on the parallel: a native by the odd name of *Hoot The Redeemer*. Hoot had been contacted by an Agent who had briefly spent time in the parallel seven years ago. The dossier has a phone number and an address: *7 Stewart Street*. W.O.T.A.N has calculated that the address maps onto Hanover Street or Castle Street on Zero-Zero and displays a map on the viewing screen. Lingstadt reminds the Agents to memorise the information because protocol dictates that no hard copies of contact information be taken into the field.

W.O.T.A.N has been able to determine that ground zero for the crisis is somewhere within a 24 kilometre radius of that parallel's central Edinburgh, which is why the Agents have been called here. Fortunately, their contact is in the Edinburgh area.

There were no prior warnings of problems on this parallel so the Valhalla Project is unprepared. They haven't been able to find a psychic in contact with an alter-self on the parallel and the Mark II Van is undergoing some repairs. If they use Mark I Van, it is likely that the Agents won't be able to reach Edinburgh using local transport before the parallel collapses. So, they are going to try a direct translocation, which is where Professor Quinscombe comes in.

Direct Translocation

Direct translocation is experimental, limited, and one way only. It requires, a powerful psychic, several gigawatts of energy, and a stable place that is echoed in the destination parallel. W.O.T.A.N has calculated that a tomb in Greyfriars Kirk graveyard offers the best connection. The psychic – Althea Rivers – is on site right now while Quinscombe is helping a hazard team set up a portable fusion reactor in the tomb of the Mackenzie poltergeist.

The problem (well, *one* of *many*) is that direct translocation doesn't allow the Agents to take anything more than the clothes they're wearing and a small amount of equipment. Plus there's no way to use the technique to get back. So, as part of their equipment, they are given a homing beacon. This small thing shaped like an egg gives off a brief pulse to Zero-Zero indicating the Agents' presence. As soon as the signal is received, The Van is moved into position and sent to them. The signal is necessarily brief to minimise the chance of the Disruptors intercepting it.

It takes eight hours to set up a Mk I Van in Edinburgh. Lingstadt is installing it in the graveyard, so that is the recommended extraction point. Failing that, the team here can reinstall it anywhere else in Edinburgh in about three hours. If no signal is received, The Van will be sent, unmanned, to the graveyard in their parallel from 13:00 to 15:00 the next day. W.O.T.A.N has indicated that the risk of The Van being destroyed raises exponentially from 14:57 tomorrow.

Lingstadt recognises that this is a difficult and dangerous mission. The Agents have limited information, limited equipment, and limited time. There is a risk (7.1%) that the parallel might collapse before 15:30 tomorrow and extraction will be, Lingstadt looks meaningfully at Quinscombe, *problematic*. The main guidance that W.O.T.A.N has been able to provide is that any six sigma event is likely to be surrounded by other coincidences so Lingstadt advises the Agents to look out for any coincidental phenomena.

Right now, the Agents have time to pick up equipment they can carry by hand, the homing beacon, and clothes fit for spring in Edinburgh: cold, wet, and windy usually. Lingstadt can answer further questions but makes it plain that time is passing. Some answers to frequently asked questions are as follows.

- They are only being provided with one homing beacon because the Disruptors have a 100% track record of finding Agents who use a second in the same parallel.
- The Agent who visited the parallel is 'Agent 4th'. She left on a five-year mission to explore new parallels but never returned. They had communication with her after she left the parallel, so there is no reason to believe she is there now or came to grief there. She provided basic socio-political information and described the parallel as 'harmless'.
- According to 4th's report, that parallel's Edinburgh is coterminous with their own so any city map should be approximately correct.

Travelling Light

The Agents are provided with small, handheld equipment packs with technology appropriate to an early computer age parallel. For reasons that become apparent shortly, don't let the players agonise over what to take and gently suggest that taking valuable personal items might not be a great idea due to the experimental nature of direct translocation. If they request lethal weapons, they are cautioned that Scotland has strict gun laws and Lingstadt recommends against it. If they argue for long enough, Lingstadt authorises handguns only to Agents with an appropriate combat style of 70% or greater (i.e., a confirmed weapons specialist).

HERE WE GO (AGAIN)

Once the briefing is over, the Agents are given their equipment along with £500 in Scottish notes that have a high probability of being legal tender, and then summoned by Prof Q. He's fretting over the power generation of the fusion unit and annoying McAllan. Once the Agents arrive, he immediately latches onto them. If he knows the Agents from previous experiments with translocation technology, he starts to quiz them about their experiences until Lingstadt puts a stop to it.

As the shadows lengthen, the Agents find themselves standing outside Bloody MacKenzie's Tomb: lair of the Mackenzie poltergeist. Even with arc-lights adding crazy shadows into the mix and the high-pitched whine of the fusion reactor, the tomb radiates a chill and swallows noise. Scrawled on the floor inside is a chalk circle and small metal baskets that contain smouldering rosemary twigs. Quinscombe hurriedly explains what's going to happen. First though, he has some sparkling, orange liquid that he instructs them to drink. If the Agents balk, he assures them 'it's for the hangover'. When someone points out that they don't have a hangover, Quinscombe simply says, 'No, but you will. Look, Lingstadt tells me there's not much time, so drink up, stand in the circle, and hold hands. I'll explain as we go.'

The fizzy liquid is a mix of sugar and stimulants that makes the Agents' teeth ache. As they enter the tomb, Wishaw is powering up the generator and Althea Rivers is standing in the centre of a circle, holding a long, ash spear tip upwards, and whispering a mantra. Prof Q keeps up a high speed and somewhat baffling commentary.

'The rosemary's for atmosphere. Don't touch the psychic, she's opening the way. Nothing to worry about, I'm told it feels a bit like stretching. Got a headache yet? Good it's working. Hold hands and form a circle around Althea. That's the way. Anyone feeling longer yet? Hmm. Wishaw, more power! Don't worry, Lingstadt, this is within operational parameters. I think. What if we use thyme next time? Wishaw, why's that light red? It shouldn't be red.'

Quinscombe's voice fades as a screaming envelopes them. They can't tell if the screams are coming from the sudden wind gusting through the graveyard, the storm front boiling into existence, the generator, or themselves. Then they are stretching.

It feels as though someone has hooked thumbs into their eyeballs and is pulling them into the sky while shackling their feet to the ground. The world is twisting around them, enveloping them in a crazy smorgasbord of colours and distortions. Their very being is stretching like rubber. For an infinitely long, timeless second, it is as if they can see galaxies burn and feel strands of dark energy wrap around them. As their minds shatter and reform, they can see everything: two magpies butchering a seagull chick while it shrieks; two lovers in intercourse, each cheating on their partner; their own bodies still holding hands in the circle.

Then, as if pulled around into a Moebius strip, they can see inside another tomb. They can feel themselves anchored in two places at once. The agony is intense, as if somehow they are being turned inside out, and then something goes wrong.

Each Agent needs to make a Hard Tenacity skill roll. On a Success, they lose 1 Tenacity Point; on a Failure, 1d3+1 points.

They are ripped asunder. Their infinitesimally thin substance is torn by razors and teeth. Their anchoring points come loose and they are falling upwards and downwards at once, spinning out of control. The last thing they see are two hooded figures watching them, holding their hands to their heads and screaming. Then everything goes black.

FIRE WALK WITH ME

20:41 Scottish Summer Time, 30-04-1981 parallel 11.24.10 Calton Hill

The Agents have arrived on Calton Hill in the east of Edinburgh sometime around 9pm in the middle of the Beltane Fire Festival: an outdoor party featuring plenty of sex, drugs, and fire juggling. Depending on the Agents' Dependencies, they may have problems staying focussed on the job at hand.

At the moment, they know nothing of this. Those who succeeded at their Tenacity skill rolls are standing; the rest have collapsed to their knees. They feel stunned, as if in the area of an explosion. There is a dull roaring in their ears. Random, blurred colours drift by out of focus. There is an incessant pounding from somewhere, possibly the inside of their own heads and something that sounds almost like a mass cheering. Those who made their Tenacity skill rolls now find the world come into focus and can start to act.

They are standing on a stage in the cold, night air. Around them, semi-naked men, painted red, are pounding on huge drums. Behind them another man, green-painted, crowned in antlers looks down at them from a throne whilst blue-painted women attend him. Everywhere is fire. Sconces, torches, bonfires, and a huge crowd in front of them holding fire to the darkening sky. The crowd has been worked up into a frenzy by the drummers, many are naked and cavorting like whirling dervishes. It certainly doesn't look any sort of Edinburgh in the 1980s.

Speaking of naked, it's at this point that the Agents who are most aware realise that they are completely naked themselves. Some of the drummers are looking over at them, clearly puzzled but doing their best keep the rhythm going. The cheering from the crowd seems focussed on these naked strangers who have suddenly appeared from nowhere.

Anyone who made their Tenacity roll notices two hooded figures in the distance. One is gesturing at the stage and issuing orders, the other is stumbling away. It's only a brief glimpse before the Agents get swamped by dancers bounding across the stage. The hooded figures are the twins, Jamie and Jimmy Krankie, who are as shocked by developments as the Agents. Jamie is ordering a group of police (aka the 'copters') to arrest the intruders on stage. As soon as the order is given, the twins make a fast escape because their psychic senses have been neutralised by the events.

Now those who failed their Tenacity rolls are able to get back to their feet and the Agents need to think quickly. It's a cold night, they have no clothes, equipment, or money; don't know where they are; are surrounded by approximately 10,000 revellers; and police are bearing down on them. They seem to be most of the way up a hill with what looks like an unfinished Greek temple at its peak. Some of the crowd are naked bar loin-cloths or capes, but most of the crowd are dressed for the cold and enjoying watching the festivities. On the plus side, at least the Agents' nudity isn't too out of place here.

On the minus side, 3-6 police (see page 152) are making their way to the stage intent on arresting them. (There are more police than Agents.) The Agents need to act. The simplest option is escape: handle it as opposed Athletics rolls. The huge crowds and darkness should make it fairly easy. Alternatively, they could stand and fight or start a riot. The festival goers are primarily Scottish, full of beer and up for a riot. They may even rock out on stage and dare the cops to come to them; the audience won't take well to having the cops mess with the performance and things are likely to get violent.

Assuming that they escape the police, the Agents need to get some warm clothing. How they go about doing it depends on their personalities. Simply asking for something warm to wear is the easiest way to get clothed. Agents who start mugging innocents for their jeans ought to be reminded that they are supposed to be the good guys.

Assuming they manage to avoid hypothermia, the Agents can start to gather information: not the least of which is where are they and what is going on.

On that front, the Agents can learn a few things quite quickly. Fashion (for those actually wearing clothes) seems diverse: everything from jeans and parkas to Victorian great coats. The technology in use matches early 80's normal: analogue cameras (selfies with Polaroid Instamatics are all the rage), digital watches, and no sign of mobile computers or phones. The language is strongly accented Scots-English and the Agents (assuming they are not all Scottish) definitely stand out. Any Agent with an appropriate Cultural skill notices that the audience is surprisingly homogenous: normally in a capital city, one would expect a lot more visitors at an event like this.

Of particular interest is that a short while after the Agents arrive, the Northern Lights begin to appear to the north of the city. It takes a while for the revellers to notice them due to the amount of light at the festival. Once they do, it causes a lot of excitement because the lights are rarely seen down this far south of the Arctic circle. The best view of them is from the top of the hill. The show lasts about 30 minutes and seems to be centred to the north and west of Edinburgh over the Firth of Forth. An Agent with an appropriate Lore skill recognises that these lights are far too low in sky; they may look like the Northern Lights but they are not.

There is a heavy police presence, including a total of four chimpanzee police (see Killpanzees on page 153) and a helicopter is circling overhead. Several armoured police vehicles are parked at the top of Calton Hill around the national monument and a mast bristling with CCTV cameras overlooks the festivities. Two chimpanzee police swing idly from the top of the mast, scanning the crowd. A van with a large communications disk is also present, presumably broadcasting footage of the main shows; it is well protected by the police. Agents with any sort of psychic perception notice that the CCTV cameras and broadcast dishes are tuned in part to psionic wavelengths. Agents with appropriate technological knowledge realise that the cameras are strangely constructed with odd-looking lenses. Trying to get close enough for a proper look is not possible without dealing with the police. Finally, anyone with a sense of geography notices that the van and mast are pointing towards the north-west in the direction of the Firth of Forth rather than the city centre. Any Agent thinking to look at the CCTV cameras closest to the stage on which they appeared notices that they have been fused and various puzzled police are trying to fix them.

What went wrong with the translocation? In a word: the twins. They are rips in the multiverse and the translocation anchor broke in their presence. They were monitoring events at Beltane, ensuring that psychic energy was directed back at Forth Bridge, when they felt an explosive wave of psionic force almost overwhelm them. They attempted to determine the source, but the pain was intense so they quickly backed off. More worryingly for the Agents, though they don't yet know this, the disruption has left copies of the Agents back on Zero-Zero. The 'husks' are physically whole but mentally inert, responding only to direct orders. As far as Lingstadt knows, the translocation was a failure and has destroyed the minds of her Agents. Now, she is making plans to seal the parallel before it collapses.

The Agents are completely alone.

Exploring Edinburgh

A general map of Edinburgh is provided and the main locations relevant to this scenario are indicated overleaf. On the whole, the Agents can assume that this parallel's Edinburgh is broadly similar to our own except where noted. If street details are required, Google offers many answers.

Once the Agents arrive in Edinburgh, the following questions need answering:

- Is this the right parallel?
- What is the six sigma event that led to the events?
- What is the catastrophe that is about to occur?
- Where is our only contact, *Hoot the Redeemer*?

Observations of the streets and people of Edinburgh match the briefing notes the Agents received. Posters celebrate the reign of King Alex 1st and the Scottish Saltire flies from hotels. Pubs are full and rowdy and the tabloid papers in convenience stores are full of scandal. Spending 1d3 hours gathering evidence provides certainty that they are at least in the right parallel. There are, however, several indications that things are not as simple as the briefing indicated:

- There are crazy juxtapositions of fashion and technology as if some sort of neo-Victorian renaissance started then gave up. Motor vehicles include everything from steam-powered trams to five-wheeled cars with propellers: not the flying

Killpanzees?

The Agents' attention should be drawn to the chimpanzees to give them some hints before they encounter them on the bridge. If the Agents ask around for information, they learn that the 'SPG' (Special Primate Group) was formed two years ago to counter the threat of terrorism. There are supposedly several groups who patrol the rooftops and high points of Edinburgh. Most people regard them as a harmless, cute novelty but some more radically inclined Edinburghers claim to have heard stories of drunks being savagely beaten. The Agents may also notice posters of a friendly looking chimp in a stereotypical, Scottish police uniform with the caption 'The long arm of the law!'

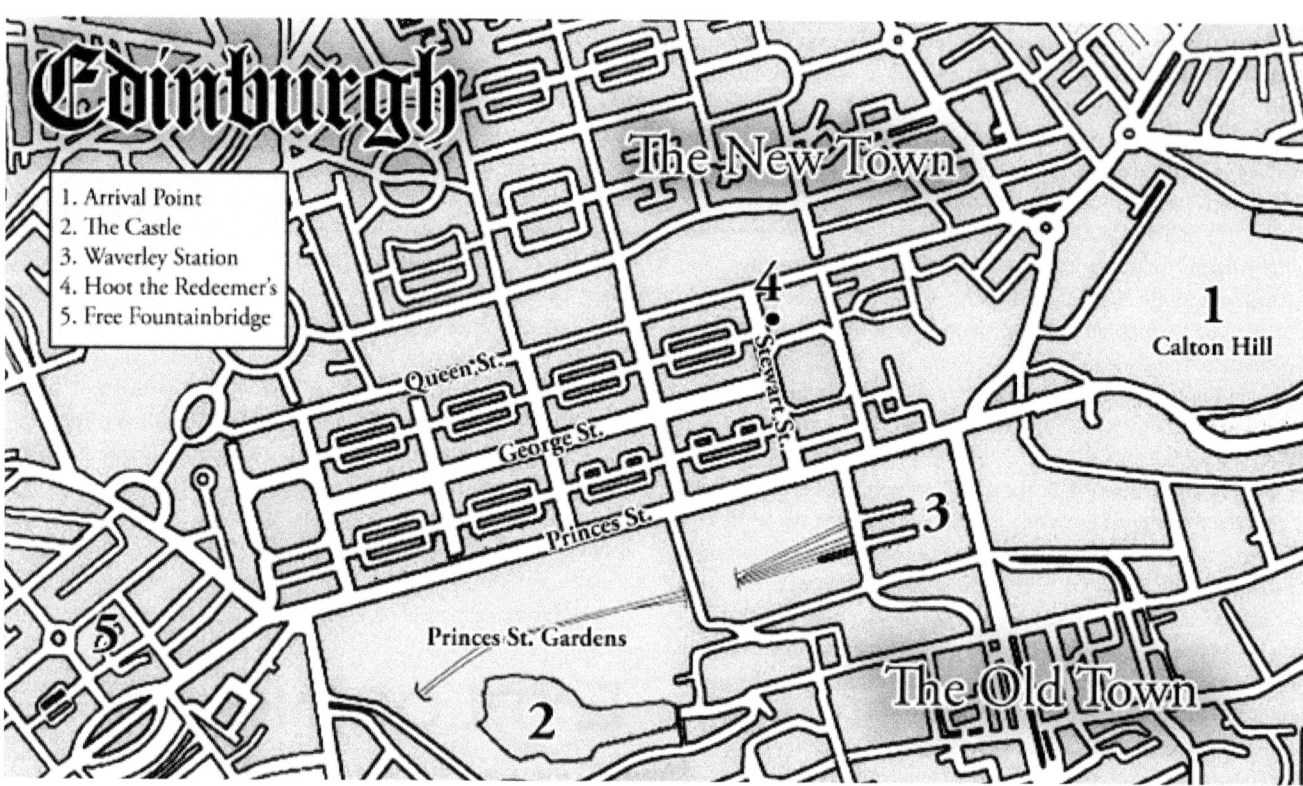

type though. Modern CCTV cameras are as ubiquitous as gas-powered lights.

- There is a distinct sense of barely supressed hostility and suspicion of any Agent speaking with an English or American accent. A popular piece of graffiti reads 'E.T.'s go home'. Agents quickly learn that this refers to 'English Terrorists'.
- Most worryingly, there are occasional glitches in time. A sentence is repeated with no one but the Agents noticing. An old building looks as clean as if it were just built. A darts game is in progress with the darts landing in the exact same place every time. And so on.

Taken together, the events are enough to indicate that something strange is happening but not enough to explain what.

The six sigma event was the completion of the Forth Bridge. In the mundane world, this is represented by the seemingly 'impossible job' of managing to finish painting the bridge. The morning papers (still available in most convenience stores) have cringe-worthy headlines such as 'King Alex 1st does the impossible!' with photos of the chubbily delighted king applying the final paint strokes. It is also still a minor item on most television news reports. If the Agents don't know this, those making a standard Home Parallel skill roll remember that the impossibility of painting the Forth Bridge is an old piece of folklore. If the Agents come from different parallels, they note that this piece of folklore is constant across all their home parallels.

The temporal glitches are a symptom of temporal decay in this parallel. They fan out from the south end of the Forth Bridge with the highest frequency being found in and around central Edinburgh. A crucial point that the Agents need to spot is that the locals don't notice the glitches. Trying to point out a glitch to a local resident causes confusion and, depending on the Agents' accents, suspicion. The table opposite gives some ideas for glitches and can be used for further inspiration. To see whether a glitch occurs, periodically roll 1d100 and consult the table anytime a double is rolled, or pick and choose events that seem to make sense.

As time progresses, these events become more frequent and last longer.

The easiest way to contact Hoot is to find some change and use a public phone box to call the number. The call is answered by one of the bar staff at Hoot the Redeemer's. If they ask to talk with him, the bar staff passes the phone over. Hoot is suspicious but suggests they meet him at the bar. If they have forgotten the number, they can try to find the streets that W.O.T.A.N named. They fairly quickly find the bar on Stewart Street: it is this parallel's analogue to Hanover Street.

HOOT THE REDEEMER'S

A discreet door with peeling red paint marks the entrance to Hoot The Redeemer's. It promises fortune tellers, crystal ball gazers, palm readers, and sundry marvels plus happy hour from 2pm-7pm daily. Through the door, a flight of poorly illuminated steps leads around a corner into the main bar. As they head down, the Agent with the highest Psionics skill (or highest POW if no one is psychic)

Edinburgh & Environs

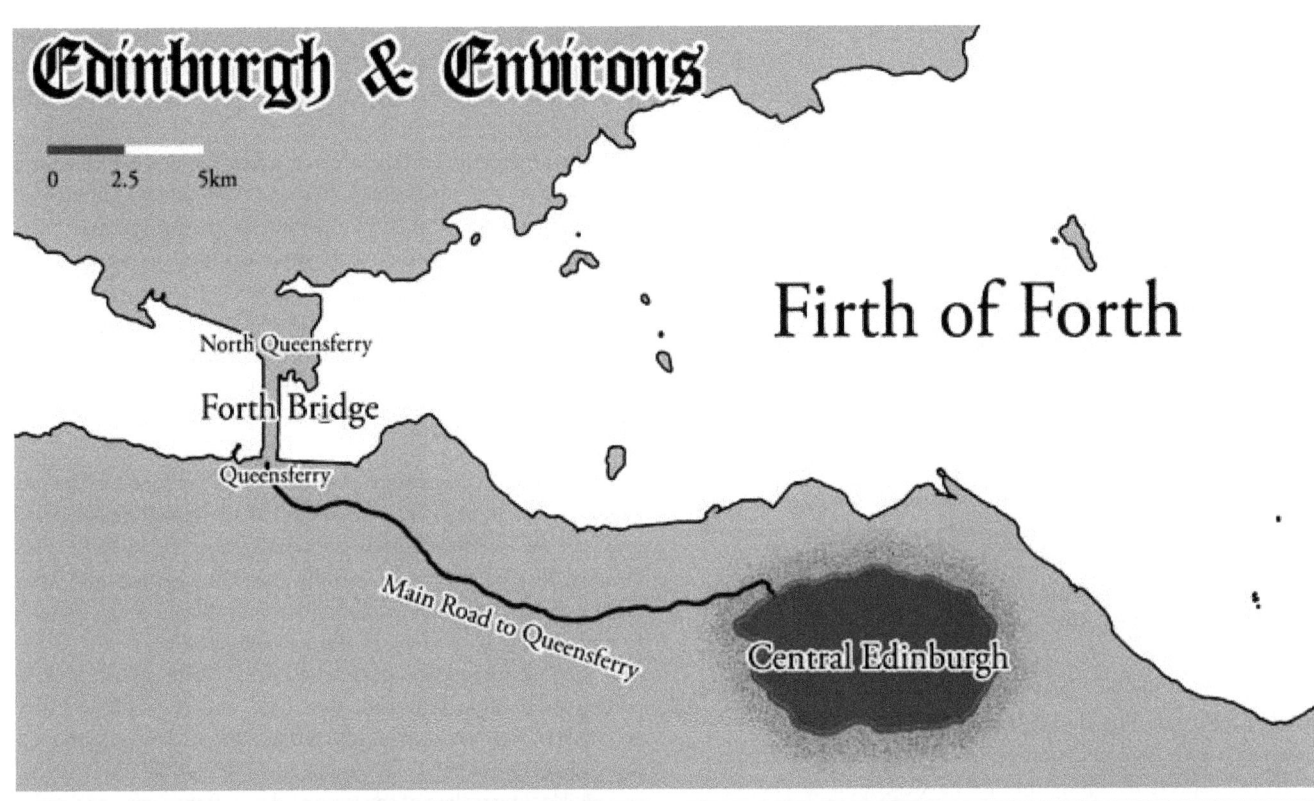

1d100	Temporal Glitch
01-10	For 1d6 seconds, a mundane event (drinking a glass of beer, opening a door, etc.) scrubs backwards and forwards before continuing normally.
11-20	For 1d6 seconds, all activity in an area 1d3 metres wide ceases then continues normally.
31-40	A tiny event is frozen in time permanently, e.g., a pigeon eating breadcrumbs, a drip from a tap, a telephone ringing (but no one answering it; it continues ringing if answered.)
41-50	A mirror shows events from 1d6 seconds in the past (or future).
51-60	An unusual looking person (dwarf, very tall, bearded woman) is talking backwards yet everyone is able to understand them.
61-70	An animal (pigeon, cat, dog, owl) is startled by an Agent, then the action repeats itself.
71-75	Graffiti ('E.T.'s go home', 'Neither King nor Kaiser', 'There will be blood', 'The owls') appears to write itself on a desolate piece of wall.
76-80	An object crumbles and decays over a period of 1d6 seconds, then returns back to normal.
81-85	The Agents hear a snatch of conversation from sometime in the past lasting 1d6 seconds 'did you set the...', 'tonight at seven...', 'och, I'm scunnered...'
86-90	A game of some sort is in progress (darts, backgammon, dominoes, cards), but the same results keep repeating.
91-95	A temporal glitch the Agents have seen before repeats itself and begins to loop permanently. Any attempt to interfere in it requires an Easy Tenacity roll or lose 1 Tenacity Point when the Agent realises their heart has stopped beating. Leaving the glitch returns the heart to normal.
96-100	All Agents present suddenly see the city as it was in approximately 1890. Succeed at a Tenacity roll or lose 1d3 Tenacity. They remain in the past for 1d6 minutes.

notices that a filament bulb is flickering in sync with their heartbeat. Easy Willpower roll or lose 1 Tenacity Point.

The room is dimly lit in red. In one corner, an ancient jukebox is playing a Bowie song: Time. *'It flexes like a whore, falls wanking to the floor'*. The jukebox always plays that song when someone new comes in. On the far wall in front of them, a fortune-telling machine stands idle. A bar man (Willie) or a woman (Gracie) is reading a cheap paperback novel.

There are 1d10 patrons at any given time, along with Hoot himself relaxing in a battered armchair and a group of three (2 women, 1 man all in their twenties) sitting in one of the booths talking intently; the latter are the members of The Writers Bloc. One of the Writers Bloc members (a slight woman with long hair piled on her head in a type of Celtic knotwork bun) pays attention to the Agents as they enter. This is Emma McGregor, an agent in the service of the twins. She has seated herself so she can watch the door. Any Agent on the lookout for watchers who makes an Insight skill roll notices that Emma does a badly hidden double take when the Agents walk in. The Agent must make a Deceit roll opposed against Emma's Insight (40%) if they don't want Emma to realise she's been caught looking.

Aside from the usual, there's at least three things the Agents may wish to do:

- Speak with Hoot
- Speak with the Writer's Bloc
- Try the fortune-telling machine

Hoot

Anyone in the bar can point out the man sitting in the armchair. He's at least 2 metres tall, built like a grizzly bear, is wearing large horn-rimmed glasses that magnify his eyes hugely, and is chain smoking. He looks like a cross between an owl, a bear, and pyroclastic cloud. Any Agents wishing to talk with him must pull up a chair and, once they do, find that all their Perception and Insight skills are a grade more difficult than normal due to the eye-watering smoke.

Hoot is cagey but intrigued by the Agents, giving the impression of knowing something about them. What he doesn't say is that his contacts have told him that the police are looking for a number of terrorist suspects matching the Agents' descriptions. The police have been told that these suspects are armed and dangerous, and that only a stroke of luck prevented them from detonating a bomb at the Beltane festival. There is, however, a security blackout about this to prevent public alarm.

If the Agents initiate a conversation, they find Hoot speaks in a soft voice with, at times, an almost metallic rasp. As they talk, the Agents find that Hoot evades answering any topics about himself and, if pushed on that front, becomes irritable and ends the conversation. If the Agents mention Agent 4th (he knows her by the name 'Sally Forth'), he becomes quite gregarious and is interested to find out more about her. He had a romantic liaison with her and is keen to know more about her.

Hoot can provide any general information the Agents might be interested in. He describes Edinburgh as a simmering cauldron ready to explode at any time and blames the twins' repressive policies for making it worse. If pressed for more information he tells them that the twins were appointed head of a new Ministry of Internal Security (MiniSec) about four years ago in response to increasing terrorist attacks by the English. They have been responsible for reinforcing The Wall (Hadrian's Wall), building a network of CCTV cameras to track suspects, and issuing national identity cards. There has also been increasing propaganda over the last few years leading to some ugly events where suspected 'E.T.'s' were assaulted in the streets.

Asking about the twins confirms Hoot's suspicion that these outsiders are surprisingly clueless. He explains that they're called Jamie and Jimmy Krankie, but that referring to them as the Krankies is not a good idea. They hadn't been known of before their promotion and little is known about their past. Hoot has done some digging and is pretty sure that there is nothing on record about them before 1976, but he won't mention this in a public place.

He first met Sally Forth seven years ago. She was working for a company called Val Industrial Products (VIP) and was interested in opening up a new market for private security products in Scotland. He saw her again some three years ago. She was only in Edinburgh for a weekend, then took a train north to Aberdeen and he hasn't heard from her since. This information is new to the Agents. As with the twins, Hoot won't mention immediately that he did some digging and discovered that VIP is a front for a non-existent company and that Sally Forth seems not to exist in any records he can find.

As far as he knows nothing 'unusual' has happened in the last few days, unless you count finishing the Forth Rail Bridge paint job. And the Northern Lights over the Firth of Forth earlier this evening. He also says, meaningfully, that some people have been talking about an explosion or some sort of sabotage at the Beltane Festival. He knows nothing of any 'time glitches'.

If the Agents reveal a connection with Agent 4th or start to talking about other universes, then Hoot cuts them off and suggests that they continue in his office: a small, luxuriously appointed room to the side of bar. He sits them down, dishes out some expensive whisky (regardless of the time of day), offers cigars, and quizzes them about Sally. If they manage to convince him that they work for the same company or something similar (very easy to do because Hoot half-suspects this), Hoot makes a decision. Last time he saw her, Sally asked him to look after some belongings. He calls for his 'accountant' (Weasel) to fetch the box. Weasel, a small, short-sighted man looking oddly like his namesake, brings in a plain, steel box with 'VIP' marked on it. The Agents recognise this immediately as a standard issue safe box from Valhalla Prime. Sally told Hoot that anyone claiming to be her colleagues would know the combination to open the box and should be allowed to do so. So, Hoot (who doesn't know the combination and has never seen inside it) suggests they open it. This is a test for the Agents; they know these boxes require three double-digit numbers, but clearly they have no idea what Agent 4th's code would be. She has left a huge clue on the box – a pair of *parallel lines* – because the code is the parallel's designation: 11.24.10. She figures any halfway competent Agent from Valhalla Prime should be able to figure this out.

If the Agents open the box, Hoot relaxes. The contents include money (£13.47), a journal containing briefing notes on the parallel that has been updated to 'probably harmless', a list of potential contacts in other parts of the world, a blank Identity card, a vibrator, a business card from Hoot the Redeemer's with 'Big Tam?' written on the back, and the front page of the *Daily Record* (dated 7 February 1978) with two stories likely to catch the Agents' attention. The main story contains a large photo of the Forth Bridge with the headline 'The Great Paint Job Begins!'. The text explains that a specially designed paint has been invented by the Ministry of Internal Security, which will last far longer than any other paint. Intriguingly, Agent 4th has scrawled a series of lines over the photo, which turn the bridge into a mandala. For the second story, see the Buzby Murder box.

Providing the Agents don't make Hoot suspicious, he offers them help and resources. The Agents may quiz him about the items. He doesn't have much to add, but depending on how the Agents have behaved he clarifies that Big Tam can usually be found at a lawless camp in an abandoned brewery in the west of the city known as 'Free Fountainbridge'. He also mentions that the authorities are looking for terrorists matching the Agents' description. He can't harbour them or get them to the bridge with the cops on the look out, but he suggests instead they talk with the three young kids in the booth and ask about Big Tam at Free Fountainbridge. The kids are the Writers Bloc and they have contacts there who may be able to help.

The Writers Bloc

Three young writers in their 20s who believe that literature can make the world a better place: they are the Writers Bloc. Their leader is a blonde named Jo. She is dynamic and passionate about the cause of building a world ruled by neither kings nor communists. The man, Charlie, is working on a goatee, wears a black t-shirt with 'Free Nelson Mandala' on it, and takes a 'suitcase' computer weighing 25kg with him everywhere. The third member is Emma: a slight, pale-skinned, lightly freckled woman in her mid-20's; she has an otherworldly, Celtic vibe about her. There are many others in their group, but they aren't present at this time.

Aside from Emma, the Bloc aren't much interested in the Agents unless they get an introduction from Hoot. Hoot has got them out of trouble a couple of times so they figure he's one of the good guys. Jo is interested in the merits of republican democracies as the ideal form of government. Emma is friendly, though a successful Hard Insight roll reveals that she's on edge. Charlie is more interested in getting his computer plugged into the wall and only pays attention if one of the Agents seems technologically savvy. He has heard, via ScotNet, that there was a disturbance at Beltane and the copters are looking for the culprits but it's unclear what actually happened. A suitable skill roll from an Agent can help Charlie access the net via his state-of-the-art 28 Kbps modem.

The members of the Bloc are naïve and idealistic but not stupid. If Hoot vouches for the Agents, the Bloc members are happy to answer fairly innocent questions, but the more the Agents ask, the more the Bloc are surprised by their ignorance. It should be obvious to the Agents that the members can be useful allies if properly motivated. In particular, Jo can get them a meeting with 'Big Tam' using Emma as a go-between if the Agents seem trustworthy. If the Agents quiz the writers about Big Tam or the camp they can fill in the basic details, but do not provide any possibly compromising information. They do have varied opinions about Big Tam himself: Charlie admires him, Emma thinks he is too prone to violence, and Jo has something of a love-hate view of him.

Buzby Murder

The minor story in the Daily Record is headlined 'Fireball at Surgeon's Hall!' and has a grainy, low-resolution photo of someone dressed as a wizard with pointy hat appearing to point a wand at a building. The text reads:

'The police have released this grainy CCTV image of a man wanted in connection with the arson attack at Surgeon's Hall three days ago. The man, dressed in wizard's robes and a pointy hat, can clearly be seen pointing his wand at the building just before the fire started. A shocked onlooker claims that he heard the man shout 'Incendio' in an English accent before disappearing down the alley. (Continued on page 4...)'

Sadly, page 4 is missing.

Interacting further with Charlie can lead him to mention 'The Banksman'. As far as Charlie knows, this is the username of someone who passes on secret information about the Scottish Government's use of false flags and other techniques to make the threat of terrorism seem worse than it actually is. In his or her most recent post, The Banksman, claims that the government set off an experimental psychic bomb at Beltane to see what would happen. Charlie says that no one knows the true name of The Banksman but that the ID refers to someone who controls traffic, so he believes that The Banksman is controlling information traffic.

Emma is, reluctantly, working for the twins. About 5-10 minutes after the Agents entered the bar, she went to the toilet to use a pager and inform her handler that the potential terrorists had just arrived. She got a message back saying 'make friends and stay close'. That was not what she expected. To complicate matters, she is finding one of the Agents extremely attractive: choose one who seems most appropriate or roll randomly.

Zoltar The Fortune-Teller

This ancient, wooden arcade game features a wooden head wrapped in a turban and a glowing crystal ball. When someone places 10 pence in the coin slot, the eyes light up, the crystal ball glows, and in a terribly stereotyped middle-eastern accent the machine says, *'Place your hands on the box if you dare to hear your future'*. A bell strikes three times and then a piece of paper emerges with a fortune written on it (see table overleaf). If the petitioner's Power is 15 or greater, or they have psionic powers, there is a different level of intensity to the machine. Somehow it seems alive, the head swivels to look them directly in the eye, and the chime of the bell actually leaches 1 Prana Point from them. Hoot is aware of the different tone and that it usually means there is something interesting about the petitioner.

Attack of the Copters

While the Agents are at Hoot's, a police patrol enters. The three copters are routinely checking identity badges as part of the heightened security measures after the incident at Beltane. They have not been furnished with descriptions of the

1d10	Power Less Than 15	Power 15 or More
1	You will meet a beautiful stranger.	You will meet a beautiful corpse.
2	Hope can be found where you least expect it.	The great work can heal as well as destroy.
3	You will marry a girl from along the street.	Choose a hint from a future scenario in the book.
4	You will travel to many exotic places.	The goldfish knows more than you realise.
5	If you stop looking, you will find what you are looking for.	You must seek the mandala.
6	You will live in a beautiful house.	You must go forth.
7	Nothing will be impossible for you.	A stitch in time is what is needed.
8	Avoid stressful situations while Mars is in the ascendant.	No one knows that you are alive.
9	If you embrace your destiny, it will embrace you.	All parallel lines meet eventually.
10	This week is a good week to look up old friends.	The future has been cancelled.

suspects but Emma assumes that they are here because she paged her handler. She is now extremely confused and nervous because this contradicts what she expected from her orders.

Shortly before the police enter, one of the bar staff notices a subtle red light flashing and signals to Hoot that the police are about to enter. Hoot acts quickly, recognising that the Agents probably don't have ID cards, and sends one of the bar staff up the stairs with several bags of rubbish to delay the patrol on their way down.

The patrol comprises three copters: two of them are older men more interested in their retirement cheque than hunting down terrorist and one of them is a zealous young man burning with desire to finally arrest a real life E.T.

What happens next depends on the Agents and the friends they have made so far. The Writers Bloc members grumble and start fishing around for their identity cards. There are no other obvious ways out apart from the stairs into the bar. There are toilets, but they don't have windows. If the Agents stay put, then the copters demand their identity cards and arrest them if they can't provide ID. Give the Agents a chance to quickly improvise a plan first. If they can't, and assuming they have Hoot on their side, he hurriedly ushers them into a stock room behind the bar and gets them to move some beer kegs. There's a trap door leading to a tunnel that emerges around the corner in Rose Street into an abandoned police box. He tells them to 'get out of here' and that there'll be someone waiting for them at the other end of the tunnel.

Assuming that the Agents manage not to get arrested, Jo and Hoot arrange for Emma to lead them to Big Tam's camp at Fountainbridge in the west of the city. She either waits for them at the police box or wherever makes sense based on the

> ### Escape?
> What if the Agents don't escape? Frankly, if they can't outwit three regular copters, they shouldn't be working for Valhalla. There is a chance to escape in transit to the police station built in the courtyard of Edinburgh Castle. If the Agents have decided that getting arrested is the best way to get to the centre of the villain's lair, then Games Master should improvise an interrogation scene followed by an escape: Hoot contacts Big Tam and cashes in some favours to have some of his contacts arrange an escape. They end up with Big Tam, who is curious about what motivated Hoot to take such a chance on them.

events as they unfold. She explains that she's going to take them to 'Big Tam' in Fountainbridge. Emma takes them on various back routes that avoid CCTV cameras and known copter observation points. During that time, the Agents may take the chance to find out more about her and the world around them.

EMMA MCGREGOR

Emma is worried and reluctant to talk much. On the other hand, she is very attracted to one of the Agents and wants to make a good impression. She talks cautiously about the political situation, the Writers Bloc, and Big Tam, but it's clear that she's holding back information. She comes across as someone worried about the way in which the world seems to be sinking into violence and repression; surely people can just learn to live in peace – even the English. Should the Agents try to find a way of getting her to talk freely, her t-shirt with *Marion was no Maid* written on it is a good place to start. If they show any interest, she'll talk at length about how she's working on a script for movie in which Robin Hood is really the descendant of an ancient pagan god (Herne the Hunter) who stands not just for justice but for a new era of spiritual peace connected to beauty and nature and Celtic knotwork.

It is more than possible that at least one Agent suspects her. If she is allowed to talk about Robin Hood, then any Insight skill roll is Formidable, because her passion inadvertently protects her. On the other hand, if they explain that they're trying to save the universe from imminent destruction, she mostly believes them. She says she saw a figure of a giant wolf head in the Northern Lights earlier and feels that the ancient gods are under threat, though she doesn't really know how.

She doesn't know much about Big Tam. His camp, *Free Fountainbridge*, is a refuge for artists, singers, writers, and dreamers, but she wishes he would kick out some of the more aggressive elements there. She thinks that the police may be tempted to try and break it up if they keep causing trouble.

UNMASKING EMMA

Emma is not really a very good double agent and most Agents should be able to rumble her quite quickly. The question is: when, how, and to what end. Stupid Agents will kill her and dump her body. Clever Agents will know that information is power and use her to lead them to interesting discoveries. Very clever Agents will realise that she can be easily turned if they play on her sympathies. Should they search her, they find one piece of evidence that she is a spy: a pager. While she works as a nurse at the Royal Infirmary hospital and has a pager when on call, any examination shows this one is far more sophisticated and exhibits elements of Disruptor technology. For instance, it can send 140-character messages and has a tracking device built in (normal pagers only support 70-character messages and have no tracking tech). Appropriate skills and knowledge allow the Agents to deactivate it or even crack it to monitor communications, using it to trace back is not possible.

FREE FOUNTAINBRIDGE

In the west of Edinburgh, centred on the shell of an abandoned brewery, a tent city has sprung up. It is a home for revolutionaries and artists, bohemians and radicals, terrorists and the homeless. Its leader is the charismatic and mysterious Big Tam. It is watched closely by the authorities, yet for all the cries in the media to close down 'Freak Town', the government never seems to act beyond the occasional raid. If the Agents can make allies here, they may find a way to save the parallel but there will be a price to pay.

The Agents are likely to end up at Free Fountainbridge at some point, if for no other reason than they'll be safe from government surveillance once they're in the camp. At the main entrance, a makeshift arch bears the words 'Free Fountainbridge – neither King nor Kaiser'. Behind it, the site sprawls along wasteland on both sides of the Union canal. The old brewery has lost its roof and part of the north wall, but canvas and lean-tos cluster around it providing shelter while a fleet of narrow boats float on the still waters of the canal. Flags and banners flutter bravely in the biting wind proclaiming organisations such as *Vox Ultra, The Shooglenifty Alliance, The Freedom Proclaimers, Dumbiedykes Army, The Big Country Martyrs*, and many others.

The Agents can come and go freely, but the main entrance is watched by several copter emplacements. Everyone coming and in and out is photographed as well as monitored by CCTV units. Emma knows a long way around, which is not routinely monitored, but if they arrive under their own steam, the Agents must wait for or arrange a diversion to slip in unnoticed. Various vehicles come in and out, but the copters stop and search a fair number. One option for easy entry is the daily 'moonrise'. Each morning, a selection of hungover Fountainbridgers head out to moon the copters accompanied by loud music. It's a daily ritual that the copters do their best not to watch and provides perfect cover for those willing to face such a sight.

BIG TAM, REPUBLICAN MILKMAN

Each morning one of the last horse-drawn milk carts does it round of the west of Edinburgh before heading back to Free Fountainbridge. The driver is Big Tam, though the copters and Edinburgh residents only know him as 'T.S.' – Thomas Sean. The watching

> ### Sleepy Baby
> If the Agents are starting to feel the effects of fatigue, Free Fountainbridge has plenty of pill pushers to take the edge off. A new stimulant called 'Sleepy Baby' has recently hit the market. It prevents normal fatigue for about six hours and gives the imbiber a sense of immense well-being. The user can keep on taking doses, until it hits a critical point, then the user simply falls asleep wherever they are. No game statistics are provided, because the Agents won't be on the parallel long enough for it to be a severe risk. Simply assume that any users of it fall asleep in the middle of their post-mission debriefing.

copters know him well and most are personally friendly with him, not sussing his true identity. If the Agents have an introduction to him, then he is keen to see them. Otherwise, they need to persuade various people to take them to their leader.

In any audience with Big Tam, Hansie the German inventor is present. The Agents immediately recognise him as this parallel's version of Quniscombe. Other likely attendees include Illegal Jack (a Mexican refugee) and Wee Tough Janet (Big Tam's enforcer). Occasionally, Jo from the Writers Bloc attends.

At a meeting, Big Tam quizzes them closely, while Wee Tough Janet scoffs at anything they say. The Agents are in an odd situation; they suspect that something is happening centred on the Forth Bridge and could do with help to get there undetected, but they have no obvious leverage. If they start talking about the world ending in less than 24 hours, they sound like crackpots, even more so if they mention anything to do with other universes. However, Hansie pays close attention. He also watches one Agent (choose randomly or as appropriate) as if he recognises them from somewhere. In this meeting, smart Agents should focus on Hansie; it's clear he's Big Tam's closest advisor. Alternately, they may try to arrange a meeting with Hansie afterwards (if they don't, he does). If the Agents reveal that Emma is a spy and have concrete proof, Big Tam is shocked and orders her held whilst the group decides her fate.

HANSIE QUALMANN

When the Agents talk to Hansie privately, they find he's very open to them. All of his life he's had waking dreams where he sees other worlds and other times through others' eyes. A lot of his inspiration for his gadgets and inventions come during these dreams and, sometimes, when he's trying to solve a difficult equation he feels as if he's working with these others to find the answer. He's sure he's even seen one of the Agents several times before in these waking dreams. If the Agents explain the true nature of the multiverse to him. Hansie becomes excited, claiming that he knew that must be the case. He also explains that recently he's been having dreams about the Forth Rail Bridge and starting to experience odd hallucinations during the day where he sees time jump. If the Agents keep their eyes open for a temporal glitch and share

it with Hansie, he almost cries with relief as he realises he's not going insane.

Provided they make an ally of him, Hansie can aid them in talking Big Tam into providing whatever help they need. In essence, he 'vouches' for them, which carries a lot of weight with Big Tam. Hansie then goes on to reveal his greatest invention: his Magnum Opus.

THE MAGNUM OPUS

The Magnum Opus looks something like a giant set of bagpipes made from an old copper still. It weighs about 2 tons and is mounted on the back of an army surplus truck. It usually hidden beneath the truck's canvas, but Hansie is keen to show it off. He completely forgets to explain what it is until prompted, merely inviting them to wonder at its marvellous workmanship. Once prompted, he explains that it is a sonic quantum funnelling device and lapses into indecipherable technobabble involving quantum foam. Eventually, exasperated, he says, 'It blows things up. With sound.' It's a once-only device, but one shot is all they will need.

BIG TAM'S BIG PLAN

Hansie won't share Big Tam's plan immediately, but it is quite simple. In a few days, the annual May Day Monday parade takes place down Edinburgh's main street: Princes Street. Because the Magnum Opus looks like a giant musical instrument, no one will suspect it of being a weapon. They plan to fire it to destroy Mons Meg, the giant cannon overlooking Edinburgh from the Castle. Hansie has assured Big Tam that the sonic beam is so tight that the cannon essentially just implodes with no collateral damage. This will strike against government power and it won't even be obvious what caused the implosion. Some planted Agents will raise a flag in the castle reading 'Neither King nor Kaiser' and videotape the destruction of Mons Meg.

It's a mad plan, can never work and, anyway, the twins know about it: Big Tam's lack of secrecy is his downfall. However, once the Agents finally uncover what is destroying the world, they may find a use for Hansie's creation.

MiniSec and Free Fountainbridge

The twins have never attempted to destroy the tent city, because they find it a useful propaganda tool. They have several spies working for them and are aware of Big Tam's plan. As far as they are concerned, they will be off the parallel before the plan comes to fruition and it appeals to their love of chaos to let it go off. Should they ever think that the town presents a risk to them, the twins move against it mercilessly with maximum force. The slaughter would be comprehensive and sickening. As the end draws near, the twins are no longer feeling the need to operate covertly.

The Forth Bridge

In the briefing, Lingstadt suggested that the Agents should follow coincidences to find the six sigma event that threatens this parallel and many others. The Agents should have found several by now, all pointing towards the Forth Rail Bridge – usually just known as the Forth Bridge: the painting, the northern lights, Hansie's dreams, the mandala in Agent 4th's box, even the name of Agent 4th herself. What the Agents don't know until they go there is what these clues mean.

Forth Bridge is one of the engineering marvels of the 19th century and is still the second-longest single-cantilever bridge span in the world, crossing 2.5 miles of the Firth of Forth. It is situated some nine miles north and west of central Edinburgh. The same bridge is situated in the same place in every parallel that Valhalla Prime knows of; it is a constant. When the first bridge was built, it was accidentally built as a mandala, opening gates across the cosmos. Each bridge is connected to each other bridge. Should the bridge ever be finished, it would form a multiversal crossing point. The result would be catastrophe with parallels bleeding into each other. Yet with the first bridge came the first Banksman. The Banksman's job was to ensure that the bridge would never quite be finished and that no traffic could pass between parallels.

Normally, hundreds of trains thunder across each day, but on the morning after Beltane, a train enters from the south and never comes back out. All train traffic is immediately stopped. News of this starts to spread unofficially, despite a communications ban from MiniSec. The Agents may hear this on the grapevine at Free Fountainbridge or from Charlie who hears about it online. Shortly after dawn, an intense haar (sea fog) starts to roll in from the east.

By 10am on the day the world is due to end, the bridge is lost in the fog and no trains go. For the first time in 100 years, the bridge falls silent.

Getting to the Forth Bridge takes time and the trains have been stopped. That said, there are no lack of options for the Agents. Once there, the main issue is how to get onto the bridge. The nearest station is Dalmeny: about ½ kilometre away. They can enter the station, jump down off the platform, and walk along the rails. They are chased by a single, overweight railway cop who quickly gives up the chase and radios in to his superiors, which causes problems later. There is a train held on the platform, which particularly enterprising Agents could steal. Alternately, they can travel to Queensferry by the Forth and climb onto the bridge from below. It is a Hard climb without proper equipment, but with the heavy fog no one notices them.

Once on the bridge, an eerie silence descends along with the cold, clammy fog. There are CCTV cameras attached to some of the girders that loom out of the fog, but they continually rotate and refocus as if confused. Normally it takes about 45 minutes to walk across the bridge, but no matter how long they walk the bridge never ends. The longer they are on the bridge, the more they hear the groans of stressed metal. Occasionally, they hear indecipherable voices and at least once the sound of an onrushing train that never appears. If they climb, the same thing occurs. There is an infinity of ladders attached to the struts; the more they climb, the deeper into the fog they go. Agents with the appropriate traits or skills begin to realise that many parallels seem jammed together here, almost bleeding into each other, and as they do so, the time glitches multiply and intensify. This is a good time for Willpower rolls or lose 1 Tenacity Point.

Attack of the Killpanzees

A while after the Agents first enter the bridge, they start to hear soft hooting calls. An Agent with the right background recognises that it sounds like chimpanzees. Unlike everything else though, these chimpanzees are on the same parallel as the Agents and tracking them using sound and scent.

Jimmy Krankie, the intellectual of the twins, has trained a squad of murderous, psionically uplifted chimpanzees that he acquired from Edinburgh Zoo two years ago. The least violent ones are spread throughout Edinburgh, but the ones on the bridge are the twins' shock troops when the mandala opens. For now, they are covertly guarding the bridge. Once the killpanzees become aware of intruders, a squad is sent to stalk them while they await orders. If it is after dawn on the second day, an instruction comes through: kill with maximum murder-death; otherwise, they are told to observe only. This is a critical time in the twins' plan and they can't afford to have intruders on the bridge. The killpanzees are delighted. Apart from a few rough sleepers, they've never had a chance to go full killpanzee. So with shrieks of rage and delight, they attack.

The squad consists of six killpanzees (see page 153), one of whom has a VLAD pack (see page 148) and flamethrower and is determined to use it. In all likelihood, the Agents are horribly outmatched and should quickly realise this. Their one advantage is that the fog is reducing visibility to 3-4 metres making it hard for the VLAD pack flyer to get a decent line of sight. It won't stop him firing incessantly at various beams and struts in frustrated rage.

They need to find a way off the bridge quickly, but the bridge appears to be infinitely long and the killpanzees keep coming. Luckily, the deus ex machina is watching out.

THE BANKSMAN

The Banksman is the spirit of the bridge (see page 148) and has been watching developments with increasing alarm. He recognises that the Agents are from another parallel. He also knows that the killpanzees have been ordered to try to find his office and are getting increasingly close to doing so. Finally, he can see the temporal destruction spreading from the bridge and his ability to hold it back is failing. So he gambles on saving the Agents and exposing himself in the hopes that they can help him save the bridge.

At a critical moment during the killpanzees' attack, a wrecking ball swings out from the fog and scatters several killpanzees, leaving the brains of one oozing off the ball. The ball swings back for another pass, the chain disappearing up into the fog. This time the killpanzees are ready and two manage to jump onto it, immediately climbing up the chain. In the confusion, the Agents notice a door entering one of the struts of the bridge is open. They didn't see it before and only have a few seconds to get into it. If they do so, it shuts behind them leaving the remaining killpanzees to pound on the door, shrieking with rage and frustration.

The door leads to several ladders heading down to The Banksman's shed. The building is a simple affair. There's a cot to sleep in, a sink to wash in, and a couple of gas hobs and a kettle, which is just starting to whistle. On one wall is a collection of vinyl LPs, many clearly from different parallels. The rest of the shed is taken up with a desk with a huge pile of antique monitors balanced precariously on it and each other. They show graphics of various parts of the bridge, radar sweeps of the area, and several screens of abstract vectors that provide information about the intersections of several parallels. Many of the monitors have flashing alerts and more appear every minute.

The Agents may be particularly interested in one monitor, which is hooked up to ScotNet. If they look, they notice various usernames including Charlie's ID: 'Antipopecat'. It is likely that Charlie is currently logged in, so the Agents could message him. The Banksman has been feeding all the information that he dares to a group of Scottish radicals whilst trying to keep his identity secret.

The Banksman himself looks tired; his bushy black beard is streaked with grey and shadows beneath his eyes indicate that he hasn't slept properly for a long time. He pours himself an extremely strong, sweet tea, sits down, and refuses to say another word until he's finished his mug. The Agents have a brief pause in which they can tend injuries, look around, and gather their breath. Once The Banksman's finished his tea, he tells them to follow him. He'll explain what he can as he walks.

THE HEART OF THE BRIDGE

The Banksman leads them down several ladders and across various vertiginous walkways to what he describes as the heart of the bridge. During that time, he imparts what he knows either as a monologue or, preferably, in conversation. In brief, it goes like this.

Five years ago there was a catastrophe in the 'next door' bridge. He doesn't know what exactly transpired but two survivors, 'the twins' were propelled through the bridge mandala, tearing a hole between the parallels and appearing in Edinburgh. He has been desperately trying to patch the tear, but he doesn't have the power to fix it permanently and fractures in time have been spreading from the bridge to infect this parallel.

He doesn't know much about the twins except that they have superhuman psionic skills and were involved in the destruction of their home parallel. About a year after they arrived, they started poking around the bridge and soon they managed to discover that it could open the way to thousands, maybe all, of the other parallels. Seeing the danger, The Banksman tried to lure them into parallels where they would get trapped but they outwitted him and then started to hunt for him too. Shortly afterwards, they started attaching psionic receptors to the bridge and beaming psychic energy there to weaken the barriers between the parallels.

The Banksman is trying to prevent the bridge mandala from becoming fully active because otherwise the time fractures will spread like a contagion across the multiverse. However his strength is almost spent and soon the bridge will be open to the

multiverse. Time will fracture and the twins will be free to travel wherever they wish.

Even as they talk The Banksman is ageing. His step slows, his breathing becomes laborious, and he starts to mumble and repeat himself. The Agents do have time to ask questions. He recognises Agent 4th's description but can only say vaguely that he 'sent her away'. He has heard of Zero-Zero, the only truly 'stable' parallel, but never gone there. He has heard rumours of the forces that the Agents call 'Disruptors' and he thinks that maybe some of them are helping the twins. He doesn't remember who he was before he became The Banksman.

At the very centre of the bridge, a geometric implausibility hangs in mid-air. It is a beating heart, moving in time with unknowable parallels, seemingly made of liquid glass. It gives off an intense cold that instantly freezes anyone approaching – something The Banksman warns them of if the Agents try to get too close a look. As it beats it rotates and the Agents get glimpses into bridges in other parallels. Then they see the bruise on the heart as it turns, necrotising black flesh/glass, tendrils of it spreading into other parallels. As they watch, they see themselves looking back out of the most infected part of the heart. Once the mandala is complete, the infection will spread into all of the connected parallels. There is little The Banksman can do now: the Agents are his last, his only hope.

Escaping the Bridge

The Banksman can give the Agents a map showing how to exit the bridge secretly through one of the supports onto the beach at South Queensferry. He can also let them in the same way provided he is warned; the door is in a different parallel so the mandala must be operated to connect it for a few seconds. In order to get to and from central Edinburgh quickly, the Agents may need to indulge in a spot of carjacking.

Heart of Darkness

The Agents need to come up with a plan. And quickly. There are various ideas seeded in the scenario but players being players are likely to come up with ideas as unexpected as they are unlikely. Providing that the plan follows the logic of *Luther Arkwright* and is suitably dramatic, the Games Master should make it possible but only if it pushes the players' Agents to the extreme. Bear in mind that the Agents may have to choose to sacrifice untold billions in one universe to save all the rest across the multiverse. The consequences of such a choice should weigh heavily on them.

- *Prevent the mandala from opening before the parallel collapses:* The twins are trying to funnel psychic energy to the bridge to activate the mandala before the time fractures become critical. If the Agents can destroy at least three of the receiver dishes, then the parallel starts to consume itself from the inside. The Banksman has one more crane and wrecking ball left and can use it to destroy one of the dishes. He can also seal off traffic to this parallel so the two dead parallels are no longer a threat to anyone else. Problems with this include dealing with the remaining killpanzees and Jimmy Krankie. Meanwhile Jamie finally gets his wish and leads an attack against Free Fountainbridge. He plans to harvest enough psychic energy from the massacre to provide additional power to the bridge. The other big problem is how do the Agents get home? The Banksman can use the last of his strength to hold open a passage to another parallel for a brief time but he can't guarantee that it will get them to Zero-Zero and there is a risk that if Jimmy is still alive that he races through after them.
- *Destroy the bridge:* This has the same effect as preventing the mandala from opening, but is much harder to pull off. Particularly ambitious Agents may try and take control of Mons Meg and blow up the bridge from the castle. It takes several shots and requires holding off several squads of copters.

An easier approach is to persuade Big Tam or Hansie to use the Magnum Opus. This is complicated when Wee Tough Janet learns that Jamie Krankie is covertly marshalling forces for an attack against Free Fountainbridge. The Banksman hacks into Charlie's computer (much to his surprise, though it'll give him an idea for a story if he survives) and shows how to connect and aim the Magnum Opus from Free Fountainbridge to a precise spot on the bridge.

It takes about 90 minutes (1d20+80) for the Magnum Opus to build up to a full charge, during which time Jamie starts his attack on Free Fountainbridge. The Free Towners have no realistic defence against the attack. A few idealists with some guns and Molotov cocktails slow things down for a bit. If any of the Agents are there they can find a few ex-army types who can act with some discipline. Wee Tough Janet has been stockpiling some dynamite, has a cache of handguns and is determined to go out in a blaze of glory.

There is no need to run the battle in detail; all the Agents can do is help prolong the inevitable and protect the Magnum Opus. The first hour mostly consists of small-arms fire as the copters are reluctant to push in and overwhelm. Eventually, Jamie loses patience. He orders Mons Meg to fire three times, destroying sections of the walls, and the copters pour into the breach. If the Agents are protecting the Magnum Opus, they must fight off 1d3+2 waves of attacks each one lasting 1d6+3 Combat Rounds. Then a final one is led by Jamie himself who has recognised the Magnum Opus as an existential threat. If the Agents have no appropriate skills, it takes the Magnum Opus another 1d6+3 Combat Round to fire. If they have some skills and use them successfully, it reduces the time somewhat.

During this time, Hansie approaches the Agents and says that he realises that if they succeed that the whole parallel is doomed. Assuming they level with him, he tells them that he had a waking dream a little while ago and he thinks he saw their parallel's Hansie. He was talking to a goldfish and seemed to think that the Agents had failed. Hansie found himself trying to shout at other Hansie that no they hadn't, there was still time, and it was as if other Hansie heard him. He heard other Hansie say, 'Dammit, Lingstadt, send The Van. We owe them that much.' This ought to remind the Agents that their scheduled extraction is right now on the other side of town. If they leave Free Fountainbridge to be massacred, they can save themselves. Providing the Magnum Opus is fired, all the other parallels are saved, though this one is doomed. When they get to the graveyard, The Van is indeed there, counting down its scheduled departure. The team back on Zero-Zero are surprised, to say they least, when they emerge with it.

The Agents are likely to offer to take as many as they can save in The Van. If they do so, while The Van is starting its countdown, they notice time glitches starting to happen within the bodies of natives of the parallel; they are vectors of the contagion. The Agents also notice glitches happening in their own clothes and items. The Agents can take absolutely nothing from this parallel with them or else the infection will spread; they must leave as naked as they arrived. For some groups, this may seem harsh, in which case, ignore this paragraph but the Agents may still be faced with an agonising choice of who to save and who to doom.

KILL THE TWINS

This is satisfying but ultimately futile. The bridge opens and time is infected. One problem with this plan is at this point is that the twins are in two different locations, so they can't just take them both out with the Magnum Opus. Should this occur, solving the crisis is now beyond the Agents. W.O.T.A.N's resources will be stretched to the maximum trying to track the infection across the parallels and suggesting countermeasures whilst avoiding the attention of the Disruptors. In the short term, the infection will occur only in the background, but W.O.T.A.N calculates that its spread will be exponential and will reach their home parallel within 100 years.

OPEN HEART SURGERY

This is one way to save this parallel and all the rest. If the Agents can get the Magnum Opus onto the bridge, The Banksman can help them aim the sonic weapon so it cuts out just the blackened, dead bit of the heart. That is, of course, easier said than done, especially as they have to get the device 10 miles up the road away from one super-powered murderous psychopath and his army and then face an attack by killpanzees and the other super-powered murderous psychopath. Again, this is probably easiest if the Magnum Opus is extracted secretly while Jamie Krankie leads the massacre of Free Fountainbridge. If they succeed, the temporal infection is halted and the parallel starts to heal. However, if the Agents don't destroy the dishes as well, the mandala is completed and Jimmy Krankie can escape into another parallel. With the last of his strength, The Banksman can open a gate to Zero-Zero for the Agents.

The Agents find themselves walking off the bridge onto Dalmeny Station in parallel Zero-Zero. There are plenty of onlookers who are watching the odd atmospheric phenomena. As the Agents turn round, they see the bridge start fold in on itself like paper. The Banksman is dying and there is no one to replace him. Now that the heart is healthy again, he cuts it free from its supports, heedless of his freezing flesh. For a split-second, onlookers see a bright shape at the centre of the folding and then it is gone, leaving just silence, empty water, and an awed impression of cosmic beauty.

THERE'S NO PLACE LIKE VALHALLA

If the Agents get back to Zero-Zero, Lingstadt hauls them in for a debrief immediately. She is clearly perturbed. The Agents know this is unusual and quickly spot that they are being kept isolated from their colleagues. It is worthwhile playing this out. Lingstadt has two concerns: the fate of their mission and what to do about the 'husks' of the Agents. She has slapped the highest priority black-out she can authorise on everyone who knows about them, including the rest of the team. This does mean that her questions are more focussed on the events around the direct transition than seems necessary. After a longer than normal debrief, she praises or damns them depending on their actions but also sends them to a 'decompression unit' for five days where they have no access to the outside world.

Lingstadt's dilemma is what to do with the husks. They are sentient individuals with rights and needs, but they also shouldn't exist. The husks have been sent to a research base in the Antarctic whilst very high-level discussions are held. Several section heads insist on termination of the husks but Lingstadt disagrees.

The Agents become aware that clearly something happened but that no one is talking about it and asking questions reveals that their security clearance is not even close to giving them access.

GAMES MASTER NOTES

This section collates some background information about what just happened and suggestions for what happens next. The Agents don't need to have discovered all this – indeed the assumption is that there are several unexplained threads left dangling – but the information can help the Games Master ensure that the Non-Player Characters react logically to the Agents' actions.

SALLY FORTH

Her main role is to provide a trail of breadcrumbs, but not to be found. She got off the train at Dalmeny Station and snuck onto the bridge, convinced that something very odd was going on. As with the other Agents sent on the five-year missions, she had the ability to sense the presence of other parallels and sometimes to be able to find ways to move between them. The Banksman watched her and realised she was able to sense the main paths in the mandala. Worried in case she was allied to the twins, he subtly steered her through a one-way gate into different parallel dominated by intelligent dinosaurs. Now she's in an alliance with a monocle-wearing velociraptor in an attempt to find a way back to Zero-Zero.

THE TWINS

Neither Jimmy nor Jamie remembers their home parallel. The transition opened their minds fully, soaking them with psychic energy and power, but the time fractures tore their psyches to shreds. They are now high-functioning, insane psychopaths. Jimmy loves to emotionally abuse people; Jamie loves violence. They both love to see things go up in flames. Their only goal is to escape this parallel before it is torn apart. Most of their conflict with the Agents is through proxies rather than directly and it is likely that at least one of them will escape. Their backstory is left to the Games Master to determine.

THE TWINS' ACTIONS

As the Agents act, so do the twins. Their goal is to open the mandala and free themselves, so they respond to the Agents based on their perceived risk to the twins' plan. A typical breakdown is something like the following.

- Calton Hill. The Agents' arrival acts like a psychic attack. The twins flee, unsure of what is happening.
- One to two hours later, as they recover, they start calling in CCTV footage, but discover that most of it has been burnt out. They send copters out to get eye-witness statements, then circulate an alert about possible terrorists. They also discover that the 'attack' has reduced the amount of

psychic energy funnelled to the bridge. Jimmy calculates that they will need more.
- Depending on how careful the Agents are, the network of CCTV cameras start to filter information to the twins. Jamie wants to take a force and neutralise them, but Jimmy is more cautious and alerts his network of agents to watch for and befriend the strangers.
- Once they make contact with Emma, Jimmy feels confident he can watch them and determine what their plan is. Then the police patrol accidentally flushes them out and, probably, Emma goes under radio silence. Her last report is likely to be that they're heading for Free Fountainbridge.
- At this point, everything is fluid. Jamie heads to Free Fountainbridge and starts pushing to be able to raze it. Jimmy is convinced that these attacks are something to do with the spirit of the bridge that has been opposing him. As they argue, a report comes in of strangers on the bridge, and Jimmy finally agrees with Jamie that it's time for maximum violence.

THE BANKSMAN

A *banksman* is someone who controls traffic on a site. *The* Banksman controls traffic between the parallels. When the bridge was first built, a psionically sensitive worker found herself becoming the first Banksman. Every ten to twenty years, a new Banksman is called and the old one retires. The current Banksman was called nine years ago. During their years of being The Banksman, each gradually forgets their previous life and becomes progressively altered by the experience. The implication is that The Banksman is a creation of 'The Five' but the precise details have been left open-ended so that they can mesh with other campaigns.

THE DISRUPTORS AND LOKI

There are various hints of Disruptor activity seeded throughout the scenario, but no direct confrontations with the Agents. At this point, the Disruptors are in shadow-boxing mode, testing out the forces that seem to be rising to oppose them. Should the Agents dig deeply, they find that Jimmy is the one with the interest in technology who seems to be adapting some elements of Disruptor technology to his ends. He has occasionally been known to refer to the (or a) 'genius loci', but has never expanded on what he means. If Games Masters wish Loki made contact with the twins' creator and helped guide him to the fateful experiment that destroyed their parallel. Loki was acting independently according to his own agenda and didn't expect the destruction. He wasn't able to track down what happened, but Jimmy's fractured brain has pieced together some technological clues. It is possible that if one or both of the twins escape that this will trigger some of Loki's sensors and enable him to track down the survivor(s).

NEW EQUIPMENT

PROP-PACKS & VLADS

A standard issue prop-pack looks something like a jet pack powered by a turbo-prop. The power pack provides roughly one hour flight time or 30 minutes hovering. They have been issued to the newly enhanced police force with one out of every five police patrols consisting of a 'Flying Squad' officer trained to use the prop pack.

Prop-Pack
Hull 1, structure 8
Speed: fast
Systems: 3: controls, power, turbo props
Traits: V.T.O.L. (inherent), superior handling
Shields: none
Weapons: none

VLAD (Vertical Lift and Destroy) Pack
Hull 1, structure 10 (essentially just a jet pack with turboprops)
Speed: rapid
Systems: 4: controls, power, turbo props, weapons
Traits: V.T.O.L. (inherent), Weaponised
Shields none
Weapons: Flamethrower
Uses the stats of the Flamer rifle (see page 106 of Luther Arkwright)

A small number of VLAD packs have been issued for extreme crowd control purposes. The flamethrower mix weighs down the unit, reduces it speed and cuts down its flying time by half.

PSIONIC MIND CONTROL HELMETS

These enable Jimmy Krankie to control the killpanzees. They are specially designed for properly prepared chimpanzees and won't work on anyone else.

Non-Player Characters

Hoot the Redeemer

Big, burly, and wearing huge glasses, Hoot talks softly for a big man, rarely able to speak above a slightly metallic sounding whisper. He has a need to collect secrets of all types and presents an air of knowing a lot more than he actually does, although what he does know tends to be interesting and relevant, and what he *doesn't* know, is not worth knowing.

Hoot isn't a fighter. If violence breaks out, he manages to find a safe hiding place and never gets involved.

Hoot the Redeemer	Attributes
STR: 16	Action Points: 2
CON: 10	Damage Modifier: +1d4
SIZ: 19	Prana: 9
DEX: 8	Tenacity: 5
INT: 13	Movement: 6 metres
POW: 9	Initiative Bonus: +11
CHA: 13	Armour: None

1d20	Hit Location	AP/HP
1 – 3	Right Leg	0/6
4 – 6	Left Leg	0/6
7 – 9	Abdomen	0/7
10 – 12	Chest	0/8
13 – 15	Right Arm	0/5
16 – 18	Left Arm	0/5
19 – 20	Head	0/6

Skills	Passions, Traits & Dependencies
Athletics 24%, Brawn 85%, Commerce 71%, Conceal 47%, Customs 66%, Dance 21%, Deceit 66%, Endurance 50%, Evade 16%, First Aid 21%, Home Parallel 46%, Influence 66%, Insight 67%, Native Tongue 86%, Perception 52%, Politics 56%, Sing 22%, Stealth 21%, Streetwise 72%, Swim 26%, Unarmed 44%, Willpower 68%	Passions: Love The Bar 80%, Loyalty to Regulars 60% Dependencies: Secrets 75%

Combat Style & Weapons	Traits & Notes
None	

Big Tam

Six foot two with languid brown eyes, the square jaw of a male model, and the toned torso of a body-builder, Big Tam has broken the heart of many a lonely Edinburgh housewife while driving his horse-drawn milk cart. His real passion is leading the rebels of Free Fountainbridge; he dreams of day when men are free of both kings and kaisers. He is charismatic and impulsive: inspirational but prone to whims and attacks of melancholy. His closest (possibly only) friend is the German engineer, Hansie. His oddest quirk is the way he pronounces 's' as '*sh*.' The Agents are likely to be introduced to 'my *closhesht* friend and mad *geniush*, *Hanshie*'.

Big Tam	Attributes
STR: 16	Action Points: 2
CON: 10	Damage Modifier: +1d4
SIZ: 16	Prana: 8
DEX: 9	Tenashity: 4
INT: 10	Movement: 6 metres
POW: 8	Initiative Bonush: +10
CHA: 14	Armour: None

1d20	Hit Location	AP/HP
1 – 3	Right Leg	0/6
4 – 6	Left Leg	0/6
7 – 9	Abdomen	0/7
10 – 12	Chesht	0/8
13 – 15	Right Arm	0/5
16 – 18	Left Arm	0/5
19 – 20	Head	0/6

Skills	Passions, Traits & Dependencies
Acting 43%, Athletics 55%, Brawn 62%, Conceal 17%, Cushtoms 60%, Dance 33%, Deceit 24%, Drive (car) 47%, Drive (Horsh and Cart) 47%, Endurance 35%, Evade 18%, First Aid 19%, Gambling 63%, Home Parallel 20%, Influence 58%, Inshight 18%, Native Tongue 64%, Perception 18%, Pilot (Microlight) 34%, Ride 32%, Shing 22%, Shtealth 19%, Shtreetwise 52%, Shwim 26%, Unarmed 70%, Willpower 31%	Passions: Love (Freedom) 70%, Hate (Tyranny) 75%, Loyalty (Free Fountainbridge) 70%, Love/Hate (Jo) 60% Dependenshies: Alcohol 80%

Combat Style & Weapons	Traits & Notes
Shaken and Shtirred 55% (Handguns, Molotov cocktails)	Shkirmisher

Weapon	Damage	Range	Ammo	Rate/Load
Walther PPK	1d6	50/100/200	7	1/3

Weapon	Damage	Range
Molotov Martini	1d4 - 25% chance of igniting clothes, with 1d4 damage per round until extingishued	5/10/20

Illegal Jack

Not in the least bit Mexican, Jack is tall, pale and skinny, and sports a luxuriant moustache. If the Agents need a high-speed getaway or a damn fine bowl of chilli, Jack's their man.

Illegal Jack	Attributes
STR: 11	Action Points: 3
CON: 12	Damage Modifier: +0
SIZ: 10	Prana: 17
DEX: 13	Tenacity: 17
INT: 14	Movement: 6 metres
POW: 17	Initiative Bonus: +13
CHA: 16	Armour: None

1d20	Hit Location	AP/HP
1 – 3	Right Leg	0/5
4 – 6	Left Leg	0/5
7 – 9	Abdomen	0/6
10 – 12	Chest	0/7
13 – 15	Right Arm	0/4
16 – 18	Left Arm	0/4
19 – 20	Head	0/5

Skills	Passions, Traits & Dependencies
Athletics 54%, Brawn 42%, Conceal 54%, Craft (Cook Mexican Food) 60%, Deceit 72%, Drive 80%, Endurance 45%, Evade 38%, Influence 74%, Insight 60%, Lore (Mexican Food) 50%, Lore (Secret routes through Hadrian's Wall) 80%, Perception 60%, Streetwise 60%, Stealth 60%, Unarmed 40%, Willpower 65%	Passions: Loyalty to Big Tam 75% Dependencies: Speed 35%

Combat Style & Weapons	Traits & Notes
Self Defence (Pistol) 30%	

Weapon	Damage	Range	Ammo	Rate/Load
Revolver	1d6	50/100/200	6	1/3

Hansie Qualmann

Use Professor Quinscombe's statistics (see page 7). An old injury to his left leg means he walks with a limp and occasionally uses a walking stick.

Wee Tough Janet

At less than 1.5 metres tall, Janet is tiny but her pale blue eyes glint with a love of violence. She dresses oddly in schoolboy style shorts, cap, Doctor Marten boots, and several hidden knives.

Wee Tough Janet	Attributes
STR: 17	Action Points: 2
CON: 11	Damage Modifier: +1d2
SIZ: 8	Prana: 7
DEX: 11	Tenacity: 5
INT: 13	Movement: 6 metres
POW: 7	Initiative Bonus: +12
CHA: 9	Armour: None

1d20	Hit Location	AP/HP
1 – 3	Right Leg	0/4
4 – 6	Left Leg	0/4
7 – 9	Abdomen	0/5
10 – 12	Chest	0/6
13 – 15	Right Arm	0/4
16 – 18	Left Arm	0/4
19 – 20	Head	0/6

Skills	Passions, Traits & Dependencies
Athletics 59%, Brawn 36%, Endurance 62%, Evade 52%, Influence 58%, Perception 60%, Survival 66%, Unarmed 65%, Willpower 44%	Passions: Loyalty to Big Tam 75% Traits: Brutal Dependencies: Violence 75%

Combat Style & Weapons		Traits & Notes		
Glasgow Welcome (Bite, Knives) 80%		Hidden Weapons		
Weapon	Damage	Size/Reach	AP/HP	Effects
Bite	1d2+1d2	S/T	As for Head	Bleed
Knives (x6)	1d4+1d2	S/S	6/6	Bleed, Impale

THE WRITERS BLOC

Treat the Writers Bloc as Casual Bystanders, but with the noted skills.

EMMA MCGREGOR

Emma was recruited by the twins just over a year ago after her uncle was badly injured in the Linlithgow pub bombings. She is worried by both terrorist violence and state violence and thinks she's trying to find a way to reduce both. She is an idealist and quite fixated on the character of Robin Hood.

Skills: Art (writing) 75%, Art (Poetry) 55%, Insight 40%, Lore (Paganism) 65%, Lore (Robin Hood) 80%

Passions: Love (Celtic stuff) 80%, Love (Robin Hood) 90%, Hate (Violence) 70%. Naïve 50%.

JO

She is the leader of the bloc. She's passionate and determined about the cause and also the power of writing. She is in an on-and-off relationship with Big Tam.

Skills: Art (Writing) 87%, Language (Latin) 55%, Influence 70%, Insight 50%, Oratory 50%

Passions: Love/Hate (Big Tam) 70%, Love (Freedom) 90%, Hate (Violence) 70%.

CHARLIE

Charlie is a geek long before geeks were cool. He takes his suitcase computer everywhere with him and lives on his own with his cat.

Skills: Art (Writing) 78%, Computers (83%), Lore (Cthulhu Mythos) 70%, Lore (Spycraft) 50%

Passions: Love (computers) 70%, Love (his cat) 80%, Fear (Eldritch forces) 60%

THE TWINS

Jamie and Jimmy are identical twins by design. Both red-haired and freckled with plain faces and scrawny physiques, they look nothing like the supremely talented killers they actually are.

JAMIE KRANKIE

Jamie is the physically violent one. He has no time for subtlety or planning. He wants violence and needs it now. He is finding it harder and harder to restrain his murderous impulses as he is gradually losing control of his shattered mind.

Jamie Krankie	Attributes
STR: 11	Action Points: 3
CON: 13	Damage Modifier: +0
SIZ: 13	Prana: 16
DEX: 11	Tenacity: 11
INT: 14	Movement: 6 metres
POW: 16	Initiative Bonus: 13
CHA: 11	Armour: none

1d20	Hit Location	AP/HP
1 – 3	Right Leg	0/6
4 – 6	Left Leg	0/6
7 – 9	Abdomen	0/7
10 – 12	Chest	0/8
13 – 15	Right Arm	0/5
16 – 18	Left Arm	0/5
19 – 20	Head	0/6

Skills	Passions, Traits & Dependencies
Athletics 62%, Brawn 54%, Computers 38%, Conceal 27%, Deceit 75%, Disguise 55%, Drive (car) 57%, Endurance 26%, Evade 52%, First Aid 25%, Influence 72%, Insight 30%, Lore (Multiverse) 58%, Meditation 70%, Native Tongue 85%, Perception 50%, Pilot (prop pack) 65%, Politics 45%, Stealth 75%, Streetwise 77%, Swim 24%, Unarmed 82%, Willpower 82%	Passions: Hate (normal people) 100%, Love (Jimmy) 100%, Fear (Death) 80% Traits: Psionic Dependencies: Violence 80%

Psionics
Warped Homo Novus 77% (Body Fortress, Inflict Pain, Mental Shield, Shatter)

Combat Style & Weapons	Traits & Notes
Murderous psychopath (Hand Guns, Daggers, Stupid big things like chainsaws and flamethrowers) 72%	

Weapon	Damage	Size/Reach	AP/HP	Effects
Dagger	1d4	S/S	4/6	Bleed, Impale

Weapon	Damage	Range	Ammo	Rate/Load
.38 Pistol	1d6	50/100/200	6	1/3

Jimmy Krankie

Jimmy is cold and calculating and all the scarier for it. He loves to cause pain of any type but emotional pain is his true love. His abilities are what have raised the twins so high so fast.

Jimmy Krankie	Attributes
STR: 11	Action Points: 3
CON: 10	Damage Modifier: +0
SIZ: 13	Prana: 17
DEX: 11	Tenacity: 14
INT: 15	Movement: 6 metres
POW: 17	Initiative Bonus: 13
CHA: 11	Armour:

1d20	Hit Location	AP/HP
1 – 3	Right Leg	0/5
4 – 6	Left Leg	0/5
7 – 9	Abdomen	0/6
10 – 12	Chest	0/7
13 – 15	Right Arm	0/4
16 – 18	Left Arm	0/4
19 – 20	Head	0/5

Skills	Passions, Traits & Dependencies
Athletics 32%, Brawn 24%, Computers 60%, Conceal 28%, Deceit 86%, Disguise 56%, Drive (car) 68%, Endurance 20%, Evade 52%, First Aid 26%, Influence 82%, Insight 32%, Meditation 72%, Native Tongue 86%, Perception 52%, Pilot (prop pack) 66%, Politics 56%, Probabilities 60%, Sing 28%, Stealth 46%, Streetwise 58%, Swim 21%, Unarmed 22%, Willpower 84%	Passions: Love (Jamie) 100%, Fear (Death) 100%, Love (Pain) 70% Traits: Psionic Dependencies: Sadism 80%

Psionics

Warped Homo Novus 79% (Empathic Push, Mental Shield, Sense Psi, Synaptic Puppetry, Thought Implant)

Combat Style & Weapons	Traits & Notes
Cunning psychopath (Hand Guns, Daggers) 52%	

Weapon	Damage	Size/Reach	AP/HP	Effects
Dagger	1d4	S/S	4/6	Bleed, Impale

Weapon	Damage	Range	Ammo	Rate/Load
.38 Pistol	1d6	50/100/200	6	1/3

Copters

The regular police force are known as the 'copters.' During last three years, they have become increasingly violent and repressive. They don't routinely carry guns but do carry batons. Specialist patrols ('The Flying Squad') include armed flying cops with 'prop packs' that run on propellers, sort of like a gyrocopter crossed with a jet pack. An elite core of these have been secretly armed with flame throwers to deal with traitors and terrorists.

Copter	Attributes
STR: 10	Action Points: 2
CON: 9	Damage Modifier: 0
SIZ: 11	Prana: 10
DEX: 10	Tenacity: 10
INT: 11	Movement: 6 metres
POW: 10	Initiative Bonus: +11
CHA: 11	Armour: Ballistic Vest & Helmet

1d20	Hit Location	AP/HP
1 – 3	Right Leg	0/5
4 – 6	Left Leg	0/5
7 – 9	Abdomen	2/6
10 – 12	Chest	2/7
13 – 15	Right Arm	0/4
16 – 18	Left Arm	0/4
19 – 20	Head	2/5

Skills	Passions, Traits & Dependencies
Athletics 53%, Brawn 57%, Bureaucracy 35%, Conceal 19%, Customs 60%, Dance 18%, Deceit 18%, Drive (Car) 49%, Endurance 35%, Evade 20%, First Aid 35%, Home Parallel 35%, Influence 16%, Insight 34%, Lore (Police work) 50%, Native Tongue 58%, Perception 19%, Sing 17%, Stealth 20%, Streetwise 32%, Swim 23%, Unarmed 38%, Willpower 18%	Most copters have one or more of the following passions Loyalty (Copters) 60%, Hate (E.T.'s) 60%, Love (a bit of violence) 50%, Loyalty (King Alex 1st) 50% Dependencies (Greggs Sausage Rolls) 40%

Flying Squad copters have Pilot (Prop Pack) 59%

Combat Style & Weapons	Traits & Notes
Stop In The Name Of The Law! (Batons, Riot Gear) 53%	*One in five copters have gun handling skills and can add handguns to their combat style. Note that no copters are routinely armed.* *Some flying squad copters have training in using VLAD pack flamethrowers.*

Weapon	Damage	Size/Reach	AP/HP	Effects
Baton	1d6	M/S	4/4	Stun Location
Riot Shield	1d4	H/S	6/15	Bash, Stun

KILLPANZEES – 'THE SPECIAL PRIMATE GROUP' (SPG)

These chimpanzees were acquired from Edinburgh Zoo and put through intensive conditioning then fitted with psionic helmets. These helmets provide the chimps with INT (rather than INS) and enforce loyalty. The helmets were invented by Jimmy Krankie, but he doesn't realise that he is aping a design that was used on him as a child. Consequently, Agents familiar with Disruptor technology recognise some give-away features. A useful side-effect of the helmets is that they fuel the chimps with a constant sense of rage. Some of the less violent chimps are used publicly in Edinburgh.

A total of 18 killpanzees are stationed secretly on the bridge.

Copter	Attributes
STR: 14	Action Points: 3
CON: 13	Damage Modifier: +1d2
SIZ: 13	Prana: 4
DEX: 16	Tenacity: 0
INT: 11	Movement: 6 metres
POW: 4	Initiative Bonus: 14
CHA: 6	Armour: none

1d20	Hit Location	AP/HP
1 – 3	Right Leg	0/6
4 – 6	Left Leg	0/6
7 – 9	Abdomen	0/7
10 – 12	Chest	0/8
13 – 15	Right Arm	0/5
16 – 18	Left Arm	0/5
19 – 20	Head	0/6

Skills	Passions, Traits & Dependencies
Acrobatics 60%, Athletics 80%, Brawn 57%, Conceal 20%, Customs 22%, Dance 42%, Deceit 17%, Endurance 56%, Evade 62%, First Aid 27%, Home Parallel 22%, Influence 12%, Insight 15%, Native Tongue 27%, Perception 60%, Pilot (Prop pack) 57%, Sing 10%, Stealth 42%, Survival 47%, Swim 27%, Track 39%, Unarmed 60%, Willpower 38%	Passions: Loyalty (Jimmy Krankie) 100%, Hate (Humans) 70%, Fear (The Twins) 80%, Loyalty (Killpanzees) 100% Dependencies Psychic Feedback from helmet (80%)

Combat Style & Weapons	Traits & Notes
Murder, Death, Killpanzee! (rocks, assault rifles, flamethrowers) 60%	At this point the Killpanzees have been trained in weapons but not issued them because Jimmy isn't convinced of their discipline. However two particularly trusted chimps have been issued with VLAD packs

Weapon	Damage	Size/Reach	AP/HP	Effects
Fists	1d3+1d2	M/S	As for Arm	Stun Location
Rock	1d4+1d2	S/S	6/4	Bash, Stun

There is a way to neutralise the killpanzees without killing them. If an Agent can tear off the helmet (doing 1d3 Hit Points damage to the chimpanzee's head), the chimp is stunned for 1d3+1 turns and then begins to realise that it has been manipulated. As its INT gradually returns to INS, its fury is directed towards its tormentors: the twins. If either of the twins are around, the freed chimp attacks him with fury; otherwise, it tries to grapple one of the other chimps and remove its helmet. However, it also tries to prevent anyone from using lethal force against its fellow troupe members.

CASUAL BYSTANDERS

The vast majority of people the Agents meet have no combat skills and zero interest in combat. Treat them as Rabble (MYTHRAS, page 111) with the attributes and skills listed below.

Casual Bystander	Attributes
STR: 10	Action Points: 2
CON: 9	Damage Modifier: 0
SIZ: 11	Prana: 10
DEX: 10	Tenacity: 10
INT: 11	Movement: 6 metres
POW: 10	Initiative Bonus: +11
CHA: 11	Armour: None

1d20	Hit Location	AP/HP
1 – 3	Right Leg	0/5
4 – 6	Left Leg	0/5
7 – 9	Abdomen	0/6
10 – 12	Chest	0/7
13 – 15	Right Arm	0/4
16 – 18	Left Arm	0/4
19 – 20	Head	0/5

Skills	Passions, Traits & Dependencies
Athletics 20%, Endurance 20%, Evade 20%, Home Parallel 22%, Perception 21%, Unarmed 20%, Willpower 20%	

Combat Style & Weapons	Traits & Notes
Self Defence (Unarmed) 20%	

Hanging on the Telephone

Set in a grimy, depressing alternate London, the Agents must investigate a series of brutal killings known as the Buzby Murders. Along the way they come to attention of a ruthless Disruptor Knight known as The Shopkeeper....

OVERVIEW

Parallel 02.87.51
British Empire Variant
Disruption Likelihood: 100%

This scenario assumes that the Agents have completed three or more of the other scenarios in this book. It can be used as a standalone climatic finish to the campaign or played piecemeal between other adventures.

The Agents are sent to look into a series of interdimensional anomalies that have been occurring in parallels contiguous to their previous missions. They must find out whether they themselves are indirectly responsible for creating these problems or if something more nefarious is going on.

Soon after their arrival, the Agents discover a series of bizarre, telephony-linked murders, each victim dressed in an outlandish costume. During the course of their investigation, they eventually cross paths with a reclusive group of mystics, hiding beneath the commons of Wimbledon. Despite first appearances as the perpetrators of the telephonic-related deaths, the mystics are actually trying to close down a network of dimensional rifts threatening their parallel.

Belatedly realising their mistake, the Agents need to backtrack and hunt down the real architect behind the murders. Clues lead to a fancy-dress shop in Putney, which the Agents must penetrate under cover, experiencing first hand what happened to previous victims. Once the source of the anomalies has been ascertained, the Agents must make a move against the shopkeeper – now revealed as a Disruptor Knight running a trans-parallel assassination cabal – pursuing him into another parallel to finally defeat him.

British Games Masters and players of a certain age should recognise many of the themes and characters appearing in this scenario; these are all drawn from television shows popular in the 1970s and appear here as affectionate pastiches from a time when storytelling for children was central to television Programmeming in Great Britain. Some Games Masters need no prompting to see the analogies, but for those who were born after 1980 or from outside the UK, we strongly recommend doing a little research on *The Wombles, Mr. Benn, The Clangers,* and anything else produced by Peter Firmin and Oliver Postgate.

NON-PLAYER CHARACTERS

The following key characters are encountered during the scenario:

- **Great Uncle Moldova:** Leader of the London Yeti enclave
- **Mr. Bren:** Unwitting trans-parallel assassin
- **Orsk:** Large and intimidating Yeti mystic
- **Philip Percival:** Professional hunter and safari guide
- **Pilcomayo:** Laconic and somewhat lazy Yeti mystic
- **Professor Quinscombe:** Head of interdimensional translocation research on Zero-Zero
- **Smasher Garou:** Bodyguard and assistant to the Shopkeeper
- **The Shopkeeper (aka Baron Zartram):** Disruptor Knight in command of *Operation Industrious*

Key Points & Timeline

The scenario should be guided by the following timeline:

1. Day 1: Briefing on Zero-Zero.
2. Day 2: Early morning arrival on parallel 02-87-51, information discovered about the Buzby Murders.
3. Day 2: Evening detection of first 'anomaly' leading to initial encounter with Orsk the mystic.
4. Day 3: Afternoon detection of second anomaly and follow up vehicle chase.
5. Day 4: Mr. Bren assassination attempt against the Agents.
6. Day 4: Evening examination of Mr. Bren's home and subsequent sewer chase to the Wimbledon mystics.
7. Day 4-5: Location and investigation of the fancy-dress shop, possible changing room side trips, and final showdown during the Great Balloon Race.

Background & Introduction

Parallel 02-87-51 - Post War Depression, Raj Rises
Designator: 02.87.51
Classification: British Empire Variation
Cultural Type: Southern Asia (British Raj)
Political Type: Bureaucratic
Technological Type: Industrial Age (Early 1970s)

Description: This parallel diverged soon after the Second World War, when American banking links to the Nazis were exposed by British newspapers, provoking the US to call in the staggering debt owed to it via the lend-lease Programme. Aggravated by what it saw as a deliberate attempt to bankrupt its empire, the British defaulted. The American banking system subsequently collapsed, leading to violent civil disorder fuelled by its own war-repressed minorities and an eventual return to isolationism.

Britain consequently suffered its own financial backlash. Faced with a capital bombed almost flat from the final waves of V2 rockets and facing rebellious discontent in India, King George VI decamped to Delhi taking parliament with him. Since then, the Empire has reclaimed the Pacific and maintained a stranglehold over the East, manoeuvring against the Soviet Union in a continuation of the Great Game, whilst the other colonial territories have become second-rate nations turned over to mass industrialisation.

The British Isles, in particular, has become a dreary place to live. The majority of the population are disenfranchised working class, employed as factory labour or coal miners. The London smogs are worse than ever, many people suffering illness or death from respiratory problems. Despite the economic and societal depression the British people have suffered for thirty years, a grudging feeling of optimism has arisen. Small improvements in wages have led to a resurgence of social activities outside of the local pub, although private home or vehicle ownership is still beyond the means of most.

The Agents' Briefing

The scenario starts during a post-mission debriefing session held on Zero-Zero. Professor Quinscombe has discovered that interdimensional anomalies are occurring on every parallel the Agents have visited. Although not precisely synchronous with the geographical location of each mission, they occur just prior to, or simultaneously with, their visit.

So far, it is undetermined what the source of these anomalies are, nor their precise form, whether it is a hitherto undetected flaw in Van operation or if something is pursuing the Agents' movements in an attempt to neutralise them.

Progression from this point depends on how the Games Master wishes to incorporate the scenario into a campaign. Professor Quinscombe does one of the following:

- Ask the Agents to keep their eyes peeled for unusual para-psychic activity on their subsequent missions, gathering clues as to what is going on (such as witnessing one of the costumed assassinations), before the scientists conclude which parallel is responsible.
- Inform the Agents that his science team has already discovered that each anomaly is linked to a single parallel, although what is causing the interdimensional disruptions is yet unknown.

If and when the Agents are ready to progress, they are issued with clothing suitable for 1970s London, £200 of pre-decimal currency, and a bulky Signature Sensor (*Luther Arkwright*, page 76) to help them track down cross-parallel radiation. Each Agent is also permitted to take personal equipment up to what can be held in a handbag or briefcase.

No firearms are permitted, since this is supposed to be an investigative mission, not an assault, and British law on parallel 02.87.51 strictly forbids the ownership of small arms. This fact alone may radically change the approach Agents take to completing the mission.

Buzby Murders

The Van deposits the Agents just before daybreak on the muddy southern bank of the River Thames under Putney Bridge at low tide. Somehow shunted away from their original destination, their arrival is further hidden by the morning smog, which is thick, yellow, and burns the Agents' lungs when they breathe. Visibility is reduced to 10 metres, but the sound of a few vehicles to access it except for an hour, twice per day, when the river ebbs to its lowest point.

It is simple enough for the Agents to discover a ladder up the brick embankment, granting them access to the fog-obscured graveyard of St. Mary's church. From there, it is easy to follow the warm glow of street lamps along Putney High Street to a bus stop at the end of the bridge. Agents who take a moment to look about notice that the illumination comes from gas lights rather than electric lights. Next to the bus stop, a young boy, muffled in a scarf and felt coat, is setting up a newspaper stall. On the display placard is a copy of the London Times, its headline reads 'Buzby Murderer Strikes Again!'.

The murder reported in The Times newspaper is only the latest in a series of serial killings, identified by the strange circumstances of the victims: each of whom have been found wearing some outlandish costume, along with some sort of small odd item found near the body. The police are, of course, bewildered.

Although the scenario assumes the Agents eventually start following the murders, it may take a while before they catch on that the trans-dimensional anomalies are directly related. The Games Master should not force this realisation, but hope that one of the Agents recalls other strange incidences already experienced on other parallels. Hopefully, they have an 'Aha!' moment when all the disjointed episodes suddenly click into place.

As a reminder, here is a summary of the publicised fracases (clues) incorporated in other scenarios of this book, that are actually part of the Buzby Murders on this parallel – which can be uncovered if the Agents think to check for news stories of previous victims:

- ○ *Wizard in robes and pointy hat covered in stars* (*Bridge Over Troubled Parallels*) – Oliver Postgate, 79 Gloucester Road, South Kensington. Found electrocuted, wired into a (telephone) exchange box, with a jar labelled 'Magic Dust'.
- ○ *Cowboy* (*Hot Metal and Methadrine*) – Anthony Jackson, 13A Finborough Road, Chelsea. Found dead behind the wheel of a stolen (telephone) repair van, which had crashed into a tree, with a sheriff's badge on the dashboard.
- ○ *Big game hunter* (*One Way or Another*) – David McKee, 40 Waterford Road, Fulham. Crushed to death by a huge roll of electrical (telephone) wire, stupidly positioned on a slope. In his hand, a photo of a herd of mastodon.
- ○ *Pirate* (*Mattanit*) – Olwen Griffiths, 10 Rillington Place, Ladbroke Grove. Struck down by a falling (telephone) pole during a gale, which had been sawn through the bottom, a Jolly Roger flag in his pocket.
- ○ *Cook with a French chef's hat* (*This Corrosion*) – Peter Firmin, 10 Stanmer Street, Battersea. 'Fell' from his office window onto a (telephone) line, neatly decapitating himself. A discarded wooden spoon nearby.
- ○ *Scuba diver complete with snorkel, mask, and flippers* (*Silver Pictures Move So Slow*), Baxter Biddy, 20 Bawdale Road, East Dulwich.

> ### Buzby Murderer Strikes Again!
>
> 'In Normand Park, Fulham, there was perpetrated on Tuesday morning a mysterious death, which appears to be the latest in a series of shamefully brutal murders plaguing the impoverished slums of South-West London. Normand Park is an area of ill repute, which lies across from a number of streets and alleys in which some of the poorest of the poor, together with thieves and roughs and prostitutes, find protection and shelter in the miserable tenements bearing the name of houses. Amongst such ill-favoured conditions Sir Robin Gillett, Lord Mayor of London has laboured for years, trying by means of his philanthropic mission to raise and elevate the moral and social life of the inhabitants of the district.
>
> The first intimation of wrongdoing occurred when a local milkman was drawn to the sound of glass being smashed and rushing to the scene through the fog, discovered the body of a man lying in a pool of blood next to a shattered public phone box. He at once shouted for aid, alerting police constable Barrett, 26H, who was on his beat in the vicinity, and Dr. Keeling of Moylan Road was sent for, and promptly arrived.
>
> The doctor made an examination of the man and pronounced life extinct, giving it as his opinion that the victim had been brutally murdered, there being multiple wounds in his breast, stomach, and neck in which large shards of glass had been impaled. The body was that of a man about 35 years of age, 5ft. 7in. in height, pale complexion and hair dark. This time the victim wore a partial suit of medieval plate armour, which was totally disarranged and torn, stained crimson head to foot with the man's own blood. The only other thing of note was a box of matches decorated with a dragon picture, crushed into the grass nearby.
>
> The victim was quickly identified as John Faulkner, 10 Rylston Terrace, Fulham, well known in the neighbourhood. What he was doing, wandering the streets in such bizarre costume in the early hours remains contradictory and uncertain. Scotland Yard was immediately notified and detectives sealed off the area, bringing in Philip Percival, a noted tracker to aid with their investigation.
>
> The circumstances of this latest in a series of awful tragedies is not only surrounded with the deepest mystery, but there is also a feeling of insecurity to think that in a great city like London, the streets of which are continually patrolled by police, a civil gentleman could be foully and horribly killed next to citizens peacefully sleeping in their beds, without a trace or clue being left of the villain who did the deed.
>
> Despite the protestations of Inspector Reid of the Criminal Investigation Department that no pains are being spared to bring the criminal to justice, the police seem no nearer to capturing the now infamous Buzby Murderer whose modus operandi is to dress his victims in grotesque costume.'

rumbling above their heads shows that the morning rush hour is just beginning.

Exiting The Van is disgusting; the thick river mud that clings to their legs smells foul with effluent and is full of rotting fish. For this mission, the trans-parallel vehicle remains available to the Agents, but since there is no way of moving it, The Van quickly becomes covered by rising river waters. In fact, there is no way

Previous Trans-dimensional Events

The first five assassination events have occurred in parallels that may have already been visited by the Agents in the other scenarios. Clues to each are tangential items of background description that players might not immediately piece together in the context of this scenario. However, once the Agents start investigating the victims, the Games Master should start dropping hints that the faces of the victims or extrapolated costumes seem tantalisingly familiar.

To definitively link the strange disturbances on other parallels to specific Buzby Murders, the Agents must actively search for clues and reports. Anomalies linked to the preceding murder victims have long since faded, but pursuing new cross-parallel signals soon reveals the underlying correspondence with the serial killer news story. The London papers do not carry photographs of the victims, only sketched artists impressions of each murder scene. This may be enough to jog memories, however, if only due to the unusual costume worn by each fatality.

The sequence of new murders is up to the Games Master to decide. It is suggested that at least two further incidents occur prior to progressing to *My Name is Bren, Mr Bren* on page 159. Which murders are chosen doesn't matter as specific in-game events can easily be applied to each one. The list of available costumed fatalities, along with their associated 'souvenir' items, are as follows:

- Spaceman in full astronaut suit – Lump of moon rock, with flecks of gold. Bernard Cribbins, Gatehouse of Granard Lodge, Putney Park Lane, Putney. Found drowned in Beverley Brook with the cord of a dozen rotary dial phones snared round his legs.
- Caveman – Stone Age hammer. Ivor Wood, 8 Colestown Street, Battersea. Head staved-in by repeated impact with the door of a blue police box.
- Zoo keeper (old style official blue suit, brush, and bucket) – Parrot's feather. Michael Hordern, 16 Shouldham Street, Paddington. Mauled to death by a bear in London Zoo, after lowering himself into the enclosure using a line of braded telephone cable.
- Scuba diver with air tanks – Seashell. Sandra Kerr, 34 Pembridge Gardens, Kensington. Blown up in her bedroom, which had been flooded with gas, triggered by an electric spark from an electrical device (rotary phone).
- Aladdin with carpet – Stopper from a genie's bottle (seal of Soloman). Gordon Murray, 28 Chiddingstone Street, Fulham. Plummeted late one night from the General Post Office (GPO) tower, riding a Persian rug.

Gathering Intel

Despite the prominent news article at the Putney Bridge bus stop, any trans-parallel vibrations related to the murder have since dissipated. The next multiversal signal does not occur until early evening, leaving the Agents an opportunity to explore SW London, perhaps even find lodgings since The Van is inaccessible for the majority of the time.

More focussed teams may well begin their investigations by searching newspaper archives in one of the local libraries, trying to bluff some information about weird happenings from the police, or simply venturing to a public house to ask subtle questions.

Past editions of the London newspapers are conspicuously absent of stories linked with mystifying happenings or conspiracy theories. Most news of the last couple of months is dreary. A few articles stand out concerning activities of the Royal Family in the Raj; otherwise, its reports of daily smog deaths, local politics, and petty crime.

The only unusual stories are those concerning the Buzby Murders, which started several weeks ago with the death of a Mr. Brian Cant of 15 Perham Road, West Kensington, who died dressed as a circus clown, apparently attempting to balance on an overhead phone line, which snapped, plunging him to his death. This would have been bizarre enough, if not for an elderly witness who claimed that a hulking yellow 2 metre tall figure with a huge beak for a face fled from the scene at his approach. Sadly, the witness died shortly after the encounter from heart failure, unable to further clarify his terrified ramblings or the odd animal tracks left in the vicinity.

Approaching the police is a fruitless endeavour. Asking questions about mysterious lights, insectoid dressed assassins (Disruptor Rooks), or supernatural events gain the enquirer a raised eyebrow and query about how much alcohol the individual has imbibed. The only line of questioning that garners a reaction, and a nervous one at that, is anything to do with monsters or ghosts, raising the recent spate of killings known as the Buzby Murders. The bobbies of SW London are good-natured souls, but lacking in imagination or the desire to speculate. Neither can they be bribed and take a dim view of such behaviour. Other than recommending the Agents keep off the streets after nightfall, the only information they impart is that the entire investigation has been taken over by Scotland Yard.

Hanging about in any one of the hundreds of SW London pubs is an education in the poverty and hopeless depression of industrialised inner city life. The majority are working class labourers seated in the public bar, with sawdust-covered floorboards and hard benches. The saloon bars only hold a handful of slightly better off middle class patrons, favoured with threadbare carpets and cushioned chairs. Clothes have a dirty grey tint from the omnipresent coal dust and most people are lean, even though post-war rationing has now ceased.

Although the grim life of the average Londoner is normally left behind in the social bonhomie of the pub, a distinct feeling of edginess pervades most establishments. Conversations are held in quiet whispers, often drowned out by somebody's hacking, smog-induced cough.

One possible avenue of investigation would be to track down the Philip Percival mentioned in the Times. A noted hunter,

Mr. Percival is currently lodged at the Ritz, where he can eventually be convinced to spill a little information over a glass or two of single malt. The tall, distinguished man is obviously in a state of passionate intensity over the strange animal tracks he's discovered near several of the murders. They are wide and padded, of some large predatory species as yet undiscovered by naturalists. Yet strangely, none of the victims has shown any sign of bites or claw marks. If convinced by their sincerity, Philip offers his services to the Agents if they need his help (which could be invaluable when tracking through the subterranean sewer pipes in *Underground, Overground* on page 160).

THE FIRST ENCOUNTER

That evening after preliminary investigations are completed, the Agent's Signature Sensor issues an alert chime. Using basic triangulation, they eventually discover the location of the next murder victim (as selected by the Games Master from the list on page 156). By the time they arrive at the scene, the police are already in attendance along with concerned members of the public.

A close perusal (successful Perception roll) of the crowd reveals a hulking figure watching events from afar, seemingly ignored by everyone else despite its bulk. Gaining a clear view of the figure is difficult at distance; all they can see is that the figure is wearing a huge seaman's duffle coat, with a trilby hat pulled down low over the eyes, and a bulky scarf wrapped round its lower face. Stranger still is that, if the Agents think or are able to check, the figure registers psychic activity.

Attempts to approach the mysterious figure all fail. As soon as the Agents close in, the hulking shape nips down a side street. By the time the Agents arrive, the figure has utterly vanished, along with the psychic signal. Attempts to track the figure using Track, Streetwise, or any other means all fail; the mysterious stranger has disappeared leaving no trace of passing.

Not all is lost, however, for if the Agents remain at the murder scene, they get the chance to bluff or sneak their way past the police cordon and discover the still resonating 'souvenir' item, overlooked near the corpse. Although appearing (relatively) inoffensive, the item is packed with Disruptor micro-circuitry broadcasting a psychic wave – which, unbeknownst to the Agents, is a self-destruct suicide trigger.

Picking up the object without any form of psychic protection (such as Mental Shield) exposes the Agent to an overwhelming desire to ring a particular telephone number, then immediately kill themselves. Resisting this mental assault requires the Agent to win an opposed test of Willpower against a Thought Implant attack of 89%. If failed, the Agent is compelled to seek out the nearest telephone away from public scrutiny, make a call to an unknown number, and then just as they are about to commit suicide, the transmission ceases leaving them fully aware of what just happened.

If they think of it, Agents that possess the Assimilation Trait might attempt to locate this phone number by painstakingly searching through the Greater London Telephone Directory, providing another route to *The Fancy-Dress Shop* (see page 161).

THE SECOND ENCOUNTER

The following day the Signature Sensor chimes again, denoting another multiversal traveller in the locale. This time the weather is much nastier, tipping down with dirty, yellow-tinged rain. Fortunately, the Agents locate this body before it is discovered by anyone else. They arrive to see the same hulking figure from the night before, bending over the corpse. Unless the Agents are exceptionally stealthy, the muffled figure detects their arrival and flees the scene, leaving the death's associated souvenir item lying broken behind it.

Before it can be intercepted, the figure dashes across a road, causing a battered rubbish truck to screech to a halt. The driver takes one look at the presence in front of his cab, yells in panic, and abandons the vehicle, allowing the figure to climb in. In a grind of gears, it drives off, spilling bin-men off the rear, the nearest Agent just inches away from leaping aboard.

The only other vehicle nearby is a double-decker bus, its conductor having a cigarette on the rear platform, and driver listening to 'Summer Holiday' blaring away on the radio. If the Agents purloin the bus, they can keep the truck in view and attempt to chase it down. The bus is a typical red Routemaster double decker, ubiquitous to London. Driving such a large, unwieldy vehicle is a Hard task unless the Agent has some prior experience of such transportation.

Treat the rubbish truck as having a lead of 3. Each stage of the chase requires the Agent driving to make an Opposed Roll of Drive skill against truck driver. Each level of Success the Agent wins reduces the lead by an equal amount, and vice versa. Although this sounds like an intimidating challenge, the driver of the rubbish truck is obviously unschooled in the control of heavy vehicles with a Drive skill of only 36%.

Due to serendipity the streets are mostly empty, so there is little danger of placing other traffic at risk. In addition to the Drive checks to catch up, the madcap chase can involve a number of close shaves based upon alternate skills. Select from the following:

- *Low Bridge* (Perception check): A steel girder railway bridge crosses above the road. If the skill check is failed, the driver misses the warning sign and must screech to a halt to avoid wedging the vehicle under the bridge, costing the Agents so much time that they potentially lose the rubbish truck before they find a way round. A Fumble automatically traps them, half removing the upper deck in the crash.
- *Lollipop Lady* (Influence vs. Willpower): A redoubtable lollypop lady steps out behind the fleeing truck and presents her sign sternly. The driver must win an opposed test of Influence against the traffic lady's Willpower of 80%

otherwise she stands her ground, forcing the bus to swerve into a small public playground and collide with a set of swings, fortunately devoid of children. As a consequence, the rubbish truck pulls further ahead before the bus can regain the road.

- *Barrow Boy* (Insight check): A barrow boy has the ill luck to be crossing the road. He comically wheels his vegetable-laden barrow back and forth barely avoiding the truck, ending up back in the middle of the street when the bus arrives. Unless willing to screech to a stop, the driver must succeed in an Insight check to guess which way the barrow boy will evade. A fail results in the bus splattered with pumpkins, onions, and the like, but not falling behind. A Fumble means a fatal traffic accident.

Unless the Agents catastrophically fail, they catch up with the labouring truck. Making it stop requires another opposed Drive roll to force it off the road, or something more heroic or violent. However they achieve it, the rubbish truck eventually crashes through the front windows of a shop. Moments later, the mysterious figure is spotted fleeing the scene.

This time, however, the following Agents are close enough to see what happens. The figure mistakenly runs into a cul-de-sac, turns its oddly shaped, scarf-covered face towards the Agents and literally fades away! The figure is merely an Astral Projection, conjured to distract pursuers whilst the real driver slips off in a different direction, under cover of its Aura (Nondescript) power.

Returning to the cab of the rubbish truck reveals no body, but investigators do find a small amount of blood, permitting anyone with the Track skill to follow the drips to a nearby sewer manhole through which the mysterious figure escaped.

My Name is Bren, Mr Bren

By now, the Agents' investigation has alerted the Disruptor Knight controlling *Operation Industrious*. Notified by an informer within Scotland Yard's Special Branch, the Knight sends his latest patsy, Mr. William Bren of No. 52 Festing Road, Putney, to neutralise the team.

Operation Industrious

Unsuspected by anyone on Zero-Zero, The Van assigned to the Agents for their missions has either developed an undetected fault or has been deliberately sabotaged by a member of the core science team. Thus, in recent months, the perturbations given out by The Van's arrival on distant parallels have been sensed by the precognitive powers of the Omega (see *Luther Arkwright*, page 123). *Operation Industrious* was a set up to covertly act upon these forewarnings.

A Disruptor Knight (Baron Zartram, aka *The Shopkeeper*) has been assigned to send a series of sabotage and assassination missions sowing destructive chaos on parallels The Van visits, in the hope of fouling any plans laid by enemies of the Disruptors. He alone is fully aware of the Valhalla Agents' identities and has long been prepared for their arrival.

Zartram reports to Loki, but *Operation Industrious* is Zartram's own fiefdom. If caught and interrogated, Zartram has the wherewithal to look contemptuously at any attempts to extract information about Loki's whereabouts and plans, while mocking his captors with references to things Loki has succeeded in doing: '*And how is Ms Lingstadt these days? I hear psychotherapy can be very... stimulating*', or; '*Such a shame that nice King of England exploded so messily...*' In short, Zartram will not give away his associate, even under the most extreme of tortures.

An English Assassin

The first hint that something may be amiss is when the Agent's Signature Sensor triggers a psychic signal proximity alert. Perceptive Agents see a man calmly walking down the road dressed in a pin-stripe suit and bowler hat, carrying a bulky looking umbrella under one arm. When he reaches close range (or just outside if the Agents are located inside a cafe or some other building), Mr. Bren unlimbers the poorly disguised WWII light machinegun (his last mission souvenir) and fires off 30 rounds of 7.62x51mm in a seemingly never-ending burst.

It has been a few years since Mr. Bren was de-mobbed from National Service, so the psychically dominated man automatically misses the Agents, provided they dive for cover. If not, he has a skill of 58%, which is further halved for firing on full auto.

In the few moments the Agents pick themselves up, Mr. Bren changes the magazine and leaps into a rather conveniently passing London cab (arranged by Baron Zartram), vanishing off into the thickening smog. If one of the Agents was foolish enough to rush the assassin instead of diving for cover, Bren attempts to club the Agent down with the machinegun before jumping into the taxi. If two or more Agents rush him and it looks like he cannot escape, the black cab runs them down to give Bren the time needed to clamber in.

Either way, in his haste to escape, Mr. Bren manages to drop his wallet on the pavement. As well as three 10 shilling bank notes, it contains his Identity Card (on which is his address), which should provide the Agents the next target for their investigation. If not, they can always use the Signature Sensor to track Bren back to his home.

52 Festing Road

Mr. Bren's home, No. 52 Festing Road, Putney, is an orange-fronted Victorian terraced house, drab-looking in the smog. Along the street, there are no dog walkers or children playing, and even

Unbeknown to the Agents, the hulking stranger who continues to dog their investigation is actually upstairs performing its own search. Agents that decide to venture up to the first floor cause the stairs to creak loudly, alerting the intruder who jumps out of an upper floor window to make an escape.

A quick search shows that one of the two bedrooms has been turned into a small study. Inside (assuming Bren wasn't captured) can be found the corpse of Mr. Bren slumped across his desk, strangled by the spiral cord of his rotary telephone. The light machinegun is nowhere to be seen unless the Agents look out of the open window, whereupon they spot it slung over the back of the fleeing intruder making a beeline for the road works tent.

A more thorough rummage through the room locates the ashy remains of a receipt in the fireplace. It seems to have been issued from a shop located in a back street in central Putney, but only the address remains legible.

UNDERGROUND, OVERGROUND

Agents who pursue the mysterious intruder find that the road works tent covers a hole leading down into a large surface water drain. Wet marks on the brick wall lead off one direction, prompting Agents to follow the trail into the claustrophobic maze of sewer pipes under South London.

> ### Questioning Mr Bren
>
> If the Agents manage to capture him, Bren collapses unconscious and, upon awakening, claims to recall nothing about the attempted assassination. This can be verified by Mind Probe or successful use of the Insight skill. Unless the machinegun he was carrying is physically destroyed, as soon as he is left momentarily unsupervised, Bren attempts to commit suicide. Anyone else touching the weapon, as with the other intact souvenirs, must resist in a test of their Willpower versus a Thought Implant attack of 89% or take the gun and open fire on their companions.

a nearby workman's tent stands abandoned, its two paraffin road lamps glowing red in the thickening gloom.

The Agents have a variety of different approaches open to them. Simply knocking on the front door of No. 52 elicits no response. However, the door is secured with a feeble latch lock that can be forced by passing a Hard Difficulty Brawn check. Even easier would be to walk to the end of the street and enter the alley running behind the tiny back gardens. Somewhat suspiciously, the rear gate has been splintered and the back door to No. 52 stands wide open.

Inside the house is as depressing as the rest of the city. Downstairs the furnishings are threadbare and decades old wallpaper is stained from years of occupation. Heating is provided by wall-mounted gas fires, although these remain unlit giving the dwelling a cold chill. Since television is not yet commonplace on this parallel, there is only a radio in the living room.

Providing they find themselves a source of light (such as the paraffin road lamps), it requires a successful Track roll to follow the intermittent prints along the main Low Level No.1 Interceptor drainage pipe, back up the High Level No.1 Interceptor, eventually reaching 'The Crypt' where it intersects with the main Wimbledon Park Sewer. (If the Agents lack knowledge of the skill, they may be able to call upon the aid of Mr. Percival, the game hunter.)

No footprints are visible from herein, but the occasional fresh mark in the slime on the brickwork (and the sound of far off splashing) eventually leads the Agents several kilometres southwest. The subterranean journey seems endless, but fortunately free from faecal waste. Eventually, looming out of the darkness in the wall of the Victorian sewer is a riveted steel door, badly rusted. On its face is a black and yellow radiation warning sign and the words 'Wimbledon Common Civil Defence Fallout Shelter – Entry Prohibited'.

Trying the door, the Agents discover that although it is extremely heavy, the portal is unlocked. Directly inside is a line of large duffle coats neatly hanging from pegs. Stranger still is the fact that the walls are covered with newspaper, seemingly stuck there by wallpaper paste. On the floor, clearly visible on the dry linoleum is a trail of what appears to be paw-prints.

It quickly becomes apparent that the nuclear bunker has been re-purposed into an extensive warren, filled with weird items seemingly created out of recycled junk. It is the secret home of a small enclave of Tibetan Yeti, non-human psychic mystics who covertly supervise the British Empire. Over the last few months, they have detected an increasing threat to life on this parallel, namely, a growing proliferation of trans-dimensional tunnels, which are weakening the physical stability of the parallel itself. If not constrained, their reality could collapse completely.

Provided the Agents do not become psychotically violent with shock or xenophobia, the yetis resignedly communicate with them, seeing a chance to eradicate the parallel disruptions without needing to reveal themselves to the British government. Great Uncle Moldova, an elderly, once snow-white yeti who wears reading glasses and a tartan shawl for warmth, explains that although they can detect the psychic resonances of the souvenir items (through which the Disruptor Knight projects his Thought Implant talent), they have not, as yet, located the source of these deadly gadgets but are sure they are related to the threat they sense.

In addition, the Agents are introduced to Orsk, the large and intimidating trilby-wearing yeti with an interest in vehicles whom the Agents have seen several times previously; and Pilcomayo, a laconic and somewhat lazy mystic with a love of food of all types, which has made him somewhat plump. These latter two are made available to the Agents if help is requested, Orsk being the muscle (Endurance 71%, Combat Style 76%, +1d6 Damage Modifier and +1HP per location) and Pilcomayo having the better psychic skills (Meditation 86%, Mysticism 94%, Willpower 52% – halved when resisting food or snatching a quick forty winks).

The only clue as to the whereabouts of the source of the evil remains the half-burnt receipt in the fireplace of No. 52 Festing Road, although if the Agents missed it and find themselves at a dead end, Great Uncle Moldova reveals the yeti's confusion as to why each suicide victim is dressed in such an outlandish manner.

Hopefully this jogs the Agents into thinking not only why the victims are dressed so, but also where they got the costumes from in the first place. After all, thus far there has been a wizard, cowboy, hunter, pirate, cook, clown, and knight, amongst others – an eclectic collection, and logically only available from a fancy-dress shop.

THE WIMBLEDON YETI

These ancient creatures originated in the high mountains of the Himalayas where they have long practised their own version of Transcendental Mysticism. Disturbed by the disrupting imperialist acts of the British Raj, several enclaves of yetis were sent to outlying political centres of British power to keep a judicious eye open against looming extra-dimensional threats sensed by their greatest yogis.

The Wimbledon Yeti have the appearance of furry bipedal creatures with long conical snouts and prehensile paws, their once glistening fur now matted yellowish-grey from London's exhaust fumes and sulphurous coal dust. Evolved to a high-altitude existence, they usually burrow under glaciers, creating labyrinthine passages where they remain sheltered from weather extremes, and farm fungi upon which their herds of tahr feed.

Unable to blend in with humanity except by use of extreme mental effort, the yeti have created a hidden burrow excavated beneath Wimbledon Common, taking advantage of an abandoned nuclear fallout shelter and Victorian sewage lines to pass unseen under SW London.

THE FANCY-DRESS SHOP

Located in a back lane of central Putney, the headquarters of the Disruptor Knight is an innocuous little shop filled with all sorts of things to wear, sandwiched between a boutique selling antiques and a clock mender. Displayed in the window is a suit of bright red armour and a 17th century sea captain's hat and coat.

Despite its modest appearance, the fancy-dress costume shop is surrounded by a field that negates detection of all psychic and trans-dimensional activity within. Behind the plate glass window and door (which are both armoured – 8 AP) can be seen hundreds of different outfits, but no serving staff. In the rear right corner are two doors: one behind a curtain, which leads to the changing room, and the other to a staircase up to the living quarters above the shop.

Entering the shop rings a little bell above the door (and an electronic alarm upstairs) and, as if by magic, the Shopkeeper appears!

An unassuming, short, plump man with round eyeglasses, the smiling Shopkeeper emphasises his fawning congeniality by wearing a white shirt, red waistcoat, bowtie, and fez. He smiles and asks the Agent or Agents whether they are interested in any of the costumes on display. In reality, this is the Disruptor Knight himself, who possesses an unusual combination of talents: *Synaptic Puppetry, Thought Implant,* and *Translocate* – the latter used to disarmingly appear out of nowhere. In addition, his fez actually contains micro-circuitry providing him with a *Mental Shield*.

Further investigation of the fancy-dress shop is likely to take one of two paths. Either the Agents attempt to subvert the Shopkeeper using subtlety find out what is going on or take the more direct option of assaulting the place.

Efforts to trick or deceive the Shopkeeper automatically fail unless, ironically, the Agents make an effort to disguise their appearance. He has had them under surveillance soon after they began to show an unhealthy interest in the Buzby murders. In spite of this, the Shopkeeper sees this as an opportunity to subvert the Agents into fulfilling his own agenda, by eradicating a few key targets of *Operation Industrious*.

Leading them on with the chance to survey his property, the Shopkeeper suggests they try out a range of costumes. If they accept, they are led into the 'Changing Room', a red-walled antechamber with a full-length mirror and a further pale green door in its side wall.

The room is not all it seems, however. The doors and walls are not only soundproofed, but embedded with Disruptor technology that amplifies the psychic talent of Thought Implant on those within the confines of the shop (Resistance rolls are one Difficulty grade harder). It is here that the Disruptor Knight brainwashes random customers to perform acts of timeline-altering sabotage in alternate parallels, i.e., *Operation Industrious*. The door behind the curtain connecting it to the shop is DNA locked, opening only if the Shopkeeper himself grasps the handle.

The pale green door on the other side of the Changing Room is even more disturbing, its frame functioning as the static end of a Disruptor Tunnel allowing trans-dimensional travel to other parallels. If no destination is set, the door opens onto a plain brick wall. Normally, the Shopkeeper gifts each returning brainwashed saboteur with a souvenir item, permitting the option of recalling the patsy in the future or, more to his sadistic tastes, forcing them to commit suicide to cover his own tracks.

Any Agent tempted into trying out a costume are provided one of the following options: a dinosaur suit, cowboy clothes, or

Prussian officer uniform. Once inside the changing room with the door closed, the Agent is assaulted with a Thought Implant attack at 89%, which plants the mission keyed to that costume into their head (see *Just Go Away*). Those that successfully resist are merely left with a bad headache, but no knowledge of what was attempted against them.

Agents who decide to take direct action (whether before or after visiting the Changing Room) face an alert enemy. The Shopkeeper is fully prepared to be attacked, and thus, for the first round, gains a +5 bonus to his Initiative roll if combat breaks out. His first action is to Translocate to the upstairs rooms, where he alerts his assistant, Smasher Garou.

If the Agents attempt to rush upstairs, they must first pick the lock on the staircase door or bash it down. The door has 4 AP and 15 HP. Whilst this is occurring, the Disruptor Knight attempts a Synaptic Puppetry attack on a random Agent he can see on his security monitors, and then destroy his invaluable psi-electronics manufacturing tools.

In the meantime, Smasher Garou shucks-on his gladiatorial armour, standing guard at the top of the narrow staircase. Wielding a shortsword in either hand, he tries to intimidate the Agents long enough for the Shopkeeper to finish his task and Translocate again, down to the Changing Room to escape through the Disruptor Tunnel, taking Smasher with him if possible.

THE GREAT BALLOON RACE

Assuming that the Agents were unable to predict his escape plan and stop him, the Shopkeeper uses the Changing Room's Disruptor Tunnel to flee. Instead of reporting directly back to the Omega on the world-ship, the Disruptor Knight conceitedly decides to handle the Agents himself – cleaning up all loose ends whilst indulging himself at the same time. Therefore, he sets the trans-dimensional tunnel to a neighbouring parallel, leaving the coordinates locked so that his hunters can easily follow.

Transiting the Disruptor Tunnel risks the same psychological dangers as described in Just Go Away previously. Pursuing Agents emerge inside a lavishly furnished pavilion, its door half unlaced. Outside can be heard the excited background chatter of a large crowd of people. Indeed, upon exiting the tent, they discover themselves amidst a huge fairground filled with people dressed in Victorian period garb. Before them, floating above the heads of the crowd, are the multi-coloured canopies of hot air and helium balloons. Cheers erupt from that direction, which should prompt enquiry of the commotion.

Pushing their way to the front of the crowd reveals a dozen magnificent flying machines of odd types. Although each is supported by a lifting sack, the structures supported beneath are a collection of fantastical Heath Robinson contraptions, using items like

Just Go Away

Agents who enter the red-walled Changing Room and fail to resist its mental Programmeming are sent on a deadly sabotage mission. The costume selected not only defines the assignment, but also controls the specific parallel the green door opens into. Stepping into the spiralling Disruptor Tunnel is very disturbing. Agents who fail a Formidable Willpower roll lose 1d6 Tenacity from directly experiencing the warping of space-time and glimpses of mind-shattering cosmic horrors.

Only the outlines of what occurs on each mission are given here for the Games Master to relate to the Agent. However, nothing prevents further expansion of each into an actual gamed out session, if so wished:

Dinosaur: The Agent awakes holding the reins of a massive diplodocus-drawn wagon, upon which is a huge egg. As the Agent guides it along an arrow-straight paved road, they behold a primitive Flintstones-like world, but one where the mega-fauna are controlled by intelligent velociraptors. After defending the cart against pterodactyls and convincing the gate guards of a neophyte city to let it pass, the Agent is rewarded by the king of the smart dinosaurs. Moments later the Shopkeeper appears to take them away, gifting the Agent a lizard tooth just as the egg undergoes a multi-megaton fission explosion.

Cowboy: The Agent is a frontier trader in the Wild West. Captured and brought before the chief of the local First Nations tribe who blames white men for the kidnap of his daughter, they must travel to Fort Pitt to prevent war breaking out. The Agent is given gifts to negotiate with the fort's captain for the return of the girl. Most are mere trinkets, but included is a small bag of precious rubies that cause a feeling of revulsion. Using these seals the deal, but at the later celebration, the skin of the captain and his cavalrymen start to break out in pustules. The Shopkeeper extracts the Agent, presenting them with a native American headdress feather.

Prussian Soldier: The Agent is a member of Otto von Bismarck's personal entourage. In drunken celebration of the petulant young duke's birthday, the British ambassador has arranged a game of cricket. The duke is batting and the Agent discovers a cricket ball in hand. Whether the Agent bowls it or gives it to the ambassador to cast, when the duke strikes the ball it explodes in a cloud of poison gas. The duke and several very important heads of state die frothing at the lips as the Shopkeeper appears to take the Agent away, pressing a cricket ball into their hand.

On exit from the Changing Room, the Agent discovers that only a few minutes have passed and memories of their experience are already fading, like a dream after waking. Unbeknownst to each Agent, an additional command has been Programmemed into them – to terminate anyone asking questions later about what happened in the room. The souvenir objects are, of course, psychic transmitters, with which the Shopkeeper intends to force remaining Agents to commit suicide.

bicycle-driven fans, steam-pumped bellows, and other such oddities to provide motive power.

In one of the closer balloons can be seen the poorly disguised Shopkeeper still wearing his fez and a false handlebar moustache stuck to his face, which he twirls sinisterly. He bows deeply in the direction of the Agents, resulting in more loud cheers from the audience. Atop a nearby tower, an official with a megaphone introduces the masquerading Disruptor Knight, as Baron Zartram, the last-minute substitute captain of the Ottoman team.

Asking anyone in the crowd what is going on reveals that this is the first ever London-to-Paris cross-channel balloon race. A pan-European event comprising national teams, the race would have already started save for the fuss caused by the Swiss, who are about to be disqualified, being too inebriated to sign in.

Sure enough, the entire Swiss team are drunkenly expostulating their desire to participate, despite their inability to stand, let alone hold up a half-empty magnum of celebratory champagne. Several bobbies are politely trying to cart them off to sober up. This prompts their intoxicated leader to lament the loss of honour if no one flies the Swiss Guard's yellow, blue, and red striped balloon.

Openly assaulting the obviously popular Baron Zartram would draw the wrath of the crowd and arrest by the bobbies present. Volunteering to crew the Swiss balloon, however, allows the Agents a chance to keep up with the maliciously smiling Baron; unwitting that this is exactly what he wants them to do.

The balloon race itself is merely an incidental backdrop to the Shopkeeper's deadly agenda to kill the Agents. The motivation of the Agents on the other hand depends entirely on their ethics and whether they think that capturing the Disruptor Knight is of value to the Valhalla Programme.

Baron Zartram waits until after the race starts before he makes his first move. Using his Synaptic Puppetry to control the crew of other balloons, he stages the following attacks on the Agents – until no competing teams remain and only they are left:

○ Manipulates the pilot of the Austro-Hungarian team, who attempts to swing her balloon over the Agent's flying machine and slice open the canopy with the razor-sharp keel. Unfortunately, the violent manoeuvre, if successfully opposed by the Agents, capsizes the attacking vehicle spilling its crew into a lake passing below.

○ The Serbians conspire to lasso the Agents' balloon with a long rope connected to a heavy anchor, just as both vessels pass over some woodland. Descending a few metres before they can transfer the line, causes them to become snagged instead, ripping off the rear section including their bicycle-driven prop.

○ One of the German team emerges on deck with a lit stick of dynamite, obviously intending to cast it into the Agents' balloon. Depending on the methods used to stop him, he drops it into his own vessel. The subsequent explosion causes their own canopy to rupture, but they are saved by German engineering when a huge emergency parachute is deployed.

○ The Russian balloon, its paddlewheels propelled by a dancing Cossack driven treadmill, briefly looks like it will be a threat until its mentally subverted officer gives an untoward command, at which point the Cossacks rebel and a fistfight breaks out.

○ In the meantime outright cheating is rife. The British team of Oxford Dons in their sawn-through oar-powered balloon is soon left far behind; the Spanish team's string of tethered seagulls are attacked by a Peregrine Falcon released by the Moroccans; and the sail-driven Swedish longship balloon goes down in axes and flames against the Danes. Perhaps the most entertaining conflict occurs when the French engages in a boarding action against the Italian balloon, overwhelming their crew with Parisian courtesans.

By the time the balloons reach the English Channel, only Baron Zartram's and the Agents' remain to duke it out. Heavy use of his psionic talents has drained well over half his Prana, leaving him with less elegant physical options to finish them off. Of course, being trained as a Disruptor Knight means that the Baron is no slouch in hand to hand combat, but he still attempts to rig the odds in his favour first with a couple of shots from his blunderbuss.

The first shot targets the Agents, whilst the second is aimed at their gas canopy if they dive for cover. Considering the size of the balloon there's little chance of missing unless he rolls a 96+ or the Agents somehow jog his aim. A successful hit causes the Swiss balloon to slowly sink towards the sea.

In spite of the fact that they are several miles out to sea, Baron Zartram wishes to finish them off personally. If the Agents fail to make an attempt to board his balloon, he attempts a Thought Implant against anyone carrying a still intact souvenir object, forcing them to turn against their compatriots, then zip across to their vessel using his Translocate talent.

On arrival, the Shopkeeper is armed with a rapier in his left hand, a loaded flintlock in his right, and a wickedly supercilious smile. His tactics are to pick off individuals and not let himself be outnumbered. He saves the shot from his pistol to help extract himself from difficulty and can Translocate one last time to change position – but would rather reserve it to escape back to his own balloon. Note that the Baron possesses the Swashbuckling combat style trait, allowing him to jump and swing about the crowded deck at no penalty, whilst the Agents are at a Difficulty grade of at least Hard when fighting amongst the clutter of machinery, unless they have the identical trait.

If faced with defeat and no Translocate jumps remaining (or as his anti-heroic Last Action), the pudgy Baron salutes his foes then takes a step backwards over the edge of the deck, diving into the sea 30 metres below. He does not surface.

Conclusion

The Agents' eventual soft crash into the sea is not quite the death sentence envisaged by the Shopkeeper. Provided they can make a Swim roll at a Difficulty grade of Easy, survivors remain afloat long enough to be rescued by a French fishing boat.

If Baron Zartram was not killed, he floats off towards Paris where he claims victory before returning to parallel 02.87.51 to close down the shop. *Operation Industrious* is considered a resounding success by the Omega who focusses its efforts to discover where The Van originates from and ultimately locate Zero-Zero unless the Agents have figured out how they were tracked.

If the Baron is killed and Smasher Garou is aboard the Ottoman balloon, the latter breaks free of his brainwashing. Taking command, he rescues the Agents before they can drown and instead it is they who arrive in Paris to win the first ever cross-channel balloon race.

Whether accompanied by Smasher or not, it is then an easy voyage back to the pavilion in the fairground where they can reopen the Disruptor Tunnel back to parallel 02.87.51 and collect some scraps of vital information concerning *Operation Industrious*, before returning to Zero-Zero in The Van.

What Next for Mjollnir?

While this is the last mission in the *Parallel Lines* book, Mjollnir's work continues, as does the hunt for Loki. Through the various scenarios the Agents should have picked-up an idea of Loki's modus operandi, although this master villain remains a few paces removed from them for now.

Further adventures for *Luther Arkwright* aim to use Loki further, so there will be more opportunities for the Agents to put a stop to his activities; however, Games Masters are encouraged to develop their own scenarios involving the elusive Disruptor Knight, or those he has managed to corrupt. If Disruptors such as Siavan and Zartram have survived and escaped, they should be used as recurring villains in personal scenarios.

Non-Player Characters

Mr Bren

A mild-mannered, middle-aged man, Mr Bren habitually wears a dark three-piece suit and bowler hat. He lives alone in Festing Road and leads a humdrum life until his fateful encounter with Baron Zartram and the Disruptors. He served as a conscript in the British Army where he learned how to use a variety of weapons, but is otherwise a peaceable chap.

Mr Bren	Attributes
STR: 11	Action Points: 3
CON: 10	Damage Modifier: +0
SIZ: 13	Prana: 10
DEX: 11	Tenacity: 10
INT: 15	Movement: 6 metres
POW: 10	Initiative Bonus: 13
CHA: 11	Armour:

1d20	Hit Location	AP/HP
1 – 3	Right Leg	0/5
4 – 6	Left Leg	0/5
7 – 9	Abdomen	0/6
10 – 12	Chest	0/7
13 – 15	Right Arm	0/4
16 – 18	Left Arm	0/4
19 – 20	Head	0/5

Skills	Passions, Traits & Dependencies
Athletics 30%, Brawn 24%, Conceal 28%, Deceit 26%, Disguise 30%, Drive (car) 58%, Endurance 40%, Evade 42%, First Aid 26%, Influence 32%, Insight 32%, Native Tongue (English) 100%, Perception 42%, Stealth 33%, Unarmed 32%, Willpower 30%	Passions: Love Putney 60% Dependencies: Tea 30%

Combat Style & Weapons	Traits & Notes
British Squaddie (Rifle, Light Machinegun, Bayonet, Club with Firearm) 58%	Formation Fighting

Weapon	Damage	Range	Ammo	Rate/Load
Bren Gun	2d6+2	50/100/200	2 x 30 round clsips	1/3/20 3

Wimbledon Yeti

The Wimbledon Yeti have the appearance of furry bipedal creatures with long conical snouts and prehensile paws, their once glistening fur now matted yellowish-grey from London's exhaust fumes and sulphurous coal dust. Evolved to a high-altitude existence, they usually burrow under glaciers, creating labyrinthine passages where they remain sheltered from weather extremes, and farm fungi upon which their herds of tahr feed.

Unable to blend in with humanity except by use of extreme mental effort, the yeti have created a hidden burrow excavated beneath Wimbledon Common, taking advantage of an abandoned nuclear fallout shelter and Victorian sewage lines to pass unseen under southwest London.

Wimbledon Yeti	Attributes
STR: 2d6+9 (16)	Action Points: 2
CON: 2d6+6 (13)	Damage Modifier: +1d4
SIZ: 2d6+12 (19)	Prana: 16
DEX: 2d6+3 (10)	Tenacity: 16
INT: 2d6+6 (13)	Movement: 6 metres
POW: 2d6+9 (16)	Initiative Bonus: +12
CHA: 3d6 (11)	Armour: Thick Fur
Abilities	Burrower (Snow), Formidable Natural Weapons, Night Sight

1d20	Hit Location	AP/HP
1 – 3	Right Leg	3/7
4 – 6	Left Leg	3/7
7 – 9	Abdomen	3/8
10 – 12	Chest	3/9
13 – 15	Right Arm	3/6
16 – 18	Left Arm	3/6
19 – 20	Head	3/7

Skills	Passions, Traits & Dependencies
Athletics 56%, Brawn 65%, Conceal 66%, Craft (Recycle Rubbish) 83%, Disguise 34%, Endurance 56%, Evade 50%, First Aid 53%, Healing 59%, Insight 69%, Language (English) 72%, Mechanics 43%, Meditation 76%, Mysticism 79%, Perception 59%, Stealth 63%, Survival 59%, Track 56%, Willpower 72%	Passions: Recycling 90%, Hate Chaos 90% Traits: Mystics Dependencies: Collecting 65%

Mysticism

Transcendental Yeti Mysticism [Astral Projection, Aura (Nondescript), Awareness (Danger, Dimensional Threats), Denial (Temperature Extremes), Indomitable, Psi Sense]

Combat Style & Weapons	Traits & Notes
Tidying Up (Retractable Claws) 66%	Batter Aside, Excellent Footwork

Weapon	Damage	Size/Reach	AP/HP	Effects
Paw Strike	1d4+1d4	M/M	As for Arm	Bleed
Grapple	1d4	M/M	As for Arm	-

Smasher Garou

An ex-prison convict who took up a career in road construction, Smasher is a huge thug of a man; big, bald, and a prominent broken nose. Selected by the Baron Zartram for his physical strengths, Smasher has been repeatedly brain washed in the Changing Room to impose loyalty, becoming a Disruptor Pawn.

Smasher is actually reluctant about fighting and especially killing foes – or 'squidging' as he calls it. His need to vandalise is a direct consequence of the stresses caused by the mental conditioning conflicting against his submerged personality.

Smasher Garou	Attributes
STR: 15	Action Points: 2
CON: 14	Damage Modifier: +1d4
SIZ: 17	Prana: 7
DEX: 9	Tenacity: 7
INT: 12	Movement: 6 metres
POW: 7	Initiative Bonus: +11 (+5 in armour)
CHA: 11	Armour: Roman Gladiator

1d20	Hit Location	AP/HP
1 – 3	Right Leg	5/7
4 – 6	Left Leg	5/7
7 – 9	Abdomen	5/8
10 – 12	Chest	5/9
13 – 15	Right Arm	5/6
16 – 18	Left Arm	5/6
19 – 20	Head	5/7

Skills	Passions, Traits & Dependencies
Athletics 69%, Brawn 84%, Conceal 54%, Craft (Mason) 71%, Customs 61%, Deceit 49%, Drive 63%, Endurance 82%, Engineering 77%, Evade 53%, First Aid 27%, Influence 54%, Insight 55%, Locale 64%, Perception 60%, Stealth 39%, Streetwise 68%, Swim 46%, Unarmed 81%, Willpower 59%	Passions: Loyalty to Disruptors 65%, Road Building 90% Traits: Menacing Dependencies: Vandalism 58%

Combat Style & Weapons	Traits & Notes
Gladiatorial Combat (Shortsword) 74% Unarmed 81%	Do or Die Knockout Blow for Unarmed

Weapon	Damage	Size/Reach	AP/HP	Effects
Fist	1d3+1d4	S/S	As for Arm	Stun Location
Shortsword	1d6+1d4	M/S	6/8	Impale, Bleed

The Shopkeeper: Baron Zartram

On the outside, this Disruptor Knight adopts the caricature of a short, unassuming, plump man with round eyeglasses, who dresses in a white shirt, red waistcoat, bowtie, and fez (which contains micro-circuitry providing him with an Intensity 5 Mental Shield). Always smiling, he stealthily appears as if from nowhere to take customers unawares.

In reality, the obsequious Shopkeeper is a cerebral sadist who delights in unleashing chaos. Based on 02.87.51, he uses his scientific skills to overthrow key parallels of interest to the Omega. He arrogantly believes himself far too clever for anyone to catch, to the point he deliberately allows victims to retain their costumes so he can Thought Implant journalists, police, and detectives to build a network of complicit spies.

Zartram reports to Loki, but *Operation Industrious* is Zartram's own fiefdom. If caught and interrogated, Zartram has the wherewithal to look contemptuously at any attempts to extract information about Loki's whereabouts and plans, while mocking his captors with references to things Loki has succeeded in doing: *'And how is Ms Lingstadt these days? I hear psychotherapy can be very... stimulating'*, or; *'Such a shame that nice King of England exploded so messily...'* In short, Zartram will not give away his associate, even under the most extreme of tortures.

Baron Zartram	Attributes
STR: 9	Action Points: 3
CON: 15	Damage Modifier: None
SIZ: 14	Prana: 17
DEX: 15	Tenacity: 17
INT: 17	Movement: 6 metres
POW: 17	Initiative Bonus: +16
CHA: 16	Armour: Ballistic Cloth

1d20	Hit Location	AP/HP
1 – 3	Right Leg	3/6
4 – 6	Left Leg	3/6
7 – 9	Abdomen	3/7
10 – 12	Chest	3/8
13 – 15	Right Arm	3/5
16 – 18	Left Arm	3/5
19 – 20	Head	3/6

Skills	Passions, Traits & Dependencies
Athletics 58%, Boating 64%, Brawn 36%, Conceal 79%, Customs 76%, Dance 49%, Deceit 83%, Drive 55%, Electronics 92%, Endurance 66%, Evade 62%, First Aid 57%, Influence 74%, Insight 65%, Locale 51%, Perception 70%, Pilot (Airships) 64%, Politics 65%, Probabilities 95%, Ride 43%, Science (Psi-Electronics) 88%, Science (Psychology) 93%, Sing 61%, Stealth 85%, Streetwise 56%, Swim 50%, Unarmed 61%, Willpower 98%	Passions: Loyalty to Disruptors 90%, Contempt for Enemies 95% Traits: Psychic, Technical Dependencies: Risk Taking 78%

Psionics

Biokineses (Synaptic Puppetry, Thought Implant) 89% and Translocation (Translocate) 97%, the latter of which he uses to disarmingly appear out of nowhere.

Combat Style & Weapons	Traits & Notes
Firearms 71%	Marksman
Fencing 87%	Swashbuckling

Weapon	Damage	Size/Reach	AP/HP	Effects
Rapier	1d8	M/L	6/8	Impale, Bleed

Weapon	Damage	Range	Ammo	Rate/Load
Blunderbuss	2d6	5/10/25	Single (Scatter)	1/4
Flintlock	1d10	15/100/200	Single	1/4

Index

3Jane Tessier-Ashpool 58
4th, Agent 132, 133, 138, 139, 143, 145
10 Rillington Place, Ladbroke Grove 14, 156

A

Aerodrome, the 58
Aigues-Mortes 27, 28, 29, 30, 31, 32, 33, 35, 37, 38, 39, 40
Airship Key 101
Alex 1st, King 131, 132, 135, 136, 152
Alfred II, King 87, 89, 101
Algonquin Tribes 18
Alien, the 20
Alph Flophouse, the 3, 48, 54, 57
Analissa-753 53
Ancestor Coil 19, 20, 21, 22
Andre-300 47, 52, 53, 55, 56, 57, 60
Aref 27, 31, 32, 33, 34, 36, 37, 38, 39, 41
Armando-888 51, 52, 57

B

Baby 31, 33, 34, 35, 47, 48, 49, 50, 51, 52, 53, 54, 55, 56, 57, 58, 59, 60, 61, 62, 64, 78, 141
Balloon Race, the Great 3, 155, 163
Banin, Count Mikhail 65, 71, 72, 75, 79
Banksman, the 130, 131, 139, 143, 144, 145, 146, 147, 148
Barwick, Daniel 11, 18, 22, 24
Battersea 38, 87, 88, 156, 157
Beltane Fire Festival 134
Big game hunter 156
Big Tam 130, 138, 139, 140, 141, 142, 143, 146, 149, 150, 151

Bloody MacKenzie's Tomb 133
Bohdan, Volodymyr 89, 91, 93, 95, 96, 97, 98, 100, 101, 103, 108, 109
Boston, Mass 12, 13, 16, 17, 18, 22, 24
Botany Bay 3, 28, 29
Bradbury Suites, the 52, 53
Bridge Over Troubled Parallels 10, 156
British Regulars 24
Burroughs, Sarah 11, 12, 13, 15, 20, 23
Buzby Murder 4, 14, 38, 56, 73, 103, 139

C

Calton Hill 134, 135, 147
Camargue 10, 27, 28, 29, 32, 37, 42, 43, 46
Caravan Vehicles 30
Chariot 31, 77
Charlestown, Mass 17, 22
Chicken Hut, the 48, 52, 53, 54, 55
China 88, 95
Chita 68
Clangers, the 154
Cli˜ord 15
Colby, Holden 121
Cook 150, 156
Copters 139, 152
Cossacks 65, 66, 77, 84, 164
Cowboy 156, 163
Crimean Separatists 89

Index

D
David-36 53
Devil's Swamp, the 3, 19
Diamante, Nikolai 74
Direct Translocation 132

E
East Dulwich 156
Edinburgh 3, 10, 130, 131, 132, 133, 134, 135, 136, 138, 140, 141, 142, 143, 144, 145, 149, 153
Edward VIII, King 89
Eldritch, Michael 47, 48, 49, 50, 51, 52, 53, 54, 55, 56, 57, 58, 59, 60, 61, 151
Emma McGregor 137, 140, 151
Empire Down 3, 48, 54, 55, 56, 57, 62, 64
Empress Katerina 10, 75, 78, 87, 88, 89, 90, 91, 93, 94, 95, 101, 102, 104, 105, 106
Engineer, the 11, 19, 20, 22, 25, 89, 93, 99

F
Faberge egg 75, 77
Fancy-Dress Shop, the 3, 158, 161
Fedotik, Gregor 89, 94, 95, 96, 97, 98, 104, 111
Festing Road 159, 161, 165
Fighter Aircra° 76
Finborough Road, Chelsea 56, 156
Firmin, Peter 38, 154, 156
Firth of Forth 135, 138, 143
Fog Generator 22
Forth Bridge 130, 131, 138, 141, 143
Forth, Sally 138, 147
Free Fountainbridge 139, 140, 141, 143, 146, 147, 148, 149
Fulham 73, 156, 157

G
Galina 65, 71, 72, 75, 80
Gate, Disruptor 33, 37, 38, 39, 40, 122, 147, 160, 163
Georgy-845 3, 47, 48, 51, 55, 56, 57, 58, 59, 60, 61, 63
Gerhard 89, 90, 91, 92, 95, 96, 97, 98, 100, 103, 107
Gleb, Wilhelm 89, 91, 92, 93, 96, 97, 98, 99, 100, 101, 103, 104, 109
Graves 89, 90, 91, 94, 96, 98, 100, 103, 104, 107, 109
Great Uncle Moldova 154, 161
Greyfriars Kirk 132
Grime 27, 31, 32, 33, 34, 35, 36, 37, 38, 42

H
Hallucinatory Gas 57
Hanging on the Telephone 4, 10
Heart of the bridge 144
Hermit, the 27, 28, 32, 33, 37, 38, 39, 40, 43
Hockomock Swamp 11, 12, 16, 17, 18, 21, 28
Hoot the Redeemer 130, 131, 135, 136, 138, 149
Hot Metal and Methadrine 10, 78, 156
Howling Wolf Pass 66, 77

I
Illegal Jack 141, 150
Irkusk 68

J
James-444 54
John-613 53

K
Khabarovsk 68
Killpanzees 135, 143, 153
Kingÿsher, the 3, 114, 115, 116, 117, 118, 120, 126
Klass, Pieter 9, 71, 73, 82, 87, 91, 92, 100, 103, 104
Klym, Klara 89, 91, 93, 96, 97, 98, 100, 104, 109
Kor˜, Major Vladimir 65, 68, 70, 71, 72, 74, 75, 77, 78, 80, 83, 84
Kovalenko, Archduke Rostov 72, 74, 75, 82, 87, 88, 89, 90, 91, 92, 93, 94, 95, 96, 97, 98, 99, 100, 101, 103, 104, 106, 107, 113
Krankie, Jamie 130
Krankie, Jimmy 130, 131, 134, 138, 143, 146, 147, 148, 151, 152, 153
Krasnoyarsk 68
Kyland 27, 28, 29, 30, 31, 32, 33, 34, 35, 36, 37, 38, 39, 40, 41, 42, 43, 46

L
Lazarev, Irena 65, 71, 73, 81, 89, 92, 96, 104, 113
Lingstadt, Freyr 4, 5, 6, 7, 9, 12, 50, 66, 88, 132, 133, 135, 143, 146, 147, 159, 167
Lisl-418 48, 52, 53, 54, 55, 56
Loki 5, 7, 8, 9, 10, 51, 59, 60, 67, 73, 78, 82, 87, 88, 89, 92, 100, 101, 103, 104, 148, 159, 165, 167
London 10, 13, 14, 49, 50, 56, 58, 73, 78, 87, 88, 89, 94, 98, 100, 101, 103, 104, 105, 132, 154, 155, 156, 157, 158, 159, 160, 161, 164, 166
Lutz 95, 99

M

Mad God, the 38
Magnum Opus 142, 146, 147
Malone, Samuel 15
Marshal Suvorov 65, 66, 67, 68, 70, 75
Mary-589 53
Mathias-015 48, 49, 51, 52, 53, 54, 55, 61
Mattanit 3, 10, 11, 12, 16, 18, 19, 20, 21, 22, 25, 26, 28, 37, 38, 156
McAllan, Mortimer 5, 6, 8, 9, 13, 51, 66, 133
McAvoy 114, 120, 121, 122, 123, 124, 125, 126, 129
Meeting Place, the 15
MiniSec 132, 138, 143
Mjollnir 3, 4, 5, 6, 7, 8, 9, 11, 12, 77, 114, 130, 132, 165
Mjollnir Command 4
Mjollnir Equipment & Field 5
Mjollnir Operations 6
Mjollnir Resources 6
Mjollnir Technical & PSI 5
Modya 65, 68, 74, 75, 81
Mohicans 12, 14, 18, 19, 20, 25
Moon, the 1–172
Mors, Captain 88, 89, 93, 94, 95, 96, 97, 98, 100, 111, 112
Moscow 65, 66, 68, 70, 71, 75, 78
Mr. Bren 154, 155, 159, 160
Mud Lurkers 29, 34, 37, 45
Multiversal Mandala 131

N

Ned the Gaoler 14, 23
Neural Neutraliser 22
Neuro-Sedative Strips 116
Norman 15
North-East Broadcast Network 49
Novosibirsk 68
Nu-Atlantis 10
NuAtlantis Law 118
NuGenesis Protocol 114, 115, 122, 123, 124, 126, 128
Number Nine 27, 28, 32, 33, 35, 37, 38, 40, 42, 43

O

Octobriana 3, 65, 66, 67, 68, 71, 72, 73, 75, 77, 78, 79
Olesko, Maksim 89, 93, 94, 96, 99, 100, 101, 110, 112
Omsk 68
Once-Men 31
One Way or Another 3, 10, 65, 88, 156
Operation Industrious 154, 159, 162, 165, 167
Orsk 154, 155, 161

P

Palmer, Petra 47, 50
Parasites 29
Parsons, Dr Natalia 114, 115, 122, 124, 126, 128
Pavlov's Serum 76
Percival, Sir Phillip 154, 156, 157, 158, 161
Perm 68
Pilcomayo 154, 161
Pirate 156
Postgate, Oliver 154, 156
Pretty Baby 47, 48, 49, 50, 51, 52, 53, 54, 55, 56, 57, 58, 59, 60, 61, 62, 64, 78
Prop-Packs 148
Psionic Mind Control Helmets 148
Putin, Sarah 74
Putney 154, 155, 156, 157, 159, 160, 161, 165

Q

Qualmann, Hansie 130, 141, 150
Quinscombe, Professor 5, 7, 8, 9, 13, 20, 21, 22, 29, 33, 38, 132, 133, 150, 154, 155

R

Reid, Inspector 74, 156
Reid, Sir Oliver 74
Rib Ripper 27, 30, 43
Rivers, Althea 5, 6, 7, 8, 50, 132, 133
Roach, giant 54, 64
Rolling Horrors 34, 36, 44
Rufus-075 56
Ruslana, Olga 89, 93, 94, 95, 96, 97, 98, 99, 100, 110

S

Salem 3, 11, 12, 13, 14, 15, 16, 17, 23, 29
Salem Gaol 14
Schumann, Otto 88, 89, 94, 95, 96, 99, 103, 104, 112
Scuba diver 156, 157
Ship's Tavern, the 15
Shopkeeper, the 154, 159, 161, 162, 163, 164, 167
Shur, Anton 65, 68, 71, 72, 73, 74, 75, 76, 77, 81, 82
Signature Sensor 155, 158, 159
Silver Pictures Move So Slow 10, 65, 75, 78, 82, 156
Smasher Garou 154, 163, 165, 166
Snow leopard 65, 70, 72, 75, 85
Sonic Pistol 118, 127, 128, 129
South Kensington 156
Special Primate Group, the 135, 153

Starship 19, 20
Steppe, Siberian 66, 85

T

Tayshet 68
Temporal Glitch 137
" ames, Anna 89, 94, 95, 96, 97, 98, 100, 106, 111, 155
"i s Corrosion 3, 10, 22, 27, 28, 156
TPT 12, 16, 29, 38, 55, 57, 66, 67, 78, 88
Trans-Siberian Express 3, 10, 65, 66, 68, 78, 92, 113
Traviche, Olin 114, 115, 124, 125, 126, 127
Trench Digger 29, 36, 45
Tunguska 66, 74, 85
Turtle of Unusual Size 25
Twins, the 130, 146, 147, 151, 153
Tyumen 68

U

Ulan Ude 68
Ural Mountains 66, 77

V

Valentova, Gertrude 65, 71, 72, 73, 74, 75, 77, 81, 82, 87, 88, 89, 90, 91, 92, 94, 95, 96, 97, 98, 99, 100, 101, 103, 104, 106, 112, 113
Valhalla 3, 4, 5, 6, 7, 8, 9, 10, 11, 12, 13, 14, 15, 16, 20, 23, 31, 37, 40, 47, 48, 49, 50, 51, 52, 54, 55, 56, 59, 60, 66, 71, 77, 78, 87, 88, 92, 94, 99, 100, 114, 115, 116, 126, 130, 132, 138, 140, 143, 147, 159, 164
Val Industrial Products 138
Van, the 5, 6, 8, 10, 13, 21, 27, 28, 29, 30, 32, 37, 38, 47, 48, 50, 51, 55, 58, 59, 60, 66, 67, 78, 115, 116, 132, 133, 146, 155, 156, 157, 159, 165
Vehemence Drake 27, 31, 40
Ventman, Padraig 114, 115, 127
Vittorio-089 53
VLAD 148
Vladivostok Station 66
Volkov 65, 70, 71, 72, 73, 74, 75, 78, 80, 83
Volyinski, Ruprecht 89, 91, 92, 93, 95, 96, 98, 99, 100, 101, 103, 108, 109
Vyatka 68

W

Wee Tough Janet 141, 146, 150
Wimbledon 154, 155, 161, 166
Wimbledon Common 161, 166
Wishaw 13, 66, 133
Witch Hill 14
Wizard 156
Wolves, Mutant 75
Wombles, the 154
W.O.T.A.N 4, 5, 6, 8, 13, 20, 47, 48, 49, 50, 65, 87, 114, 130, 131, 132, 133, 136, 146
Wrigglers 34, 44
Writers Bloc, the 130, 137, 139, 140, 141, 151

Y

Yaroslavl 68
Yekaterinburg 68
Yerov Warehouse 66
Yeti 154, 161, 166

Z

Zartram, Baron 154, 159, 164, 165, 166, 167
Zoltar " e Fortune-Teller 139
Zulu 48, 50, 51, 52, 56, 57, 60, 63
Zykhov, Countess Anzhelika 65, 70, 72, 75, 76, 83

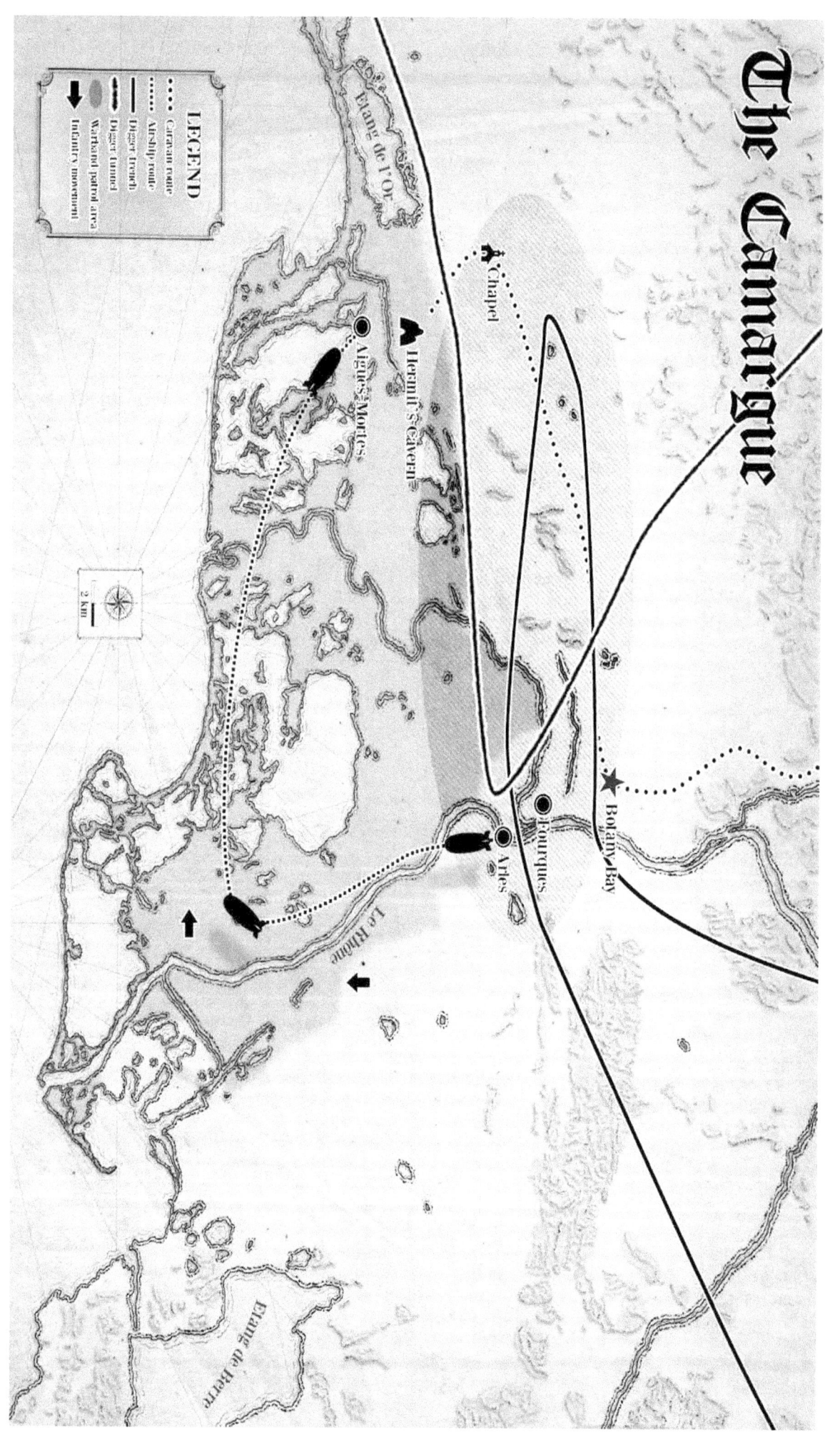

AREA MAP FOR THIS CORROSION

www.ingramcontent.com/pod-product-compliance
Ingram Content Group UK Ltd.
Pitfield, Milton Keynes, MK11 3LW, UK
UKHW050703160426
5217IPUK00038B/2075